EMMIT W. BOYER

Harbingers of Fate

The Sentinels

First edition

ISBN: 978-0-578-98463-6

This book was professionally typeset on Reedsy. Find out more at reedsy.com

To my incredible parents, who not only supported me along my journey to create this story, but also raised me into the man that I am today. Without them, I would not have possessed as strong of a drive to continue my passions and seek to share it with the world.

Contents

Prologue

Sometimes I ask the void of this place I call my world where I am or why I'm still lingering here alone, just to see if the emptiness of this locus will ever become a malleable reality. But deep down I knew the truth of it all. This place was nothing but a prison, with the walls of my own mind filled with memories of what I had endured through all these years.

The blackness of this world was overwhelming, filling every orifice of my being with its corruption. It oozed out of every corner of wherever I was as I drifted aimlessly through a void of absolute nothingness. Dream-like visions from the past lurked in the shadows, but they were often too far to reach out for. Liquid shades shifted and moved like coherent beings, mimicking real creatures in an almost mocking way. Everything about this place is so…putrid.

This world…if it could even be called a world…was absolutely agonizing. Creating any form of thought was incredibly strenuous on my mind, as my surroundings lacked any inspiration I could draw upon to make anything cohesive.

Without warning, a light flashed through the limitless darkness, blinding the eyes that were so used to the lack of coloration of this world. I tried to latch onto it in desperation, but it was gone before I could even grasp it.

And there stood a figure cloaked in absolute shadow, a shadow far darker than anything in this realm. He looked like a solid silhouette despite the surroundings.

For once in my existence, I could not tell who this person was. He was...

Different...

He looked nothing like any being I had ever seen in my lifetime.

He sneered at me, speaking to me in a tone I knew was sinister and yet, he spoke words that for now I cannot even fathom to remember anymore.

Words woven together became splintered, as the only sentences I could gleam mentioned a young boy that the figure spoke of in an elated tone.

Of a collection of familiar sounding gems lingering in a memory far beyond my reach.

And finally, of a singular girl, one whose mere name produced immense anger in the figure, making the shadows flee in terror as the man's aura of malice shook the void itself.

He disappeared almost immediately, and so did the dreaded darkness I had grown so accustomed to.

Soon, I was in a blanket of darkness yet again, but light now poured into the shadows.

I stared at my scarred hands, finally able to see the color I had missed for so long. I chuckled to myself as I relished the sudden change.

Turning around, I began to run towards the beautiful light in absolute glee.

Sprinting towards freedom!

My body crashed against a pair of bars that materialized in front of me. A shock jolted through my body, a body that had never truly realized what pain was. I was propelled backwards from the shock, with the stone walls soon materializing on all other sides.

I screamed out in anger as I pushed myself off the cold stone floors beneath me. Freedom was at my fingertips for a moment, and yet someone felt the audacity to immediately snatch it from my ravenous grasp.

Anger replaced the darkness as my yells of defiance shook the very walls that now entrapped me, my face burning in the dark as the screams of anguish and the almost nostalgic feeling of betrayal filled my soul.

1

Connor: Alone

The shrill chirping of a bird in the distance knocked me out of my present thoughts, glancing away from the ancient book I held within my grasp. The pages crinkled as I leaned my head back against the tree I was sitting under, glancing up at where the sharp calls were coming from. The two different styles of handwriting still lingered in my mind as I gazed up, one of the pair being incredibly purposeful and neat, whilst the other was sloppy and dug into the other person's words.

The neat expressions would always tickle a form of nostalgia within me, whilst the sloppier ones always elicited a form of curiosity, always wondering whose hands crafted the other half of this book. Or better still, how each piece of writing was connected to one another.

Directly above where I sat, a black and white magpie sang its radiant song, its head directed to the heavens as the branch quivered with every motion. It appeared to enjoy where it perched, calling out to others as it wove wonderful melodies with its sweet chirps and squeaks. It didn't appear to hold a nest of any kind, so perhaps it was instead searching for food, or maybe even calling for a mate.

Regardless, I took it as a sign I've been out here for too long.

1

Closing the worn book I held in my hands as I lowered my head from the branches above, I glanced over the tattered title that was carved into the front so long ago.

Inside the Mind of a Tactician...such a simple title for a book like this.

A melancholy smile curled across my lips as I glanced back one final time at the pristine view I sat in front of. Of the calm stream that silently flowed west about twenty feet from where I sat. Of the many other trees that towered around me, creating an ocean of green that I just so happened to be swallowed in. Of the towering mountain sides that housed imposing cliff sides, which if proper courage were built up would provide the greatest perspective of this entire valley.

Of the absolute silence and peace of all, allowing me to leave the aching web of my thoughts behind as I took it all in.

Standing up, I brushed the loose grass off my grey pants and shirt as I snatched my brown cloak from the branch I hung it from, checking it twice to ensure no bugs or rodents somehow crawled into it. Latching it around my neck, I took one last fleeting glance as I began walking down the path I had torn down many times, almost to the point of memorization.

How long was I out this time? Maybe an hour...it's hard to tell when you don't really care where you're going.

Feeling my worn boots crunched against the pebble ridden path I had carved what felt like years ago, I let out a deep sigh as I stared off into the forest, my vision distorting as I became lost in my own mind. My feet knew where to go, so it's fine if my mind takes a short break.

I wonder if I'll get to explore the entirety of this place?

Probably will, after all I have quite a bit of time now.

A depressed laugh shook its way out my system involuntarily, glancing down at the book that still rested within my right hand.

Yeah...sure do have a lot of time.

I glanced up at the bright blue sky that hung directly overhead as I ran my left hand through my coarse black hair, noting the sun that now hung directly overhead.

Three to four hours then. I left that thing I call home right when the sun peeked above the mountain tops.

Combined with this twenty-minute walk, I'll probably be back right when Jack finishes his daily training.

A shiver abruptly ran down my spine as something sharp daintily poked into the small of my back, freezing me in my aimless stride. An unrefined chortle echoed behind me, followed hastily by the pacing of another set of heavy footsteps. I attempted to crane my neck around to see who my assailant was, but whatever blade he was holding jabbed harder into me, forcing me to revert my gaze. My face shifted into a frown as another gravely laugh rang out.

"What do we 'ave here?" A gruff male voice gleefully murmured behind me as the form of his companion came into view, "Zain told us that we wouldn't find anything by glancing around the area, and yet here I find a scrawny child wandering aimlessly through the forest. How old do ya think this kid is? Fourteen? Fifteen?"

"Sixteen." I growled out as I raised my hands up, allowing them to know I wasn't carrying any weapons. Well, unless they considered an old book a weapon.

The only man I could see was stocky in stature, probably a few inches more compressed than I was. He was dressed like an ordinary civilian, wearing a ragged brown tunic and pants. He held a small dagger within his hands, holding it in a manner that showed he had absolutely no idea how to properly use one. The point directly facing me, he flashed an almost innocent grin as he stepped closer.

Yellowed teeth, dirtied skin and secondhand clothes...some form of wandering bandit even all the way up here.

"I don't have anything you ruffians would care about," I calmly explained, motioning to the book still present in my raised hands, "A simple tome is all I took with me on my walk, and I'm unsure if you all can even read in the first place." Hearing a grumble directly behind me, the man holding me in place pushed what I now assumed was a dagger slightly deeper, piercing through my shirt. I cringed as the metal poked into bare skin, a minuscule amount of blood beginning to trickle from the scrape.

"Don't give us that attitude kid. As you can see, we're the ones in control here." The man in front of me laughed as he began rifling through the pockets of my pants, blatantly ignoring the book that rested in my raised arms.

Grunting in annoyance over finding absolutely nothing within them, I almost let out a snicker as the man grew progressively more agitated the more he searched.

You can examine me all you want; you'll have nothing but pocket lint and loose scraps of paper. I'll let you disappoint yourself, and when you let me go in irritation I'll be on my merry way.

"Ya gotta be hiding something kid," the short man groaned as his search of me traversed higher, "You may be some runt, but no one walks 'round with nothing." Breaching up into my shirt, I realized that the man was almost complete with his search, having already torn through my boots and pants for absolutely nothing. Freezing at my chest, I let out a sigh of relief, only to notice the crooked grin spread across the man's face. My relief washing away, a coldness overwhelmed me as he wrenched his hand into the cavern that was my shirt, ripping out something that made his grin grow even wider.

My emerald pendant...

Resting within his palm and with the metallic band now being pulled tightly around my neck, I could feel the man's intrigue as he stared into the swirling green pools. Every second he stared at the gem was another extra moment I desired to pummel him into the dirt, my jaw clenching and my eyes boring into him the more he placed his filthy hands upon its pristine surface. His yellowed teeth pulled back like a dog's, he shot up to his partner and let out a hoarse chuckle.

"Now this," he began as he turned it over in the sunlight, examining every angle as I noticed the many smudges now adorning its surface, "This ought to fetch us a pretty penny. Oi Maurice? Would you kindly unhook our ticket to riches out from around his neck so we can share what we found with the others?" Feeling the blade shift further as he nodded, I almost gasped in disbelief as he lowered the dagger slightly off my back, growing marginally closer to unhook the pendant from my neck.

Fool...

Whirling around with my hands still raised, I threw a kick into the other short man's direction, only able to watch in disbelief as a boot-covered foot cracked into his ribs. He let out a pained groan as he stumbled to the left, dropping his dagger on the way down.

Hearing his equally as inept partner sprinting up in surprise, I ducked past a haphazard strike and threw my right hand forward, making sure I threw the fist that still held the book in it. While most of the pages and cover of the small book were incredibly worn down due to the test of time, the spine remained as stiff as it once was when it was created.

Smashing that side of the mini book into his mouth, his eyes rolled back as a drop of blood cascaded through the air and plummeted to the ground below. I could even feel a couple teeth shift from the force of the blow.

Lurching to the floor I snatched up the dagger left behind by the first goon as the pendant bounced against my chest, the cool metal shining brilliantly with every movement.

Without letting up I threw the dagger into the unnamed man's knee, watching as he crumpled to the ground as the blade dug into his damaged appendage.

Hearing the distinct sound of feet bounding swiftly behind me, I realized that the one I had brought down earlier wasn't content with staying that way. Ducking on instinct, a heavy swing whooshed above me as the bandit Maurice had made his move, still clutching his potentially bruised side.

I have to create an opening. Difficult considering I don't have a weapon, but I'll make do. I always have.

As I pushed myself up to jump to the side, I slung my right hand across the coarse path, grasping onto as much loose dirt as I could. As my body lurched to the side, I hurled the mass into his face, landing on my feet as the dust particles invaded his retinas. He let out a sharp bellow as his offhand immediately went to his face, wiping his eyes frantically in a desperate attempt to regain his vision.

Utilize whatever control you possess...see options that others cannot.

Taking advantage of his sudden blindness, I threw myself at him and drilled another fist into his side, aiming for the spot where I kicked him previously. He gasped in a mix of surprise and pain, swinging wildly in an attempt to connect with his invisible opponent. Dodging the sloppy punch with ease, my eyes locked onto a broken branch that rested on the ground nearby, most likely snapping from its source due to the previous week's spring storm. I snatched it up immediately, stepping out of the way of another rage-induced punch.

His chest or the spot where he's bruised. I need him awake.

I swung the hardened branch into the man's side as hard as I could, my assailant letting out a sharp gasp as the air forcefully left him. Before he could react any further, I slammed it into his ribs, sending him sprawling back as he finally collapsed to the ground below. A few soft pants escaped my lips as I dropped the branch, turning back around to my original opponent. He still sat defeated on the ground, gripping onto his damaged knee.

With both of my threats neutralized for now, I marched over to the unnamed man who shook me down in search of riches.

Still crying out in pain through a few blubbering tears, I grabbed hold of his aged greasy hair. Keeping him in place for a moment, I made sure the man known as Maurice was still crumpled to the ground before turning back to the one who touched the gem.

"You absolute wretch," I seethed out as he stared up at me in pain and terror, "I would've let you just walk away if you hadn't touched that with your disgusting paws." I reached down and tore the dagger from his ruined knee, eliciting another pained scream.

"You aren't worth my time; just a petty obstacle set in my way by the universe." Not letting him even cry out another time, I gripped into each hair and slammed his already battered face into the hardened dirt path below, knocking a couple more teeth loose as he was forced into unconsciousness.

As the dust billowing up from the blow began to fill the air, I marched over to the thug Maurice. He gripped multiple places on his battered body as he attempted to stand, groaning in pain through heaving breaths as he finally opened his eyes.

One hand on the bloodied text, another on the dripping dagger, I strove over to the man, pointing the dagger at his throat before he could even react. He stammered between words, unable to find his own pleas for mercy as I stared him down like the afternoon sun above me.

Sighing to myself, I lowered the dagger from his face, staring down as his reddened eyes widened in surprise.

"Scoop up your friend and leave; back to Bellhollow or wherever you crawled out of," I calmly demanded as I already began to walk away, hearing the soft droplets of blood drip off the once clean metal and pattering onto the dirt below, "I've never killed anyone with these hands, and I'd rather not start it with you. So leave, and while you're at it forget this area ever existed. If I find you back here, I don't think I'll be as forgiving as I was now." Giving a scared nod as I stepped over the prone form of the unnamed bandit, Maurice lurched over to his friend and threw him over his shoulder with a strained grunt. The slow dragging of their feet echoed into my ears as I ensured the book wasn't damaged by the strike I had utilized it for. To my relief, aside from a drop of blood the book was unscathed.

Without even glancing away I hurled the dagger to my side, hearing it clatter against either a tree or its roots deep within the brush.

I have no need for the tool of a thief.

Pulling the pendant out, I spent the rest of my calm walk buffing out any smudges or marks that man might have made, making sure it was in the same condition as it has always been.

As it was...when you once held it...

* * *

As my meticulous cleaning finally came to an end, I noticed the path I was treading was far more familiar than anything else I'd already traveled. Finally averting my gaze as I let the pendant fall back into my shirt, my hazel eyes locked onto what I'd been marching towards this whole time.

My home...

Well...the ramshackle cabin I call home now...

My feet involuntarily beginning to drag, I stepped up to the rickety wooden door, watching as it wobbled as I stood near it. I averted my gaze towards the sky, noting the sun was already beginning its downward descent.

No sounds of fighting either. Jack probably just finished.

Easing the door open into the entrance way to the kitchen area we threw together, I glanced around the room to see if he was in here or if he decided to pay an early visit to Eincrest.

The former proved true, as leaning against the leftmost wall of the building was my brother, Jack. At the moment, he was cleaning off his massive two-handed broadsword, pointing it up single-handedly whilst cleaning it off with the other. He set a now grey cloth down on the nearby kitchen table and began cleaning it off with his grey shirt. The coat that was always attached to him rested nearby, hooked onto the handle of a cabinet that housed our dry food.

"You're later than you usually are, Connor," he announced in the smooth, almost jovial tone he's carried for most his life, not even bothering to look up as he already knew it was me.

"I got distracted." I simply stated, already walking past the man who was still glancing into the reflection of his sword, ensuring it was pristine.

"Well anyways I'm glad you're back. I think we should-" he clearly paused mid-sentence, finally noticing I was already far past him and at the door of the room I always frequented.

"Well uh bye I guess," he sarcastically said with a sigh as I opened the door, already stepping inside, "Is that...are you dripping blood right now? Were you late 'cause you got into a scuffle with a squirrel or something?" Without responding I closed the door behind me, although the walls were thin enough where I could hear him mutter a curse or two under his breath.

Still have time before nightfall, although I suppose that hasn't stopped me before.

Setting the tactics book back down on the desk it usually sat on, I stretched out my arms as several joints popped, much to my relief.

Haven't fought against another human being like that since then... hopefully this means everything hasn't been for nothing.

I gripped the green pendant within my shirt, feeling an odd comfort with it around my neck safe and sound.

You had to try and take this didn't you?

Pulling back the wooden chair that screeched against the ground with every movement, I planted my tired self within the chair with an aching sigh.

I stared up towards what I've done in the days prior, before I finally resumed the work after the long excursion I had just gone on.

2

Connor: The Terror of Dreams

"He possessed armor like an eastern soldier of Bellhollow, the mystique of someone from Pyrnesse, and yet he still managed to tear his way into the center of Solaton. We're in the heart of this country and he somehow still arrived here anyway." The single candle sitting in front of me wavered with every word that exited my mouth, threatening to flicker out and leave me in darkness if I spoke any more. It towered over the inkwell I dipped my white feather into, the blackened ink oozing from the tip of the quill.

My eyelids began to grow even heavier as words meshed with previous sentences I'd already established by now. My fingers shook with every motion, making me have to go back and redo the word I had already gone over once already. It took almost a full minute to finish one sentence.

Letting out a sigh of relief at finally finishing the theory I had in mind, I chucked the feather to the side without glancing up. The hardened material clattered into the inside of the base of the inkwell, the sound echoing within the enclosed space.

Pulling out another metallic pin, I attached this new paper to the wall in front of me, allowing it to dry.

Letting it blend in with the mesh of papers and files that adorned this particular wall, the paper made it appear far more organic and disrupted than it originally was. I can't even remember a time when this portion of the wall was brown like the rest of it.

So hard to think...can barely keep my eyes open long enough to jot a single character down.

I gripped the sides of my head as I moaned in annoyance, the walls of my mind crumbling as my thoughts became jumbled and confused.

"Everywhere it conflicts...dammit. Why does everything I find have to be so paradoxical in nature?" My finger involuntarily tapped against the desk I sat at, rapidly pattering against the hollow wooden base. I let out an exacerbated groan as I rocked the chair back, staring into the loose boards that made up the rickety ceiling. A sigh rolled off my tongue as the chair creaked back and forth.

What am I doing?

I crumpled forward as I laid my body against the desk, pressing my face down into the other swathes of paper I had yet to fill out with ideas. Many were fractured theories and hypotheses, not making any sense until I crafted another one to match it.

I've been sitting for hours, and yet even in that excruciating amount of time I have nothing to show for it.

No new theories.

No confirmation of old ones.

Just the same emptiness he left behind for me to pick up the shattered pieces of...

As I pushed myself up off the shifty desk with an elongated yawn, I glanced down once I thought I properly shook the tiredness off.

The papers in front of me began to swirl and spiral, almost appearing as if they were liquid in nature. They were spinning like they were gripped by some form of tornado, twisting around my desk. Despite the strange occurrence, my brain did not initially process the oddity occurring in front of me. I began to try and write in the swirls as if they were solid objects, only to witness the feather slowly sink into the whirlpool as if it were a puddle of ink.

My brain finally understood the new reality I had been dipped into, snapping to attention as the feather fully disappeared.

Succumbed to sleep again...why does this always happen?

With legs that didn't feel like my own, I stood up from my chair, tipping it over as I stumbled out. Not that it mattered to the chair anyway, defying physics as it rebounded against the ground with a resounding clatter. Turning back, it was already back in the position it was when I was sitting in it.

Lurching forward, I grasped the wooden doorknob, tripping right at the moment I ripped open the wooden gateway. To my surprise, as I collapsed never once did I hit solid ground or experience the ever-growing pain that comes with it.

Instead, I was met with an endless void of shadows and darkness, swallowing me up. The door above me disappeared into a faint light.

And I fell...deeper and deeper into this blackness.

I shut my eyes as some form of wind rushed past my face, hoping to awaken anywhere else besides this void.

Soon, light began to brush over my eyes; not any form of aimless ambient light familiar to dreams, but one that carried an ounce of warmth to it.

Opening my hazel eyes, I found myself in a room that I never thought I would be in ever again.

My house...

Not that dilapidated shack that I currently reside in with my brother, but my actual home.

The wooden and stone walls; the same wooden roof that once sloped upward in a triangular fashion. Same photographs that lined the cabinets and walls as proud trophies.

Maybe a little off in some of the minute details, but it's all the same.

I sat down at the wooden table at the center of the room, passing the other three empty seats and plopping down in the chair I always knew; the one that creaked every time I sat down.

I glanced over, trying to see if this dream truly held every detail, when my eyes widened in surprise over what I saw.

My mother...

The long black hair that matched my own swayed momentarily over her face as she shut the cabinet she was shuffling through previously. She turned around with a bright smile, hiding a flickering annoyance beneath. In her left hand she carried a small clear case, one which held a multitude of medical equipment from gauze to bandages. She always kept it in the closest cabinet to her room, knowing full well she would be needing it soon. She crouched down beside me as her smile drifted into a scowl.

"I swear to whatever god or deity exists above that if your father does this again, I'm throwing him off a cliff." My mother's tone never shifted from the calm and collected manner she always spoke, making her promise sound even more venomous.

I winced as she tightened the somewhat patchy gauze around my right arm, making sure the bleeding I hadn't noticed previously was covered. Another gauze found its way around my forehead, looping around as she pushed my matted hair up and to the side. She gingerly lifted my right hand as I involuntarily flinched, eliciting a sigh of annoyance from my current caretaker at the state of my currently bent pointer finger.

"There's a slight fracture in this finger too," she commented in an almost chastising manner, although I'm sure that scolding was directed to wherever my father was, "I just...I don't understand why he didn't hold anything back against you today. He should know his strength compared to yours, and yet I didn't see him even try to hold back anything." I could feel the muscles of my body sag as I let out a sigh, almost forgetting the troubling pain I was still in.

"I don't know," I said in a voice that sounded like me, but in so many ways it felt so different. It was almost peppier, more far-sighted. I suppose that maturing over a couple months from this would bring down the tenor in my voice.

Or...did I simply shift away from those ideals all on my own?

"Maybe he was trying to push me to become stronger all on my own? I've only been fighting against a training dummy this entire time, not actually against him. It felt so...different and wrong, and perhaps that is what he was going for."

My mother just bit her lip and sighed, "Well your father utilized the same methods with Jack, but he didn't come out of all that with as many injuries as you have right now." Another groan shook out of my throat, making me slump back in my chair at the mention of the man my brother was.

How much of a prodigy he was with that sword.

She grasped my finger gingerly, eliciting a frantic yelp of pain as a tear came to the corner of my eye. Without letting go, she took two small sticks and placed them on the sides, before immediately wrapping it swiftly with gauze. She continued wrapping until it grew incredibly tight, my finger remaining immobile even without the tremendous pain coursing through my fingers. I knew the splint was temporary before we visited another town's doctor, but I was always impressed with what my mother could do.

"Well, this proves it," I muttered to myself, "I'll never be able to surpass Jack in a fight, much less match father's skill with a weapon. If I ever got into a fight on my own, I'd be dead before I could raise a weapon. Maybe I would be better off just reading the book that you and your friend wrote." My mother just gripped my hand once again and looked at me with her bright blue eyes. Even though my finger was secured for the time being, it was still incredibly tender to the touch. I let out a muffled grunt of pain at the contact.

"Connor don't you dare say that," she whispered, "Jack may be incredibly skilled with a sword, but the way you can gauge how your opponent will act is absolutely remarkable. Remember everything I've taught you when you fight your father again. You have gifts, Connor, and if you give them proper attention then you'll be far more renowned for those instead of just being a simple-minded warrior."

She released my hand, and within it now was a vibrant, emerald pendant my mother always wore. It was smooth, with the cold stone sending a single shiver up my body. I was entranced by the swirling pools of emerald-green, staring into every varied angle. I looked up at her in confusion, curious as to why she would ever give me her prized pendant. A pendant which for as long as I have been alive had never left from the safety around her neck.

"A charm for good luck, and to help you think before you fight," she teased while knocking me on the head, before picking up the pendant and looping it around my neck. A faint metallic click echoed out as the gem fell, bouncing against my shirt once.

"Remember everything I've taught you Connor, and please don't stop reading that book. My friend and I put a lot of time into that, so even if her writing is basically illegible it still may provide you with significant information about the outside world." She ruffled up my hair as she flashed a smile, standing up from her position on the ground as I did the same a small distance away from her.

"But that isn't going to help you at all, is it?" My mind recoiled momentarily as words foreign to my mother's sweet and calming tone echoed from her mouth as if it were a normal occurrence. The creepiest factor of it all was the ever-present smile on her warm face as she said this, perhaps even growing wider after the fact. A deep heat began to overwhelm my body as I involuntarily stepped back in surprise, and perhaps even in fear.

"M-Mom?"

"So much weakness in you...even if that piece of jewelry had an ounce of luck within it, you'd still be too useless to actually make it worth anything. And don't get me started on that book you're so adamant on reading over and over ad nauseam." Another hesitant step, this one feeling far heavier as my leg began shaking. I stared up at my still smiling mother, her head lowered as her silky hair covered the rest of her expression. It swayed just barely enough to reveal her ever present grin.

"What're y-you saying? Y-You're scaring me, stop it!"

"Oh Connor," she chastised as the heat continued to grow stronger, almost to the point of being overwhelming, "Why are you so afraid of the mother you let get taken away?" I stumbled back, tripping over the chair I once sat in. Collapsing to the floor, something gave way beneath me, scraping off the wooden boards my father once hammered in. I nervously looked over my now prone shoulder.

The planks were blackened, charred by some kind of heat or *fire*...

What I had knocked loose from the boards was the ash attached to it, now fluttering through the air as it assaulted my lungs. I violently coughed into my hand, my eyes beginning to burn as a familiar smell and taste overwhelmed my senses. I stumbled wildly, attempting to gather my bearings as the room spun around me. I propped myself against a wall, recoiling immediately at the intense heat I was met with. I finally was able to open my eyes, now completely turned around from where I once started.

What I smelled was the putrid stench of rotten smoke, perforating the air with its repugnant odor. The walls shifted and creaked, threatening to cave in as the fire had not quite reached the interior of the building. Instead, it lurked on the outside, a beast stalking its prey as it waited for me to come outside.

As he waited for me to come outside.

Hearing heavy footsteps approaching behind me, I chose not to hesitate and be another victim of this horrific nightmare. I latched my hand onto a sword that always rested on our nightstand, one my father said he once wielded when he was a soldier.

Whirling around, I plunged the blade into whatever was stalking behind me, lowering my body to deliver a fatal strike to the stomach. Hearing the distinct tone of metal piercing flesh as my head crashed into the heavy stomach of my assailant, I almost smiled at my victory. Only, something was wrong. The boots they wore…they weren't the blackened steel boots of enemy infantry. They were the worn brown boots of a common man who maintained his home and his family as if it were his job. I shakily glanced up, not wanting to see the man I had just run through.

"F-Father…?" My father stared down at me in surprise, the man who once towered over me feeling rather small in my grasp. Every ounce of defiance he always held dissipated, instead replaced by the obvious look of betrayal.

"C-Connor?" I could feel him fading within my grasp, but for whatever reason I couldn't pull the blade from his body. Hearing a low, almost distorted laugh, I glanced around to the source. The being that took my mother's form was holding the sword in place with a single hand, the smile remaining present beneath her midnight locks.

"Sorry, can't let you do that," she chided out in a giddy tone, flashing her now manic blue eyes, "Maybe you aren't so useless after all. Fairly decent strike, maybe if it was a little deeper…" Without warning, she tugged at the metallic part of the blade, inching it closer to her as my father squirmed in agony. His betrayed brown eyes never left mine, as I couldn't build the strength to look away.

"That's more like it," she gleefully exclaimed as she stepped closer

18

to me, keeping her hand on the blade as the flames began seeping in through the roof, "You don't even have the strength to release your grip on that blade, let alone pull it out. I pity you, so much potential the universe poured into such a useless person. Maybe if Jack was the one, or if someone else was born in your stead? Maybe they'd at least have the power to actually do something." The floorboards began to creak and falter under my weight as I stared up in anger at the being in my mother's skin, taunting me with her visage.

"S-Shut up," I muttered out, still attempting to wrench free from my father's quivering body.

The being almost appeared perplexed by my outburst, the smile faltering slightly as she edged ever closer.

"Do you have actions to actually back that line up, child? Or are you just talking up everything like you always have?" My teeth painfully ground against one another as the room shifted another time, spiraling in a way unfamiliar to the real world.

"You don't know me," I muttered out in a voice that sounded like my own again, "You're nothing but an ancient visage! A whisper of the past sent to break me down."

"But can you deny anything I've said? Do you have a noble sentiment that could actually refute everything you already know?" The room shook again as I lowered my head, feeling something coalesce slowly in my hands. The being let out another shrill laugh, amused.

"So quick-witted, that you didn't even realize you had countered yourself," she chuckled as she wiped a tear away from her eye, "I have seen your bark, child, but where is that bite you've promised?" She leaned in close, smiling wider than ever as she pulled in.

So useless...

The single thought echoed in my brain as I couldn't muster the courage to stare at my mind's bastardized illusion of my own parents.

19

Everything you have done has led to failure, and death...what's the point of going on anymore?

Maybe you should just give up here...let yourself be swallowed up by your own nightmares.

"Get out..." I murmured, seeing the being's smile fold into a frown.

"Get out...of my head!" The scream I bellowed out shook the foundation of the room we were in, blasting up winds as the room spiraled and spun. All of my rage emanated throughout the walls as the visions quivered, the fire itself retreating in fear. As the room began to fade away and vanish into the same blackness as it began, a new thought rang louder than the others. A thought, which I knew when I awakened would be as present as it is now.

I will never allow myself to be as useless as I was that day...never.

3

Connor: Shattered Memories

I awoke from the dream with a violent jolt, smacking my head against the low hanging ceiling of the rickety cabin. I grasped my forehead in pain as I groaned, murmuring to myself in tired annoyance. Once the sting had largely dulled from my senses, I fully opened my eyes and glanced around my room.

The old, wrinkled curtains of the bedroom window were already pulled open, suggesting that Jack had already awoken hours before I had even stirred. I found myself resting in the top bunk of a bed Jack and I had as kids that never left this place. I always got the top of the bed, considering Jack was older and got first pick. Besides, he always talked about how he would find a way to fall off and crash into the floor while he slept.

Did he seriously take the time and effort to drag me from the office, up the ladder and into this bed?

Of course he did.

I groaned as I pulled myself out of bed and rubbed my pounding skull, knowing a headache would be coming in my near future. Placing a hand on my chest, the rapid beating of my heart hammered against the confines of my rib cage, threatening to explode out. I stared down at my hands, sighing in relief that there wasn't a drop of blood that stained them.

"Easy Connor," I reassured myself, "Just...Just a-a bad dream is all." But it wasn't a dream. It wasn't fuzzy like a dream. It may have been fractured, and perhaps even unreal in its appearance, but other moments were so clear.

Everything about it, even the most dramatic moments, still held the vividness of reality.

The dagger I had left by my bed was now clasped within its sheath. *Father always called my weapon choice...unconventional.*

I changed into an identical set of clothes as I slipped my tight boots on, slipping the tactics book into my pocket where it usually sat on my travels. I didn't have much armor, mostly because we lacked enough strong materials for a pair of gauntlets, let alone a full set of armor.

I ensured the pendant remained dormant within my clothes, hidden from prying eyes.

I could buy something in the village, but...I have no reason to go there anyway.

I glanced back into my quaint little cabin in the woods, before heading outside.

I chuckled coldly to myself, as I walked along the path right when the birds began their morning songs. In my meandering stride, I passed by the ruins of my old home.

The wood was still charred, crisp and black. Shattered glass adorned the outside and chunks of wood were scattered around. The remains of the door were still in front of the collapsed door frame, a hole split through the center. The triangular roof was utterly caved in, with bits of its once pristine wooden planks sticking out through random holes in the wall.

When I was young, this place was a paradise. A place my mother had us move to, away from the noise of the world. Away from the chaos of man.

And yet, despite her efforts, the turmoil found us anyway.

I kept shuffling down the dirt route until I reached the all too familiar dirt clearing, pausing in my stride as I stood there.

I pity you, so much potential the universe poured into such a useless person.

I shook out those words from my brain as I reached down to my side, brushing off the dirt covering a loose piece of metal that was lying in the dust...forgotten.

I snatched up a metal shoulder guard, once a bright silver, but now age and the stinging air had rusted its once clean surface. I stared into the dirty reflection, feeling my vision shift and shake as my mind wandered. My skull ached as day turned to night, and my brain began to travel down a path it had refused to witness for a long time.

* * *

The house I came to love was burning down, the wooden and stone roof caving in on itself with piercing crashes and bangs.

Every piece of this house that our family had taken so much time to build was breaking down. The windows were fissuring to the point of shattering. The wood was blackening and starting to crack and splinter from the heat alone.

Standing in front was my father and I, staring forward in abject shock and horror at the raging inferno. He held me back with only one arm, preventing me from diving in as I thrashed within his grasp.

I knew mom and Jack hadn't gotten out yet, so I had to get to them.

The more I squirmed the tighter my father's hold became, gripping me firmly as his body shook with pure anger.

Without warning, a darkened sword drove a hole through the front door, and a black boot kicked down the shattered remains of the door. My father and I both audibly breathed a sigh of relief as my brother Jack came lumbering through the door. His curly brown locks were covered in soot and ash as he coughed up smoke, his brown eyes watering. I almost smiled upon seeing Jack holding his massive sword and a bow on his back, weapons he cherished and the only things he managed to save from the fire. I hesitated for a moment as he staggered towards us, before I asked him the question hammering in my mind.

"Jack, where's mom?"

Shifting his expression away as his normally jovial face began to tremble, the world screeched to a halt as he softly shook his head. My breath hitched in my throat as the meaning of his silence hit me, my limbs shaking as every battered emotion crashed onto my psyche.

Mom...mom no...you can't be gone. Jack...Jack must've seen something wrong...you have to still be alive somewhere!

Every thought of denial crumbled as my father pulled me closer, his initial grip on me shifting from imprisonment to comfort as he pulled his head down, his teeth grinding together as a tear hit the top of my skull.

My body grew numb as my mind attempted to understand, slouching down into my father's grasp.

Please don't be gone...please god don't leave me without even a goodbye.

As tears welled up in my smoked stained eyes, a momentous battle cry ruptured throughout the land, puncturing through the sound of crackling fire before I could even register anymore of my growing internal anguish.

Dozens of soldiers spewed out from the forest and from behind our home, each garbed in armor black as the night. The two in the front held flickering torches, while the rest gripped sharpened black spears in their hands and on their backs. Encircling us on all sides, the two remaining members of my family raised their weapons as the soldiers raised theirs. Released from my father's grasp, I slowly drew my sword as well. Even though I was more comfortable with a dagger or a small knife, this was the only weapon I could grab on short notice.

At least I know how to use it.

In front of us, the soldiers which encircled the main entrance parted the way for someone else.

A larger knight marched through, although he was instead cloaked in a solid silver set of armor with many black accents.

A black cape with a purple interior was clasped firmly around his neck, which flowed in the midnight wind. A helmet of the same design as his armor masked all of his features, with the metal looking twisted and malformed; almost as if the blacksmith who designed it did a poor job at molding the material. At his side rested a shimmering sword with indecipherable symbols branded upon it.

Jack glared at them as the rest of us stood frozen, yet he still shakily pulled the bow from his back. The soldier's closed in further as he did so, with the commanding knight being the only one not to move. My father and I remained still, staring directly at the horde in front of us.

Jack swiftly knocked two arrows on his bowstring, a move he had perfected over years of training. These arrows were ones he had bought at the marketplace in case of emergency: arrows built with material that could pierce through armor if necessary.

He hastily took aim at the knight and fired both arrows. The first flew directly at the knight's face with a piercing speed. He caught the arrow rigidly right before it connected, the point inches away as he snapped it like a twig. As the pieces of the first still fell, the knight moved slightly to the right to dodge the second, with said arrow finding a new home in an unprepared soldier's face. He was knocked off his feet and dead on the ground in seconds.

25

Steadying my blade as Jack drew his own, I grew closer to my father as the soldiers did the same.

"What should we do father?" His brow furrowed as his face molded into one filled completely with rage. He swung his axe across the ground, kicking up large amounts of dust as he took his usual stance, resting the axe head on the ground a little behind him.

"Kids...get out of here."

"What!"

"Dad, if you think I'm going to just run away you're out of your mind."

"Don't argue with me Jack. Get as far away from here as you can and don't turn back. Try to get to the village and inform someone if you can. I can handle this." I tried to yell in further defiance, but Jack hastily grabbed me by my arm and dragged me into the forest without another word. Charging full speed at the soldiers near the forest, my brother drew his massive broadsword with one hand and slashed across, bulldozing right through them and dragging my screaming form behind him.

"After them," I barely heard an echoing voice say, swiftly followed by the clambering of soldiers as they gave chase, "Leave the patriarch of the family to me." Jack only increased his speed as we rushed further into the deep tree line.

"Jack let me go!" I screamed. I rapidly punched his arm in defiance amid my screams, but his grip only tightened around me as he continued to run. Jack only returned me a somber look, one that was still filled with genuine sympathy.

Minutes dragged on as we stormed through the forest, until I eventually noticed my brother's grip loosen on me as he finally ran out of breath. Suddenly coming to a stop, Jack released me from his grasp and stood directly in front of me.

"Our father and his blasted pride," Jack murmured as he drew the broadsword he carried like an appendage, "I think we've led the idiots far enough. Get back to dad. I can keep them busy while you do." I simply nodded my head and charged back the direction we came from, with Jack flashing me a weary smile as I sprinted off through an alternate route to avoid the soldier's rapid approach.

Taking this way through the intrusive branches and dead leaves that littered the soil below, I was able to get to my father just in time to witness him and the knight clashing against one another. With one final swing, the knight swung his glistening blade over his shoulder and into my father's axe, digging him into the ground. Just as quickly as he did this, the knight performed an underhanded swing, one which my father could barely block as he was propelled a couple feet back.

"Father!" My father jerked towards me in anger tinted with surprise.

"Connor, don't you dare take another step!" I stopped immediately at his yells, stiffening as my mind refused to comprehend my father's bizarre declaration. And yet, I still halted my approach.

Glancing away from me, my father charged forward and clashed once again with the knight. Both men were switching between their offensive and defensive stances, battering and blocking all at once. My father parried a sword swing and finally managed to strike the knight as he dodged out of the way.

The axe managed to connect with his shoulder guard, dislodging it from his armor. My father smirked as they both jumped away from one another.

"Surprised someone else didn't arrive to join you. I expected Garrick. Someone of higher status. But some nobody? Do you all think that little of me to not even send every single man you had?" The knight replied with silence. My father's teeth ground together as he glared forward.

"Why have you come here?" my father questioned, "For a mission like this I'd expect someone of higher status."

"You can't run from the life you chose Master Gaius," the knight replied in a smooth baritone voice that echoed throughout the chambers of his mask. It would almost sound pleasant if it wasn't so bone chilling to hear.

"This squalor you have established is admirable, but you can't keep running forever Gaius." My father's expression darkened for a moment, before he swiftly drew a small dagger from his side and flung it at the knight. The knight didn't move even an inch as the dagger's blade shattered against the front of his helmet, the sound breaking through the silence of the woods. My father scoffed in annoyance at his failure as he shifted his stance.

"You think I care about your petty threats? From people like you no less? Your people made me into a monster...and maybe this all is just retribution for what I have done. But, even if it is, I won't let you tear down everything I've spent so long to build." The silver marauder just chuckled to himself, his laughter a cold echo that reverberated from within his twisted visage.

"Is that so?" he laughed coldly, "I suppose you're the same stubborn man our country has known for so long." My father paused while staring at the knight, a cathartic grin spreading across his face.

"Perhaps so," he solemnly sighed, "I've done a lot of bad in my life, but I won't shirk this opportunity to make do on the foulness of my past." My father pulled out his axe and beckoned it towards the knight.

"I refuse to yield. Strike me down if you can."

With a loud bellow my father lunged at the commander. Their weapons clashed in a battle that would affect my life forever. The knight effortlessly blocked each of my father's swings with surprising ease.

28

As they clashed, axe and sword locked with one another as neither could maintain dominance over the other. Eventually my father backed off and raised his axe, swinging down with as much force as he could muster. With an inhuman reaction time the knight sidestepped the axe swing, slashing across my father's chest before the axe buried itself into the dirt.

The knight struck my father across the jaw, causing him to stumble backwards. In the midst of recovering and raising his axe, the knight grabbed him by the shoulder and plunged the blade through his chest.

A mask of shock appeared on both me and my father's faces. Time seemed to freeze as I noticed the silence creeping in, the wind dying down as their two cloaks fell still. All that could be heard were my father's pained gasps.

"Is…is that it?" he whispered into my father's ear incredulously, "I expected something more from you." He pulled the sword out of my father's body with a disgusting sound and lightly pushed my father down. I flew forward to catch him as he stumbled back, causing both of us to fall to the ground with the combined force.

"Don't…don't leave. Please don't leave me! F-Father!" He sputtered on his own breath as he stared up at me, his bloodshot eyes quivering as he choked back blood.

"Connor…please…run."

"Come on father please…get up!"

I cradled my father's shivering body in my arms. I couldn't stop the tears from falling like streams as I tried desperately to stop the bleeding. No matter how much I tried, the blood still seeped through my fingers, turning them a bright shade of crimson. My father's eyes still held the constant look of defiance even while in constant pain, but I could tell their brightness was fading. I couldn't feel the shaking of my limbs, but I could see it. I felt almost numb.

I didn't even notice the earth shake as his murderer walked slowly up to me. I coldly glanced back at the knight as he looked down at us, my vision blurred by the tears raining down my face.

"Is this truly what has become of you?" he inquired, "A man who lives in hiding…afraid of his own shadow." My father only looked obstinately back at him.

"Stay…away…from my family!" The knight remained motionless as he towered over both of us.

"You know why I'm here. Give me what I came for Gaius."

"I don't have it," he laughed to himself, "We got rid…of that old thing." The knight chuckled hollowly, with the laugh echoing in his imposing helmet.

"You threw it away? The man who destroyed his entire life to protect it simply threw it away?" My father just looked away.

"I'm not going to waste my time…talking with you." The knight gazed between my father and I in silence with his frightening visage, unnerving me.

"He sensed it Gaius," the knight continued smoothly, "It's activation called me here, and your classic defiance is only making things difficult." My father only replied with silence, making good on the promise he made earlier.

"Perhaps your tongue would loosen if I killed your children. Just imagine this boy's face turning pale as the last of his blood drains from his body," he calmly stated as my blood ran cold from his words. He paused as he stared towards the forest, completely ignoring our presence for a moment.

"Or imagine the other one in the forest. Just imagine the look of horror plastered on his face when he sees your broken forms lying in the dirt." I bolted upright at his final threat, blinded from both the tears and the anger flowing through my body.

"You…you bastard!"

"Connor, don't!"

I stood straight up and drew my sword from my side, my father's blood trickling down my hands and onto the hilt of the blade. I sprinted full speed at the knight, wielding the sword with both hands as it dragged across the dirt. I swung the blade up towards the knight's mask, flinging dust into the night air as the knight dodged. I continued to strike without rhythm or any technique, flinging my sword wildly as the knight continued to sidestep out of the way.

"You have every chance to walk away from this child," he echoed as he ignored another swing, "Step away from this battle while you still can. My quarrel is not with you." The crisp forest air was tinged with dirt and dust as his heavy steps and my swings connected with the ground.

"Connor please stop...you can't win." We both came to a halt as the knight looked at my father. He stared at him completely motionless, almost as if he was perplexed by my father's statement. I seized the opportunity he presented with glee. I swung my sword for his neck, aiming to decapitate him. My sword connected with his less protected neck directly underneath his helmet...

And shattered completely.

I froze, standing in the open only holding the hilt of what once was my sword. I gasped out in pain from the steel fragments piercing my right hand and arm, cringing as they jabbed further into me with every movement. The knight slowly craned his neck towards me as I stood immobile, almost like he just noticed my presence. He took a single thundering step towards me.

"Stubborn like your father." The knight turned and swiftly crashed his armored elbow into my face, the force of the blow audibly breaking my nose as a painful bruise swiftly followed. I crumpled to one knee, clutching my face. I could feel my own blood mixing with my father's already on my hands.

"Give me what I came for Gaius and I might consider leaving him alive. I won't stay my hand a second time." My father had somehow managed to stand and wield his axe, swaying from the weight of it all. His blood was pouring onto the ground beneath him like a torrent as he lurched forward.

"You won't lay another strike...on...my son." He tried to stand to protect me as he raised his axe, but he could not fully raise the weapon even above his waist. He collapsed from the strain with a groan, landing back in the dirt.

I tried to stand up again, but the knight swept my legs out from underneath me. Before I could retaliate, he pinned my right arm to the ground with his boot, crushing my arm underneath it. I angrily punched his leg, crying out in pain as my index and middle fingers cracked from the blow. With blinding speed he drove his other boot into my chest, a rib audibly cracking as I gasped out in pain.

"I suppose the defiant dead shall keep their secrets." The knight raised his large sword as I prepared for more pain. Instead, the sound of metal slamming against metal instead met my ears. I opened my eyes slowly.

There in front of me stood my mother...

Her radiant hair swayed in the wind, panting fiercely as the dust that billowed up from her actions sprinkled through the air. She stood proudly with the most vicious look I had ever seen painted on her face. Her weapon was a dagger, but to me its edges appeared to be uneven, and the blade appeared to be made of dazzling light.

All the pain in my body must be finally catching up to me.

"Away from my family wretched demon." The knight scoffed angrily at the new presence and pressed his attack. They clashed over and over, slashing wildly without any formal technique. And yet, it was still a stunning dance of blades.

The sound of metal against metal clashed throughout the night, cracking through the silence over and over. No matter how fast or graceful my mother could ever be, the knight was always one step ahead. She pushed harder than I had ever seen her fight, but eventually the knight deflected another blow to the side with his gauntlet and smashed her backwards with a swift palm strike. She flew backwards, her body slamming into a nearby tree. The leaves fell around her as she blew a single strand of hair out of her face, her eyes burning into the knight in front of her.

"You always ruin everything," the knight fumed with a voice tainted by malice, "Just like you always have you witch." He looked over at my father and me. Our broken forms barely even resembling humans at this point. My father's breathing had become ragged, my body being unable to move due to my broken body.

"I was so close, but no matter," he continued, "I managed to do damage, even if I did not get what I wanted. At least one threat of ours is gone now." Raising his left arm and removing the glove, I could faintly see a purple aura that surrounded his hand like a glove, along with a purple insignia that appeared to be carved into the back of his hand. It was some form of fanged beast, one with its mouth agape and a singular purple eye that pierced through my being. Clenching his fist, the emblem began to glow even brighter as the purple glow expanded into the armor around his hand. The gauntlet began to splinter and crack as the light glowed to almost a blinding degree.

The knight's figure seemed to grow dimmer, almost vanishing in front of us. The armor's colors looked washed out as I could almost see the forest through his figure.

The knight was fading away. In anger I tried to stand myself up to stop him. My chest erupted in pain as blood sputtered its way out of my mouth, making me collapse to the ground once more.

From her place under the tree, my mother stared at me as the softness returned to her face. She mouthed something to me as she gave me a faint smile; something I wish I could understand as the look of resentment returned to her face. She sprung up as fast as she could, bolting with all her strength at the knight. As my mother wrenched her blade up to stab up at him, the knight snaked his right arm around her attack and grabbed hold of her wrist, twisting it as he tried to wrestle it to the ground. My mother, with pure hatred written onto her face pushed on, latched onto one of the grooves of his armor as she pushed the dagger further and further. Her body began fading as well, both practically see-through.

And then they were both gone, the eerie silence returning to the clearing as I stared in awe over what had just happened.

I screamed out in agony before the world went black.

4

Connor and Jack: Divided Purpose

I shook my head free of everything stirring within it, standing in the same spot I once stood those months ago.

Just now...it felt like a hallucination of some kind, almost like I was reliving that very moment.

Maybe I am going mad...nothing makes sense anymore.

I hurled the malformed chunk of metal back onto the ground, hearing it clatter against the hardened earth several times before skidding to a stop.

I glanced forward at the lonely mound resting solemnly in the center of the clearing. Beneath the ground rested my father, his noble axe dug alongside a wooden headstone the neighboring village crafted for my brother. I fell to my knees and slid my hand across the smooth dirt of the grave.

"Pleasant to see you, father. It's...been a while. Apologies for not visiting. Just been a little busy on the road of life as you called it." I laughed to myself at this, repeating one of my father's lines he constantly said to my mother.

"Jack and I have been doing well. It's obviously been hard without you or mom, but we manage." *Mom...*

I know you're out there somewhere in the world.

I paused for only a moment, the loose dirt and pebbles crunching within my palm.

"I'm...so sorry that I couldn't save you from that demon. I'm sorry for not being able to save mother from him either. I'm sorry for being a failure of a child to you, and to mother. I couldn't even save you when you were dying right in front of me, so what kind of son am I?" The sound of boots crunching against the ground met my ears as I prattled on, growing ever closer with each word. I still stiffened when I felt a hand firmly grasp my shoulder, even though I already knew who it was. Glancing slowly over my shoulder, the towering figure of my brother stood above me, blocking the sun with his form.

His dark brown eyes bored into me, the dullness of them completely contrasting my shining hazel ones.

Along with his personality...

His long brown coat almost covered his entire body, extending to his feet and barely managing to cover the ordinary grey and brown clothes underneath. He held a dejected smirk on his face, almost looking uncomfortable wearing it.

"Connor, you're the brightest man I've ever known, so you of all people should know we can't bring back the dead."

"That may be true," I rasped out, "But I can still do everything that they would have done if they were here." The unusually solemn man visibly sighed while he lowered his head, his grip on my shoulder tightening.

"Do you really think you can spend your entire life like this?" he rhetorically asked in his usual boisterous tone. I swatted his arm off my shoulder as I rapidly rose to my feet. I stood face to face with him, my fiery hazel eyes not completely staring into his dull brown ones as I was slightly shorter than my older brother.

"And what should I do Jack?" I countered with a slight snarl to my voice, "Stand on the sidelines like you do while our mother is still out there? While that demon is still out there?"

How can he just stand there and do nothing while people are suffering out there because of me?

"Connor, have you ever heard the words that exit your mouth?" Jack attempted to say calmly, although his signature snark was bleeding through, "I've never met someone who is somehow so brilliant and yet so stupid." He shifted slightly, taking a slight glance at the gravestone behind me, his train of thought breaking momentarily before turning back to me.

"I'll say this one time as clearly as I can. It was not your fault. None of it was. That *thing...*" he enunciated that word with venom, "...that man came here for a reason we couldn't have understood. He took the most precious people from us, but that does not mean we should spend our entire lives searching for him. He could be anywhere on this whole continent at this point." My jaw painfully clenched as I pushed an accusatory finger towards him.

"How could you not place the life of our mother above everything else?" I screamed out in frustration, his face remaining the same, "It doesn't matter what it takes to find her, it never has. That monster is some malevolent force that thrives on nothing but pain and he took everything we care about." I jabbed my finger into his chest aggressively, his steady stance wobbling slightly at the sudden force. He looked genuinely surprised at my response.

"And what have you been doing Jack?" I continued, "You are living your life as if nothing happened. As if that brute is just another man and as if the absence of both of those two in our lives meant absolutely nothing to you!"

As the final words exited my mouth, an unknown force swiftly cracked against my cheek. I reeled back in pain and crumpled to my knees, clenching my face. I strained my eyes up at the source of the attack, who still had his fist held in the same position.

"Oh, I think you're doing a fantastic job at wasting away in your room while you obsess over that knight. Excellent work if that was your intention Connor. Bravo." His voice was filled with nothing but exhaustion and sarcasm as he gazed down at me, peering into my thoughts with those dark brown eyes.

"What you're doing is unhealthy Connor," he proclaimed with concern, "I know you Connor; you're my brother after all. They were my parents too, you know? You think I don't wanna track him down and kick his ass for everything he's done? He killed our dad! Our dad was better than both of us combined and would undoubtedly kick us down if we even attempted a true duel with him."

He extended an arm to me, which I begrudgingly took. He gave me his signature smirk as he pulled me back up onto my wobbly feet.

"I want to track him down too, but we are in no shape to do it just yet," Jack insisted, "You need to just breathe and relax for a little. Then one day we're gonna show up and beat the armor right off that smug bastard." Laughing at his own remark, he stared at me waiting for what I was going to say.

"You've been incredibly jovial lately." I finally remarked sarcastically.

"I've had to make up for your absence," he wistfully grinned back. I slid my arm away from him as I plunged my hands into my cold pockets, lurching away back down the winding dirt road towards the wooden shack.

"You still haven't found a purpose even after all this time," I called out in response, "I have."

* * *

I lowered the arm I instinctively raised up as he walked away, my body's vain attempt at trying to do whatever I could for my brother, easing him through the pain.

But I know he wouldn't let me.

Forcing my arm down, I straightened the collar of my long brown coat and turned around in the opposite direction to walk down the opposing path.

Although, that was the closest I've ever gotten.

I couldn't help but smile at my success, managing to suppress a jovial fist pump.

Jack Illium, you are the greatest older brother ever.

Watching his silhouette vanish in the distance, I traced my hand along my dad's headstone one last time, before I fully departed from the clearing.

Walking downhill away from our home and towards my destination, I thought back to how my brother had lashed out at me while I tried to comfort him. Every conversation of ours always ended terribly.

Most of the time he'll completely walk away from me as if I wasn't even there, or stay silent the entire time I'm talking.

Or sometimes, like now, he'll lash out, yelling in anger about what has happened and everything that could have been done.

What he doesn't realize is sometimes nothing can be done.

I shook my head from my thoughts when I heard the familiar chatter of people in the distance, not realizing I had already walked the almost mile to get here.

Fifteen minutes just now felt like fifteen seconds...must've been too stuck within this empty head of mine to notice.

Vendors screaming at people passing by, children laughing and hollering as they play, or just the familiar greetings of friends and family.

I couldn't help but smile when entering this modest merchant town, despite how much Connor disliked it. Everyone is so ecstatic to meet each other when they cross paths considering the small population of around maybe two hundred. Especially me, just because I'm a rare stranger in this town, even though I've visited many times.

"Jack!" the gatekeeper hollered, knocking me out of my thoughts, "Another supply run?" I make a trip every two weeks for food and other supplies for my brother and I, so most of the people I talk to here have recognized my schedule.

"As always Lundhard," I replied as I paused in front of him, "Anything noteworthy going on lately?" He shook his head with a smile, his large helmet covering most of his head.

"Nothing to report," he exclaimed with a joking salute, "But then again this town has almost nothing of note. Nothing suspicious in a simple merchant town such as this. Makes my job boring."

"Well, that's about what I expected," I smirked back at him, "Although it's always enjoyable to enter Eincrest anytime despite that." We lived somewhere like this long ago, I only know that much. It's troublesome to remember specifics that far back, but I do recall that we lived there for a few years before moving to the house under the cliffs, until that was destroyed by that demon's men and we had to go to another one nearby.

"Well take as much time as you need Jack," Lundhard stated as he straightened his overbearing helmet, "Try not to annoy her too much with your visit." I gave him one last joking wave before I walked into town, leaving him to his boring duties.

Immediately I passed by a group of foreign merchants, each trying to sell me something of theirs that was extravagant and definitely overpriced.

"Sir! Sir! Would you care for silk rugs from the capital?"

"Sir! You look like someone who could use some famed amulets from the mystical land of Pyrnesse."

"Or perhaps the supposedly unbreakable armor of Bellhollow soldiers? A rare commodity to see in Solaton, or any other country in all of Aelton besides Bellhollow."

I waved them away with a smile creeping onto my face. They were clearly exaggerating, but I'll give them credit for their effort.

Other adults I passed gossiped and conversed with one another as they went about their day, with some even giving a wave as I walked by.

"Did you hear? Someone in town said they ran into a group of bandits while traveling about! Barely made it by the skin of his teeth he said, spouting off about a colorfully dressed man and his goons."

"Don't listen to every rumor you've heard dear. You forget how old that man is. He probably just saw some traveling circus that attempted to sell him some exorbitantly priced tickets." I chuckled at the way they spoke, wishing I had more time to listen to the crazy stories brought in by travelers.

A posse of young children aged around six or seven charged around a corner, almost taking out my legs as they surged past me. I chuckled at how they barely even noticed me; so caught up in their silly game that they didn't notice the stranger they almost took down. I kept marching on, closing in on the store I always frequented nearby Eincrest's entrance. A giddiness overcame me as I grasped onto the rotting doorknob of the shop.

Avelina's shop...

"Avelina!" I proclaimed as I burst through the wooden door, "I'm back!" As soon as the words left my mouth, I barely had enough time to dodge an incoming wooden dagger hurtling towards my face. It cracked a plank in the wooden wall beside me before clattering to the ground. With a flickering smile, I cautiously turned towards the source.

There stood the purple haired merchant who threw said dagger.

Her sleek hair was matted over her amber eyes, with her green sleeved arm still extended from the throw. She kept her attire relatively simple: long sleeve green shirt and brown pants, with matching brown gloves and a metal plate over her right shoulder. I assumed she was in her mid to late thirties, but I wouldn't dare ask.

"H-hey Avelina!" I exclaimed with a slight crack in my voice, "What seems to be the issue?" I plastered on a smile as I rubbed the back of my head innocently. Her disappointed frown remained.

"Jack Illium…" she growled out, sending goosebumps up my arms, "What did I say about coming into my shop like that?"

"It slipped my mind," I replied with as much confidence as I could muster, "After all, it was such a long time ago and you know I've been busy with a lot of things." Her brow furrowed as she placed her hands on her hips.

"That was only two weeks ago," she deadpanned, "If you can't even remember that far back then that toy wouldn't have done that much damage." She leaned against the store counter with her arms crossed, exhaling a sigh to blow the hair out of her eyes.

"Another supply run I assume?" I nodded as I walked towards the counter. She pointed towards the now closed door.

"If you come into my shop like that again, or if you're unlucky enough to break the door like you did two weeks ago, consider the discounts you get here void," she chastised as she moved towards the back of her shop, "You're lucky I feel bad for you two, otherwise I'd make the effort to ban you from every shop in this town." As I waited against the counter, I decided to push again for my daily dose of my mysterious mother's life here.

"You've said before that you met my mother a while back," I started, "Or rather when my mother and I would come here for supplies and I'd run off to converse with people. How did she act around you?" I heard her excavation of the back room pause for a moment before

42

the scurrying continued.

"You're trying to pry into your mother's private life again?" she yelled out, "I've already told you that she wasn't in here very long. It was only one time if I recall. A couple months back when I moved in, before all your craziness happened."

"Yeah, but you never told me what that was like." I heard her let out her classic grating sigh as the searching intensified.

"You know if you had half the intelligence and perception your brother supposedly has, you'd be able to figure out every conversation your mother had that day." She responded sarcastically.

"That's a trait my brother and I both gladly share." She scoffed as she reentered the room, carrying a massive box in her arms.

"You just like to speak," she countered, "According to your stories, your brother knows how to actually use his words to further what he wants." She set the box on the counter, narrowly missing my fingers as I leapt out of the way. Without skipping a beat, she flipped a knife out of her sleeve and sliced the top open as I gave a fake hurt expression.

"If your brother still has that skill I mean," she continued, "Connor doesn't seem like much of a people person." I sighed as I examined the contents of this first box. There was an assortment of dry food such as wheat, oats, and honey, all items Connor and I couldn't really hunt or grow ourselves. It was no secret Connor and I were absolutely terrible cooks.

"It's been maybe four months since then, and he still can't shake that mindset. No matter what I do or say I haven't even seen a single genuine smile or laugh," I commented solemnly, "But enough about that. You didn't answer my question." She groaned as she retreated back to her pantry to retrieve more boxes, as the sound of clanging metal and shuffling boxes intensified.

"You just won't give up will you?" she exhaled, "Fine then." She

43

promptly came out with two boxes: one I knew held materials to build certain tools and another filled with miscellaneous goods she decided we needed. Dropping them on the counter, my view of her was partially obscured as she leaned against its wooden surface.

"When your mother came here, you had decided to converse with the gatekeeper instead. She and I are close to the same age, although I knew she was a bit older," she began, "She mostly talked with me as if I were her best friend in the world, discussing her social life and children as any mother would. We both laughed together before your mother bought her things and left. I'm not sure what you were looking for...but that's all that I remember." She squinted her eyes as she pushed the last box towards me, sliding it into my awaiting grasp.

"Were you expecting anything different?" I sighed to myself as I carried the large boxes in my arms, blocking my field of vision slightly.

"I don't know what I was expecting honestly," I admitted, "I'm her oldest child and yet I probably knew the least about her. Connor and I would probably be in the same boat if he wasn't so meticulous in his examination of people." Confirming that the boxes remain balanced in my arms, I placed a bag of gold coins on the counter as I stumbled my way towards the door.

"Pleasure doing business with you Avelina," I proclaimed, "I look forward to our next meeting." Avelina scoffed in exhaustion before picking up a long spear and cloth, looking away as she began to wipe the surface clean.

"And I look forward to the day you find a new person to take your business to." Chuckling at her remark, I ensured that the boxes remained balanced within my arms before kicking back the door behind me, allowing me to step out into the dusty town. I heard her grumble one last scathing insult to herself before the door closed back on her shop, allowing me freedom from her hawk-like gaze.

* * *

Setting the heavy boxes on the aged wooden floor with a creak, I heard my back pop out as I stretched it with my sore hands. Extending my arms out, I glanced around the cabin momentarily as I pushed the front door closed and cracked my neck.

It took two weeks to refurbish this home, since after our new home was built back then we largely left this temporary home alone. I don't really care much for it, but it serves its purpose well until we figure something else out.

The first week was the worst of them all, as Connor laid comatose for the entire time, leaving me in such a foreboding empty house. I knew he was breathing, but I never knew if he was ever going to wake. Once most of the rooms were cleaned up and refurbished, and a doctor from Eincrest was called in to examine him, he finally woke up.

When he did rise, I knew something was different about him. His sharp hazel eyes held no emotion behind them as they usually did. Their dullness unnerved me; he didn't speak the entire time we reorganized the small cabin aside from the occasional "okay" when I asked him to bring me any form of tools. He would just sit against one of the walls alone, staring at a green pendant I wasn't aware he even owned.

I walked over to the room directly next to the bedroom we shared, softly knocking on the wooden door thrice. Most days I could only find my brother in two locations: outside beating a dummy half to death, or in this room. I always knocked, but I always knew I wouldn't get a response from him.

Easing the door open with a creak, I gazed into the dark room lit only by a singular dying candle, noticing my brother's silhouette crumpled against the lone desk in the darkness. Tiptoeing my way towards his figure, I briefly leaned over to examine his collapsed form. He was sound asleep; his mouth partially open and pressed against a parchment he was writing on, his words trailing off into indecipherable scribbles. His right hand still firmly grasped the feather he was using, the ink already dried to the tip of it.

Shifting my gaze from his dozing body, I sighed as I examined the collage of documents and papers pinned to the wall in front of him. Written pieces and sections of maps were pinned to the wall, connected by heavy black lines of ink. Dark splotches blurred many words, and the recent paper written by him was basically illegible. However, every piece held one topic in common.

Bellhollow. Our neighbors to the east.

Rumors flow in and out from there. Some say our neighbors aren't even human; that they are monsters raised by their king. Others whisper in secret that their armor and weapons are unbreakable, and that if they so desired they could destroy this entire continent. What we do know is that their soldiers are trained from birth to be weapons, and although their military is small it's still incredibly formidable. I don't know why they don't just attack our country, but I am sure there's a perfectly logical reason that I don't understand.

"Lucky us they decided to stay secluded in their famine ravished land." I chuckled to myself. Returning to the wall, I knew his thoughts only lingered on searching for that…that knight. My blood boiled even imagining that monster.

I want to find mom and kill that knight as much as Connor does. My brother has always been the smartest between us; always able to see details that I couldn't even fathom perceiving. But now… something has changed.

And I'm sitting here useless, unable to help him.

"Why won't you let me help you Connor? Why won't you let me into your brain to ease your suffering?" Perhaps hearing me in his sleep, he mumbled and groaned as his body stirred on the desk. If his gibberish meant anything to me, I already knew he was undergoing another nightmarish memory of that night.

Turning to him again, I laid a dark woolen blanket that sat nearby over his shoulders, patting him on the back and blowing out the candle as I crept my way back out of this room.

"May your dreams be filled with more pleasant memories Connor. Perhaps a memory that can allow you to smile tomorrow."

5

Connor: Stepping Out of Asylum

"If he was a soldier of Bellhollow, then perhaps that would explain the armor shattering the blade and the dagger?" Mumbling to myself in the darkened room, I hugged a woolen blanket I must have placed on myself while I was half asleep last night. My eyes beginning to strain in my skull, I traced my eyes along my writings one final time.

"His armor was seemingly invincible, which plays into the rumor that Bellhollow soldiers possess such advanced weaponry. Based on his stature and the strength of the armor he was the general. Since he was the only one with such unbreakable armor, then if it exists it's incredibly scarce, as it appears to only be provided to said commanders." Pinning another aged piece of paper to the wall, I placed the stained feather back into its ink well.

"The knight spoke of my father in such a familiar way, but why? And if he were truly from Bellhollow, what could that emblem have possibly been on his hand? Was that how he vanished?" Gritting my teeth, I swept all of my dusty papers off of my desk, listening to them float across the room as they devolved from their stack.

Hurling the coarse blanket to the ground, I walked to the door of my office, refusing to turn back as I slammed the door behind me.

Judging by the opened aged curtains, Jack had already been awake for some time now. His worn coat still rested on its stand, meaning that he had chosen not to head anywhere today. Securing my sole dagger to my waist, I snatched an apple from the kitchen before I made my way to the door.

When this house was built so long ago, it was split into four rooms. A living space sat by the doorway, containing a kitchen area Jack constantly used. A dusty set of chairs rested around a table, which since their creation have been lonely from lack of use. Down a hallway to the right sat three rooms: A cramped room that Jack and I shared, a somehow even more confined room I used for my research, and a room I hoped to keep empty.

That would be mother's room when we find her.

Stepping outside as I clasped the brown cloak around my neck, I paced a couple steps as I listened to the stillness of the outside. No birds chirped. No rivers around us to flow. Just the calm chill of the morning wind, flowing around us as the only form of nature remaining.

The sound of steel splintering through wood shattered the silence, displacing me from the moment of calm I found. Sighing, I threw my almost finished apple to the ground and turned around, making my way behind my house. The sounds of metal cracking against weakening wood grew louder, along with the familiar yells of the wielder.

Entering the clearing, I could see Jack resting against a massive tree, panting sharply as he held his broadsword in his left hand. Noticing me, Jack eased himself up with a tired smile, giving a soft wave as he did so.

"Mornin' Connor," he began while repositioning his large sword to his right hand, "Care to actually join me for some morning sparring?"

Setting the broadsword on a rack nearby, I noticed him repositioning a leather chest plate I had not seen previously. Seeing the direction my eyes were going, he motioned to his new piece of armor as he finished straightening it out.

"Oh yeah this," Jack declared, "Avelina slipped this into our supplies when I wasn't looking. That woman, not trusting us to be safe, but I can't say I'm ungrateful." The armor looked almost brand new: the stiff chest plate perfectly fitting the stocky, yet lanky frame of my brother.

"Anyways if we're actually gonna spar, I have a bet for you Connor if you really wanna take it." Raising an eyebrow, I drew a small wooden dagger from the weapon's rack, turning back to him as I flipped it over in my right hand.

"A bet huh?" I asked with a curious tone, "What sort of bet are you proposing?" Noticing his smirk, I was beginning to regret even considering his deal.

"Eh, just a test is all. If you somehow win, I'll be kind enough to let you have this leather chest piece," he explained, drawing a wooden broadsword of his own, "But when I win, you'll come on down with me to Eincrest to give Avelina some money for the same chest piece." Hearing those words, I immediately felt my mouth move to deny his request. The gift victory would provide was not even worth it to me, especially with an item as trivial as that.

However, I know how much Jack wants me to leave this horrid cabin. He keeps telling me how terrible it is for my psyche. It's been difficult to focus lately, and if I can't focus, I won't be able to track down that knight. It's also an opportunity to truly see if I've grown any.

And besides...don't want Jack worried enough to stop me...

"Alright Jack," I replied with a confidence I forgot I had, "Make sure you thank Avelina for the gift when you get there." Grinning, my brother advanced to the opposite side of the clearing.

Flipping the dagger around in my right hand as I bent my knees slightly, I analyzed Jack's position across me. He gripped a wooden broadsword in both hands, drawing it behind his left side as he stepped forward with his right. He was already tired from his training session beforehand; his arms already shaking from the weight of the sword.

Jack has always been an incredibly offensive fighter, so I can't give him that chance.

Before Jack could scan my stance in any way, I sprinted towards him at full speed, swinging my training dagger up at Jack's face hoping to end this fight as quickly as it began. Flashing the sword in front of his neck, the dagger rebounded off of it as he flung the sword across. Evading the blow, I lunged at Jack again, this time aiming for his chest. Ducking under his sword swing, I struck his chest with my right palm, hearing him groan as I swept his legs out from under him.

Hoping to catch him before he could react, I brought a fist down towards his face hoping to force him to surrender. Unexpectedly, he caught my fist in his right hand before he sprung up from the ground with a savage head butt. My eyes blurred from the pain, unable to properly react as he fiercely jabbed me in the ribs. As soon as my vision recovered, my dagger was launched out of my hand by Jack's broadsword.

Grasping my hand in pain from the sudden loss of my weapon, I only had a couple seconds to react before the broadsword crashed against the side of my knee. Crumpling to the ground, I glanced up just in time to catch a powerful uppercut to the jaw, sending my body cascading back down to the ground. Before I could spring back up, I found the wooden sword placed at my neck.

"Sorry Connor," Jack gasped through heavy breaths, "Couldn't afford…to hold anything back, but I'm afraid you've lost this one."

Placing the sword back on the ground, he extended a hand down towards me. I gladly took it as I rubbed the back of my skull, wincing as I passed over the spot where I collided with the ground.

"I'm afraid you've lost," Jack repeated, "You've been training for so long and yet you still can't beat me."

"Losing to you doesn't mean I haven't improved any," I retorted as a genuine grin crept onto my face, "If I fought you when we were younger, you'd be flat on the floor." My brother chuckled slightly, making his way back over to the weapons rack.

"Ah yes you would beat up my fifteen-year-old self," he remarked, "That's low, even for you Connor." I smiled again as he latched his metal broadsword onto his back, readjusting his clothes as he turned back to me.

"Any advantage I can take Jack," I joked, "And if that means fighting your younger self, I'll take that as well." Guffawing from my joke, my brother walked up side-by-side with me with one of his famous smiles. Without warning I was swiftly tugged into his warm embrace, pulling tightly at my grey shirt as he let out a sigh.

"It's good to talk to you again Connor," he gasped out, "I know you're still not all there, and I know your pain still is. But...I'm so happy that some piece of my brother is back with me." Being only two inches taller than me, my face was about level with his right shoulder, causing my chin to be buried in his chest. Without thinking, I wrapped one arm around him, my left one remaining limp at my side. I let out a single dry laugh as he stiffened in my arms.

"I know you think something is wrong with me," I started, releasing my brother from my grasp, "We experienced the same pain, yet I saw it in person while you fought to ensure I could get there." Crumpling my fist together, I brought it up into the air as my brother watched on in curiosity.

"This whole time, I know I haven't just failed father or mother, but

I failed you," I continued, "You entrusted me to protect our father through the battle, and I failed."

"Connor you know that's not…" I held up a hand to stop him.

"I know what you believe Jack," I interjected, "You believe there was nothing I could've done. Perhaps if this man is from Bellhollow like I suspect, then our defeat might have been inevitable." Staring at him, I could see the concern littered in his brown eyes, almost like he was waiting in fear over what I would say next.

"What I do know is that I will protect everyone I know, especially you, with everything I have in me. That knight is a threat to everyone, and I highly doubt he worked alone based on what our father said b-before he died." My voice hitching in my throat at the memory, I let out a cough as I extended a hand to a confused Jack.

"Jack… I have no idea what on earth our future holds for us. But, in this moment of clarity, I want to ask you if you'll stand with me. I know it sounds rather simple, but will you stand by my side no matter what obstacles we face? You're the only family I have with me, and I hope to keep us on the same page." Initially listening to my ramblings in slight confusion, Jack's mouth curved into a genuine grin and grasped my right hand firmly with his own, shaking my arm from his strength.

"Connor I should've asked you that question," he responded, "Of course I will. You're my only brother after all, and my superior skills as a fighter can't change that." Laughing at his own joke, all I could muster was a light chuckle as I let go of his hand.

"I'm glad to see the Connor I remember return, even for a little," he commented sadly, "Far different from the Connor of yesterday." Briskly walking past me, Jack motioned for me to follow him while maintaining a smile.

"Now if I recall correctly, someone said they would come down to Eincrest if they lost. And since that someone lost rather handily…

" Letting out a sigh, I trudged back to the front of the house after I ensured my dagger was still secured to my side, hearing my brother let out a soft snicker.

Walking to the front of our cabin in the woods, I examined the rickety shack we were forced to call home for months now. I didn't care much for it. I would abandon it in a heartbeat if another option were presented. Not as much care or hope was placed into this building as our previous one; a home that represented the freedom our parents felt for living out on their own. They hoped to establish their home to raise their children away from the corruption they saw in the real world.

No matter how much they sheltered us, the corruption found us anyway.

The creaking sound of boots against wood met my ears, breaking me from my thoughts as the front door eased shut. Jack walked out to meet me at the front, wearing his worn brown coat over his armor and his two-handed broadsword, exposing only the hilt slightly above the coat's collar as its silver edges poked out from behind his back. A bag of coins jingled on his waist as his boots crunched against the dead leaves littering the ground.

"Ready when you are," he exclaimed to me. I nodded in agreement, motioning for him to lead the way.

"There is no way I am going to let Avelina give me this brand-new chest piece for free, so we'll see if any of them will be surprised at me visiting two days in a row." I nodded at his sentiment as I kept a decent pace beside him.

In his place, I would hope I would be able to do the same thing.

With nothing much to talk about, I placed myself within my thoughts as our feet dragged across the dusty road.

Taking away the extra couple of inches the helmet and boots gave, the knight who attacked us that day could be around six foot two or six foot three, a couple inches taller than my father.

His voice was cool and calculated, meaning that he was a man who was not new to the brutality and bloodshed of battle.

He was right-handed, but he could potentially be ambidextrous like Jack due to the way he carried his blade once the energy was drawn from his right hand. I still don't get that blasted aura.

He could be a member of the Zevron...

I've toyed with the idea a couple times in my mind.

The Zevron were a race of people that lived in the secretive nation of Pyrnesse in the northern region of Aelton. I don't know much about them, their past shrouded in mystery even from the teachings of my mother. What I did know was that their appearance is almost identical to that of a human, with their distinguishing traits being a full head of pale white hair, and piercing blue eyes that peered into the soul. With those two traits, it would be fairly simple to identify one.

While it is true the Zevron have not been seen outside of their homeland for centuries, the rumors circulating around their supposed "gifts" have been around for generations.

I visibly shook my head, drawing the attention of Jack who moments ago only was focusing on the path ahead.

"Something up?" he questioned.

"Do you recall the energy I brought up that the knight used to escape?" Jack visibly groaned at my question.

"Yes Connor I remember," Jack replied with a grumble, "You rambled about it while you slept, not to mention it's kinda hard not to hear it with how much you talk to yourself in your tiny room." Letting the silence perforate in the area, I faced him as we continued in our stride.

"Do you think that he could have been a member of the Zevron?" Jack stopped in his tracks at this question, curling his face into a frown as he did so.

"Connor, he was a Bellhollow soldier if you read his armor correctly," he commented, "Do you really think a nation as secluded and...selective as them would allow a Zevron to rise in their ranks to such a commanding position?" Hearing my silence, Jack shrugged his shoulders and continued to walk the now downward sloping path, swiftly followed by myself.

No, he's right. A Zevron would never be made a Bellhollow soldier but... That emblem of that beast...

Maybe he learned it from a Zevron? Or perhaps the soldiers of Bellhollow know more than we realize.

After all, aside from appearance and their location in Pyrnesse, our mother didn't know anything else about them. There were of course a large amount of rumors, but how many of them could possibly be true? The tales of them possessing magic have always surfaced, so what if...

"Connor!" I was shaken out of my thoughts by my brother's yelling voice. Startled, I looked over at him to see a smile creeping to his face.

"Ah that's something I forgot you did," he chuckled while shaking his head, "You're mumbling to yourself again. You might as well be having a conversation with me because nothing you're saying is staying within that brain of yours." I awkwardly laughed again at his comment while putting a hand behind my head, embarrassed he noticed my old habit resurfacing. For some reason, it felt good to feel awkward about something again, let alone laugh about it with my family.

A foul stench crept into my nostrils as we reached an elevated form of path, my nose instinctively crinkling due to the noxious aroma. Although I didn't recognize it at first, the putrid smell instinctively caused me to reach for my dagger, feeling my knuckles turn white as

I stopped dead in my tracks. I tried to force myself to walk, but my shaking legs remained bolted to the ground.

I recognized what that despicable smell was…the distinct aroma lingering in my mind like a pesty disease.

It was the virulent smell of billowing smoke.

Jack, noticing my panic, stopped as well, turning to me with a furrowed brow and tilting his head towards me in mild confusion.

"Connor?" he asked, "What's the matter?" Panicked, I flipped the dagger around in my hands as I began to hyperventilate, unintentionally breathing in the rotten air, with my lungs beginning to burn. Firmly grasping me by my right shoulder, Jack began to shake me.

"Connor snap out of it! Why are you…" Pausing mid-sentence, Jack craned his head up to the sky, obviously sniffing the air as he did so. *He smelled it too.*

Looking up, I could finally see a billow of blackened smoke enveloping the morning sky like clouds. The distinct sound of fire crackling and popping enveloped our ears, drowning every one of our senses with a truth we now immediately knew.

"Jack…" I rasped out.

"I know," he replied, already pacing down the road several steps, "Don't tell me it's…" Cutting himself off, my silence told him what my assumption on the matter really was.

"Jack, we need to move now!"

Nodding in acknowledgment, we turned down the path and bolted as fast as we could, kicking up dust with every pounding step. Ignoring the harsh lungfuls of smoke we continuously breathed in, both of us ran without pause for two agonizing minutes. Near the end, I could see the faint outline of a village up ahead.

Its silhouette shifted and changed as it was burned to the ground.

6

Connor: The Village Inferno

"No no..." Sliding to a stop in front of the gateway, we arrived just in time to see the sign of the village collapse from its archway. The words *Eincrest* became no longer visible as the sign blackened into nothing; my brother and I recoiling with our hands up to shield our faces from the flames enveloping it.

Glancing up, it became obvious the fire began its rampage here before it slowly danced its way across the many village rooftops. The discarded, burned out torch nearby was proof. Leaning back to cover my face from the flames, I took a step back in shock, almost crumpling to my knees as they buckled in fear. Hearing a retching sound to my right, I turned to see Jack bent over, puking his breakfast out to the ground below.

"Bastards," he growled out while wiping his mouth clean, "What kinda sick twisted bastards would do this?" I tried to reply to him, but the dryness of my throat barred any words from exiting my throat. My body was shaking, quivering at the mere sight of the blazing inferno that towered over us. Every backwards step I took caused my knees to buckle and sway as the image of the flames burned into my memory.

But what about Jack and mom! We can't leave them!

"Connor...are you still with me Connor?" A faraway voice faintly called.

Jack let me go!

My vision blurred for a moment as something crashed into my face, causing me to grasp my face in pain.

"Get a hold of yourself Connor," Jack yelled, "I don't like having to hit you but you keep forcing me to! People are dying in there, and the longer we stand here the more people are going to die. So, push those fears inside you for now, because I need everything from you right now, okay?" Removing my hand from my still burning cheek, I slowly nodded as I attempted to steady my stance.

"S-somebody...g-guh...p-please..." Jack and I whirled around simultaneously, each of us drawing our weapon instinctively as we did so.

"It came from the bushes next to the entryway," I informed my brother in a shaky tone, "A young man, and by the sounds of it they're wounded in some way." Creeping our way to the bushes while shielding our faces from the flames, I cautiously stepped over them. Jack was the first one to arrive at the source of the sounds, tearing the bushes away with his broadsword resting in his right hand.

It was a young man who appeared to be in his twenties. Judging by his attire, he was the guard for this village, based on his position outside of town and the silver chest piece he wore with the town's first initial branded onto it. The helmet to match was nowhere to be seen, revealing his flowing locks of auburn hair splayed against the ground. His spear laid by his side, broken in half at the shaft.

Buried in his chest was a two-headed axe, its blackened teeth glistening in the light of the flames. The crimson blood oozed out, disguising his once clean and well-kept silver breastplate with its corruption.

His eyes held nothing but fear as he stared up at us, his ragged breathing barely making a sound under the crackling flames as his body trembled.

"L-Lundhard?" I could hear Jack gasp out, dropping his sword with a heavy clatter at his side.

"J-Jack?" he quietly replied, "Is that y-you?" Jack somehow managed a smile in this situation, kneeling to his eye level with someone who I believe he knew. His lip quivered as he fought to maintain the mask of joy.

"It's me, friend," he mumbled with a solemn smile, "I suppose you found the excitement you were hoping for." The man known as Lundhard somehow managed a laugh as he appreciated some form of irony in the situation, before devolving into a fit of coughs. His mouth spewed blood as Jack grabbed him by the arm. With his other hand, Jack moved to remove the axe from his body.

I immediately jumped out to stop him.

"Connor, what're you doing! I need to…"

"I know you want to help him Jack," I cut in, "But, you'll only hasten his demise if you remove that axe. It's the only thing preventing him from bleeding out immediately." I heard another laugh by my feet as I too crouched to meet him.

"Y-You must be Connor," Lundhard asked, "You appear as brilliant as the stories Jack told us about." Staring up at the sky, Jack grabbed his friend by the hand as he stared at the smoke above.

"I know you are in pain Lundhard," I began, "But, I must ask you for any noticeable features of what your enemies looked like? Any descriptions to help us pin down the perpetrators once we wipe them out of this village?" His eyes widened in fear as his pupils shrunk, the pained smile vanishing.

"T-they were barbarians!" he exclaimed, "They stormed in here f-full speed and hoped to set this…this t-town ablaze. I took down five of them…but many more came and…" He closed his eyes as the memory tore into his soul. Tightening his grip on Lundhard's hand, Jack closed his eyes as well.

"Lundhard, you served your duty like a hero," he cried out, "You risked your damn life for these people without question. Even though it's been boring for a long time like you said, you risked your life just to give others a chance." Turning to Jack, Lundhard grinned as the fear finally dissipated from his eyes.

"T-Thank you…Jack," Lundhard whispered, "For being a friend… and for being here to reassure me I did the right thing…" Laying his head back, Lundhard breathed his last, never losing the content smile adorning his face. I could almost feel Jack's shakes as he grasped onto his friend, his eyes hidden by the shaggy brown hair that had already begun to collect ash and soot.

"You were a friend I would tear through the veil of heaven to protect," Jack whispered, "Farewell, and may the memory of your life live on forever." Finally releasing his hand, Jack choked back sobs as the sound of flames snapped and hissed behind him.

"He was just an average man," he started, "He was loved in this town. He stood there day after day because he was the only one to volunteer for a seemingly rudimentary job. He just lived a simple life." He stared into the distance, causing me to stare at what he was looking at. What we had not seen while sprinting to get over here was the five bodies that adorned the ground near us. They each were incredibly muscular, and most appeared to be in their thirties and much taller than the both of us. All of them rose up in droves against this town, and now they lay dead each from puncture wounds to the chest. Marching up to them, I examined each body for any form of identifying emblems or insignia.

Nothing…

"Connor…" Jack growled as he stood up, picking up his giant blade, "Do you have a plan of any kind within that twisting head of yours?" I gave him a nod as I flipped the small dagger around in my grip, drawing it up near my face as I did so.

"I need you to fan out to the eastern side of this village and look for any survivors you can. I'll take the western side and do the same. There's no time to put out any of these fires. We need to focus on saving as many lives as possible." Jack gave a smirk through his indignant features as he repositioned the blade that was almost as tall as he was, almost baring his teeth at the flames.

"Will do," he replied in a serious tone that was foreign to him.

Illuminated by the light of the flames, Jack wielded his broadsword in his right hand, his darkened figure making him appear like a reaper. His brown eyes burned with refined hatred.

"Make sure the guys on your side get what's coming to them Connor!"

Splitting from Jack completely, I sprinted through the west side of the village, carefully ensuring I wasn't crushed by flaming debris that came crashing down around me.

Every single body I passed, villager or enemy, made me almost roll over and puke. Every breath was pained; each gasp of smoke I inhaled almost caused me to collapse.

But I didn't care.

Finding any trace of survivors is the top priority, no matter the cost.

I sprinted past groups of bodies strewn against the dirt floor. Many had been charred from the flames creeping up to them after their demise. Most of them carried red slashes across their backs, meaning they weren't even aware they were being attacked before they fell. Some lucky few appeared to have brandished weapons and fought back, as shown by the several barbarian corpses that lay beside the villagers. However, much like the rest, these brave men and women soon also fell.

The most sickening part of this was the number of children lying through the carnage, halting me dead in my tracks. From what I could see, there were at least three children laying in front of a shop, littered with the same slash wounds. One of them, a boy around seven years old, gripped a rubber ball within his charred hands.

These kids were just playing when this all happened.

"What kind of monsters would cut down children?" I shivered aloud, not able to keep the cavalcade of emotions confined within my mind.

"The kind that's gonna slice ya to bits ya little runt!" Whirling around at the gravelly voice, my world went dark for a moment as a large fist crashed full force into my face. My body buckling slightly from the attack, I was able to somehow react quick enough in a daze to sidestep the axe swing of a large barbarian, followed closely by another one of his cronies. Back-stepping a couple of feet, I took a moment to examine my grinning attackers.

The first man was almost a full six inches taller than I was, along with being significantly more muscular. He held a massive battle axe in his right hand, not bothering to balance it with his left. He wore almost no armor. In fact, he had almost no clothes besides the brown cloth pants he had on.

The second man was just as muscular as the first, albeit around my height and holding the axe with both hands. He was similarly dressed, except he had a recent sword cut across his chest, revealing to me that he was far sloppier than the man beside him.

Unrefined bandits...just like the ones that attacked me back home.

"So, you lot are the ones who decided to ransack this village," I deadpanned as the dagger was raised by my face, "No one, not even empty-headed fools like yourselves would attack somewhere like this at random. So then…what would you be doing here?" Widening their sneers, both men raised their glistening axes in both hands, staring me down as my rage began boiling over.

"Isn't it obvious kid?" the first man replied, "We're here to plunder! The boss said that if we tear this village a new one then we'd get ourselves a tasty reward."

"So, you're all nothing but greedy bandits?" I asked rhetorically, my face involuntarily twitching at the sight of them, "This boss of yours…where would I find him?" While the first guy remained silent, the second, shorter man grinned as he stepped forward.

"He was at the town 'all last I saw," he yelled out like an idiot, "But you aren't gonna live long enough to get to him!" Charging full speed, his body language showcased him preparing to swing over his right shoulder. Ducking past the swing, I slashed up under his armpit before whirling around and slashing him across the back. Before he could react, the dagger pierced through his chest. I felt the life leave him as he crumpled in my grasp.

I drew the dagger out his body as I stared back at the first man, hearing the distinct crash of my opponent's lifeless body colliding with the earth.

I suppose my training has actually done something. Excellent.

"Your friend was idiotic and sloppy, letting a kid like me take him down," I deadpanned with a cold expression directed towards the only one left standing, "I'm assuming you'll give me something better?" Yelling as his face twisted into a mask of utter rage, the first man charged with a speed I did not anticipate due to his size. He cut through the air just as I dodged out of the way, slicing a shallow cut into the surface of my left arm.

I staggered briefly as the man charged again. I noticed he was dragging the axe across the ground, kicking up ash and dust as he did so.

Diagonal slash up and across.

Waiting for him to do so, I dodged to my left before striking him across the face with the fist holding my dagger. Stumbling back, the man angrily grasped what was most likely a shattered nose, letting out a low groan.

Before he could recover, I slashed up and across his right arm, making him drop his massive weapon. Now empty handed, I sprinted confidently up to him as the axe boomed against the ground and sunk the dagger deep into his chest. Expecting him to go limp in my grasp, the man instead stared down at me with hatred brewing in his greedy eyes.

Somehow unfazed by something that should have been a deadly blow, the gargantuan man backhanded me across the jaw, propelling me across the dirt road of this town. Skidding across the ground, a billow of dust clouded around me, taking in pained breaths of either smoke or dust as I grasped onto the side I landed.

Leaving the blade within his body, the man skulked towards me as I lay on the ground, grabbing onto my jaw as I attempted to sit up. Crawling backwards, my hand collided with cool steel laying just out of my grasp.

A discarded sword covered in a layer of loose dirt and soot sat behind me, one that I assumed was once wielded by one of these villagers.

Laying myself against the ground, I slowly grabbed the handle of the sword as the man grew ever closer, careful not to draw his gaze.

Without a second to glance up, I waited until his shadow came directly over me, protecting me for just a moment from the glare of the flames. Without a second thought, I instinctively swung the sword up into the shadow, hearing metal pierce through skin.

Easing my eyes slowly up to him, the sword was piercing through the upper right portion of his chest. His axe was held above his head, recovered from the last blow and ready to end my life in an instant. His eyes still held a glimmer of hatred in them, the only emotion his last moments could muster.

Lying in this frozen space, the air stood silent, the only noise filling the void being from the snapping and popping of the flames.

Eventually, any form of emotion disappeared from his eyes, and his body fell limp as I released the sword from my grasp, hearing them both clatter to the ground. I stood up slowly, staring down at the man I just vanquished, along with the other man a couple feet away. The adrenaline I'd been running on this entire time began to fade away as I came to the realization of what I had done, stepping back with wobbly legs.

"I…I killed them…oh god…" I gasped aloud, stumbling to my knees between the two bandits I defeated. I didn't know what to feel. I felt almost numb, my fingertips tingling as I stared down at my own hands. Foreign blood caked my shaking fingers, permanently staining me with their vile essence even if I managed to wash them clean.

They were animals, nothing more. They deserved what was coming to them, even as my first kills.

They were human beings too, no matter how evil they were.

It was either him or me, and I chose to save myself.

I took a human life, no matter how vile.

I was supposed to be prepared to slay that knight. How can I kill him if I can't even muster the courage to kill a measly bandit?

I could feel the corners of my eyes water slightly as I shakily slid the dagger out of the second man's body with a disgusting slink. I stared down at the weapon my father once gifted me, teasingly chastising me for picking such an unorthodox tool to train with. How he hoped I would never have to use it.

The crimson blood of those two men now glistened off its once pristine edges.

Spinning it within my grasp once, I threw the dagger behind me, watching it spiral through the air and cut through the flames of a building currently burning to the ground. I could hear a faint clang as it struck something in the house before the roaring fire became the only sound once again.

Keeping the sword at my side instead, I took one final look at the two men I had slayed, their bodies almost faceless in the sea of villagers.

"You men were monsters," I lamented to the corpses, "But…to take your lives was nothing I could have imagined. It felt so…wrong to steal another person's life from them, even ones as unsavory as yours."

This path I am treading is necessary to rid the world of evil like that knight. I have to remember that.

As I rigidly stood up, my attention was drawn towards a pair of amber eyes that were watching me within an alley, unaffected by the raging inferno. At first, I thought they were the eyes of a village cat, or perhaps those of some rodent unfortunate enough to be caught within the town. Upon closer inspection, I found how wrong I was. These glimmering circles showed a certain level of fear only human eyes can portray.

Walking towards the alley in as casual of a manner as I could, the eyes instantly vanished from view. My ears locked onto the soft pattering of feet running away even through the now whispering flames. The alley I had waltzed into was completely made of high stone walls, which allowed for it to be sheltered from the blaze. Inside was nothing but a pile of trash, currently rustling quietly. Creeping up to it, I warily moved the rubbish aside.

Within the pile rested a young girl, no more than twelve years old. Her frightened golden eyes stared up at me, shaking horribly as she lay within the trash. She wore a torn blue shirt that had clearly been hit by some form of fire, along with a white skirt that extended down to her feet, caked by mud and soot. Her reddened puffy eyes showed she had just stopped crying, but it was obvious that more tears were threatening to burst out at any moment.

Realizing I still held the blood-soaked blade in my right hand, I swiftly threw it to the ground with a clang as I crouched down to meet her at eye level.

"Easy," I reassured her, "I'm not one of them. I...I came here to help." Putting on a smile for her, I gently extended a hand towards her. She instantly recoiled at my movements, leaning back to escape my grasp. She huddled up into a ball, purposefully avoiding my gaze.

"Sorry sorry," I explained, "I...I know it's common sense for you not to trust me, and you probably shouldn't. But I need you to work with me for just a moment so your safety can be assured." Motionless, she still sat within the ball, silent.

Letting out an exasperated sigh, I ran a shaky hand through my black hair, now coarse from the amount of ash that came to rest within it.

"I didn't use that weapon on any villagers by the way," I noted with a forced smile as I motioned to the nearby sword, "I mean...I took it from one but he was dead, so I didn't steal it." She let out a somewhat terrified squeak as she huddled further into her ball, clearly unnerved by my words. My awkward grin faltered slightly as I realized what I just told a child, kicking myself for the way I worded what I wanted to be comforting.

Never been good with kids...dammit she's worse off than before...

I shuffled my stance just a tad, making sure that I was blocking her view of the bloodied blade as I crouched down.

"If I tell you more about myself, will that prove to you I'm an alright guy?" She stayed motionless for a few seconds, before a brief nod shook her entire body as she remained in her curled-up state.

"My name is...Connor Illium. I live about fifteen to twenty minutes away from here. I also have a brother named Jack who is two years my senior. We both came here to visit initially, but we realized something was wrong and arrived to help you." She remained still, yet I could now see one of her bright amber eyes staring into me from under her folded arm, watching my every move. I cringed as I heard the rafters in a house snap and collapse, letting out a loud crack that cut through the infernal roars.

"Alright I started, now you have to at least tell me your name." For a moment, nothing could be heard except for the crackle and pop of the flames, echoing off the smooth stone walls around us as dying sparks drifted into the alleyway like cherry blossom petals.

"...C..Catherine," a muffled young voice eventually muttered, "M-My name is C-Catherine." I gave her a soft smile, hoping to alleviate her concerns about me.

"That's a lovely name Catherine," I replied, "Do you know where your parents are?" Hearing a distinct sniffle, my smile dropped as I knew I just asked the wrong question. Remaining in her position, Catherine extended her arm from her body, and shakily pointed it up to the smoke covered blue sky.

Understanding what she meant, I couldn't stop myself from waddling forward and pulling her into my embrace, genuinely not knowing what else to do. Flinching for only a moment, the ball she sat in crumpled as she melted fully into me. She threw her arms around my chest, burying her tear-stained face within it. Not truly crying, she simply sat there and shook as I gripped onto her.

"Catherine, I need you to be as strong as you can for a moment," I began, "There are very, very dreadful people in this town right now, and if they see you they will hurt you. What I need you to do Catherine is hide in the greatest hiding place you know. Do not come out of there until you are absolutely sure that these people have left. Come find anyone else who is still here or find me if I am still present.

69

Do you understand?" She nodded in my arms, causing her tears to be further spread along my soot covered shirt. Loosening my grip slightly, she came to look up at me. Her golden eyes were watery, as she nodded repeatedly.

"Then go do it," I ordered with a warm smile, standing up as I did so, "You're a brave young lady Catherine, and I know your parents are looking down on you with warmth. I have to go now to make sure these bad men don't go anywhere. Stay safe, Catherine." Rising to my feet and sprinting off so I did not draw any unnecessary attention to her, I glanced back one more time. While I could see that her eyes still had tears sheltering within them, I could see a glimmer of hope in her amber eyes as she carefully stood up, standing slightly taller with a renewed determination to survive.

7

Jack: The Bogeyman of Bellhollow

"Is this the best you jesters can do?" I challenged the ruffians, "I don't think I have ever fought anyone as predictable as all of you." In front of me stood five of these bandits, each of them being much taller and larger than I was. They each wielded a one-handed steel sword like they were boring clones of one another, apart from the man in the middle being a lefty. Three of their buddies lay dead at my feet, each with conspicuous slashes across their chests.

"Now I will ask you all again," I yelled with a cocky smirk, "Have any of you seen a demoness with purple hair? Perhaps she put new holes through some of your friends." Sneering at my response, the man in the middle charged forward with a growl.

"Ye cocky bastard! I'm gonna tear you in half!"

"So is that a no?" I replied with a sneer, "Oh well then…have it your way I suppose." Flicking the sword up in my right hand, I drew it back behind my shoulder as I pointed it at the man currently charging at me. Dragging the sword along the ground, the ruffian swung the massive blade up towards me. Sidestepping the strike, I slashed my sword down across his chest, causing him to stagger back as the jagged cut tore across him. Before he could properly recover, I sliced the massive blade again across his torso and neck, finally making him collapse to the ground with his already dead comrades. Swinging the blade up and wiping it on my left sleeve, I returned to stare coldly at the four remaining men.

"I'll ask one final time," I repeated at nauseam, "Have any of you seen a woman with purple hair around here? I know she probably would have killed you all but as everything is going absolutely mad I need something to go off of." Judging by their expressions, none of them had seen Avelina, and even if they had they're either too sharp or too pissed off to tell me what I need.

"You thugs have no place in this village," I announced as they gradually walked towards me all at once, "You'd better pray your end is as swift as your friends over here, or this could be painful." Just as they all began barreling their way towards me, a long arrow plunged through the neck of the guy on the far left, dropping him instantly as the black and red feathers came into view. The bandit next to him turned to look for the source of the attack, only to catch an arrow in his leg and a second one in his chest. As he collapsed with an agonized scream, the other two scanned frantically around in the hope of finding the one taking them out so quickly. I almost twirled my sword with glee.

"Forgetting about little old me that easily?" Charging full speed, I drop-kicked the first person on the back, sending them tumbling to the ground with me. Whilst in the dirt I plunged the sword deep into the second man's stomach before he realized where I was, dropping him with an elbow blow to the chin as I stood up. As the first bandit lay dazed on the ground, I threw another swift elbow into his jaw, knocking him unconscious as a couple teeth flew out. The final man remained standing, attempting to pull the arrow that was currently poking out of his chest. Just as I flew up to stab him, a green blur lunged out of a building that wasn't on fire, before phasing over to the thug. As I pierced through him just above his right pec, the green blur jabbed a lance further through the man's stomach, the head of the weapon colliding with the dirt. The man finally fell dead, still standing before we both pulled our weapons out of him.

"And for a minute there I thought you were swallowed up by this wretched fire," I joked as I gave a smirk to the one who assisted me, "Then again Avelina, you would probably kill every bandit attacking here if they even breathed near your shop." Scoffing at my attempt at humor, Avelina blew another wave of her purple hair out of her face as she strapped the lance she had on her back alongside her bow. Her quiver was completely void of arrows, so she tossed it off her shoulders and onto the ground.

"A joke at a time like this?" she asked, glaring at me. I nervously chuckled as I used the same sleeve to wipe off the blood, the material growing damp. She sighed again as she looked around at the carnage her village had become.

"Never mind why you're even here in the first place," she continued, "How many have you brought down?"

"Seven," I reported, stealing my expression, "One as I made my way over here, and the other six you can clearly see here." Staring at Avelina even further, I noticed that the metal plate that usually guarded her upper shoulder was completely gone, with an indent replacing where it should have been. Dusting off her brown pants, she waited patiently as she obviously knew I would continue.

"I had those two handled you know," I proclaimed, "I could have easily pummeled all four of them."

"Or you could have been smashed into the dirt," she countered, "You getting hurt was something I couldn't risk." I couldn't help but chuckle at her reply.

"Aw so you do actually care about my well-being, how kind of you." She gave a hearty chuckle at my words, lowering her gaze as she tried to suppress her snickers.

"Don't get too cocky about it kid," she proudly proclaimed as she returned her gaze with renewed fire, "It'll just be a lot harder to deal with these bandits without your help."

"Whatever you say, Avelina," I joked to myself, suppressing a callous laugh. Returning to the problem at hand, I dropped the smile as I examined the fires slowly beginning to die out on their own; already having consumed all they could as the afternoon sun bored in directly on top of us.

"Avelina," I began, "I still can't quite understand it. Why would a group of bandits randomly ransack a town yet apparently take nothing for themselves? This fire has surely swallowed everything they could've taken, and I've seen plenty of bodies with jewelry still on them. I just don't get why they would do something so random."

"Because it wasn't in any way by chance." My blood froze as I drew my sword and spun around. I let out a sigh of relief at seeing it was just Connor approaching, his brown cloak dragging across the dirt and ash. Avelina gave a single chuckle at the sight.

"So, the unseen brother emerges," Avelina commented, unmoved despite my reaction, "What do you mean that it wasn't by chance?" Walking to stand next to us, his hollow hazel eyes stayed directed at the ground. His dagger was discarded, instead replaced by a crimson stained sword he must have picked up off the ground.

"What I mean is that this all was some form of distraction," he explained, "Sent off into the town to cause as much havoc as possible to alleviate attention from what their boss really wanted." Stiffly raising his left hand, Connor pointed towards a large building about a hundred feet east of us, untouched by the flames.

"That building is the town hall, correct?" Avelina nodded slowly.

"Whoever is guiding these barbarians is currently lying within that town hall. If I had to assume, whoever leads them hoped to distract the town's citizens while he gained some form of riches within that hall. It didn't matter how many people died as long as they got what he wanted." Connor crunched his fist into a tight ball, wielding nothing but hatred and anger within his narrowed eyes as his arm fell.

At least he isn't pointing any of that towards himself.

"I'm impressed, your intelligence surprisingly matches Jack's boasts," Avelina commented to my chagrin, "That would make sense considering my shop is currently untouched, unless the fire reaches it soon. But what would they want from there? As far as I know there's nothing they would want within its walls." Seeing the cogs turning within Connor's head, a sign of realization came over him as he scanned Avelina up and down. His look of curiosity devolved into a sideways glare.

"You're lying," he finally replied, "You know something that we don't."

"Excuse me?"

"Connor you can't just make wild accusations like that! That's how you piss people off. Why would she lie at a time like this?" Seemingly ignoring me, Connor once again stiffly raised an accusatory arm and pointed it angrily at Avelina.

"You bear the crest of the Heartwood military on your right shoulder," he exclaimed. Before she could react, I stared at the area I hadn't paid attention to due to the amount of adrenaline pumping through me.

Sure enough, a black crest that almost resembled a wolf's face was imprinted within the area where the metal plate once sat, almost as if it were branded onto it. It looked almost like it was growling. Its blackened eyes and sharpened teeth peered directly ahead, similar to how a real wolf would look after spotting its prey.

She swiftly covered the spot as a blush began to creep up onto her cheeks. Her eyes widened as she repeatedly opened and closed her mouth, unable to grasp at the proper words.

"So," Connor began again, "I know you just recently moved here a couple months back, so I want to know what a member of the capital's military is doing in this town? You were clearly hiding that crest so no one else here knows about it. I need you to tell me what their leader could possibly be looking for." Her faltering gaze shifted to the floor with each added word, shuffling her feet as she remained silent.

"I'm...I'm not quite exactly part of the capital's military, but I was sent to monitor this town since my arrival." She finally was able to look up from the ground with her signature glare, attempting to match Connor's fierce gaze. It resembled a defiant child desperately trying to stand up to a parent.

She's...she's military?

"The mayor of this town has been hiding something," Avelina finally muttered with a sigh, "But, I could never pin down exactly what. Whatever it is, it holds a considerable amount of value outside of this village. I was close to figuring out exactly what it was before these people attacked. I...I didn't think this information was imperative to you, but I would still be cautious." Glaring at her for a moment, Connor turned his back to us as he drew the sword at his side with a flourish.

"Thank you for your honesty," he stated plainly, "Jack, you and I will head towards the town hall for their leader. Avelina, I need you to spread throughout the town, taking out any stragglers we might have missed and saving any villagers if you can." Not even waiting for a response, Connor began his march towards the capitol building. As I followed him, Avelina raised her voice up to him.

"Wait a minute! How did you know I knew something about this town?" she yelled, "Just because I have the crest doesn't mean I could have known about whatever their leader is looking for." Continuing to walk, Connor only craned his head to the right slightly so she could hear him better.

"Lucky guess," he deadpanned as he paused to stare at her with his cold hazel eyes, "Besides, the military wouldn't be here unless they wanted something. They couldn't care less about a small merchant town burning to the ground." Leaving her in stunned silence, Connor continued walking as the both of us neared the entrance of the large, untouched building.

"Was that really necessary Connor?"

"Not really no, but my patience has run thin today…"

Sprinting up the stairs and crashing through the doors of the town hall, Connor and I both spotted a man huddled against the wall of the room. From what I could see he was wearing a long purple robe with a hood that obscured most of his features, extending from his head all the way down to his feet. His back was to us, but he had to be deaf to not hear the loud crash behind him.

"And here I thought my little distraction worked," he grumbled, his voice sounding like grating glass, "Too bad I suppose. One of you must've been perceptive enough to figure it out." Continuing to keep his back to us, Connor took a single step forward.

"You went to all the trouble of massacring an entire village as a distraction," Connor proclaimed, "Whatever it is you seek we will not allow you to possess, for these people's sake." A dead silence fell over the room as Connor motioned for me to approach, both of us inching ever closer to the man. Every step I took filled me with an unnatural sense of dread, making me want to turn tail and run away the closer I got. Eventually, we stood a couple of feet away from the man, well within striking distance for the both of us. As we both pulled our weapons back, the cloaked man gave a shrill laugh that shook me to the very core. It was like that laugh was a darkness that seeped into every part of my being, making me hesitate with my swing.

"You two are simply children attempting to play the hero," he sneered, "Pulling yourself into a conflict you barely understand. Willingly walking into death's door without realizing what it is you face. Such foolishness coming here, but if you desire to die like the rest that badly then so be it." Shaken by his words, I froze in my stance, unable to swing in time. Connor broke out of it halfway through the final sentence, stabbing into the man to end him.

With a speed I couldn't track, the man lunged out of the way as he finally turned to face us, Connor's sword smashing into the desk he was rifling through just a second before. The wood exploded into pieces as Connor pulled back.

All I could see within the darkness of his purple robes were his shimmering green eyes, studying us with their snakelike gaze. On his neck rested an amber pendant, its color brightened by the fire reflecting through the windows.

Recoiling from him, I could see Connor's shaking eyes staring directly at the amber pendant, his arms beginning to quiver. As the man began chuckling at his response, I stood confused as I also took a hesitant step away from the cloaked man.

"Ah you recognize this," he proudly exclaimed, motioning to the pendant, "To a common villager this pendant would mean nothing but to us, to us it means something far more powerful. The mayor here knew this and hid it in plain sight so that no one would suspect anything. You already know this of course judging by your reaction, meaning you probably have seen one of these work firsthand. Would you like to see how this one is different?" I could see Connor was visibly shaken by his words, losing the stoic expression he maintained when we first entered. Jumping in front of him, I stood at the ready as the pendant's light grew ever brighter.

No longer afraid of the ever-present light, I lunged directly for him with tenacity, my massive sword aimed directly for his heart.

78

"You are going to pierce the sword forward, then slice the sword up hoping to kill me quickly." Gasping in shock, I realized I was doing exactly what he said, as I pierced the blade forward and up. He sidestepped the slash as I stood there in shock, unable to think clearly.

How the...how did he know?

"A swing to the left next." In anger I swung my sword directly at him, watching as he backpedaled for a moment to avoid it.

"Remarkable, isn't it?" he proclaimed, "The power of the gods directly in the fingertips of a man." Before he could speak again, I lunged up from a crouching position hoping to catch him off guard.

"Your sword will pierce nothing but a cheap robe!" As if by magic, my sword pierced through the right side of the thick purple cloth he was wearing, but the feeling of steel piercing skin never occurred. Twisting his body around in order to rip the sword out of my grasp, I was distracted for a moment before he struck me across the face. With a strength I didn't even feel from the barbarians outside I was flung away, shattering a nearby chair into wooden chunks upon landing.

Staring down at me, the whitened teeth of the man grinned at my crumpled form. Before he could do anything, another chair came out of nowhere and crashed against his face, causing him to stumble slightly as it broke into many more pieces. Carrying the two broken off pieces of the chair, Connor threw them both to the ground as he drew his sword once again.

"You are a clever one boy," he growled, "Catching me by surprise like that is something no one has ever done. It's too bad you didn't go for a killing blow. Tell me, what is your name?"

"You in no way deserve to know it," he hissed, straightening his stance as he pulled the sword over his right shoulder, "And I didn't go for anything because you were standing over my brother. As far as I can tell whatever that pendant is gives you some form of foresight, and I did not wish to risk it."

"Well then boy, do you think you can fare any better?" Letting out another sneering laugh he stared down at me, before glancing up at the ceiling.

"A piece of the overhang will fall down, pinning your brother's arm so he cannot intervene." The sound of crumbling stone echoed in the large hall, before a chunk of it came loose from the low-hanging roof. I only had a moment to gasp before it collided with my right arm, trapping me.

I screamed out in pain as my vision blurred and my arm spasmed, tears threatening to cascade out of my eyes. There was a slight amount of room between the rock and the floor, so I could still feel my arm slightly, but the bone was obviously snapped in some way. I was getting a tingly sensation in my arm, meaning there was some blood flow at least. Didn't take away the fact it hurt tremendously.

Connor gasped out as my pain tore through me, however he only lingered for a moment before reverting to the main threat. He continuously flickered his eyes back to me as anger went across his face.

"How do you know what that thing is?" Connor spat, directing his attention to the pendant, "Do you even realize how much power those things contain?"

"And that suddenly makes it a negative tool?" the man barked with a snarl, "Oh I know what this is, and I know you do too. Perhaps now that you are aware of that notion you'll let me go? Otherwise, you'll force me to use its gifts on you." Connor's mouth curled into an snarl as he stared him down, keeping his narrowed eyes on the pendant that swung from his neck.

"Not a chance." The man seemed disappointed by his declaration, shaking his head as he glanced dismissively in Connor's direction.

"Every one of you keeps adding unnecessary casualties to the steep pile I've already created," he sighed in a loud voice, "As soon as you charge me, I will simply jump out of the way. With you right there I will knock the sword from your grasp like you were a child. Then I'll cast you aside like the unnecessary garbage you are." Connor's stance shifted momentarily at those words, the sword looking awkward and clunky within his shaking grasp. Staring the man down, Connor lunged towards him full speed as the man stood utterly still.

"Or perhaps he changed it to a diagonal swing!" Seeing the shock come to his eyes, Connor did the exact move the man predicted, slicing with one hand diagonally up to the left. Jumping out of the way, the man struck Connor on his right wrist, causing Connor to release the blade. Before Connor could retaliate in any way a hand was clenched around his throat. Somehow being picked up with one hand by the man, Connor scratched and clawed at his throat as he was held midair.

"Attempting to perform a move I couldn't jump out of the way of?" he questioned, "Very impressive, but very predictable. After all, I did tell you what I believed you were going to do." Connor's scratching and clawing began to die down, his face turning red as he gasped for air. I slammed and punched at the rock holding my right arm hostage, recoiling in pain as my fingers bruised upon impact.

I'll be there Connor, just hold on!

Eventually, Connor went limp in the man's grasp.

"I admire the determination of you two," he acknowledged, "Nobly risking your lives to save a couple of petty villagers who refused to give up a world changing gift." Holding him next to a nearby window, the man shook Connor one last time to check that he was truly out cold. Realizing he remained motionless, he grasped Connor by both hands and cast him through the hall's window.

"Connor!" I screamed, still punching at the rock as my left knuckle began to bleed, hearing something crack. As if just now remembering

I was here, the man apathetically stared down at me for a moment before slowly walking back over to me. Bending down and staring deep into my eyes, his sinister green pools looked almost bored as he looked me up and down.

"And what would your name be?"

"My name is Jack you self-righteous pompous arrogant bastard!" Sneering at my response, the robed figure picked up one of the wooden legs of the chair I shattered, testing its weight in his slimy hands.

"Do you want to kill me, Jack?"

"In a heartbeat dumbass!" I sputtered out, attempting to yell but lacking the strength to do so, "You killed all these people for a stupid pendant!"

"Ah you still don't get it," he lamented, opening his green eyes as he stared into the cracked ceiling, "These people were too idiotic to understand the value of what their village owned. This pendant is remarkable, and these people just didn't get it. If they knew what this could do…they wouldn't have left it within this place to collect dust." Swinging the chair piece back, the wooden piece smashed against my face as my vision became dazed, turning the robed man into a purple blob. Again, the piece slammed into me, this time bashing into my chest. Before I could even gasp for air, he smashed the piece into my body again and again, my trapped form spasming as his gleeful blows hammered into me. Finally, his barrage ended with a swift strike to the head, tinting the edges of my vision in darkness as the world began to spin around me. The broken, red stained chunk of wood landed beside me as the purple form approached, barely representing a human being as the top portion shook in annoyance.

"Your world will go dark in a moment," he slurred, "A shame you two had to die here without even comprehending my grand ambition…"

8

Connor and Jack: The Strangers

Easing my eyes slowly open, I covered them with my left hand immediately as I was blinded by a sudden piercing light, the dreamlike grogginess still affecting my mind. Feeling my way around in confusion, I realized I was lying in some form of thin bed. Based on the haphazard way the corners of the sheets were aligned made it seem like it was hastily set up for my comfort.

Examining it further, the blankets contained no abrasions or tears and the mattress of this cot had no human-like indent within it, meaning that whoever sheltered here had set this bed up recently. Attempting to stand up and explore further, a shock of pain erupted throughout my back and shoulder, sending me recoiling back to the makeshift bed.

Daintily touching the area of pain, the same shock wave flared up throughout my body, shocking up my spine and throughout my upper torso. I crashed back onto the thin cot, shifting and shaking at every motion I made.

Judging by the lack of direct sunlight and the uneven, damp textures of the walls around me, I was in some sort of cave or other form of earthen cavity. Furthermore, the light I saw earlier came from many different lamps surrounding me, with a small crack of sunlight hitting me in the face. Examining the source, I noticed a large boulder resting in front of what appeared to be the entrance, the light coming from a small crack large enough for someone my size to crawl through.

Thinking back, the world swayed as I recalled a vague memory of lying against a group of burnt wood and ashes, with my eyes pointing directly towards an unnaturally blackened sky.

I was...thrown through a window, and...through a wall? It was...a house already extinguished of fire.

In that same memory shortly after, a pair of hands began to drag me across the ground, appearing unable to lift me fully from it. The hands were covered in a pair of brown leather gloves without fingertips, allowing me to notice they were a woman's hands. The memory gets fuzzy when recalling the rest of her appearance, aside from a last fleeting glance of Eincrest.

"Oh god the village," I thought aloud, "Jack!"

Forgetting about the debilitating injury, I sprung out of the bed, the dirty sheets flying into the air along with me. As soon as the motion was made, the pain plunged throughout my body again, crumpling me to the smooth stone floor below before my foot even touched the ground. Grinding my teeth together as I attempted to ignore the persistent pain, I crawled completely prone towards the entrance of the cave, thrashing violently with every motion. Grabbing hold of a table nearby, I attempted to rest my weight on it for support to catch my breath momentarily. The minute I applied pressure the table was thrown off balance, completely flipping over as I fell back down to the cold ground.

"C-come on body move!" I screamed as my fingernails screeched against the stone ground, "I have to g-get back to them and my family. I have to make sure that man doesn't hurt anyone else!" My cry of desperation echoed throughout the cave, sinking into its walls utterly unheard. I writhed in agony as I flipped myself over onto my back, panting as I stared at the stone walls in which I now resided.

Helpless…again.

The pattering of feet on some form of dirt outside caught my attention, but all the thrashing I had just done made me unable to shift myself onto my stomach to see who or what it was. The sharp gasp of a woman filled the cave as the pattering grew ever closer, evolving into a trot. Coming to a stop near my ears, I steadily glanced up to see the source of the sounds.

It was a radiant young woman who looked about the same age as me, perhaps older by a month or two. Her long, chestnut brown hair flowed down slightly past her shoulders before abruptly coming to a stop, looking like it had been roughly cut by a warrior's blade instead of calm hands wielding scissors. She wore a red and white long-sleeved shirt, with layers of leather plating poking out slightly at the bottom of the shirt serving as proper protection. I could see the beginnings of her burgundy pants and judging by the sounds of her steps she was wearing some form of small boot.

Her emerald eyes stared down at me with a look of concern, however that concern seemed a bit distant, hidden deep within the pools of green. Her face held no emotion on it, making her look as if she held no care for almost anything.

"Are you alright?" she blankly said, staring at me on the ground.

"Yeah…yeah I'm alright," I strained, "Could…could you help me up though?" Without a word, she extended a rigid gloved hand down to me, which I gratefully grabbed. Pain shot through me again as she pulled me up, but it was far less than before. Standing up with a slight wobble, I glanced at the girl who had already begun walking me back towards the bed, taking a moment to further examine this mysterious woman.

Regarding weapons, she possessed a straight sword on the left side of her hip, but upon closer inspection the blade looked…odd. The blade had a silver line that went across its side, making it appear parallel in design. Its hilt was almost golden in appearance, with clashing pieces of gold and silver flowing throughout. It wrapped around the user's hand like a cutlass, further entrancing me with its unique design.

Setting me down on the bed, the woman now stood directly in front of me with her arms crossed, examining me up and down.

"Sir," she began in the same steady tone, "I want to ask exactly who you are and what happened in your village over there? I found you inside your home after it had collapsed from some form of fire." Examining her stance, I could see that she was incredibly formal in her demeanor, but something about it rang odd. The way she stood exemplified a certain tenseness, almost as if she was prepared to run away or strike at any moment. Ever since she entered the cave her mossy eyes never left me, continuously examining me as if waiting for me to spring up and attack.

"N-No miss you have it all wrong," I awkwardly explained, "My name…is Connor. I don't live in that village, but I live fairly close to it. My brother and I went in to hopefully save as many people as possible from that carnage you saw." Her eyes widened momentarily, before reverting to the blank stare she held.

"I…I see," she hesitantly acknowledged, "Do you have any idea what happened there?" Staring up at her, I locked eyes with her emerald pools as I repositioned myself on the bed, pulling my legs up onto the mattress. I decided to test something.

"With all due respect, I would like to know who you are before I answer any more questions." Her eyes narrowed as she took in my statement, her blank stare curling into a frown.

"What gives you the right to…"

"Easy easy," I stammered with hands raised, realizing I had touched a nerve, "I didn't mean anything by it. All I know about you is that you saved my life, and I am incredibly grateful to you for that. What I wish to know is who you are so it could clue me into why you are here, and why you went to the trouble to save me? A name wouldn't hurt either." A light blush went over her face as she turned away from me, perhaps realizing she probably overreacted.

"I'm...sorry," she reconciled, her blank stare returning, "I just... my name is Mara." Trailing off from what she was initially saying, I raised an eyebrow as this Mara clearly hid some form of information from me.

"I'm...a traveler around here," she continued, "I was...looking for a specific group said to be in this area, when I stumbled upon a village blackened by flames. Searching through it, I found you, lying in rubble and injured."

"Did...did you find anyone else there?" My heart sank as she shook her head slowly.

"No, the town was completely abandoned after I placed you here." Saddened for a moment, I shook my head firmly.

My brother wouldn't simply lie down and die.

After I get out of this cursed bed I'll look for him.

He couldn't have gone far. Besides...that Avelina woman probably found him or something like that.

"In any case, I won't be able to stay here for long, as I need to continue searching around this area. You can recuperate here while I do." Turning away from me, she marched towards the cave entrance with her right hand on the shimmering blade, her footsteps softly pattering in a way which exemplified her tense demeanor.

"I am in no way trained as a medic, but from what I can see, your condition is in no way dire," she reported, "You have no broken bones, but there is a substantial amount of bruising and torn muscles covering your back." She paused for a moment to see if I would respond, before continuing.

"Your cloak and shirt are completely ruined as you can see. I've thrown out the cloak, but I can bring you a new shirt if you want." Taking a single step away, she appeared to immediately hesitate in her stride, tilting her head back to stare at my injured form.

"Who are you, really?" she asked in the same tone, "No one with any sense of self-preservation would've willingly dove into that pit of fire and brimstone I stumbled upon." Her eyes traced over me as she froze in place, waiting for a proper response.

"I'm just some kid who thought they could affect the…undesirable outcome that this village faced. In the end, it wasn't enough." Her eyes continued to scan my own as she stood motionless, her blank expression softening into a look that almost resembled pity.

Or more likely…it was an expression that portrayed a level of sympathy.

"I suppose we have that in common then, don't we?" she eventually breathed out, catching me slightly off guard, "I'm sure what you did saved lives, or maybe prevented them from dying in the long run. Who's to say really, but if you're anything like me, you did all you could." As she turned to walk away, I felt my hands attempting to prop myself back up in bed, hoping to slide onto my feet and walk after her.

The pain said otherwise, and I found myself back on the bed, almost feeling the pained twitching of my nerves.

I feel…drawn to her in some way. Almost like my body on its own wants to follow her out that door.

"This group you are looking for," I called out since I couldn't move, causing her to hesitantly turn around, "Do you have a description, or maybe a name? I might be able to help if you tell me." Never changing her expression, Mara stared at me for a couple awkward seconds before replying.

"They are…a group of skilled soldiers," she mumbled steadily, "I have to get to them soon. They call themselves the Sentinels."

* * *

"Sir…are you alright?" Gradually opening my eyes, a groan choked out as my groggy vision came into focus, almost being blinded by the sun. Immediately attempting to shelter my eyes from it, I realized my immobility as I turned to the side, dull pain pulsing through my arm. My eyes widened as I remembered the circumstances, noticing the rumble which confined my bloodied arm.

Still trapped here…that bastard got away.

Everything feels so sore but somehow, I'm alive. That idiot really thought that would kill me.

I winced as I felt my chest tentatively, pain shooting through me at even the lightest touch.

Doesn't take away how much it hurts…I'm gonna chase that bastard to the ends of the earth if he did something permanent.

It still had some form of feeling in it, which meant I wouldn't have to deal with the horror of losing it, although that came with the caveat of feeling every stupid twitch of pain. Glancing around slowly, I carefully searched for who was calling out to me.

Standing above me were two distinct figures, one being a girl who looked around my age and a boy who looked slightly older. The girl had short, cropped tangerine hair that only extended to her neck, along with a pair of bright grey eyes. She had a dark red skirt that extended slightly past her knees, along with a white long-sleeved shirt and light brown boots.

The man…well…

I could barely tell anything about the skinny man who stood in front of me. Not only were his pants and long-sleeved shirt a deep

89

shade of black, but he also wore a black cloak with a hood to obscure his hair. The shirt looked like it had leather sewn into it, taking away as much of a need for a chest piece. On top of that, he had a pair of black gloves and a grey mask that covered his entire face. All of these obscured every possible detail about him except one: the piercing blue eyes which glared into my soul.

I stared up at the both of them, motioning with my eyes to the stone pinning my arm as I took in both strangers.

"Lady, do I look at all alright to you?" I remarked without malice. Seemingly just noticing my condition, she gasped in surprise as she took a shocked step back. Nudging the other man in the side, the second stranger sighed as he walked over to the rock and crouched down beside it. Picking it up with relative ease, he hoisted it over his head and threw it against the hall's wall. It exploded into pebbles and dust.

The tangerine haired girl extended her hand to me on the ground, one which I took carefully with my left. As I stood up, my right arm jerked up at my sudden movement and slammed into my side, filling my body with horrifying pain. Yelping in surprise, the girl accidentally let go of my hand, dropping me back down to the ground with a painful crash. It almost would've been comical if it didn't hurt so bad.

"Sorry sorry!" she exclaimed in surprise, "Okay I got this. Just… look away from your arm alright." Listening to her instructions, I stared away from her as I grasped my right shoulder in absolute agony.

Somehow, the pain got considerably worse, as I could feel my bones being shifted and twisted around.

"Lady I don't know what you're doing but I am about to…" As my words faded away, the pain began to dissipate, as the twisting and turning of bones ceased as well. Taking a hesitant glance over, my mouth opened in shock as the cuts and bruises slowly faded as this girl gripped my arm tightly. Her hands glowed a shimmering green, one which spread throughout my entire body like an odd warmth.

After a moment, the pain was completely gone and I could feel the inner workings of my arm again, albeit with a bit of soreness.

How...how in the...

"Oh thank the Goddess," she exhaled, "At least my power extends to bones too." Noticing my confusion, the girl gave a light giggle as she finally helped me up. She flashed a bright smile as she turned back to me, booping me on the nose like a child.

Alright now I know I've died...this is just fantastic...

"If you're wondering, the amazing woman who just saved your life, otherwise known as me, is Serena. The one brooding over there would be Henry." Simply turning to me, the gaunt man simply gave me a nod, continuing to stare at me with those bright blue eyes. Marching towards me without a word, Henry kicked up my broadsword by the hilt and caught it in his right hand. Grabbing me with his left, he pointed my own blade at my neck without even a hint of shakiness.

"Tell me," he exclaimed with his voice dripping with venom, "What would you be doing in this village of corpses? Please give a proper answer. It would be such a bother to add another body to the piles."

"I would do what he says," Serena gleefully proclaimed, "His methods are a lot less apologetic than mine." Raising my hands in surrender, I tried to match his gaze as my prized weapon now held me hostage.

"Hey take it easy," I babbled, "The name's Jack, and if you used your eyes earlier you'd be able to tell I clearly wasn't responsible." I pointed around the town hall desperately, eventually settling on the destroyed chair close to me.

"I was thrown against that chair and a couple other places until I landed there," I proclaimed, pointing around the room, "The man responsible pinned me to the ground with that stone, and eventually knocked me out with that chair piece. Now, could you please let go of me and give me back my sword. I'm really fond of that thing, and I'd rather not have to take it back by force." I motioned to the chair leg currently lying next to me as proof, carrying a slight streak of my own blood across it.

"Let him go, Henry," a familiar voice commanded, "And give the child the heap of metal he calls a sword." Almost instantly releasing me from his grasp, I gulped up the sweet air as I was finally free from his clutches. I gripped at my neck with my right hand, the appendage miraculously fine aside from some light tingling.

Looking up from a coughing fit, I could see the purple-haired shopkeeper, Avelina, walking into the room, now equipped with her metal guard back on her shoulder. She also now possessed a worn brown cloak clasped around her neck to match her pants.

"Good to see you again Ms. Rockwell!" Serena exclaimed with a beaming smile.

Rockwell...

"Serena, how many times have I told you to just call me by my first name?" Avelina chastised with a light smirk. Serena blushed in embarrassment, standing up from where she was sitting with a fake salute.

"Sorry Miss...Avelina!" Laughing at her antics, Avelina stood next to me and helped me off the ground, yanking me up by my other arm.

"Damn your brother for being clever enough to figure out I'm in some form of military," she sighed, extending her hands out to showcase Henry and a smiling Serena, "Well, here are the ones who were already gonna pay me a visit before all this crap happened."

Connor...

"Oh god Connor!" I yelled out, startling Serena while Henry remained unfazed by my outburst, "Avelina did you find..."

"No, we didn't," she sadly lamented, placing her hands in her pockets as she did so, "I scoured everywhere for anything, but there was absolutely no sign of him, not even a body. I am assuming some kind soul found him and is nursing him back to health as we speak."

Clenching my fists tightly together, I turned to pick up my broadsword, hooking it onto my back as I examined myself.

My brown coat completely shredded, I threw it down on the ground as its back and right sleeve were covered in rips and tears, possibly torn to ribbons by any number of things.

"…ruined my favorite coat," I mumbled to myself, "…those assholes." Serena giggled at my pouting, while Avelina and Henry seemingly conversed about something I couldn't hear.

"Jack," Avelina asked, finishing her discussion with Henry, "You and Connor entered this hall to engage with the perpetrator. Did you catch any descriptions about their leader that would help us find him? Anything at all?" Thinking back on his features, I realized I never saw anything about his face besides his teeth and eyes.

"Well, he wore a hood, so obviously he's got some self-esteem issues there."

"Jack seriously." Avelina chastised with a scowl, but it faded into a smirk she couldn't keep hidden.

"Fine. His robes were a distinct purple, and his eyes were a deep green. He…made off with this amber pendant of some kind, and he was able to predict exactly what Connor and I would do. It was almost like he willed it into being, as he was the one who somehow made that blasted rock fall onto my arm." The room fell deathly silent, as the smiles of Avelina and Serena dropped. All three of them stared at me as if I just described a mass murder.

"What's the matter with you guys?" Grabbing me by the shoulder, Henry turned to stare at me.

"Jack," he growled with a coldness to his voice, "Did you catch a name?" I shook my head.

"No, but as Avelina could attest, the chumps following him had no connection to any outside nations. They were just dumb raiders listening to the call of their master." Henry released me from his grasp as Avelina came up in his stead, staring at me with something that almost resembled desperation.

"Jack, I need you to come with us." Raising a hand in protest, Avelina immediately shut me down with a swift hand raise. Seeing the seriousness in her gaze, I decided it was an excellent time to shut up.

"I need you to come with us to explain all of this to our leader. I know you want to find your brother, but we will bring him to her as well to explain his side of the story afterwards. We'll send a team out to find him once you arrive." I crossed my arms stubbornly, staring at all three of these supposed soldiers at once.

"Why do I have to come with you to explain a story I just told you? I have to find wherever my brother trounced off to after all."

"Because that guy took something really dangerous!" Serena shouted, before blushing and twiddling her fingers.

"Serena is right, Jack," Avelina said, "If your story is anywhere near correct, he snatched some form of weapon from Eincrest, something I was trying to track down before he got his hands on it. You have firsthand experience with what it could do, so if you come with us you may be able to help. Besides, if your brother was dead I would've found his body lying around here, so keep a level head about all this." Thinking of her offer, I stood in awkward silence pondering their proposition.

I would be leaving a simple life behind, a life I wanted to live away from all the chaos and torment that took our parents away. I am not my brother, the boy who wants to charge into the chaos and attempt to tame it.

But what else do I have to lose?

"I'll come with you," I finally relented, "But only because this man destroyed a village full of people I enjoyed company with." Avelina nodded, clearly experiencing the same feeling as I was.

Motioning forward, Henry took off in front of us while Serena walked shortly behind him, acting as the spearhead of the group we had.

"The Sentinels will appreciate your company." Avelina remarked, before marching forward to follow her two fellow members.

9

Connor: Unknown Invaders

L aying in this stiff cot for this long has been absolute agony. I sat alone in this cave with almost no human contact, my only source of the outside world being the ray of sunlight that crept in through the crack the boulder didn't block; the massive rock that just so happened to be positioned in front of this cave, sending away any prying eyes.

My inability to study or train was driving me to a breaking point as I lay trapped within the confines of my own thoughts. I traced over some notes within my tactics book as it still lurked undamaged within a pants pocket, but I could only read the same sections so many times before the boredom once again reared its ugly head. I could almost feel my muscles stiffening at my solitude.

Occasionally, Mara would crawl through that crack to express her lack of success thus far, before handing me some food and a blue shirt when she came back for the first time. I hastily put it on, relishing the cleanliness of the garment even with my ash coated skin. She would stay for maybe an hour, simmering in silence before immediately exiting the cave once again.

I don't think I ever saw her eat, or even sleep. She resembled a living statue.

Today was exactly like yesterday: I awoke from a restless nap in the cave to unsurprisingly find Mara absent yet again.

Mara.

This woman who had stumbled upon me was a confusing enigma. She appeared to be a woman of great skill and perception, based upon the way she glanced over me repeatedly as if I were a threat. Even more so, she seemed frantic about finding this group of individuals, almost to an obsessive degree. Some cavalcade of people known as the Sentinels.

The Sentinels.

Of all the lands and names my mother repeatedly studied with me, none of them ever mentioned a group with that name. If I had to assume, they could be a group of mercenaries that lurked in this area. Perhaps they're a branch of the military, working independently from the Solaton army. Although both are just theories.

I would never have assumed any military could be around here, but after seeing the crest on Avelina's shirt I suppose anything could be true.

There was another pendant.

The single thought panged through my mind as I reached into my shirt, staring into the green pendant I still wore after all this time. I made sure to hide it when I changed shirts, even though Mara already turned the other direction when I did so. I wasn't sure if she knew the power that resided within these things, not taking the risk that she'd just assume it was a normal pendant.

So...the pendant isn't unique, but gifts that reside within them may be.

Since that day, I've kept this pendant locked away within the prison of my shirt.

It somehow led the knight to them. Its activation led to their demise.

Compressing the cool stone within the palm of my hand, I allowed

97

it to fall back within the confines of my shirt, the cool stone rattling against the warmth of my chest.

Could there be...anymore? Are they connected? Could...could finding that user in Eincrest lead me to more evidence on my mother's whereabouts?

The user...that man...

My achy fingers involuntarily gripped at the bed sheets with venomous ferocity, my brain spiraling as I had all this time to review that horrific moment again and again. My thoughts remained hyper-focused on that man, and how he so easily dispatched my brother and me.

"His powers...what on earth were they?" I mumbled to myself, thinking back to the reason why I now lay collapsed in this bed, and why Eincrest was now a pile of ash. All of this chaos, all thanks to the help of that...pendant.

Could it have been the ability to read minds?

No...no that's unlikely. He would never have been caught by surprise if he could do so.

Perhaps a form of mental control? Or maybe a way of forcing us to adhere to his actions?

Then why not have us kill ourselves on the spot? It would have been simple.

"Doesn't make sense." I punched at the side of my bed as I groaned, with all of my thoughts cascading all at once like a rampant storm.

I'll think about this more later, but for now I need to get out of this blasted bed.

Sitting up from the cot with considerably less effort, the soreness of the previous day still cracked throughout the muscles in my back despite the day of rest. Luckily, the feeling was far more muted, allowing me to move my body without stabbing pain erupting through my muscles and nerves.

I sighed in indignation, stretching my arms out with a groan as I glanced again at this cave I had to reside in.

On a table to my right rested a full map of our continent Aelton, although not as detailed as some others I had seen. The corners of the paper each held conspicuous tears throughout, looking as if it were ripped from a wall it was stuck to.

The massive nation of Solaton rested in the west on the map, comfortably taking up the most amount of land within it. To the east was Bellhollow, the desolate place it was. Its landmass of sweltering plains rivaled ours in size, but the Falcon Ridge Mountains tore through the center of the map, making any large-scale confrontation between us virtually impossible.

Any more since the Century War that is...

I chuckled to myself at my own thought.

The Century War...a war almost no one knows anything about, and yet it's still used as a way to tell the year, and that it was a time where every nation fought each other. No one else is still alive to tell any more details, only leaving us with notations on a calendar.

Before and After the Century War...leading us to the current year of 441 A.C.W.

Above the two almost identical nations sat Pyrnesse, the land of the Zevron. The significantly smaller nation was only about a quarter of the size of Solaton, even though it took up the entire northern coast of the continent. Almost nothing was known about what lurked within their borders, as no human from either rival nation had ventured into there for centuries. Even this map left the interior of Pyrnesse barren, unknown even by its creators.

Other than a couple of lamps that were haphazardly strewn across the cave, my current living quarters remained largely empty. There wasn't even a place for this Mara to sleep if she ever decided to stay.

Slowly edging my legs over the side of the bed, I tested to see how much weight I could place upon them. My knees buckling in surprise,

I gradually stood for the first time in a day, using the slightly rickety table for support. I simply stood there for a moment, taking in the fact that I was finally out of that cursed cot and letting my body get used to the weight. Steadily removing my hand from my wooden crutch, I stood tall with arms raised, carefully ensuring my legs wouldn't collapse underneath me.

I stepped forward once, carefully raising my leg before setting my bare foot down on the cool stone beneath.

I took another step. Then one more.

I glanced towards the massive boulder, forcing another rigid step forward as I was now a few feet away from the entrance's barrier. I shakily extended my right arm out, pressing it gingerly against the stone.

It was obvious the boulder had been here for years, with moss growing around its edges and several parts of it darkening from the weathering of time.

With renewed confidence I placed my other arm upon the boulder, taking in a deep breath as I trudged ever closer, pondering the best way I could possibly scale this with how terribly my body ached.

For a moment, I thought of the woman Mara, my mysterious savior who had still not returned yet from her most recent exploration. A woman who in some fascinating way I couldn't understand I felt drawn to; drawn to whatever ambition was driving her to find this ever-elusive group.

I know I haven't even uttered a simple thank you to her yet...but there are more pressing matters at the moment.

Jack...Eincrest...I'll be back to you all soon I promise.

Just as a plan to scale this obstacle entered my mind, my ears caught on to the sound of rustling outside, like boots dragging along dirt as their wearers brushed by branches and shrubbery. Assuming it was Mara, I stepped away from the boulder as my strength returned to me, thankful she was here so I could explain my reasoning to her in person rather than simply leaving. I wobbled back a couple of steps so I wasn't directly in her line of entry, almost smiling gleefully as I relished being able to move around. As I was about three paces from the center of the room, I stopped dead in my tracks as my smile dropped from my face. My blood ran cold as I realized something about the sounds outside.

There wasn't a single set of pacing feet outside. There were three.

Flying back in shock, I slammed painfully against one of the cave walls as a gloved hand crept over the boulder, snaking their arm inside its depths. Before I knew it, a man of average height slithered into the cave, landing on all fours inside. His head shot up immediately, completely shrouded by black wraps that disguised every feature except his eyes. Meeting my hazel eyed gaze with his dull brown ones, time felt as if it was coming to halt as we stood motionless.

Holding my ground as I knew I was incapable of sprinting, I brought my fists up as the man suddenly charged at me. A short-sword was gripped within his hand, barely visible in the poorly lit room.

The swordsman sprung forward at me with incredible speed, looking almost like a blur as he directed the sword at my throat. I rolled out of the way of his strike at the last possible second with a yelp, the blade I narrowly dodged skidding off the stone walls with a series of bright sparks. Dust and shards of rock rained onto the ground, echoing in the small chamber I was now trapped in with an unknown foe.

I grabbed hold of my left shoulder as I stood up, having put too much weight onto it when I dodged as shivers of pain pulsed through it. I stood for a moment and stared at the man who held the ability to effortlessly end my life.

From the way he held his sword to the way he stared at my wounded form revealed years of experience, all written in how closely he came to ending my life. He stood there again painfully still, hanging the sword at his side as he examined me, waiting.

"Who are you?" I questioned, my words echoing within the cave's walls, "Are you a member of those marauders we fought against in Eincrest?" Silence met my ears as my question's echo faded away, his dead eyes continuing to stare into me.

"Alright then...not as openly chatty as the ones in Eincrest I suppose."

In another burst of surprising speed, he lunged forward at me again with almost the exact same technique. Crossing the space between us in just a second, my silent attacker was upon me almost instantly.

Recognizing the pattern he was utilizing, I lashed out behind me and grabbed hold of the cloth covers I laid in for all this time and enveloped the swordsman with it, slinking to the side as I hurled it over my assailant.

The sword pierced through the blanket instantaneously, however the sharpened blade once again only found stone instead of my body. Trapped beneath a blanket of darkness, the man grunted and flailed as his sword jutted out several more times, narrowly missing me at least once. After one of his stabs struck the stone once again, I came at the form like a raging bull, my brain trying to figure out what on earth I was supposed to do through all the searing pain. Pulling back my right arm, I slammed by fist full force into what I believed was the outline of his face.

The man's head only rocked back slightly, releasing a small grunt as he took the force of the blow, my mouth involuntarily gasping from his impassive reaction. Now with the knowledge of where I was, the man pierced through the blanket another time, barely slicing a narrow cut in my left arm as I managed to stumble out of the way.

Finally managing to throw the covers off his face, the man glared at me with that blasted cold expression, affirming his weapon's position.

Raising my fists again, my right arm spasmed in pain as it fell to my side, clearly affected by the force I put behind my last punch.

Without pause this time he lunged at me, drawing the sword back at the ready to end my life. Without anything else for defense, I grabbed hold of a lamp resting nearby, gripping onto the handle in my left hand awkwardly. I swung underhanded up at the man, catching him in the chin as his sword swung up, slicing another thin cut up and across my left arm. The lamp snapped from the handle as it connected with my attacker, crashing into the ground with a new dent in its side and a dead flame. Finally getting a reaction of pain, the man staggered back with a groan as he gripped his face, somehow maintaining that emotionless visage.

How is he still standing? I threw the bent handle of the lamp onto the ground with a clang.

Only able to raise my left hand in a feeble defense, I knew I could only dodge two or three more attacks before he struck me with some form of fatal blow. I maintained my defiant glare, hoping to strike him in the face or chest before he could get a stab in.

Charging at me one final time, I thought back to the knight who stole away peace my brother would have hoped to hold. The hopelessness I felt then.

The hopelessness I feel now…

* * *

"Come on son, stand up and fight!" my father yelled angrily, "We're doing this

until you get it right!" I stood up begrudgingly and took my stance again. My father's breathing was ragged, his frayed dark brown hair splayed wildly over his sweaty forehead. His dull brown eyes bored sharply into me as I readied myself the same way I had during the hundreds of hours of our training. This time, I let my father charge first.

He slammed the wooden axe down on me, slowly battering my feet further into the ground as I tried to detect any form of an opening. I was getting angrier and angrier at my father, but instead I took a deep breath and remembered one of my father's lessons.

Keep your anger under wraps while fighting. Anger only makes you predictable and sloppy in a fight, and a predictable opponent will very quickly be a dead opponent.

I slid out of the way of his axe, with his weight carrying him down to the ground and digging him into the dirt. I practically flung my sword downwards as I tried to get a hit in, but my father was always one step ahead as he rolled out of the way. He popped back up as he attempted to catch his breath. He stood completely still ten feet away, giving me the opportunity to charge at him again.

He swung at me while caught off guard and off balance, giving me the opening I was trying to find. I maintained my momentum as I ducked under his swing and struck his elbow with an open palm, causing his grip on his axe to loosen. I struck my father again at the center of his sternum, drawing a pained groan from the older man. A powerful sword swing to the knee brought him down. He struggled to stand once more, but the practice sword at his neck stopped his stance.

"Ha....Ha...I d-did it." My father's face turned to one of pure wrath as he smacked the sword with such force that he snapped it in half. He kept hitting against the remains of the sword with his axe, knocking me to the floor.

"In battle never let your guard down!" he screamed as he kept beating down at my hands, over and over again. "You hear me! The real world will never be fair!" He raised his axe high above his head, preparing to swing down.

I instinctively threw my hand up in a desperate attempt to block the axe. It was a reaction. Something I didn't mean to do. As the axe was about to collide with my hand, a single flash changed everything I had dreamed would be possible, shattering the realms of my reality and creating something new. Something…unnatural.

* * *

Look at you…you haven't grown at all since then have you Connor?

My memory flashed back as the world seemed to slow to a crawl, right as the man stood above with his sword diving down.

You're still the useless boy who doomed the life of his father, and that's who you'll still be even in death.

As if by instinct, my body moved in pure desperation to strike the man with my palm before he could bring the sword up, one last feeble attempt to keep on living.

As I did so, a brilliant light shined around the room, blinding myself and my assailant as the darkness scurried into the furthest corners of the cave. For a moment, everything was still, as my hand was about to strike the man in his ribs as his sword slashed down above me. It was in that split-second moment that I realized the light was emanating from me.

A brilliant shine of green-tinted air coalesced around my entire hand like a miniature hurricane, swirling and dancing at the tips of my fingers as the green winds enveloped my hand like some form of glove.

This is…the same as that day…

In that brief millisecond of time, my hand struck the man just as quickly as I noticed its glimmer, crashing into him with as much force as my last-ditch defense could possibly muster. His dull eyes widened as we stood in milliseconds of frozen space, the blow catching him by surprise.

With a loud bang, the man was propelled away from me at high speeds, my left arm recoiling back from the immense force of the ethereal blow as I yelped out in surprise and pain. Dropping his blade as he flew, my attacker spiraled through the air before his body collided headfirst into the nearest wall with a resounding crack. His body slumped to the floor, as the tiny bit of life that was once in those brown eyes faded away.

The same green air quickly retreated from the rest of my hand and emanated in a circle around my hand like a puff of smoke momentarily, before fading completely, allowing for the darkness to swallow up the light once more.

I stared at my hand in disbelief, my left hand unintentionally shaking as I crumpled to my knees. I didn't check, but I knew beneath my blue shirt my emerald pendant shined brighter than it ever had before, generating heat against my skin just like that day.

"No...oh please no..." I frantically rasped to myself, shaking as the darkness itself began to spin and sway around me.

I did it again. Oh god I did it again.

Snapping to the cave entrance, I frantically stared at the only way to enter the cave, my senses blurred as I waited for someone to burst in.

For him to burst in...for him to recognize the foul stench this pendant gave off and home in on it like a rabid dog.

For a full agonizing minute, I sat there slumped to the floor like a wounded animal, biding my time as I waited for that demon of a man to barge in and end my life. I couldn't quell my immense shaking. I sat there and waited for what felt like decades of my life dragging on, waiting for the moment my life would come to an end.

But, even after all that time, all I did was sit in silence.

Nothing...

There was nothing...

No demon...no monster to come and end me where I stand.

Gripping my face with my left hand, a snort of laughter escaped my lips as I knelt in utter silence, the involuntary shaking of my body coming to an end.

He...isn't coming...

Tears almost escaped my eyes as I finally unleashed my own manic laughter, cackling like a madman as the realization fully hit me. I stared down towards the earth in triumph, hearing the cries of my hysterics' echo around me.

He didn't know it happened. For some reason this was...different from the last time.

I snorted and laughed uncontrollably as I stared down at the floor, no longer afraid of whatever abyss could come riding in through those doors.

Because that demon doesn't know where I am.

Eventually managing to shake off the fits of laughter that had overcome me for a moment, I recalled the two other sets of heavy footsteps outside with a final snort, hearing them wildly pace around just behind that boulder as if startled by something.

Knowing his companions would be here any second to tear into me, I swiftly limped over to the sword he cast aside, swiping it up as I whirled around to face the cave entrance in whatever stance I could create, gripping the sword over my left shoulder. However, something about this sword was...odd.

Taking the time to examine it within my grasp for a moment, the sword that was once held by the man beside me now was about the size of a dirk. Its razor-sharp steel edges were tinted in some sort of black metal, making it appear far deadlier than a common blade. The handle was covered in a brown cloth of some sort, bringing an odd comfort while holding it. I sorely swung it twice, awkwardly flipping it around into my usual grip in my left hand before swinging it again.

The weight is somehow perfect for my fighting style, even with it being slightly longer than a traditional dagger.

After analyzing the weapon I decided to keep, my ears noticed an odd factor about the sounds that were going on outside.

The shuffling that I had heard previously had gone utterly silent. The sudden shift of sounds sent shivers up my body.

Mustering up the courage to survey what had happened, I detached the sheath from the man's body and attached it to my own waist.

He wasn't going to be using it anyway.

With the weapon secure, I lurched forward towards the boulder in front of me, hoping for the safety of the one who saved me from that village of fire.

10

Connor: A Greeting and A Goodbye

Rigidly grabbing hold of the boulder that blocked my path, I arduously hoisted myself over the top of it as my muscles stretched and panged, having to squeeze through a little as it was obviously more suited for someone like Mara.

I hope she is alright wherever she is. I hope she's still out there searching and didn't get ambushed by the two lurking outside.

Finally reaching the top of the massive rock, I ensured my balance on it was perfect as I stared out at the area, taking in the crisp air of the leaving winter.

Glancing down at the ground first, I immediately noticed two male bodies crumpled onto the course dirt below. They were both collapsed face-down, but it was obvious they bore similar body structure and attire to the man slain inside.

Standing above them was Mara; her once pristine blade now painted red as she peered at the dead men at her feet. From the looks of it, she had not even broken into a sweat while fighting them, her breathing completely even as she stood the victor.

In a flash she had the sword pointed up directly at me, pausing before realizing it was the man she had saved earlier. Lowering the scarlet blade slowly, her gaze never left mine as we stood triumphant over our assailants.

"You survived," she finally breathed out as if it were an afterthought, keeping her sword at the ready as I crawled off the boulder's face carefully. I eased onto the ground below as I stepped down, making sure the weight was evenly distributed between my legs.

"Did you expect anything else?" I retorted, almost sounding like my brother in my snark. Ignoring me, the brown-haired girl sheathed her blade as she stared out at nothing, seemingly lost in thought.

I relished taking in the landscape around me, realizing we were surrounded by trees and foliage. We were on a mountain side of some kind, as a sea of trees engulfed the area beneath us. Several different shades of green and brown filled my vision, the cleanliness of the air reminding me of the old home in the mountains. I breathed it all in with a smile, relishing the upgrade in air quality from the cave and the smoke.

In the far distance I could see Eincrest, its blackened and malformed shape no longer resembling the bustling merchant town Jack often told me about.

Reverting away from the moment of reprieve, I turned away from the cliffside as I knelt down to examine the body of one of these men who attacked us. Turning him over, I could tell that his armor was slightly thicker than the swordsman I conquered inside, made up of some form of leather with the same blackened coloration as this dirk. However, the thick leather now proudly showcased a large puncture wound where Mara clearly found her target. A spear laid in the dirt beside him, the darkened point glistening as it lay covered in dust.

I could assume these men came from the same group that butchered Eincrest, but that wouldn't make any sense.

I stared out at the town once again, remembering the robed man who was willing to not just butcher a town, but willingly push his men into a distraction knowing full well that it was likely that they would be killed.

"In no way did he care about them," I mumbled to myself low enough so that Mara couldn't hear, "None of them would have survived the ransacking of that village. Even if they did, how would they even know I did, or even who I was?" Along with that, none of those bandits had the same temperance as these soldiers. They were too well focused; too well experienced.

Too...dead.

How would they even know we were here?

Standing up slowly without any noticeable pain or soreness, I stared at the emerald-eyed woman who stood only a couple feet away from me, still lost within the tangled web of her own mind. Her hand was gripped tightly onto the handle of her slim blade, the bits of her hand exposed from her gloves turning white as some form of troubled emotion finally filled her eyes. Her lips curled and her eyes widened in a way that almost resembled fear.

"Have any problems holding these two off? The one inside was troublesome to say the least."

"No." She replied plainly without ever averting her eyes from the skyline. I noticed the way her fists clenched when I mentioned those two; how much anger it clearly brought out of her. It was almost impossible to tell due to the emptiness in her gaze.

But I knew better...

"Something off about these men," I noted as I stared down at the two she had slain, awkwardly attempting to hold conversation, "No emotion or passion behind their strikes. I don't think I even heard a single word come out of them." She kept staring forward without a word despite my sentiments, never once even glancing at me or the bodies I discussed.

"Yeah I...I noticed that too." Her tone was shaky, yet at the same time it still came off as distant. It was almost as if she was vaguely listening to what I had to say, losing herself within the confines of her mind as she fought to keep her tone passive.

"Still unsure of where they came from though, or why they would go through so much effort to attack some kid in a ca-" Everything about this scenario hit at once, almost rocking my mind as it all became so clear. I turned to the woman who was practically ignoring everything I said, opting to think rather than speak.

The woman who would have been in that cave if she wasn't searching.

"You knew these men would come, didn't you?" I asked her, even though I already knew the answer. Clearly knocking her out of whatever train of thought she was in, she swiveled around with a wide-eyed expression. Just as quickly as that emotion surfaced, her blank expression returned in an imperfect way, a tinge of fear lurking behind her forestry eyes.

"I don't know what you mean," she responded, lying through her teeth as she did so. I could not help but grit my own in irritation.

"Cut the crap Mara." I demanded with venom, my anger at her passiveness getting the better of me. She was startled by it, the blank stare fading back into the visage of a terrified girl.

"It's clearly visible in your expression that you're afraid of something," I asserted, "Whoever these people are, you knew them in some way. You may not have known they were following you, but you knew of their existence. I can see it in the fear you're trying to hide away." I took a step closer to her, her body tensing up with every word.

"I don't like when people lie to me, so I just want you to tell me the truth," I admitted in a softer tone whilst maintaining my assertiveness, "Let me help you." Staring down at the ground, the Mara standing in front of me was far different from the woman who came in and out of the cave beside me, not even muttering a hello as she scurried by.

112

This Mara was clearly spooked by the appearance of these men, and no matter how hard she tried she could not move past it.

"They..." she muttered, barely beginning before she trailed off, "I didn't know these people would follow me. I came looking for these people...the Sentinels, hoping that they held the key to solving my problem." Even though her voice and demeanor returned to the same reserved self, it was obvious she was keeping everything purposefully vague.

"And what would that problem be Mara?" I asked with just as venomous of a tone, catching her off guard.

"I'm sorry," she replied, a hint of remorse within her stony voice, "But I won't say. It is my burden to carry, but I know that these people will help me alleviate it."

"But why would you go to these people for a burden you simply carry? You seem capable enough to handle it yourself." Her expression further hardened, almost shaking in the single greatest sign of emotion I have seen from her yet.

"The burden I carry could potentially grow and fester throughout this entire continent, bringing destruction and ruin throughout." A silence rang throughout the area as the two of us stood deathly still, staring at each other as the importance of her words fell upon me.

Could she mean...people who could bring chaos back to our nation? She couldn't...right?

This woman...this Mara. How could anyone at our age even involve ourselves in something as drastic as that?

"I found them right before I came back," she interjected, startling me, "The Sentinels' base of operations. It was hidden deep within this forest, impossible to find if you didn't know where to look." She stared off into the distance once again, peering down at the green sea that lay before her.

"Their leader is named Katrina," she continued, never shifting her eyes from the horizon, "She is a woman with incredibly high aspirations for this country and its people." Finally snapping back to me, her stunning emerald eyes glistened as she stared at me.

"I came back because I wished to extend to you the offer to come with me," she informed, beginning to walk towards the cave entrance to grab what she needed, "If your village story was true then you have adequate skills, and your fate seems to be drawing ever closer to her anyway. She'll need both of us if she wants her goals to be achieved."

"And why would I be needed there?" I demanded loudly, "I am perfectly capable on my own, and what I want can be best achieved alone, and uninhibited." She froze in her tracks at my words, not bothering to look at me as the silence I had grown accustomed to returned.

"Because if I am correct about my assessment of the men you fought in Eincrest, more of them will come." Although her tone had remained the same as it was before, her words chilled me to the core of my being.

"If you truly are a good man Connor, you will at least consider it," she continued with vigor, "I am...not the greatest judge of character, but even though I don't truly know who you are, I respect the fact that you so adamantly threw yourself into a town from which you had no connection. Many men and women I've seen encounter similar situations choose to flee when their life is truly on the line." Finally glancing back at me, for a moment the blankness that permeated her eyes for so long vanished, replaced by some form of determination that threatened at any moment to spill out.

"Fate has thrown a crossroads in front of you, and whether you realize it or not you don't have the option of turning around and ignoring both paths. Every person has a crossroads thrust in front of them, and every person has eventually made their choice." She glanced down at the ground for a moment, a glint of sadness filling her expression.

"Sounds like a bedtime story I was read to as a child," I replied almost sarcastically, "Is this going to be a tale of fighting between humanity's good and evil nature?" The conviction in her eyes never faded as she shifted to fully face me, standing at least ten feet away from my position with her fists clenched at her sides.

"You know that life has never been that simple," she responded in a biting tone, "If it was, then I wouldn't be standing in front of you looking for these people in the first place, because they would have already purged the world of its evil through the power of their pure hearts and minds." She took a heavy breath, staring me down with the same analytical eye she had maintained since she first saved my life.

"On one of these paths is the way your heart is pulling you, towards this group and towards something more than yourself. On the other path, there is nothingness and indifference. If you choose to go home and pretend like none of this ever happened; that a man did not enter that village and butcher innocents, or any other atrocities you have witnessed in your lifetime, you choose a path far worse than any evil." Turning away from me, she gave a fleeting glance over her shoulder as she stared me down.

"It appears fate is pulling us in the same direction, but the choice to divert course if you so desire is completely in your hands."

Without letting me respond, she proceeded toward the cave entrance once again as she turned away from me, never taking a second glance back at me.

Katrina...

That name shook throughout my head like the vibration of a ringing bell.

It's familiar to me, but I have absolutely no idea why.

I stared at Mara's fading form, watching as she was already on top

115

of the massive rock and slinking back into the cave for whatever she needed.

She is something. There's a coldness to her and yet, she clearly is hard set on solving whatever burden has been placed upon her shoulders, along with a maturity void of many people my age.

I crossed my arms in thought, placing a hand upon my chin as I mumbled aloud the thoughts that refused to stay confined within my head.

She's right you know, you have always wanted to make a difference in this country, and you've just been presented with the ideal way to do it.

You can make a better difference by staying home, by finding Jack. Then you can finally track down that blasted knight and mom.

What if those paths intertwine? What if these Sentinels are combating some greater form of evil they're all connected to?

There is no greater evil than that knight! He took everything you care about.

You selfish idiot! The man from the village is still around with that weaponized jewelry and he clearly wasn't working alone. What if his group is the one Mara is hoping to fight?

Then they've got it handled. Killing that knight and finding mom is much more imperative now.

What could be more imperative than preventing men like him from slaughtering so many more people?

"Shut up!" I screamed aloud, slamming my hands against my head as the thoughts became too much, "Shut up shut up shut up!" With my outburst ceasing as it echoed throughout the vast nature, I panted from my yells as the silence of the air truly hit me.

"Why am I so conflicted?" I questioned myself hysterically, "It should be an easy question to answer. If I find these Sentinels and join them then my life could be dedicated to preventing ruin and death in this nation. What I have always wanted! Why is it so damn hard?" I fell to my knees as the weight of my inaction hit me. I gripped onto individual tufts of grass as I stared blankly at the ground, shaking violently as everything about my life came crashing into my mind at once.

If you choose to go home and pretend like none of this ever happened; that a man didn't enter that village and butcher innocents, or any other atrocities you've witnessed in your lifetime, you choose a path far worse than any evil...

"Am I that selfish?" I asked incredulously, "Why am I so hard set on returning to my decrepit log cabin and focusing on nothing but what I want?"

It's because you love your mother...you know what she would do...

Standing back up shakily, I wiped my thumb across my nose as I stared off into the distance, seeing the blackened figure of the former merchant post swaying in the distance.

No longer a bustling and vibrant town because of one man.

One man who I could have stopped.

Who can be stopped with the right group of skilled people.

Who will be stopped with the right people.

"I refuse to be conceited," I affirmed as I brought a defiant fist up near my face, "I promised myself long ago that I would stand up and fight when I knew people were being wronged." I brought my fist down as I stared back at the cave, waiting for my brown-haired companion to come out.

"I'm not a believer in fate," I announced to no one, "So I say with full confidence that I choose to walk this path on my own terms, as a man who wishes to set this world straight." As the woman's hand jutted out of the entrance of the cave, I jogged forward as her entire body came into view, staring at me with hidden curiosity.

"I accept your offer, but I would like to make one stop before we go to find these Sentinels," I explained as she slowly nodded, "I just...have something I need to do." Her eyes gave a faint glimmer of surprise as she jumped down, landing in front of me as she stared me down.

"Alright then. What is it you require?"

* * *

I could sense her confusion as we moved up the charred building that I once called home as a child, running a hand along the blackened doorway. The walk wasn't terribly long to get here, but the silence from her certainly made it appear so. My boots crunched against the ash and chipped wood as I stared around the space one final time. Chunks of the roof lay collapsed amongst the broken glass, and the only items that were recognizable were composed of some form of metal. The rooms were completely indecipherable amongst the rubble, but I remembered the placement exactly. I knelt down as I brushed my hands across the battered terrain my home once resided in, before standing back up.

Goodbye...for now. I'll be back with Jack and mom soon.

My eyes met those of the woman named Mara, who despite her apprehensive nature still trudged along behind me this entire journey, her light footsteps and her continuous gaze upon me accenting her paranoia. Her eyes shifted over the destroyed house, her eyebrows creasing in bewilderment.

"What is this place?" I continued walking past her as she said this, motioning her to follow as I walked down an all too familiar path.

"A relic. From another lifetime." I knew she was still puzzled as to what this place was, and yet she still followed closely behind me. Her eyes continuously shifted between me and the surrounding woods, her gloved hand never abandoning the grip of her blade.

I didn't bother to enter the shack Jack and I had called home very briefly when we passed it. It meant nothing to me; no memory of proper goodness attached to it or materials I could possibly wish to retrieve. Just an empty vessel to reside in temporarily, and one which I no longer wanted nor needed.

Eventually, the two of us came upon the same clearing which ran chills up my spine every time I entered. The words and actions of that night still shook through my mind, threatening to pull me back into a horrific retelling of my life's first inflection. The same shoulder guard of that bastard rested where I had tossed it aside days prior, almost blending into the earth due to its rusted visage.

The same wooden grave gazed into me as I finally stood in front of the main purpose of this trip. The dust settled as I came down to my knees, the sun bearing down upon me as the cool breeze reminded me of the changing seasons. Of our current transition from the cold and desolate times of winter to the rebirth present in spring.

"I'm sorry to be leaving father, but it appears I'm being pulled in a new direction," I murmured as I stared at the wooden headstone, "I…wanted to give a brief goodbye before I left. I promise you that I won't forget my purpose. I'll find her and that knight soon." Coming to stand beside me, I craned my head back as I examined the women who had accompanied me. The one who promised me that soon, I would face a new beginning to my life. She crossed her arms as she flipped between me and my father's grave, the blankness I had grown used to somewhat softening.

"This…this whole place was yours?" I gave a slow nod at her question, brushing a hand over the grave one final time as I stood up, dusting off the loose dirt that had coalesced around my knees. She unfurled her arms as she looked towards the ground, her brunette hair disguising her inner thoughts.

"I'm…sorry. No person deserves to go through any of this." It was a common form of apology most people give when someone they know loses a loved one, one I had grown used to in its many derivatives.

119

But, despite the emptiness of her tone, I felt an odd warmth I had never experienced before through her words.

"I'm ready to go now. Lead the way." She gave a sharp nod as she turned on her heel, marching forward with purpose as she worked down the path I had originally shown her, trudging along after her.

I reaffirmed the position of my tactics book and my newfound weapon as we both walked down the hill, past the woods I once strove through and the mountains I hoped one day to scale. I stared one last time at the swirling pendant, the one that saved my life and set me on this path.

Through them and through that man in the village, I'll gather the information I need to find you mom. His pendant is the lead I needed, and if I work with them and find him, perhaps they'll bring me one step closer to the truth of it all.

With his downfall, I will find you.

I promise.

11

Jack: A Fated Meeting

"Wow you've gotten to work with Miss Rockwell all of this time? That's so cool!" I let out a laugh while listening to this new woman's hyper way of speaking. While Avelina and Henry remained almost completely silent at the front, Serena continuously questioned and conversed with me with enough energy to make up for their absence. Despite looking the same age as me, her mannerisms made her appear so…childish. While many would find it annoying, I very much found it a breath of fresh air from the destruction and death we were walking away from.

Almost skipping side-by-side with me, Serena and I kept a decent pace behind Henry and Avelina, who were both keeping watch with steady eyes. Serena paid no mind to any of that, keeping on a cheery smile as she continued to talk and talk about whatever topic randomly appeared within her head. We had been like this for a couple hours now, as the afternoon sun of a new day was just peeking over the tree line we found ourselves in. I didn't see her stopping anytime soon.

Against Avelina's wishes, Serena demanded that we made camp last night, claiming she was too tired to even walk another step. Agreeing as I was completely exhausted, I proclaimed that we would be staying the night whether she wanted it or not. Clearly defeated, our current group rested for the night before we continued this morning, my own grogginess not being reflected in the woman beside me.

"I wouldn't call it working together Serena," Avelina called back from the front, speaking her first words during this entire walk, "He was a frequent customer is all, and a troublesome one at that." I shot daggers at her as she let out a slight chuckle, covering her face with a hand mischievously as she did so.

"Oh shush Miss Rockwell you're not part of this conversation," Serena briefly retorted with a wave and a giggle, seemingly forgetting Avelina's words about titles just a day ago, "At least you got to see each other so much. I would kill to be able to just sit around and talk with you all day." I grinned as I peered over at Avelina, who was currently still looking back at us with a light chuckle.

"Eh I'm not so sure about that Serena," I stated, "After all, conversations with Avelina often turned rather...boring." Serena and I both couldn't help but laugh as it was Avelina's turn to glare back at us before returning to stare forward, leaving the rest of the conversation to the two of us.

While I enjoyed the general jovial attitude of the group at the moment, I couldn't help but be spooked by the one silent member of our party.

Ever since leaving the town hall, Henry hadn't spoken a single word, let alone even a simple grunt. I hope at the very least he was still breathing.

His general disposition almost made me shiver every time I looked at him. Aside from the covering attire and complete lack of any weapon that I could see, his closed off nature reminded me too much of how Connor acted.

"Is he always this silent?" I whispered as discreetly as possible to Serena, leaning in close to her ear, "Of the many negative feelings I'm getting, it's just plain eerie." Serena suppressed a giggle at my words, shaking her head with a smile.

"Unfortunately," she replied without malice as she leaned in, almost audibly rolling her eyes, "It's just the way he is I'm afraid. However, that means I can make fun of him as much as I want and he won't retort in kind."

"I hope you know I can hear you Serena," Henry deadpanned, startling me once again. Serena put a hand to her mouth as she giggled, similar to how Avelina did.

"How much farther do we have to go before we get there?" I yelled up to Avelina, who I could tell rolled her eyes before craning her head back.

"A couple more minutes," she replied in an equally as loud tone, "When we arrive, we are going straight to Katrina so she can discuss this with you." Immediately after those words she reverted to her lookout position, keeping her eyes carefully trained on our surroundings.

"Katrina?" I asked curiously as I turned to face Serena, "Am I supposed to know who that is?" Serena kept her smile on as she stared at me, lightly shaking her head.

"She's the one in charge of course!" she exclaimed peppily, "She's the greatest of us all!" I could hear Avelina let out a hearty laugh at Serena's simple words, however she didn't turn to face us.

"What I believe our hyperactive medic was trying to say is that Katrina is the creator and remarkable leader of the Sentinels. She is a noble woman who truly understands this world, along with being a prestigious soldier. I'd follow her to the ends of the earth if it meant I could stand by her side."

"I knew no one would set up shop in that town willingly," I muttered coyly, getting another childish laugh from Serena. Avelina extended a hand up in the air as she flipped me the bird, making Serena laugh even harder as she wiped a tear from one of her grey eyes.

"I am being serious Jack, something you constantly fail to do," she responded sarcastically, lowering her hand, "I admire the woman. She truly believes that what we do is imperative to the growth of this whole continent; of Aelton."

"And what is it you guys do anyway?" I asked, exclaiming the question that has been on my mind this whole trip, "You've dragged me all this way towards some vague destination you all work for, but you won't tell me why your work is so damn important." With neither of the other two responding, Avelina let out a sigh as she realized she was being volunteered to give the explanation.

"As I am sure you can glean from what your brother said in Eincrest, we are soldiers of the Heartwood military in Solaton," she explained, "Although calling ourselves soldiers would be a bit of hyperbole. Reconnaissance would be the more accurate word to describe ourselves." Henry for the first time during this trip cleared his throat with a hoarse cough, facing me as he did so.

"Our primary objective is to scope out areas to ensure the security of this country," he explained in a cold voice, "We are a small enough organization where we can be relatively unnoticed by the general public, and all of our members have to be incredibly well trained in their craft. For that reason, our missions can consist of security, reconnaissance, espionage, and a couple other items only we can achieve."

Serena gave another closed-eye smile at those words, holding up a sideways peace sign to her left eye as she grinned at me.

"We're the best of the best, no doubt about it!" she exclaimed, maintaining the comical pose as she did so, "Katrina handpicked each and every one of us herself. The only one who was in the military themselves was Ms. Rockwell." Avelina gave a slight nod at the words.

"So, is that why you're the only one with that crest on your outfit?"

I asked her. Avelina grasped onto the metal piece with her left hand, leaving it on but gripping tightly onto it with a sigh.

"I frequently work between the Sentinels and the military themselves, relaying messages and information wherever I can, so I required some form of proof of my membership. I was placed in the town in search of a weapon…that pendant apparently." She let go of her metal piece, letting her arm slink around and drop down at her side.

"I just wasn't aware our enemies knew about it too," she lamented, "Otherwise I would have been swifter about it."

"Your…enemies?" I asked in a genuinely serious tone, "I was under the impression Eincrest's attackers were just a collection of rotten bandits." I could hear Henry click his tongue at my words, crossing his arms as he hid his facial expressions behind the emotionless visage his mask was.

"It wasn't those manipulated fools we are worried about," he explained, "But the man who pulled the strings for his expendable puppets."

"Jack if your description of him was spot on then we have an immense problem on our hands," Avelina cut in, "That man is incredibly dangerous, and the sporadic nature of his actions make him even more of a threat." Serena, who was beginning to remind me of Henry with how scarily silent she was, suddenly pushed past me with a gasp. Stumbling slightly from the surprising force behind her push, I glanced up in time to see Serena shine a bright smile as she pointed into the distance.

"But that doesn't matter right now!" Serena further interrupted, "Look we already made it!" Shaking off her push, I gazed in the direction where the other two ahead of us were walking towards.

It was a large wooden cabin about a hundred feet ahead, cloaked by the towering trees and brush surrounding it.

From the outside, it appeared to be a one-story building that extended deep into the woods nearby, with much of it being hidden from my view due to the amount of nature that camouflaged it. Even then, the amount I could see was incredible.

"Wow," I breathed out, "How on earth does something like this stay hidden from unwanted attention?" Avelina lightly chuckled to herself as Serena sprinted up full speed in front of us, swiftly flanked by Henry's darkened form.

"I've frequently asked Katrina that question myself," she admitted with a smile, "To her, we're deep enough within the country and these woods to drive away both curious strangers and enemies trying to track us down."

"Besides," she continued as she walked briskly ahead of me, "According to the rest of Aelton, we don't exist. So to anyone, this would just be some random cabin some rich politician lives in during the hotter months." Catching up to the other two swiftly as the wind blew across my dirt caked face, Serena was already upon the door and had her hand placed upon the ornate door handle. Flinging the door wide open with a giddy smile, I gazed into the room that Serena was already waltzing into.

The room we currently resided in appeared to simply be the formal entryway, as well as looking like some kind of recreational room. A red couch was pressed up against the right wall, and a grand table sat in the center surrounded by wooden chairs. A collection of windows adorned the space; however, a multitude of unlit candles were strewn miscellaneously in the cabin. A large map of the continent was plastered against the back wall, with pins and other knick-knacks jutting out of Aelton's normally rocky surface. The area of Solaton was divided into six sections, with a large circle in the middle.

On the left side of the room sat a blonde-haired woman far older than I was, but one who still looked relatively young. She sat cross-legged in a hefty chair in the corner of the room, close to the map but a decent distance away from the table at the center. She was reading a small blue book in her right hand, sipping on a steaming drink in her left. Her very aura was one that proudly shouted power and wisdom. Even if I were unaffiliated with this group, I would know that I was looking at someone born to command.

"Katrina!" Serena hollered, already in the process of kicking her boots off with relative ease. The woman who I now knew was Katrina glanced up from her book with a smile, barely able to set her drink down on a stand beside her before Serena sprung forward. Somehow launching herself completely over the immense table in front of us, Serena landed in front of Katrina and practically tackled her back into her chair. Katrina gave a delighted smile as the rest of us walked around the table.

"Ah Serena, it's good to see you again," she said in a calming yet commanding voice, similar to that of a mother, "It only felt like a couple minutes ago since I sent you and Henry away." Serena gave a radiant smile as she gazed up at her commander.

"Can't get us out of your hair that easily captain!" she beamed, stepping out of Katrina's grasp as she loosened her grip, "You're gonna have to try a lot harder next time to keep us out permanently." Ruffling her tangerine locks, Katrina gave a hearty laugh as Serena gasped at the sudden tangling of her once pristine hair, now filled with knots and strays. Her laugh continued as her eyes came to rest on Henry, with the orange haired girl still desperately trying to straighten her now disorderly hair.

"And it's good to see you in favorable shape too Henry, even if you're not quite as vocal as Serena over here." Henry gave a grunt as he immediately leaned against the wall beside Katrina, becoming a gatekeeper as he stood and stared at Avelina and I. Serena stuck her tongue out at Henry after finally uncoiling her orange mane, which to her annoyance he ignored. Grabbing one of the nearby chairs, Serena turned it completely around and sat backwards within it, resting her arms and chin on top of the back portion. She swung her legs back and forth like a bored child as she waited for what Katrina was going to say next.

Coming to a rest in front of her, Avelina gave a nod and light smile as she stood with her hands behind her back. Katrina appeared genuinely surprised by her presence, her eyes widening as she gently closed the book and set it next to her drink.

"When I sent the two of them to Eincrest to check up on your progress, I didn't expect you to return with them as well. Any particular reason why?" Her face shifting into a cold expression, Avelina rigidly stood at attention.

"Eincrest...was destroyed yesterday," she somberly stated, causing Katrina to sit up in her chair, "No one else made it out besides Jack and potentially his brother." Katrina gave Avelina a quizzical expression.

"Jack?" I cleared my throat as she said my name, causing her attention to immediately divert to me.

"Ah I see," she exclaimed, "And at ease Ms. Rockwell. You know how I feel about formalities." Avelina's arms fell from behind her back and came to a rest at her sides, still maintaining a somewhat straight stance.

"And who exactly are you, Jack?" she questioned, "They had to have good reason to bring you all the way out here." As her question exited her mouth, Henry's face noticeably shot away from us, staring his icy eyes at the now closed door. Katrina also observed Henry's behavior, her eyes narrowing as she stared at him.

"Someone is outside," he growled out, still glaring at the door, "Two people actually based on footsteps. If everyone is here, then that can only mean one thing." Henry started taking slow steps towards the door. Avelina and I had hands on our weapons, while Serena suddenly stood up and pushed in the chair. Katrina continued sitting within her seat, her arms remaining crossed.

"Could it be that you were followed?" Katrina asked, although she didn't appear to be worried.

"Don't know," I replied, "Maybe they just saw how massive this building is." Avelina swiftly struck me on the back of my head in response, before returning her hand to her weapon. I yelped in pain as I could hear Katrina sigh behind me.

The door abruptly eased open, causing Henry to lurch out of the way of the opening. He pressed himself against the right side of the door, becoming a shadow as his darkened clothes blended into the darkness.

A silhouette stepped through the doorway, their face shielded by shadows as they began to peer around the room, glancing around apprehensively. As soon as he took a single step through the doorway, Henry sprung up from the wall and grabbed the figure by their shirt collar, sweeping their legs out from under them as he did so. Before he connected with the ground, Henry swiveled slightly, causing the figure to land full force on their stomach with their head facing our direction. A loud gasp of air exploded from him as the wind was knocked completely out of his body, dirt from the ground kicking up into the air by his breath.

There pinned against the ground was a familiar set of matted jet-black hair, squirming on the ground beneath the cloaked man's grasp.

His hazel eyes glanced up at me whilst widening in realization, as Connor gasped in surprise at the five of us residing within the room.

12

Connor: Katrina Ward

"Connor?" I glanced up from the incredibly uncomfortable position I was in on the ground, squirming and struggling under this mysterious man's rather strong grasp. Even though I could barely see him, I could feel his eyes boring into the back of my head as I attempted desperately to get free.

Resting all of his weight on top of me, the man pinned both of my arms between his chest and his left arm, preventing me from moving. I yelped in pain as he snagged onto my already muddled black hair, lifting my head up slightly as he continued to glare down at his prey. He was clearly composed, as his breathing remained steady to the point where it was barely audible. I could almost feel the ferocity of his gaze.

This man is fully prepared to end my life at a moment's notice.

Being held tightly within his grasp, it was incredibly difficult to see who called my name, but I knew who it was already based on the distinct tone of their familiar voice. I strained my eyes forward as I attempted to scan my surroundings.

There stood my brother with his favorite coat fully discarded, gripping his broadsword tightly as he appeared far smaller without his coat. Despite the circumstances, a relieved smile came to my face when my eyes met his.

It was probably destroyed in Eincrest, but thank god that was the only thing lost.

His right hand let go of the weapon on his back as he continued to stare at me with awe and a tad bit of confusion.

Hearing metal slice swiftly through the silent air, my attacker stiffened as a pair of soft footsteps calmly walked behind him.

"I would advise that you let go of him," Mara calmly stated, coming to a stop behind my assailant with her golden sword clearly drawn, "We aren't here for trouble, so I'd rather not be forced to weigh in." Being held at sword point, my attacker froze momentarily, clearly weighing his options.

"That's enough Henry," another familiar voice cried out, "He's the brother that Jack was talking about when we found him. Now, would you kindly let go of the poor boy?" Hearing the man grunt above me, the tense grip around my arms loosened as my assailant began to stand.

Before he did, the man I assumed was Henry raised my head up slightly, before roughly throwing me back down to the ground. The floor rapidly rushed towards me, as my face crunched into the aged floorboards with a crash. I let out an immediate groan of pain as I could hear him turn around to face Mara. The woman let out a sharp gasp as her eyes connected with my assailant, before the man turned around and took a step over my prone form, almost ignoring me.

Finally able to shift my body around, I propped myself up on my hands and knees as I caressed my nose, pain shooting through it as it took the full force of the blow. I shakily rose to my feet as I examined the people that surrounded us.

There was my brother obviously, having already taken a steady step towards me.

Avelina stood close beside him, her lance from the day before fully discarded and the metal plate returned to her shoulder, covering her true allegiances with the now slightly misshapen steel.

Staring at the two figures I didn't know, I first glanced at my attacker, the one Avelina called Henry.

Every bit of skin was completely covered by some form of darkened clothes, with black pants that extended into his black boots. He also wore a black long-sleeved shirt that looked like it had leather sewn into the material, along with a black cloak and hood. If that wasn't enough, he wore black gloves that covered every bit of his hands, and a cloth mask was hooked onto the front of the hood to disguise his features.

Well...all of his features except for his icy blue eyes, which at the moment were solely trained on me, unmoved since he let go of me.

He did not appear to have any weapon on him, which was odd considering how calm and steady he was when I was in his grasp.

That, along with the move he used to knock me to the ground in the first place...

The other unknown person was a girl who looked around Jack's age, with bright tangerine hair that extended just above her neck in a manner that was both choppy and sleek. Her eyes were a bright grey, an oxymoron as the dullness they should have held were almost completely overshadowed by the intense emotion brewing within them.

The way she dressed expressed that she did not fight directly in combat, wearing a long-sleeved white shirt and red-orange skirt without any blemishes on them.

Either she was incredibly meticulous while cleaning, or she mainly serves this group in some other helpful way.

She also did not appear to have a weapon like her comrade, essentially confirming my theory.

She appeared to be scolding the dark cloaked Henry, whispering to him with an irritated look plastered onto her face.

"I haven't even been formally introduced to Jack, and yet here I am face-to-face not only with his brother but another mysterious person." Glancing up, I noticed the older woman sitting cross-legged within a chair near the corner of the room, analyzing us with a pair of bright eyes, close to indigo in their coloration.

Katrina...

Without any form of introduction, I knew it was her. If anyone was the true leader in the room, it would be this woman. She held a powerful aura of influence on those around her, allowing me to feel the power and wisdom etched into her gaze as every person gazed upon her when she spoke. It was the gaze of someone who had been a commander for years; someone who had encountered the battlefield many times and come off as a champion.

She dressed casually at the moment, with a long-sleeved white shirt and black pants. A yellow jacket clung loosely to her, shining much brighter than her dirty blonde hair that flowed over her right shoulder. She wore leather bracers that did not extend to her hands, leaving them bare. A short-sword rested against the chair she sat on, almost completely hidden from view. If I had to guess she was in her early forties, but for anyone not looking past the surface they would assume she was in her mid-twenties.

Based on her demeanor alone, the former is most likely true.

Uncrossing her legs, Katrina stood up from her chair with heavy steps and motioned me forward. I took an uneasy couple of steps, hearing Mara do the same.

"Avelina," she proclaimed, causing the woman to snap to attention, "What do you make of these three?" Avelina scanned all three of us again for a brief second, pausing on Mara for a tiny bit longer before returning to her leader's gaze.

"While I don't know anything about the young woman standing right there, I do know these two, and they fought for that village as if it was their own home. I'd say they're both skilled for their age, and if that woman is with Connor, then I would trust her as well. I'll brief you on the details later, and how swiftly our response should be, but they may have prevented a terrible situation from becoming far more dire." Giving a nod with an emotionless visage, Katrina beckoned with her finger towards us, motioning for us to follow her.

"I trust your judgment Avelina, it's never let me down before," she proclaimed, "If you all truly desire to be one of us, follow my lead. If that isn't what you desire, and you were led here for some other purpose, then you are permitted to walk right out. I won't mind if you do it, but wait too long and we may face some...problems."

Mara immediately took two steps in front of me, before following closely behind the blonde-haired leader who had turned down a nearby hallway. Stumbling for a moment, I swiftly followed suit.

"Jack that means you too." My brother, who had been motionless for the moment, widened his eyes in realization as he swiveled on his feet and took off after us.

The young girl giggled behind her hand as we walked, the blue-eyed man continuing to watch us as we fully exited the room.

Katrina led us in a single file line down a corridor that was about as wide as my wingspan. I could hear Jack's broadsword clanging against the narrow walls, along with the curses he continued to mutter under his breath.

He gripped onto my shoulder suddenly, bringing the two of us to a stop as the women continued walking.

"I was about to go looking for you the second I was done at, wherever we are," he began with a smile, "Glad to know you've made my life a little easier." I patted him on the arm as we both continued walking, catching up to the slow figures of the other two as Jack's arm fell limp at his side.

"I had a feeling we'd still manage to find each other, even if I didn't actively look for you." Jack gave a nervous chuckle as he walked beside me, his laugh echoing in the tight chamber.

"You uh…you did actually look for me though, right?" I didn't answer his statement, instead giving a quiet smile as I reverted my gaze somewhere else. He flashed me an overly dramatic offended expression as he crossed his arms, pouting to himself in an almost mocking way. I ignored him and stared down at what we were all waltzing past.

There were five doors on each wall, each possibly individual rooms of identical design.

Four of the doors on our right side had perfectly clean door handles, shimmering as if they were just freshly installed. Despite that, a layer of dust resided on each of them, meaning that they had been put in a long time ago.

The other six ornate door handles obviously showed the wear and tear of time, with each of them containing their own individual smudges and handprints. One door even had cracks and splinters along where the door handle connected with the wood, appearing almost like someone had accidentally caved it in.

At least six people exist here.

We appeared to be walking towards a slightly larger door at the end of the hallway, lit up by several lamps in a somewhat cliche manner. A door rested ninety degrees to the right of this large one, although it looked like it wasn't another bedroom. Katrina pushed through the massive door with minimal effort, motioning for the three of us to follow through.

It appeared to be some sort of office space, most likely Katrina's. Two doors sat directly opposite of each other on both sides, but what they led to I had no idea.

Perhaps bedrooms, but in that case why would there be a second one in what is clearly Katrina's office?

A sizable desk sat at the back center of the room, surrounded by towering mountains of papers and books. I grew slightly nauseous from how tall they stood over us.

Pictures of herself with other members of the group adorned the front of the desk, further cluttering the already messy workspace. I couldn't recognize many of the faces on the desk, but it was incredibly difficult to study them as they were shielded by the mounds.

The only picture I could see rested on the right side of the wooden desk, facing us with the small picture resting just outside of the towering documents.

It was a picture of Katrina and Avelina with their arms splayed over each other's shoulders, clearly laughing about something just out of view. They appeared to be a couple years younger than they were now, perhaps in their mid-thirties, with Avelina being a tad younger than her blonde companion. Each of them had their hair tied back in a ponytail, making them appear younger than they already were. They each gave a peace sign to whoever was taking the picture, capturing themselves in a single moment of pure joy and bliss.

Between their extended arms was a woman who appeared even younger than they were, probably in her mid twenties. She had straight black hair that was cropped just below the neck, and she wore a black dress that extended down to her feet. Her eyes were closed, as she crouched down slightly to give a joyous thumbs up to the person just out of shot.

They look...almost like a family.

Aside from that, an almost empty bookshelf lay barren on the right side of the room, looking like it had been abandoned for years. Another one of those massive maps adorned the wall to the left, taking up almost the entire space. Our country was divided into six sections in a hexagonal manner, with a massive circle making up the center which I believed to be the capital. Unlike the other two I had seen previously, this one was incredibly detailed regarding Aelton, including the differences in terrain and the names of many major cities. Much of it was covered by metallic pins that clung to its edges.

Strangely, I noticed there was a singular blue pin stuck out of Pyrnesse. It was the only map that I had ever seen in my lifetime to ever place anything within the secluded land of the Zevron people.

Circling around the desk, the blonde-haired woman was briefly out of sight for a moment, shielded by the papers and books. Coming back into view she eased herself into the chair behind the desk, placing both of her hands together on the table as she studied us with her indigo eyes.

Looking at my two companions, Mara was still giving Katrina the same blank stare she maintained with me, hiding whatever festering emotions she entrapped beneath her reflective green eyes. It was hard to decipher what she was actively hiding.

Is it...admiration maybe? Or perhaps it's relief?

I groaned to myself silently, shifting my gaze to my brother instead.

Damn her for being so brilliant at hiding her thoughts. She's the first person I've met who possesses such a skill.

Staring at Jack instead, I couldn't help but smirk from how small my brother looked without his signature coat. Even though he was only two or three inches taller than me, he always felt so much more towering.

He was lanky like I was, but he had a little bit of a bigger bulk than I did. After all, you require a little bit of muscle to carry around a sword the size of another human being.

"Ms. Rede!" Katrina unexpectedly yelled out, cutting through the eerie silence of her spacious office as the three of us reverted to her. I could see Mara jump slightly at the sudden exclamation.

A small black blur burst through the door on the right side, throwing a book behind her haphazardly as she came to a rest in front of us.

It was the black-haired woman in the picture.

Her cropped hair from the picture now extended slightly below her shoulders, looking rather frizzy in its appearance. She wore a similar black dress to the one in the photo, although this one in particular had silver frills littering the ends of it and a black pair of pants underneath. There were darkened marks on her dress' shoulders, wrists, and torso, almost appearing like shadows in the room's light.

She adjusted the spectacles on her black eyes, slightly panting as she stumbled into the room. Strangely, a portion of her sleeve was slightly more elevated than the rest of the clothing, one which I tried to examine without looking strange.

Something hidden I'll see later I suppose.

"Yes Ms. Ward?" she asked, walking close to Katrina's desk with a slight blush on her cheeks. Katrina motioned towards the three of us.

"We appear to have potential newcomers among us, and I thought you should witness their arrival as well." The woman known as Ms. Rede gave a slight "Ah" as she adjusted her spectacles again.

"But let's push that aside for a moment," Katrina cut in, staring at the three of us, "I want to know why the three of you are here? Almost no one should know of our existence, and yet here you all stand. It's...intriguing, considering how I'm usually the one to seek out members." She put a hand up to her chin as she spoke to us, as Ms. Rede nervously stood incredibly close to her.

"I want to know why you three truly are here," Katrina declared, "No one finds us by chance, and our purpose is incredibly specific. So, what brings you three standing in front of my desk right now?" Upon those words, Jack coughed into his hand out loud, meaning he had something to say. Katrina's eyes shot to him as I stared at my brother, hoping he wouldn't say something stupid.

"Well, if I'm being completely honest," Jack blurted out, "I'm not totally sold on becoming a mindless dog of the military." Katrina raised an eyebrow at his words as I sighed to myself, rubbing my temples with my right hand.

"Jack..."

"However," Jack continued, his normally jokey tone fading from his voice, "I suppose that if what I want is to be achieved, I may have to become one anyway. I watched as a town I came to love was burned to the ground in front of me, the butchers responsible not caring who they cut down, as they were promised that their pockets would be filled with the spoils of their bloodshed." His fists clenched together at his sides as Katrina continued to stare at him, listening intently to his words.

"And above all that, their leader sent them off to kill so many others knowing full well they would die to distract others from him. A massacre on both sides, for almost nothing. If those are the type of people you all are against, I'd be glad to fight beside you all so I can cut those bastards down." Katrina continued to stare at Jack for a few moments, the fiery light common to Jack burning within his eyes.

"A noble cause," Katrina finally said, "Avelina is rarely wrong about people. If she has faith in you, then I will put all of my confidence into you, as long as you put the same faith into me and our group as well." She motioned to me with her off hand.

"Connor, was it?" she questioned, "I know that you two are siblings, but I wish to know if you hold the same sentiments as him." I raised a fist slightly as the other two stood around me.

"Of course I do," I began, "I have met my fair share of evil people, and amongst all of them, I have often been too weak on my own to feasibly stand up against them. I don't care if you fight those armored overlords, or random bandits in the streets of Solaton, I wish to join you. Evil is evil; it's all the same to me. I believe you all need as much help as you can get to stave off whatever your enemies are, so as far as I can see our goals coincide." Katrina gave a nod to my answer, before craning her head to the woman on my left.

"And the one I know even less about," Katrina mumbled, "The one who burst in with Connor. Who might you be?" Mara shifted her stance, her blank stare faltering under the watchful eye of the commander. Jack craned his head to the side as well, paying close attention to the woman who came in with his brother.

"My name is Mara...Mara," she unusually stumbled out, "I stand by what the other two said earlier. My...village was destroyed by a group of B-Bellhollow soldiers. I'm a survivor, and I believe that people like them must be fought at every turn." Katrina cocked an eyebrow up at her words.

"Bellhollow soldiers? This far inland with such a blatant action of violence? I am fairly certain I would have heard of such an occurrence." Mara stiffened at her words, curling her fists up like she did before. She hid her gloved hands behind her back in a motion that appeared as if it were an act of respect. While that may have been true, I knew better.

Her palms quivered and shook just out of view of the blonde commander.

"We were a uh...a small town deep within a v-valley. We weren't even put on most maps due to our location in the F-Falcon Ridge Mountains at the border. It makes sense it would go unnoticed." Katrina and Mara had a stare down for a brief moment; a fiery gaze glaring into the blank void of Mara's expression. With every second that passed Mara seemed to be drawing ever closer to losing her empty gaze the more Katrina stared her down, her hands continuing to shake viciously. After a tense moment of silence, Katrina gave a shrug as she motioned for Ms. Rede to step forward, although the suspicious tint never left her narrowed indigo eyes. Mara's hands halted their shaking as she glanced away, relieved.

I took a glance at the woman who I had spent a decent amount of time around, getting used to the bland way she spoke aside from that one moment of conviction outside of the cave.

When speaking to Katrina just a few seconds ago, her tone spiked much higher than it was when we first met, losing the monotonous way of speaking I grew used to. The several pauses in her speaking solidified my mindset.

I thought finally I had gotten a glimpse of who she is just now but...all lies. Every bit of that story was tinged in deception. I don't even know if a single word of that was true.

Maybe she doesn't want to shock Katrina with too much information?

Unlikely...but whatever this is must be indispensable to her. It supersedes feelings at this point. She saved my life in that village, so I trust that she is a good person. However, with threats like that man in Eincrest and the knight out there in the world...

Aside from that, I hope that Avelina told Katrina about that man and the pendant ...he's too immense of a threat to leave alone...

"So boring," Jack whispered into my ear, forcefully knocking me out of my thoughts, "Was she like this when you first met?" I suppressed a snort as I leaned into my brother's ear.

"It was somehow more silent actually." My brother gave a slight chuckle as he leaned away from me, staring back towards the massive desk.

"Ellia..." Katrina whispered out to the black-haired woman, "What do you make of these three?" Ellia Rede took an awkward glance over at the three of us, still standing close to Katrina as she fumbled and scanned us up and down.

"Apologies for this, but a couple people who have joined us decided to keep secrets about what they could do. Ms. Rede has almost a sixth sense about trustworthy people, and if any of you were liars she would know. So, what do you think Ms. Rede?" A blush erupted on Ellia's face as she swiveled slightly around to face Katrina, pausing her study of Jack who took an apprehensive step back.

"Please Ms. Ward; you know how much I hate f-formalities. I am just simply doing my job, so you have no need to thank me. We've been friends for so long and all and you are in a higher position than me, so you really don't have to..." Katrina held up her hand to stop her rambling, flashing a quick and gentle smile that I hadn't seen at all, even when we first arrived.

"I was simply doing it in front of them, pay no mind to it," Katrina began, almost forgetting the three of us were still in the room, "Ellia, I may be your superior, but you are still my second-in-command, and as such you are within an imperative position as well. You are my ally, and my friend. In my mind we are equals. In fact, if it were not for your stubbornness and reluctance to talk to people, I would most certainly put you in a higher position than my own." Ellia blushed at this and looked away, turning back to Jack.

"Oh and Ellia," Katrina exclaimed suddenly as if it were an afterthought, causing Ellia to turn sharply with the same red tinted cheeks before she became truly lost in her thoughts.

"You should know by now I don't appreciate these grand formalities either. If Serena can address me as Katrina, you can too." Ellia nodded frantically with a nervous smile, before returning her gaze back to Jack.

Stepping away from us momentarily, the awkward expression she once held was replaced by a stoic expression of someone scanning an enemy. Her eyes traced over all three of us, lingering for a moment before continuing to the next person.

"They each seem well trained," she began, "The two on the outside probably more than the one in the middle based on the rough abrasions on their hands and gloves. The man on the right appears proficient one handed with that massive blade due to his right hand being incredibly calloused, although he appears to be able to use both since a similar effect is on the other hand. The girl has the same effects on her right hand due to the glove, which along with her stance right now showcases years of experience." Jack whistled in amazement as her eyes came to rest on me.

"This one might be a bookworm like I am Ms. Ward, based on the book in his pants pocket," she remarked, causing my hand to shoot to that side, "He has a weapon of some kind, but he may engage in combat as much as I do."

"I'm as much of a fighter as the other two," I replied back instantly, "Just like you apparently are, or did based on the armor markings on your dress and the gauntlet of some kind currently hidden in your sleeve." Her face flushed red at my words as she gripped the raised portion of her sleeve, causing her eyes to immediately shoot to the ground. She ran a hand through her long hair as she let out a nervous chuckle.

"M-Ms. Ward…" she stuttered out, "I'm a tad embarrassed h-here. He's the only person I've met who's read me like that." Katrina let out a laugh at her predicament as she sunk a quill of some kind into an almost empty ink well, the point's various pangs reverberating in the empty glass. Jack slugged me on the shoulder as my focus shifted.

"That's my brother for you," Jack yelled as I grumbled while rubbing my arm, "I've seen Connor pump out ideas and plans as if they were already resting in that twisted up head of his."

"Maybe you are right for this place," Katrina murmured to herself, "Alright, if my two most trusted advisors think you should be here, then I do as well."

Plucking the white feather from its ink well, Katrina began to write something down on the paper, her darkened words oozing onto the pages. I couldn't read any of the words, from both the distance we were at and how sloppy her handwriting was.

If she wasn't careful her sentences may accidentally overlap over eachoth-

I froze at that single notion; the flurry of thoughts wiring through my brain at that moment suddenly came to a halt as my eyes locked onto what should've been a useless piece of paper.

"Y-You...You're..." Katrina gave me a quizzical look as she set the quill back into its ink well. The drying strokes of ink continued to scream at me.

The bold, sloppy strokes of ink that seeped into the paper and the recesses of my mind as I stared at it, my entire body shaking.

Each individual character flashed in my mind as if they were floating around me, fragments of their words strewn about the air as I gazed at the powerful woman who was sitting in front of me.

"Connor," Katrina questioned, "Is something the matter?" Without speaking another word, I tore open the side pocket of my pants and ripped out the ancient text that lurked within, its decrepit pages crinkling in my grasp. I slammed it onto the table in front of her, startling everyone in the room as Katrina maintained her gaze, unperturbed. The desk wobbled and the papers threatened to fall over as the impact reverberated off its surface.

Raising a hand to retaliate, Katrina paused momentarily as her indigo eyes drifted down to the dusty tome that rested in front her. A small gasp escaped her mouth as she extended a hand towards it, daintily picking up the worn tactics book as if it were made of glass.

"Inside...the Mind...of the Tactician..." Her words came out slow and methodical, as if sounding out each word to ensure they were exactly what she believed they were. She stared at me with incredulous eyes, her tone sounding incredibly unnerved.

"Where...where did you get this?" Standing firm under her accusatory tone, I returned a fiery stare in her direction as our bright eyes met.

"My mother," I finally exclaimed, "My mother gave it to me." Jack and Katrina's eyes both widened at my words. Jack gave a sound of realization as he stared at the book gripped in Katrina's clutches.

"Ah, so that's what kept you away from the sun you so desperately needed." Ignoring Jack's remark, Katrina sprung up from the table immediately, grabbing me by the shirt collar and hurling me forward. Jack took a step forward, raising his fists up before Mara stepped in front of him to stop my brother's march.

As my legs slammed into the wooden desk that I now knew was bolted to the floor, Katrina reached forward and stuck her hand within my shirt, haphazardly digging around for something as a slight blush came to my cheeks.

After searching for a few agonizing seconds, Katrina grabbed hold of the pendant that rested around my neck and pulled it out, a gasp escaping as her eyes came to rest upon it.

"L-Liza," Katrina finally breathed out, staring into the swirling green pools, "I suppose you finally managed to get that family you so desperately wanted." Her eyes entranced by the gem, Jack spoke up.

"You knew our mother?" Katrina was propelled out of her thoughts at those words, letting go of the pendant and allowing it to sink back into the confines of my clothing as she let me go.

"I did…when we were a little younger, back at the academy," she whispered to herself, sinking back into the same chair, "I knew her for a decent amount of time, but I never thought I'd see her, let alone her children again. It's remarkable how fate intertwines certain lives together." She picked up a solitary picture frame from behind the mounds of papers, examining it with a reminiscent smile. She swiveled it around as Jack drew close by, leaving Mara and Ellia alone.

In it sat two women, smiling at the taker of the aged photograph as they gave comical salutes to people just out of frame. It was clearly my mother and Katrina, looking the same age as I am right now. They both had their hair tied up into messy ponytails, with a black cap adorning their heads with an insignia I didn't recognize. They had some form of academy uniform on, along with ceremonial swords attached to their hips.

Setting the picture down onto the desk, she leaned back in her chair as she ran a hand through her messy hair.

"Why are you here really?" she asked with an inquisitive glare, "The Elizabeth Macherral I knew would never allow her children to join such an...involved group." A deafening silence filled the air as I heard Jack's breath catch in his throat, my own breathing stilling as I inhaled the musty air.

"Her last name is Illium now, and mother...mother is gone," I lamented to Katrina's visible surprise, "Not dead...I think, but I have no idea where she was taken."

"What do you mean...taken?'

"By a soldier. Vanished into thin air after slaying our father almost half a year ago." Katrina visibly shrunk into her seat, her shuddering eyes glancing one last time at the photograph before returning to us. Her eyes lingered on the young form of a woman she thought she would never see again. I could see in the corner of my eye Mara glancing away, the emotion in her eyes hidden by a shadow.

"I'm sorry, it must've been rough for you boys," Katrina finally sighed, "Your mother was an incredible person, and she must have met an equally as incredible man worthy of her hand." She rubbed her temples as she shut her eyes, lost in the depths of her own head.

"I'll tell you two boys more later about your mother. For now...I would like you all to pick one of the three rooms on your left coming out of the office at the end of the hallway. They're exactly the same, so don't get hung up if you don't get the one you want." She returned to the paper she was writing on before, almost ignoring us.

146

"Dismissed." Ellia gave a small wave as I turned to the door, retreating to what I assumed was her bedroom nearby.

Making it to the exit first, I held the door open as Mara briskly walked through, noticing Jack was simply glancing around the office in childlike curiosity. I let the door slowly shut behind me with a creak.

Jack is still in the room. I have time.

Before she could get too far, I grasped onto Mara's shoulder, making her stumble a bit as she attempted to continue her stride. She sharply turned around and slapped my hand, her brow furrowed as she prepared to yell out before seeing me. Almost immediately, she went back to her complacent mask again, a slight flush present on her cheeks as she put her hand to her mouth.

"Sorry," she apologized, "Just a...reaction is all. Did you need something?" I folded my arms together as I studied the way she still continuously observed me, her hand still resting on her blade.

"Why did you lie back there?" I asked her. She gave a dumbfounded look as her eyes widened, the grip on her sword tightening. She looked as if she was trying to find what to say, but couldn't grasp at the proper words.

"You lied to all of us in there. Every bit of that story you told was nothing but lies, so I'm a tad confused as to why you told a fabricated story instead of mentioning the same goals you had when we were at the cave." Mara kept her gaze firm as she glared back at me with tenacity.

"How would you know anything about my life Connor?" she fired back, "Were you somehow present when I was left alone to fend for myself? Or perhaps you saw a different scenario than what I said? If you're as astute as your brother proclaims, then perhaps you should know when you're grasping at straws." Before I could respond, the wind of the door swinging open hit my back, narrowly missing me all together.

"Make way you two I'm getting first pick," Jack barged through me immediately after those words, causing me to stumble.

"Sorry Connor, but I want to scope out real quick which room is best before your damn eagle eye finds which one is the best tactically." He said the last two words with quotations on his fingers, giving a salute as I dusted myself off.

Glancing around me, I noticed Mara was already gone. I grabbed my face in annoyance.

Damn that woman! She's toying with something she absolutely shouldn't be messing with.

She got incredibly defensive just now. I'd say that confirms everything I just said, but I'll try to keep track of her.

Looking forward with an annoyed sigh, I glanced forward at the options for rooming laid out before me, knowing the three closest to me were open.

Raising my eyebrows slightly, I noticed that new smudges adorned the metal door knobs at the end of the hallway; the dust pushed aside to make room for the occupant's fingerprints.

I suppose the one closest to Katrina's office is mine.

Grasping the cold metal door handle, the aged dust clung onto my right hand as I turned the knob, stepping in as I swung the door open.

Taking a few steps forward, I glanced at the decently sized room, sticking my hands in my pockets due to the slight chill of the area. I glanced around, analyzing the length and width of the room.

About two arms lengths long on both sides, give or take a couple inches.

I glanced down at the bed I had somehow managed to end up beside. The sheets looked rather old, with a layer of dust caking the bed. No bugs appeared to have made the bed their home at least.

Before I could even glance around what was to be my new living quarters, my legs buckled and swayed beneath me as the fringes of my vision became filled with darkness, almost making me immediately keel over in nausea.

My face thudded against the dusty pillow, and before I could even muster a single thought the land of dreams consumed my mind, as I fully drifted off into a deep slumber.

13

Connor: The People of Aelton

S tirring from my sleep, my eyes steadily cracked open as the morning light shined through the window nearby, refracting directly into my eyes as I flinched.

No dreams tonight...

I murmured in annoyance as I sat up in bed groggily, rubbing the back of my head as I glanced around to see if the window was close enough to cover.

What I didn't expect to see, was that same tangerine haired girl from yesterday sitting in a chair beside me, reading a book.

A book that appeared to be my tactics book; its wrinkled pages crinkling with every movement.

Recoiling in surprise, the bed creaked loudly as dust and sheets sprung into the air. The girl's eyes widened at my own reaction as she almost fell back, most likely not even realizing I had awoken. Her cheeks grew red as she gasped in surprise, slamming the book shut as her chair tipped slightly. For a brief second neither of us moved, my hand on my chest as we both panted heavily from the shock we just experienced.

"S-sorry I came in here for something...b-but I just got a bit curious and I..." she sputtered out as I held up a hand to stop her, my breath beginning to steady.

"It's quite alright," I replied, "Although I should definitely install a lock in that door fairly soon if I am going to stay. However, I would like to ask what you are doing here, miss..."

"S-Serena...Serena," she murmured with a slight bow, "That's an interesting book by the way. Might've slipped out of your pocket or something because it was just lying on the floor when I got here. I got a little curious so I just kinda..." She rubbed the back of her head as she blushed, letting out a shaky laugh as she glanced away from me.

"I noticed it has Katrina's handwriting in it." Serena mentioned cautiously.

"My mother and her knew each other apparently," I replied, scratching my head, "Although honestly I had no idea who Katrina was before I arrived here."

"Your mom knew Katrina?" Serena suddenly cut in, the blush fading, "That's really cool! If she was friends with Katrina that means she would be super strong like she is." I chuckled into my hand as I pulled my legs up close, sitting criss-cross on the bed.

You bet. She was the strongest person I knew.

Serena rubbed the back of her head again, shutting her glimmering grey eyes. I took a moment to glance this girl over.

She wore the exact same outfit she was wearing yesterday, except now she had a pair of small brown boots slipped on. A somehow clean white headband was spread across her hair, making it appear even brighter than it already was.

She's probably close to me in age as well, although perhaps slightly older based on her features. However, her attitudes make her seem a little younger than she appears.

"Everyone tells me my head wanders a bit when I speak," she

admitted with a guilty smile, "Can't be helped I'm afraid, since I've dealt with it for so long and I haven't worked at all on fixing it. Just got too much energy to stay on one thing I suppose." She slouched a bit in her chair as I stared at her, slightly coughing from the dust that perforated the stale air of my room.

"But anyways, I came in here to explain a few things, because if I'm correct everyone is still asleep or too busy to bother talking with the new folks. I already explained it to your brother and the new girl, so you're all that's left." I gave a nod as I set my chin on my right fist, resting my head that was still a little dazed from just waking up.

"So apparently Katrina kinda forgot to explain what we're all about, which to me seems a tad bit empty-headed of her but I digress." She twirled a finger through her lush hair as she spoke. She looked as if she was fighting a losing battle to maintain her focus on me, but her eyes continued to wander throughout the unexplored room without a care in the world.

If I didn't know any better, she wasn't even paying attention to what she was telling me.

"Thank Anula I at least remember, as opposed to Katrina back there. She's always so busy though so it kinda makes sense." I cocked an eyebrow at her words.

"Thank...Anula?" I replied quizzically, "Who would that be? Someone else I haven't met?" Serena gave a soft giggle at my words, slightly shaking her head as her straight tangerine hair whipped around her.

"The Goddess you dummy!" she jokingly emphasized while suppressing a laugh, "The Woman in White? The creator of humanity and the entire world as we know it? How could you not know about *the* Goddess?" I gave a simple shrug as I ran my hand through my still tangled hair.

There must be a river or something nearby to get all this dirt and ash out. Could be hidden behind the sea of green around here.

"Sorry, I simply have no idea," I admitted with a shrug, "My parents weren't exactly the religious type, and we lived far enough away from towns to not hear simple stories passed down for generations." Serena gave an exaggerated frown as she crossed her arms, reminding me slightly of my brother.

"It's not just stories Connor," she pouted, "They're all real, and she is the reason we exist today." I raised an eyebrow as I leaned forward slightly on the bed, my doubt apparent.

"How do you know it's real Serena and not just stories your parents passed down from their parents, and their parents before them? Stories around for that long often get lost in translation, and it's possible if you go back that far that it was simply a tale your ancestors told to put their children to sleep." Serena gave an exasperated yell as she placed her hands on her knees, using them as leverage to immediately pop herself up.

"It's not just a story!" she exclaimed, her tone losing the lackadaisical edge it held before, "Watch!" Closing her eyes, Serena put her hands into fists and placed one in front of the other.

Crossing them together in an "X" shape, Serena gave a loud yell as she extended her arms out into the air at her sides, a small billow of air breezing past my face. The air caught the dust still within the room and transported it directly into my eyes, causing me to wince as I rubbed them in pain.

When I regained my vision, Serena still stood there with her hands proudly extended. The only difference now, was that her hands were covered in a strange green aura, one that wrapped around her hands like a glove as the green light gleamed throughout the room.

I stared at them in awe, almost instinctively reaching out to touch it.

Is it...similar to the pendant?

"Cool, isn't it?" Serena rhetorically beamed, "Although they don't have a name, I like to call them the Palms of Anula, just because it's got a pretty good ring to it." Setting her hands down at her sides, Serena exhaled a relieved breath before the green light began to fade, eventually dissipating all together.

"See that? That is a tad more substantial than the generational stories you talked about, right?" she said sarcastically, "It's the ability to heal most wounds such as various scrapes and even broken bones occasionally. It does happen to drain away my metabolism as I perform the magic, but as long as the wound isn't incredibly large or deadly I can seal it. I trained for such a long time to get this done, and yet I have a bunch more I need to know."

She's still incredibly young. How old did she have to be to start training?

"Who did you train with?" I asked, "I'm assuming no normal person can train in this...art?" Wagging a finger at me, Serena gave a playful wink as she grinned at me.

"That's a secret I just can't tell ya Connor," she laughed, "And no person can just learn it if you were wondering. You have to be a believer in Anula first off, which if I recall you aren't." She gave another one of her sharp giggles as she sat back down in the chair.

"We have a library nearby the office if you really want to learn more," she recalled with a glimmer in her dull grey eyes, "Ms. Rede's really the only person who goes in, so you'll have a lot of options as long as you don't scare her. You'll find all sorts of stories about how Anula created us, and her counterpart Rennak." I raised an eyebrow at the second name.

So that was the other door. If no one else is in there I would be content to check it out.

"Rennak?" I questioned, "Another one of these gods you worship?" She visibly cringed at my proclamation, allowing me to already see how wrong I was.

"Well…if you're a Bellhollow citizen maybe," she slowly muttered out, "It's said that Rennak was like Anula, and created the Zevron race that resides above us. He was corrupted by his own magic, and in the end was banished to the realm of shadows and nothingness known as the Abyss." A moment of silence billowed out as the conversation ended; an awkward echo as Serena stared at me. Her smiling visage was tinged with a certain emptiness.

"I assume you didn't come here to give me a culture lesson?" She giggled lightly at my words, whatever dark emotion brewing behind those eyes fading away.

"Straight to the point I see," she relented while still giggling, "I'm a fan of you already." Sitting with her hands on her knees, she looked almost like a child, gleefully awaiting the end of the story, or perhaps the beginning of one.

"Ms. Rockwell said you were already aware that we're a small group of people connected to the Solaton military known as the Sentinels," she resumed with a serious tone for the first time, "It's so much more complicated than that. The Sentinels' main missions involve security, reconnaissance, and espionage; we analyze the movements of the other two nations to ensure they aren't up to something nefarious." I swung my legs off the bed as she spoke to me, stretching my incredibly sore arms out a little as I did so.

"Mostly Bellhollow though, right?" Serena gave a sharp nod at my interjection.

"You got it! We know almost nothing about them, and it's been super difficult to send people into such a secluded nation to monitor them. So…we watch closely at what they send here instead."

"Sentinels…" I repeated aloud, "The ones who stand guard at the gates of towns and villages. I'm assuming that your guard was tipped off recently?" Serena gave another sharp nod as her eyes focused onto me for an impressively long period of time.

Maybe when she has to get serious, her brain just...knows when to hone in.

"It was," she somberly responded, "Tell me Connor...do you recall a man with a long purple robe and green eyes recently?" At the mention of that all too familiar description, my fists involuntarily balled up as my thoughts shot to the carnage of days prior.

That sorry excuse for a man in Eincrest...

"I do...fought him pretty hard as well."

And I'm going to be the one to find him, and through that get some answers for myself.

"In that case, then you know how appalling of a danger he is," she continued, "They call him Zain, and he escaped from Bellhollow a couple weeks ago; an admirable feat for any man confined within that barren land. What he wants, I have no clue, but Ms. Rockwell had tracked his movements between both of our nations transporting something. He's working on his own based on his avoidance of guards and other Bellhollow officials." Serena looked down at the floor.

"Ms. Rockwell notified us a while ago that he had made a stop in the inner village she was positioned in: Eincrest. Henry and I immediately set off to assist her in whatever way we could." Her eyes watered for a moment as she became lost in her own mind, looking away as she wiped her eyes with a sniffle.

"By the time we arrived a day or so l-later, it was already too late. Everything was g-gone. We were lucky to find Ms. Rockwell and your brother beneath all of that destruction." I hesitantly extended a hand out to her shoulder, her body stiffening at my touch.

"I'm sorry we couldn't do more to help them."

"No, y-you did enough. If not for you two, some of them might have gotten away....or they may have even killed Ms. Rockwell." She suppressed another sniffle as she turned back to me. I let my hand fall back down onto the bed.

"In any case," Serena restarted, "We're gonna be looking constantly for him, and we'll give out more information to you all as soon as we can." Standing up from the chair, Serena ensured her skirt was without any wrinkles of any kind, straightening out any she happened to stumble upon and pushing her hair back. Once she finished, she craned her head back to me.

"Are you really with us Connor?" I stared at her as I put a tight-lipped smile onto my face.

"I thought I had a purpose for a long time Serena, just…hiding away in my home in the woods. Hoping desperately that what I wanted could be achieved in solitude. But…it can't. You all have a purpose that fits mine and…what more do I have to lose?" All of what I just spoke was the truth, although I opted to not mention the part about mom and a connection to Zain. I don't know why I didn't elaborate on it but for whatever reason I felt inclined to suppress it for now.

"I knew there was something I liked about you Connor," she admired proudly, "Don't let me down!" She gave one final smile as she opened the door to leave, giving an excited wave as she exited the room, leaving me alone once again.

I've chosen the life of a soldier…or something of that sort…

Sliding off the bed, I stretched my arms over my head with a groan, examining the room I was too exhausted to glance around last night.

A thin layer of dust coated every object that resided within this space, aside from the bed where the dust instead clung to me.

A small desk resided within the top left-hand corner of the room, with a lamp resting upon it having been long extinguished. A dusty cupboard lay dormant beside it. Based on the almost visible layer of dirt and soot encasing the wooden contraption, it was probably left alone longer than the room itself.

Besides…I don't think it would be wise to try on any clothes in there depending on how long they've been encased in that tomb…

157

Dusting off my clothes that weren't in terrible shape, I stared out the window to see what surrounded this building.

I was met by the same sea of green that I had seen several times already. Although this time, I noticed a faint glimmer of blue shining in the distance.

Good thing there is a river nearby. Not a fan of looking like I crawled out of the ground a couple minutes ago.

Not wanting to sit for very long I made my way to the room's door, carefully setting the tactics book on the desk nearby.

As I walked over, I reached into my shirt and hoisted out the pendant, staring into the familiar green pools.

Did you know, mom? Did you know...what lurked within this gem?

You had to know....how could you not? If Zain knew himself, it would be impossible for you not to.

I placed it back under my shirt as I eased the door in front of me open.

I'll find you soon...

Stepping out into the long and cramped hallway, the sound of foreign voices immediately filled my ears as I turned my head to the left.

Four people, all sitting in that entrance room. Hard to distinguish who is who.

My interest piquing, I crept slowly out towards the room, masking myself in whatever morning shadows lurked in the hall. I cringed slightly as a wooden panel creaked beneath me, but that didn't deter the voices I heard.

Don't want to startle them; better make sure they don't think I'm an enemy of some kind.

Lurking just behind the corner of the hallway, I took a single cautious step out as I peered around to find the source of the voices. Or at this moment, the one voice that echoed loudly throughout the empty hallway.

"And you relayed every bit of this information to Katrina this morning?" Avelina proclaimed as I took another step forward, "No details shirked...or exaggerated?" An unknown voice let out a restrained chuckle as the room came into view, keeping me within the shadows but still allowing me to see what was happening. A young man stood directly across from Avelina, clutching his side with a toothless smirk as a woman and large man lurked behind him on a red couch.

"Of course Avelina, what do you take me for? Some mindless oaf who can't tell a simple story? I'm honestly quite offended by such a blatant accusation." Avelina let out a snort as she crossed her arms, staring forward at the three unknown figures who faced her.

"Nathaniel, if I had a single coin for every exaggerated half-truth I've heard exit your mouth, I'd be richer than your entire family. Let's hope that Serena patching you up earlier had a positive effect on your brain."

I hid a muted laugh behind my hand as the large man on the couch did the same, although in a much more aggressive manner. He began laughing at a rate and volume unfitting of what was quite frankly a simple joke, but his guffawing continued, almost to the point of him losing his breath as he clutched his chest.

His hair was long and blond, but it was certainly a dirtier shade than Katrina's refined hair. His brown and yellow clothes showed a more casual appearance, but the dark markings on it told me otherwise. Two one-handed axes rested by his side, curved in a way which I have never seen an axe molded before.

If I had to guess his age would be in the thirties range, but in all honesty he could be much younger.

The fire-haired woman who listened far more intently than her laughing companion was sitting with her arms crossed, her red locks tied into a ponytail that draped over her right shoulder. She wore a pair of intertwined red and dark-yellow clothes, ones that didn't appear to have any armor currently attached to it. She didn't appear to have a weapon, but I highly doubt she is a non-combatant. She held an exasperated expression as one of her eyes ticked in annoyance, although her face still carried a smile.

I can't tell her age either. Although, she's probably in her mid-twenties if I had to guess.

And finally, the man Avelina was talking to. He was a reasonably fit, grey-haired man who wore an outfit similar to the woman on the couch, except it was black and a shade of dark blue. A silver rapier clung to his side, which he also used to help emphasize the story by continuously gesturing to it.

Early twenties as well. Fitting age for the military...unlike me.

As I continued to chuckle at the scenario playing out in front of me from my side of the room, the large man wiped a tear from his eye and finally noticed me, locking eyes with me from across the space. The storyteller, noticing the direction his friend's eyes went, turned towards me and cocked his head to the side.

"Ah I didn't notice you there friend," he announced vibrantly, "Would you happen to be new here, or are you a brave bandit with a death wish?" The other two fully paid attention to me now, both examining me closely with half-squinted eyes. I stepped out of the shadows and gave a somewhat stiff wave to the strangers. Avelina, noticing my appearance let out a chuckle herself, turning to the others as she motioned to me.

"Ah of course. I'm assuming then Katrina did not go in depth about our new arrivals. While I'm unsure where the other two are, the young man standing here is named Connor Illium. A good fit for us, mostly due to how sharp-witted he is. Watch what you say around him Nathaniel, or you may end up regretting it somewhere down the line." The man named Nathaniel took a step towards me as he slowly removed his hand from his side, never losing that cocky grin. He flicked his grey hair back and suavely extended a hand, his posture relaxed. I firmly took it as he gave a charismatic smile.

"I recall the commander mentioning you while giving us the briefing on our mission. The man who entered with the other two yesterday," he announced with a stylish flair and exaggerated bow, "Nathaniel Byron, at your service." He motioned to the other two standing beside him with the same style and flair, gesturing dramatically with his hands as he planted his feet together.

"The scruffy oaf sprawled across the couch would be Gerard Roberts, and the lovely redhead over there is Joan Silverton." Gerard grinned ear-to-ear and gave a boisterous "Hello!" while Joan simply offered a soft wave.

"Of course, of these two I am the greatest warrior that we have to offer," he boasted proudly, "I am swift like the wind, and as strong as a crack of lightning." He beamed proudly as he stood in front of me with his fist on his chest.

His ego is simply astounding.

The large man known as Gerard almost immediately began laughing right as I suppressed mine. He chuckled so hard he completely fell off the couch, knocking Joan down with him. She yelped in surprise, slugging Gerard in the leg with an irritated expression, although he was laughing too hard to even notice. Avelina let out a sigh to herself as she rubbed her temples, one which Joan replicated as she picked herself up.

"Idiots," Joan sighed out as she dusted off her now wrinkled shirt. She turned to me and plastered on a weary smile; her stance much more restrained than her melodramatic male counterpart.

"Don't let these fools give a poor impression of who we are," she groaned, "Despite their...charm...their boasts still hold some truth.

We're some of the finest soldiers in Solaton. In any case, we'll be departing on a reconnaissance mission after this, so it was excellent we met you now." Gerard stood up from the ground and crossed his arms.

"Well, the finest most of the time," he relented with a lowered smile, "After all, we are here a lot sooner than we anticipated." Avelina gave a nod as she stared at me, her eyes filled with inner discussion and brainstorming as her brow furrowed.

"Although they are departing on a mission soon to ensure trade relations are going smoothly in one of Solaton's port towns, their arrival back from a different mission was...cut short." Avelina's bright eyes darted away from me as she lost herself in thought, the light in her eyes almost appearing to grow dimmer.

"During their travels back, they encountered Zain about an hour shy of here." My body froze as that singular name echoed within my brain, chilling the very blood in my system as everything flashed into my mind yet again.

Eincrest...that terrifying pendant which somehow allows him to see actions before they are done.

A singular man...somehow the distinct utterance of his name was just as revolting as thinking of what he had done, reaching levels that only one despicable knight could match.

"Are you positive?" I proclaimed frantically as I stared at the three people who had survived him, "Same purple robe, and green eyes? Was that pendant still wrapped around his neck?" Gerard gave a nod as a much more restrained nature overcame him, killing any form of laughter and joy he echoed just seconds before.

"Oh absolutely," Gerard began as his eyes went almost glassy, losing himself to his own recollection of memories, "That...jewelry of his was absolutely terrifying. It was almost as if he could see the fate of actions before we engaged in them. Even if we managed to get away...I felt so small against such a power."

"But we did manage to thrash him a tad bit before he retreated like the coward he was," Nathaniel interrupted with the same precise pronunciation and diction, "We landed a few solid blows before he sprinted away in blatant terror." Before his sentence was even finished Joan let out a snort as she shook her head, Nathaniel's grin faltering as he craned his neck back.

"If by thrashing him you mean knocking you flat on your noble ass after barely landing a strike, then yeah you did a fantastic job." Gerard's same smile returned as Joan teased the now defeated man, his boasting quelled as even Avelina let out a minute chuckle. The story seemingly over, Joan turned to me as she finally acknowledged the stranger in the room.

"We reported all of this to Katrina of course," she stated, "While she was writing down a report to send off to the higher-ups down in Heartwood, Serena told us all about these so-called newcomers as she healed us, and mostly Nathaniel of his wounds. She spoke about you and the other two in her own bombastic way as if you all were warriors that needed to be seen to be believed." Gerard let out a hearty laugh at the last sentence, turning to me as Avelina shook her head.

"Perhaps once our second mission is done, we can fight just a little bit eh? I'd be interested in seeing how long you can last against us."

"I would love to actually," I replied without hesitation, "I assume there's somewhere we can fight to test your metal against mine?" Gerard started guffawing again, while Nathaniel and Joan quietly smirked.

"I enjoy your attitude Mr. Illium," Nathaniel replied, "You'll make a perfect sparring partner. The training grounds are at the rear of the building. Know it well if you wish to face someone like me." He flashed a bright grin as Joan shook her head, putting her head in her hand. Avelina sighed to herself as she too shook her head, mumbling something about my brother.

"Don't antagonize the kid Nathaniel." Joan groaned to herself, but I almost paid it no mind. Instead, I reverted my attention to my previous thoughts revolving around these individuals' distinct manner of speaking.

"Your name and your voice scream nobility," I suddenly interjected, spooking Nathaniel for a moment, "What would a nobleman be doing in a group of people like this?" Nathaniel gave a somewhat snotty chuckle as he held his hand up to his face, laughing into his palm.

"You are a perceptive fellow Mr. Illium," Nathaniel declared while placing a fist on his chest, "You are correct my friend. I am the proud first son of the noble Byron family, born as a child of William Byron, one of many prominent politicians. I am positive you've heard of him?" He stared at me for a moment with the same proud smile, glancing into my blank expression as a realization dawned on him. I shook my head silently, watching him crumble in shame as he discovered I had no idea who his father was and thus by proxy didn't know who he was. Joan came up and patted him on the back jokingly, trying to suppress her snickers.

"My father is one of the senators from Heartwood itself," he popped up with a grin, Joan stepping back as the two companions laughed at his sudden mood swing, "He has been their representative since before I gave first breath, and as his only son I have proudly been raised as his heir."

"Raised as a naive noble fool I believe is what you meant." Joan snickered to herself, causing Gerard to laugh in kind. Nathaniel gave a dismissive sneer as he reverted to me, avoiding the gaze of the purple haired woman who was already out of the door before I even noticed her stride. As the door finally creaked closed, Nathaniel continued as he pointed to himself.

"It was I who approached Lady Ward and asked her if I could join this merry group. How else do you think they managed to keep themselves so well-funded?" My eyes narrowed as I gazed back in confusion.

"The...military itself doesn't fund the Sentinels?" Joan shook her head as she let out a sigh.

"They do...but they provide minimal benefits at best. They spat out enough money to create the group and provided some weaponry. Most of us came here with the clothes on our back and the pocket change we carried."

"I uncovered the true nature of this group while studying under my father," Nathaniel began seriously but still in his noble tone, "He was one of the few who were authorized to know about the Sentinels, and I discovered how poorly our leaders funded them. I believe that these people are noble folk and that their cause is imperative to our nation's continued survival, so I pooled as much as I could to keep you all afloat. I joined as well as they were in desperate need of a skilled combatant such as myself."

Gerard let out a guffaw as he slapped Nathaniel on the shoulder joyfully, causing his entire body to shake as his eyes bugged out in surprise. Gerard let out another bellowing laugh as Nathaniel crept out from under his arms, giving a repugnant grimace as he did so.

"Oh the money is fantastic my wealthy friend. Keeps me with new clothes and better weapons whenever I please." I suppressed a laugh while staring at the three of them; Nathaniel rubbing his shoulders, Gerard with his hands on his hips chuckling to the sky, and Joan, who had somehow found her way back to the couch and laughed at her two companions.

So, these are the other three I was missing earlier...I'm glad they seem rather connected to each other.

"Oh Connor..." I turned to the voice who called me, startled by the sudden declaration of my name. The others also turned to the new sound, with the boys fully turning to face the front door and Joan tilting her head to the side.

It was my brother standing right behind me positioned in the main doorway of the building with his signature smirk on his face and his sword latched onto his back. He leaned against the door frame as he examined us all curiously.

"Well would you look at that someone's socializing," Jack interjected, keeping his smile as his tone steadied, "Katrina asked us to meet with her as soon as we could. Your lady friend you met before is already there, so I came to get you. Not sure exactly what she wants...but based on the look Avelina gave me as she walked by, I expect something good." Listening to his words, I simply gave him a slight nod as I stepped forward, giving a soft wave to the other three as I wordlessly walked beside Jack.

"I never asked," Jack whispered to me, "How'd you manage to arrive here the same time as I did?" I shrugged my shoulders as I came up alongside him, watching as he stuffed his hands into his brown pockets.

"That woman Mara recovered me from the window I was thrown from. She's the one that told me about this place. What about you?"

"Henry and Serena. Avelina pointed out where I was and managed to get me free from that damn rock Zain trapped me under." He let out an angered groan as he wordlessly stepped out the door, gripping at his right arm in a disgruntled manner.

"That Mara girl must have great connections," Jack remarked as he motioned to me to follow behind him, "These people appear to be very...tight lipped about this organization to people who aren't aware of it."

I still find it peculiar...the fact that Mara knew about this place even though it's so secretive.

Maybe she works for the government like Nathaniel does?

It's possible, but why would the young child of a public official seek out a group like this all on her own whilst hiding her identity? It just doesn't make sense.

"We should watch if there's going to be a fight." I heard Joan say as I followed swiftly behind Jack, "We have some time before we leave, and I'm genuinely curious about these new people; that black haired kid in particular." Gerard chuckled in response, whilst Nathaniel remained in his spot.

"And see them get their asses handed to them?" Nathaniel replied with a snicker, "Perhaps it is worth it for the entertainment alone."

14

Connor: The Dueling Ground

Wandering around the back of the massive building, my brother and I arrived upon what appeared to be a large training area, one which was almost half the size of the entire building.

Several practice dummies and targets littered the area, each with various types of protection and armor, with most having leather while a couple bore steel. Some even had arrows adorning their lifelike forms. Most of them had many weapon slashes and pierce wounds. A couple had holes blown straight through them. One unlucky dummy looks like it imploded, with its blackened limbs scattered across the field.

There was also a designated field for dueling, with small benches with boxes nearby arranged for supposed spectators.

In the center of that field was Katrina.

She sat cross-legged with her eyes closed, lost in the meditative thoughts of her own mind; her sandy blond hair whipping in the wind. Attached to her back was a massive, silver longsword. She didn't even seem to notice us step into the dusty arena.

Ellia and Serena were both sitting within the benches with their hands on their knees. Ellia looked incredibly nervous as her gaze continuously shifted around, while Serena simply held an apprehensive smile as she playfully rocked back and forth.

Avelina leaned against a box beside them, smirking down at Serena as she stared back to her commander.

She must have known Katrina would test us like this when she left the main hub.

Gerard, Joan, and Nathaniel each arrived a little after us, presumably leaving a minute or so after we did. Joan positioned herself beside Ellia and crossed her arms, closing her eyes in quiet thought, while Gerard and Nathaniel both started a loud conversation with Serena and Ellia respectively.

I almost missed the darkened silhouette of Henry, leaning against the side of one of the large boxes, out of view of the people around him due to the towering darkness lurking over him like creatures.

Katrina eased her eyes open and stood up from the ground, dusting herself off hastily. Her top consisted of a shining silver breastplate, with a black long-sleeved shirt lurking underneath. She wore a long dark skirt covered in matching silver armor, along with chainmail leggings and silver plating that covered her regular boots and extended to her knees. Several small knives were attached to her legs as well, which combined with the sword made her look like a walking arsenal.

Adjusting the silver shoulder pads and the silver gauntlets that extended to her elbows, she dusted off her yellow and black cape as she stood up, facing us. I could hear Jack whistle beside me, clearly impressed.

If she didn't look like a commander earlier, she certainly looks it now, even if it is a tad on the dramatic side.

Mara suddenly came up behind us, startling the both of us as she stood a couple feet away. Her emerald expression was empty, staring straight ahead at the blonde woman.

"Glad to see you found your way here," Katrina finally said, smirking as she turned to the other Sentinels, "And with quite the audience as well. You're the first newcomers to arrive in such a long time, and I can tell we've perhaps all been cooped up with the same people for too long." She pulled the massive sword off her back. Its maw glistened in the afternoon sun as she stared at it absentmindedly, pointing the tip straight at the blue sky.

"I apologize for the sudden intrusion, but I found it imperative to test each of your skills firsthand. Your word is one thing. To actually see the fighting prowess of another is worth far more." Facing the three of us, Katrina twirled the sword around in her right hand with ease, pointing it with her left hand towards me.

"Connor," she commanded, "You will be fighting me one-on-one, however you may rest for the time being. Jack you will be facing Avelina, and you may rest on the benches nearby with the others as well. Mara, I wish for you to fight Ellia first. Then, I shall test the brothers." Without a word Katrina departed the dusty circle, coming to a rest beside her purple haired companion as she rested her sword in her left hand. They immediately began discussing something at a speed that made it sound urgent.

The name Zain occasionally could be heard through harsh whispers...

Let's hope Katrina can hone in on his location so that I can corner him soon.

Ellia shakily rose from her seat with a blush, shuffling to the center of the ring as Mara drew her sword wordlessly, stepping into the ring with the same straightened posture and delicate footsteps.

Her hands remained inhumanely steady as she shifted into her stance, showcasing a stability over oneself which takes years to master.

Jack flashed me a thumbs up as he ran towards the benches, landing haphazardly on the bench closest to Avelina. He immediately appeared to start a conversation with her, to which the cross-armed woman blew the hair out of her face and calmly listened to the words of both Katrina and my brother. I opted to sit next to the blonde captain, simply eavesdropping before turning towards her.

"What was the reason I was singled out to fight you?" I questioned Katrina, who paused what she was saying to Avelina and allowed for Jack to fully take in his conversation. She placed the sword in her right hand as she adjusted her gauntlet on that side, ensuring she was in the peak condition to fight later.

"Based on your possession of the tactics book and the pendant, you clearly studied more under your mother," she explained to my surprise, "Your mother was a talented fighter yes, but she was even more brilliant when it came to thinking on her feet. As such, I wish to see if you are as skilled as she was, and how much you truly learned... from my friend. So, when the time comes, draw your weapon, and prepare to fight like your life depends on it." Giving her a quizzical look, I motioned to the dirk that rested on my side, the deadly metal glistening in the almost afternoon sun.

"Don't worry about that," Katrina answered me, "We do use wooden practice weapons around here, but I for one believe that fighting with real weapons during our introductory fight gives a proper example of your true prowess. It'll be fine; when we fight you won't land a deadly hit on me, and I know how to not hurt you terribly. Besides... we have a trained healer on standby just in case things get ugly." As if knowing she was being talked about, Serena flashed a cutesy smile to the both of us, before reverting her attention back to the conversation she was furiously maintaining with Joan and Nathaniel.

"Ellia!" Katrina yelled out, startling the woman who now stood directly opposite to Mara, "Do not hold back anything. That woman

171

from what I can tell is no stranger to combat, so you'll need everything you have." Her eyes visibly hardening for the first time since I'd met her, Ellia gave a stern, albeit nervous nod as she slipped a pair of black gauntlets onto her fingers.

"As you wish, Ms. Ward." The two women glared at one another; their vicious stares creating an aura of unease as a hush rushed over the surrounding people.

The two bowed their heads down as they instantly sprinted towards each other, the bright red figure of Mara directly juxtaposing the black blur she rushed at.

Mara slashed to the side with her blade the millisecond they came within striking distance, startling me slightly with how fast she swung at an ally.

This is the first time I've seen her fight...and yet I can already tell her precision and speed far outclasses almost all of us. Not even Jack can attack with that amount of ferocity.

Amazingly, Ellia managed to duck under the swing, sliding on her knees painfully with a noticeable cringe as she struck Mara in the knee, buckling the appendage as the swordswoman stumbled slightly. Ellia popped to her feet in an instant, cracking her fist against Mara's dazed jaw. Mara crumpled onto her back, grasping onto her already bruising visage with surprise evident on her features.

As Ellia went for a finishing downward strike, Mara tucked her legs over her face and rolled backwards, narrowly dodging a vicious jab as Ellia's fist dug into the earth. Ellia winced as she drew her left hand back, the blackened material now cloaked in a layer of dust and pebbles. Mara was immediately back on her feet, her breathing somehow steadying as she balanced the golden sword in her right hand.

A faint tap on my shoulder interrupted my thought process in the middle of this, causing my attention to revert to the source, which turned out to be my grinning brother.

"Who do you think is gonna win this one?" Jack asked with a cheeky grin as I let out a sigh, "Bet ya fifteen gold Ellia takes this one." I reverted my attention back to the arena as I could hear the shuffling of the two women's feet on the loose dirt, both trying to determine the best path to take the fight.

"Mara, and make it thirty." Jack flashed me a thumbs up with a laugh as he turned back to Avelina, letting me swivel back to the fight with the knowledge I would have an extra thirty gold soon. I took a closer look at the woman who saved me days ago.

Her stance was an intriguing one. It was almost noble and valiant in its appearance: her left hand balled into a fist on her chest, almost like she was discarding the appendage. Her sword was pointed at the audience while resting in her right hand, its shining edges facing her opponent. Her green eyes sat utterly focused on the woman in front of her.

Her stance...of course. It's not a nobleman's stance; she appears this way on purpose to make an opponent underestimate her. If they didn't know her true speed and power, her opponent would involuntarily assume she would be unable to block a sustained barrage of attacks based on her stance.

"Genius." I muttered to myself as I stared at the audience, witnessing everyone paying close attention to the two staring each other down. Even Henry was closely watching, his ice-colored eyes staring through the black cloak with hidden curiosity.

"You see that?" Avelina muttered to me, causing me to return my attention to the battle as Mara ran at the other woman, "I knew you were probably wondering why Ellia doesn't arm herself with any weapon to truly defend herself. Watch closely Connor, I feel this may intrigue you." Right on cue, the sound of metal slicing through the air met my ears as Mara slashed towards Ellia, who was frantically backstepping to avoid the blade's savage barrage.

173

As Ellia lunged backwards a noteworthy distance, the shy woman grasped onto the hinge of her gauntlets, tugging at the leather just beyond the bracer in a dramatic fashion as she stood her ground. I wasn't sure, but I swear I could faintly hear a small clicking noise emanate through the sound of heavy breathing and slashing. Mara swung down with all of her might, yelling out as the blurred matter cut through the wind itself.

The shine of steel suddenly sliced through the air as the sound of metal cracking against metal erupted through the arena. A shimmering blade had appeared over the top of Ellia's right gauntlet, deflecting the blow and keeping Mara's attack in place.

I could hear my brother gasp as I closely examined the miraculous blade that had just saved Ellia from what would have been a match-ending blow.

It was a blade about the size of my own, extending out from the top of her gauntlet like a spike. The smaller blade was locked with Mara's, with small sparks cascading off as the metals screeched and ground against each other.

The two blades dislodged from one another, slashing light scratches into each other as Ellia was the one instead who came running back at her.

The dancing of blades surged against one another, the slashes almost rupturing throughout the air as their violent battle continued.

At one point as she deflected the gauntlet blade to the side, Mara struck Ellia across the jaw, causing the woman to stumble back in a daze. Still winded, a boot slammed into her stomach, sending her sprawling to the side a couple feet away. Ellia wiped her mouth as she stared up, noticing Mara's approach as she lay crouched on the ground.

As Mara sprinted towards Ellia another time, the panting woman grabbed hold of the glove again, the blade retracting back into its holding.

She appears to be grasping onto a different section of the glove this time.

Pulling it back, I could hear the faint sound of cogs turning as Ellia shakily brought her right hand up into the air, her balled up fist facing Mara in defiant fashion.

She's already almost upon her. Whatever Ellia is doing it's too late for Mara to dodge out of the way of it.

In fact, she doesn't even look like she's trying to dodge. Does she not realize that...?

Just as that thought cut through my brain, Mara swung her sword up diagonally to the left, a move I thought she would do. Unlike my thought, Mara swung for the gauntlet, striking the leather bracer as hard as she could as Ellia's arm involuntarily swiveled upwards from the blow. Ellia winced in surprise and in pain.

Suddenly, a small explosion ruptured from Ellia's arm, originating from her wrists as a fiery shock wave emanated from her hand. The sound of the blast met our ears milliseconds later, noticeably causing Serena to cringe in her seat.

Ellia's arm was propelled backwards from the blast; her fingers and gauntlet covered in soot and ash. Her sleeve tore and chips were dug into the gauntlet's exterior, but other than that the only thing affecting Ellia at that moment was the explosion's recoil.

At least because of the bracer the strike didn't cause any permanent damage.

Before Ellia could bring her arm back down, a swift elbow crunched against her face, sending her crashing back to earth. Ellia sputtered and coughed out a combination of blood and soot, attempting to rise to her feet a decent distance away.

The sharpened point of a sword met her back, freezing her in her motions. Realizing her plight, Ellia sat herself up on her knees and raised her dirt covered hands up.

"I...I y-yield." Serena immediately sprung up from the bench at her declaration and rushed over to Ellia, the blood already seeping down from cuts and bruises onto the dirt below. Ellia glanced up at the victor, already sheathing her golden blade. I glanced over at my brother, seeing his dropped jaw as the winner was decided so swiftly.

"Any other bets you want to make?" Jack grumbled to himself as a coy smile came to my face, almost laughing at my brother's audible pouting as he reached for his pouch.

Mara, despite taking a couple blows, wasn't even sweating from the engagement, her clothing lacking any wrinkles. She wasn't even breathing out of rhythm. She took a single step away before Ellia let out a sharp cough.

"H-How...how did you know how to counter that?" Ellia sputtered out as Serena applied the green aura to her face, the various cuts growing smaller as Serena's breath grew increasingly labored. Freezing in her motions, Mara turned her head a centimeter to the right as a way of noticing her statement.

"It's...a type of trick I have witnessed before in the past." Without another word, Mara went to sit next to a couple boxes a decent distance away, sitting with her knees pulled close to her chest. The closest person to her silent meditation was Katrina, but even then she was still a couple feet away. She shut her emerald eyes, her breathing steady.

Katrina walked over to Ellia and threw her arm underneath her, a pink tinge rapidly creeping up to her cheeks as she limped towards the benches.

"S-She surprised me is all Ms. Ward, I didn't expect her to be able to..."

"It's alright Ellia," Katrina interrupted, taking a glance at the woman who bested her protege and placing a hand on her shoulder, further flushing her red cheeks, "I don't know how she knew about it either."

Me neither...that woman grows more mysterious by the day.

"I've never seen anyone beat Ellia before," Joan whispered, out of earshot of Ellia who Katrina was resting on a bench, "She may be a timid woman but she's an incredible fighter. Probably one of our foremost and yet, she was defeated so quickly." Serena turned to Joan, brushing her tangerine curls out of her face.

"It's crazy," Serena muttered as she glanced at me briefly, "Connor did you know Mara was that cool?" I quietly shrugged my shoulders as I stood up from the ground, stretching my arms out as Jack tapped me on the shoulder.

"That fight was pretty sweet to watch, even if I was wrong about the victor," Jack commented with a slight pout to it, "Try not to disappoint Connor." I let out a snort as I turned, seeing him flash a quick thumbs up before I marched over to the dusty circle, now filled with footprints and long divots from the previous fight.

I silently drew my new dirk from its sheath, its blackened edges screaming into the air. I twirled it around in my palm, allowing it to come to rest in my traditional backwards stance as I readied for its first true encounter in better hands. Katrina gave a grin as she walked opposite of me and pulled her massive blade behind her left shoulder.

"Almost exactly like your mother's stance..." she noted with a tinge of nostalgia to her voice, "Let's see if your competence with handling it matches your skill!" Without letting her think of any form of attack, I immediately lunged at her in the open area, even catching some of the fellow Sentinel spectators off guard with my sudden lunge.

She appears to be a normally offensive fighter, judging by her stance and how her feet were already planted to rush at me before we even began.

She craned her neck backwards at the slash, stepping to the side as I stabbed forward. She aggressively swept my legs out from underneath me, using my forward momentum to send my body

177

flying forward. Thinking fast, I tucked my body underneath myself, clumsily managing a painful roll across the dusty and pebble ridden surface. I panted as I jumped to my feet and whirled around, the sharpened blade of the dirk now pointed directly at her in defiance.

She knocked me to the floor in one hit.

"Impressive recovery Connor," Katrina admired, her sword hand motionless, "That little maneuver managed to knock a certain somebody on their stomach when I did it against them." Nathaniel quietly mumbled a curse or two as the sound of Gerard slapping him on the back reverberated in the area.

"While noteworthy, you're gonna have to do a lot more than that to take me down…so come on!" She charged at me this time without hesitation, no longer allowing me to take advantage of the split-second I had previously. I was forced onto the defensive as I deflected blow after devastating blow, with the dirk somehow managing to withstand the force she was putting behind that mighty sword.

Every so often, I managed to parry a move just perfectly and go for a pierce or a slash, but each attempt would miss as she sidestepped the attack with ease.

How many years did she have to train to be this fast?

"You're quite good Connor," she commented as she rushed me again, "Any normal soldier would've been killed from any one of those strikes. But you're fighting a woman with decades of experience, so don't expect victory so easily!" She swung strongly across towards my face, moving diagonally as the momentum of her sprint carried into her attack.

That's it!

Ducking underneath her strike, I gripped my hand tightly around the handle of the dirk to ensure it didn't fall out of my hands, before swinging up and through her arms towards her face. Unable to stop her swing, her face widened in surprise as my fist connected with her right cheek. I could almost feel the capillaries in my knuckles burst upon impact, immediately bruising the area as my hand was caught between the dirk and her hardened face.

Pain rushed through my hand as her sword clattered to the ground behind me, watching as she stumbled painfully backwards. The pain grew so tremendous that I involuntarily dropped the dirk to the ground, cursing myself as I did.

Dammit! Doesn't matter...I have to take advantage of every second I have.

Rushing at her with my fists fully raised, I sprinted full speed at our blonde-haired commander who was still clutching her face, a single indigo eye poking through her strained fingers. I pummeled into the hand still latched onto her face, landing two vicious blows as more bruises painfully spread across my fingers.

Without warning she spun around full speed, roundhouse kicking me in the chest and knocking the air clean out of me. I was flung off my feet, spiraling through the air for a few moments before I landed on my back across the makeshift arena. I eased myself up slowly, clutching my chest as I took the moment of reprieve Katrina's injury provided me with.

"You're getting slow Katrina!" Gerard bellowed out, "I don't remember the last time anyone ever landed a direct hit on you." I heard Avelina scoff as I formulated what to do next, the pain shooting through my head making it hard to think.

"He's a crafty kid Gerard," Avelina retorted for her commander, "If Katrina wanted it, this battle would already be over. She's testing the kid, so beating the crap out of him doesn't really give us anything." I heard the familiar guffaw Gerard gave off as my eyes lit up, trying to formulate my next move.

"You see that?" I could hear Jack faintly whisper, most likely to Avelina, "That's the face he makes when he has you all figured out. Something tells me your commander doesn't realize what she's facing." I knew Katrina was stunned for a moment as she wiped her bloodied nose, after which she would most likely move over to grab her sword which rested on the opposite side of the arena. I gave a deep breath and grabbed onto my shirt, resting my hand over the familiar cool metal lurking within.

You activated when my life was threatened...let's see if summoning its power is just a simple test of willpower.

Taking slow even breaths, I grasped onto the outline of my pendant as I desperately attempted to call upon its gift, feeling a vein poke out on my forehead through the mental strain.

Come on pendant work with me here. I'm not strong enough yet to beat her...so as much as I disdain it, I need you if I am to fulfill my ambition.

A burning heat suddenly began to swirl around my right hand, and without even looking I knew that the familiar green glow was emanating from within my shirt, flashing a brilliant light that lurked at the corners of my vision.

I hate having to use this thing...but I need to prove that I can win. I won't use you again unless absolutely necessary.

Taking one final deep breath as the quiet pain dulled, I darted towards Katrina's direction with my right hand lying at my side, concentrating on focusing every ounce of energy this pendant could provide into it.

I would rather not use this, but since I know it won't bring the rider of death upon me, I'll see what it can truly do...if I can harness it.

It was at that moment I felt it...

The torrents of winds rushing around my hand in the same glove formation. The winds were so fast and violent that they couldn't even be contained within my grasp, with the occasional cool torrent of air rushing down my arm in a way that sent chills up my spine.

It was almost as if I had bottled up a hurricane and attempted to contain the whipping winds within my shaking human clutches.

By my guess, this energy will involuntarily spill out in a couple seconds or so. Enough time to reach her.

At this point, Katrina had obviously noticed my approach, drawing her blade in front of her as a defensive maneuver. All she could see was my fist drawn out to the side as I charged her, rushing by the silent audience as Jack gave a single cheer in my direction.

I have you!

As soon as I came within striking distance, I curled my fingers as I prepared to strike the sword she was currently using as a guard, knowing it would pierce through her defense and force her to yield.

At that moment before the blast would strike, her eyes widened in realization as she finally saw the winds whipping around at my fingertips. She had to know she had no time to truly defend herself from the attack as I stood mere feet from her, launching my fist towards the sword she was defending with.

Without warning, she let go of her weapon.

Hearing the blade clatter to the ground, I watched in shock and horror as the area I had aimed my attack for had completely vanished, rattling beneath my feet.

Katrina had already sidestepped the attack at this point, reaching out and grabbing hold of the hand filled with wind.

Grasping hold of it, my body was slammed into the ground stomach first, knocking every ounce of air out of my body. My right arm soon hit the floor, followed by my right-hand landing palm first in the dirt. The wind lay dormant in the ground for a split-second before the recoil of the blast launched my arm backwards slightly. A geyser of dirt and dust soon followed, whipped up from my final desperate move.

"I've seen enough!" Katrina shouted out, "That was an incredibly risky move Connor. I haven't seen someone perform an action like that in a long time. Who taught you how to do that?" Releasing my hand from my grip, I instinctively grabbed hold of my wrist and pressed at the points of pain, which were far more dulled than I thought they would be. I dusted myself off and cracked my neck with a suppressed groan.

"I taught myself." Grabbing hold of my side, I limped over to the audience, finally hearing the reactions they may have been giving for some time now.

Jack and Serena were giving boisterous cheers, backed up by Gerard who was thunderously clapping behind them.

Avelina, Nathaniel, and Joan gave quiet smirks in my direction, whilst Ellia wearily flashed a thumbs up from her sitting position.

Mara stared at me for a moment, before returning to her own thoughts as she closed her eyes.

And Henry…his eyes never stopped examining me. The hostility remained in those icy eyes, narrowing as he examined me with what appeared to be a renewed curiosity.

Serena gave a gasp of realization as if just noticing I had fought someone, rushing up to me and allowing me to sit in her spot on the bench. Her hands were engulfed in the same green gloves as she applied them to my sides and my wrist. The wounds began mending themselves as a warm feeling overwhelmed me.

"And you were the one asking how I got trained with this power," Serena smiled, "Turns out you have an awesome power of your own that you didn't bother to share."

"I didn't know you could do that either Connor," Jack interjected with a still surprised look on his face, "Since when do you do cool crap like that?" I shook my head and pulled out the shining green pendant, looking rather dull as it had just stopped glowing. I could feel the eyes around me shooting towards this piece of jewelry, all except for Henry and Mara, who were both out of eye-shot.

"Remember this, Jack?" I said calmly, "I don't really know what it is, but it can make me do...that. I've never used it like that either, so that was a large gamble I took for nothing." Serena released me from her grasp with a sigh, able to fade away any bruises and turn most of my cuts and scrapes into darkened bruises.

"It was impressive Connor nonetheless," Avelina insisted as she walked over to Katrina, "To have the mental determination to do that must've taken a large amount of strain, so well done."

"Indeed," Katrina maintained as Serena ran up to heal her still bloody face, "Anyone else would've lost. Don't take this as a failure. Take it instead as a testament to your skills thus far." Once finished, Katrina turned to my brother, who I could tell was practically bouncing in anticipation while waiting for his chance to fight.

"Jack you will be fighting Avelina," Katrina proclaimed to Jack's excitement and Avelina's chagrin, "But that will be later today. I think resting for a moment with some food will be beneficial. Don't want us cooking in this afternoon sun for too long." Without another word Katrina began walking back to the main building with a slight stumble, with Ellia shakily standing up and swiftly following behind her.

Jack let out a defeated sigh as he hung his head down, depressed that he wouldn't be able to fight right away. Avelina patted Jack on the shoulder as she brushed past.

"Don't you worry Jack," Avelina jokingly consoled, "I'll have time to beat you later." Walking by with a chuckle, Jack sprinted after the purple-haired woman who was still laughing at Jack's expense.

You couldn't beat her.

My body unconsciously shivered as that single thought gripped my mind like a vice.

You have lost to everyone of substantial strength you have ever fought. How could you possibly think you're strong enough to fight that knight

183

and find your mom? Or even fight Zain for that matter?

I can...I can do it. I j-just need a little bit more time to train myself.

You have been doing that for ages now. If you can't reach your threshold of strength now, there is no chance you ever will...

An arm snaked around my shoulder suddenly, shaking me from my thoughts as I turned to the person who did it.

"Connor my friend!" Nathaniel exclaimed next to me, "How about you sit next to us during lunch? We can proclaim to you the exuberant tales of warfare and victory that we've gone through in the days of yore before we leave for the day." Gerard and Joan walked side-by-side with us, along with a giggling Serena who had managed to walk beside Joan.

"If by victory you mean tales of us saving your butt last second, then yeah...tell him all about it." Nathaniel gave a scoff as we continued to walk, seemingly forgetting the two silent warriors who still lurked speechlessly in the training grounds.

They're so jovial...do they not know of what Zain has done?

"Sure...sure it sounds great." The nobleman and the commoner both shared a laugh as Gerard threw an arm over me as well, almost crushing me from the weight of both of their appendages.

"Splendid!" Nathaniel proclaimed, "Then may your ears today be filled with the tales of our noble fight for justice."

15

Connor: The Soldier's Table

"And the bear my father and I hunted had to be eight feet long and eight hundred pounds. Quite a loathsome beast, and when it came upon us, we were petrified in fear as we stared it down."

"I'm sure that was quite a thrilling experience." I retorted dryly, although it didn't appear the eccentric noble even noticed. His smile just extended as his arms waved wildly, trying in vain to explain a story apparently more complicated than words.

"Indeed it was my insightful friend," Nathaniel exclaimed as he motioned me into a chair, "I stood my ground in front of my father, drawing the dazzling silver my father crafted into a rapier so long ago. In a single thrust forward, I slew the mighty beast, watching as the foul creature fell to my feet as my father gazed over in awe. Soon the creature whose malice so entrenched us rested on my father's mantle." While the nobleman was beaming proudly after his blatantly exaggerated story, the red head walking behind my chair let out a dramatic sigh at her companion's words.

"Nathaniel you were s 'posed to tell him a story 'bout us," Joan groaned as she sat right beside the long-winded noble, taking the seat at the end of the table, "Not some exaggerated bar tale 'bout one of your father's excursions." As she sat down, I noticed the man known as Gerard wasn't present, disappearing somewhere I hadn't tracked.

To my left, Jack immediately sat himself down beside me with a wide grin, probably just realizing there was going to be food. To his left sat Avelina, her orange eyes shutting as she leaned back in a rickety chair.

"Quite a hearty group we've locked ourselves in Connor," Jack beamed as he kicked his feet onto the table, "Didn't think you'd find yourself surrounded by people who actually talk." Avelina swiped Jack's legs off the table as soon as he finished speaking, surprising my brother mid-sentence. Before I could even take another breath, Jack began exclaiming with an annoyed expression as Avelina chided my brother over something involving table manners. I almost laughed at my brother's childlike antics, their argument devolving into a trading of insults.

Directly in front of me sat Katrina Ward, having swiftly changed back into the same attire she wore when I first arrived. She removed her yellow jacket and placed it on the back of her own chair, crossing her legs as she sat down. Ellia promptly sat herself to her left, fidgeting slightly as she sat with a restrained smile. She whispered something into the commander's ear, the blonde woman's expression remaining solemnly serious as she shut her eyes in thought.

The name Zain was tossed around again, with Ellia seemingly briefing her superior on something crucial in a hurried tone.

Serena positioned herself on the other side of Katrina with a smile, with the cloaked man known as Henry notably missing.

Mara was also absent from our current gathering.

"Alright I've had this brewing up for some time since we arrived... hope you all are hungry!" Glancing up at the noise, I could almost feel Jack's excitement as the wooden wall to my left popped out and slid to the side, revealing some form of hidden room. From what I could see, the space resembled some form of kitchen, with wooden cabinets and pots that hung from the ceiling. A back door hung open outside, leading to where a campfire and any other cooking materials rested.

I didn't even notice this hidden panel was there...would be perfect as a discrete escape path.

Gerard lurched through the opening, carrying a large copper pot as he beamed proudly. He set the massive container on the table with a loud rattle, noticing the steam flow through the air like a faint whisper.

An incredible smell promptly flowed to my nose, making my stomach grumble slightly as I realized I hadn't eaten anything substantial in a couple days. Even though Mara brought food to me in the cave, it usually consisted of small rations such as a chunk of bread or berries she snatched from who knows where.

Whatever Gerard had cooked up blew those scraps out of the water, as I had to make a conscious effort to prevent myself from drooling.

"Fantastic job as always Gerard," Katrina proclaimed as Ellia finished what she was saying, "Glad you decided to piece together some stew before your departure." Gerard gave a beaming smile as he revealed a cavalcade of clay bowls from behind his back.

"Alright, I've had enough of talking," Avelina cut in as she pointed toward the large container, "Somebody hand me a bowl before I snatch up the container myself." Gerard gave his usual boisterous laugh, before systematically hurling each individual bowl across the table. They skidded perfectly in front of each chair, coming to a rest in front of everyone present. One stopped at the spot next to Serena, presumably where the chef would sit once everyone was served.

The brackish broth was dished out to everyone, with similar colored meat chunks floating just above the murky surface.

How it looked didn't appear to matter to anyone, as almost immediately everyone began to dig into the hand cooked meal as spoons were handed out. The only two individuals with some form of pacing to their eating was Serena and Nathaniel. Both were eating in a way that resembled a restrained, almost noble way of eating one's food; nothing like the way the rabid dogs around them devoured the food.

The somewhat salty meat tasted incredible compared to what I've eaten over these past few months. Jack and I aren't exactly renowned for being acclaimed cooks.

Although, it still isn't as superb as mom's.

Maybe she can show Gerard a few tricks once I find her.

Before anyone could blink, almost everyone was done, all except for Serena who was taking her sweet time with her dish. A large cavalcade of conversations soon swept through the table, as everyone began their individual topics unconcerned with one another. I wished to interrupt and ask one of the three what their encounter with Zain was like, but I opted not to.

The jovial mood that somehow encompassed this space would be ruined. Besides, most of the information on how Zain fights or where he's going is either something I already know, or has already been relayed to Katrina or Avelina.

Most of the conversation consisted of small talk common within groups of similar size to this, so I chose not to pay attention to most of them, but one of them not only caught the attention of myself, but also of my unusually silent brother.

"Do ya think Senator Richards can actually beat the Chancellor?" Joan asked Avelina in an attempt at small talk, "After all you're the last of us to actually be in the capital." The spymaster gave an indifferent shrug.

"Well uh…he's one of the most energetic and dedicated Senators

I've ever had the pleasure of meeting, Joan. But with that said, Solaton is a fickle place. The people already in charge may not even give him a platform to make his case, let alone go far enough to make it on ballots."

Jack glanced up as he tapped the table with his spoon, managing to somehow get the attention of the entire table. Unaffected by the multitude of eyes staring into him, Jack gave a smile and looked between Joan and Avelina.

"Forgive me for being ignorant...because I am. But I've been wondering how the heck your system even functions? Like those involved in politics and power. I've only really encountered a mayor of a town before, but I keep hearing talk about other politicians and leaders and whatever the heck else. Like what even is this Senator you're talking about?" I could hear Avelina groan as she set her spoon down in the bowl, audibly showing she was finished.

"Jack," Avelina began in an almost disappointed tone, "I know for a fact I've explained this to you almost twenty times."

"And I wasn't really paying attention...all twenty times." I could see a vein pop up in Avelina's forehead as she sighed, rubbing her temples in a way that showed she refused to explain one final time. Ellia perked up momentarily, looking as if she was excited to add to a conversation she was well-educated on.

"Well, we have a form of Chancellor," Ellia began as she stared at Jack with a warm smile, "We had a new one recently elected five years ago, but he can serve for one and then another six if he were to win another election. The rest comes from the hexagonally divided counties, from which every village within them votes for the Senators to represent them. Anyone can be put into that position. They just need to end up on the ballot to make it during the election cycle." I could hear a heavy snort in front of me, realizing it came from the large blond man who had prepared the exceptional meal. I took a moment to scan him over before he spoke.

Based on the secondhand clothes he wears he probably lived in one of those small villages before this...although he was not wealthy enough to be a merchant based on his mannerisms. Perhaps a farmer or small-time trader?

"Ha, elections don't matter," Gerard said sarcastically in his same tone, shifting his eyes to the nobleman of our group, "We all can vote for those Senators to send to Heartwood and our own mayors, but it's the nobles already in power who decide who ends up on that stinking ballot for each county, and most of the time they're the ones who stay. Even the mayors choose their own councils to observe them, so they can get as many like-minded yes men to watch over them as possible." There was a bitterness to his tone I hadn't ever encountered when we first met, losing the constant laughter he echoed after every remark.

"They make a crap ton of money too," Joan cut in a tad more passively, "That's why we consider most politicians noblemen as well, since they're the ones who live fancifully off the laws and taxes they establish."

Passed down clothes as well. Perhaps her upbringing was similar to Gerard's.

I glanced over at the unusually silent noble beside me, expecting him to have an exuberant retort prepared against his two companions.

Instead, Nathaniel said nothing to the aggressive remarks, keeping his attention on the spoon he swirled steadily around the rim of the bowl. Joan, sensing the awkwardness of the room cleared her throat, turning to Katrina. The commander looked as if her attention was far away, not paying any attention to the present conversation.

"Well...I believe it's time to take our leave," Joan began as she stood up, swiftly followed by her two male partners as they sensed the conversation was dead, "We'll be back from our surveillance mission in two weeks' time. Until we meet again." Serena gave a joking salute as Katrina gave a firm nod, the rest of us watching as they made their way towards the door.

"Stay safe out there," Katrina implored in that same motherly tone, "I expect to see you back here with the same ordinary proceedings." With that, the three of them exited through the ornate doorway with final waves, Nathaniel giving an overzealous bow as the door shut once more, leaving behind a further vacated room.

Avelina and Jack swiftly departed afterwards, each rapidly going down the hallway to prepare for their expected duel.

Jack's already so acclimated...

Serena already ran off somewhere to search for her cloaked companion, while Ellia regarded that she had some paperwork to finish by today. I found myself sitting directly opposed to the blonde woman who was miraculously now my commander, a woman who already trusted me despite barely knowing me. I stared down at my empty bowl.

Let's hope my hunch was right...and that through being a part of this I'll have a greater chance to find my mother.

My thoughts drifting as the world faded away around me, I thought back to the one whose power within an amber pendant may give me a clue to where my mother had gone.

Could his power be linked to his voice? These occurrences only happened when he spoke about them.

It's possible, but once again why wouldn't he just declare for us to trip and fall onto our own weapons?

I know I'm getting closer, but the more theories I debunk the more questions that...

"You really do remind me of her." I glanced up in surprise at Katrina's sudden declaration, one which she began nonchalantly as she stood up from her chair. She stared down at me with softened indigo eyes, pushing her chair in as a faint chuckle exited her mouth.

"Your distinct mannerisms are like an after image of the Elizabeth I knew all those years ago," Katrina continued as her yellow jacket clung to her shoulders, "Still so silent and content even when everyone is screaming around you about something. Same mumbling whenever your mind wanders off to another realm. Even your eyes are like hers; always somewhere faraway as your mind twists and turns about something I can't even fathom to understand." She laughed to herself again as some form of nostalgia overtook her, her eyes glazing over as memories flooded her mind.

"She never mentioned you," I plainly noted, freezing her in her stride, "I know you both were friends at one point, but I still find it odd that someone who cared about her that much was never even name dropped around me." She let out a sigh as she froze like a statue, refusing to turn her head to face me.

"I um...I only knew her for those few years before she left the academy," Katrina admitted, "That's a testament to how incredible of a person she was. Even in the brief time I knew her, we wrote that book together and dreamed of a world we could mold within our hands. But I knew deep down she always wanted something far simpler; a life much easier to mold as her own. I suppose in the end, she lived her dream of living an ordinary life, and I lived the one we hoped to create when we were younger."

"I'm going to find her Katrina," I proclaimed as I myself finally stood up, causing her to turn her head towards me, "I can't do that alone... and while I'll serve you because I know you stand for something greater, every bit of my free time and energy will be put into finding her." Her eyes hardened momentarily, a brief micro-expression that shifted back to the soft facade she was now putting on.

"How do you know she isn't dead already?"

"I know it Katrina," I immediately retorted as I took a step towards the door, leaving the table completely void of people, "If you knew her as well as you say you do, you'd know my mother wouldn't accept death that easily. I feel as if working for you or finding wherever that man Zain went is the key to all this, and I intend to make the most of it." She cringed at the mention of the man who destroyed Eincrest, confirming my suspicion that Ellia had talked to her about it.

The woman let out a sigh as she took a single step towards me, putting a warm hand on my shoulder as she stared down at me with a stern expression.

"Don't let this search consume your life Connor," Katrina implored in a faraway voice as she began to step away, "Maybe Zain will provide you with some necessary information to find where they took her, but an obsession over all of this may be more damaging than it is helpful." With that, she immediately walked away with one final warm smile, presumably towards her office.

I have to stay focused...and luckily this group is providing me with more leads.

I stepped away and gripped onto the exit doorknob, swinging it open.

Even if he's just another unaffiliated Bellhollow brute, he still wears a pendant of a similar kind to my mother's. If he's not the key, the pendant he wears will be.

"And I'm supposedly the one who knows everything." I mumbled aloud to myself, hearing my own voice disappear into the tree line.

"Perhaps not everything." Whirling around at the sudden voice, I drew my dirk as I stood at the ready for a sudden attacker. Glancing around for anything I noticed a darkened silhouette resting by the boxes nearby.

"Henry," I said cautiously, "I didn't notice you there. Do you need something?" Uncrossing his arms, Henry walked up to me with his black cloak dragging on the ground, kicking up clouds of dust with each pounding step. The mask on his face almost made my stance buckle in anxiety, his cold blue eyes the only feature I could distinguish. He stiffly approached me like a mannequin, making me unsure if he really was a human being lurking under those garments.

Without any form of warning, he grabbed hold of my right hand, entrapping it in his tight grasp. In a panic I attempted to wrench myself free, but my wrist remained firmly stuck within his clutches. Turning my hand over as I struggled, he stared at the top portion of my hand, eventually letting it go after peering at it for a couple uncomfortable seconds.

I held my tongue as the silence returned, waiting to see if he would explain himself before I unleashed my prepared retort.

"I don't get it." He murmured to himself, already beginning to walk away.

"Hey!" I yelled out, losing patience at the completely covered man, "Would you care to explain why you just did that?" Henry didn't take even a fleeting glance back as he continued to walk, the brisk wind making his cloak flow as he trudged away.

"You keep generating more perplexing questions, Connor Illium." I chased after him so that he could explain himself, but the moment I took my eyes off him he was already gone.

Dammit! Almost reminds me of Mara and her own disappearing trait.

I huffed as I dusted my hands off, wandering around the outside of the building.

Never mind then. I have time to kill, and I would rather not juggle any more theories about Zain for now...I may as well quell one of my many innate curiosities.

Wandering around outside, I decided to explore the outskirts of the thick forest we found ourselves surrounded by, making note of the almost clear river that flowed loudly nearby.

Almost immediately, I found her.

About a minute or so away from the building, the girl who pulled me from the wreckage of a burned home sat on a downed log, already beginning to rot as it had clearly been here for several days. Mara stared off into the green distance, keeping her eyes on the patchwork of trees and bushes that swayed in front of her. The sound of a river flowing beside her was the only sound that perforated through the area, almost completely masking my approach. For the first time since I'd met her, she appeared content, her hand resting in her lap instead of on her sword. Her lackadaisical gaze held a glimmer of relief as she sat utterly still, her shoulders down as she genuinely appeared relaxed for the first time.

I took a step closer.

"Didn't think this would be the type of place I'd find you." A single gasp escaped her throat as she stood up from the log, the sound of metal slicing through the air. Instantly something sharp jabbed into the center of my neck. Glancing down apprehensively, my body involuntarily stiffened as she stared me down, the sword now at my throat.

I let out a nervous chuckle as she slowly moved the point away, my hands lowering from when I instinctively raised them in fear.

"Oh…it's just you," Mara breathed out in a reticent voice, "Don't ever sneak up on me like that, or I may not be able to stay my hand a second time." Another chuckle emanated out involuntarily as she stepped away, still staring back at me.

"Sorry about that. Just trying to find where you vanish sometimes," I explained as she sheathed her golden blade, "Didn't think I could be as silent as Henry while doing so." She stared at me blankly after my attempt at humor, glancing back with vacant confusion as the silence took over the scenery.

Alright note to self…no more jokes.

After another awkward second, she sat herself down on the log she had rested on prior, letting out a sigh as she kept her now narrowed eyes on me.

"What is it you want?" she finally asked as she averted her gaze, staring back into the distance. I gave her a simple shrug.

"I was simply wondering where you vanish to," I explained again as I took a step closer, noticing her gloved hand was now back on the hilt of the sword, "Didn't expect to find you so transfixed by... all of this." She adjusted her posture as she stared away from me, her stance never fully slouching back to what it once was.

I stepped closer to the log, seeing her stiffen as I stared in the direction she was examining in confusion. While the forest was noteworthy for how many trees littered its surroundings, other than that it was like any other in the world. There weren't even any animals around, and the lake this river most likely flowed to wasn't present from this view. I looked down at the occupied woman, seeing her gaze shift between me and her surroundings.

"I don't particularly understand what has you so transfixed. It's just a bunch of trees."

"Maybe to you," Mara interrupted as her eyes never left the patches of green, speaking with a strong conviction I had gotten used to, "But...I can't help but stare at it all. The way the wind faintly whispers on every leaf, making them softly quiver in the wind. Or that river; how the sunlight twinkles off its dazzling blue surface, making it appear far brighter and livelier than it actually is." The way she gushed about her surroundings was the most genuine way I have ever heard her speak, one of the few moments in this journey she hadn't lied. She sounded like a young girl who was transfixed by one of her favorite subjects, far different from the way I thought this woman was. I let out another involuntary chuckle at her statement.

"You seem proficient at noticing these kinds of details." She scoffed to herself, the question appearing almost ridiculous to her.

"It's easy to notice when where you come from lacks any of it."

Almost immediately after saying that her emerald eyes widened, a look of shock evident on her expression as she glanced away from me in a hurry.

Still hiding things about herself...maybe that was the first true thing she's ever said about where she came from.

"Hm...in that village down in the valley, right?" I said in a curious tone, posing a loaded question she didn't seem to pick up on.

"What're you talking ab-" her words caught in her throat as she stopped her sentence immediately, the words she said fully registering, "U-Um yeah...the village was pretty far down in the v-valley, so all these t-trees didn't really reach us."

The lie was so blatant, she probably didn't even believe it herself.

Perhaps everything I've seen about her has been a massive lie...could her standoffish behavior potentially be a way she prevents herself from lying as badly as she has?

I thought about pushing the topic further, but I let her have this one after our conversation yesterday.

"I suppose the landscape is quite captivating...Do you mind if I sit with you to study it like you do?" I asked, not realizing the words that came out until they did. She still looked largely flustered and uncomfortable from the several slip-ups she had earlier, but for some reason she wasn't immediately saying no.

"D-Don't expect much conversation, but go ahead." I sat myself down beside her on the log, a red tinge appearing on her cheeks as I did so. I let out a sigh as she slightly scooted away, propping myself up so I could sit on the ground in front of the log instead. She breathed out a sigh of relief, edging back to where she once sat as her gaze shifted back to the tree line.

And there we sat in sustained silence, content with our surroundings without realizing the company we had.

16

Jack: Test of Wills

"Do you really think you can beat Avelina?" I glanced over at the woman who asked the question, watching as Serena rushed beside me with her usual smile.

Maybe someone as spunky and extroverted as her will help my brother be more social...which I can't seem to do even with how much I talk to people.

"Pretty sure I can handle it Serena," I replied with a hint of snark, "I've watched her fight for a while now and I think I'll at least be able to get a few licks in." A lie, since I'd only seen her fight once before and it was at longer range.

"I'm expecting a repeat performance of what Connor did this morning," Henry suddenly exclaimed behind me, startling both of us as we didn't even notice he was there.

"Come on give him a break Henry," Serena rebuked in the same jovial tone, "You know as well as I do no one has ever landed so many direct hits on Katrina, and since Jack is Connor's brother he's gotta be just as awesome!" Henry gave a dismissive grunt as he folded his arms, hiding them within the veil of the endless void his cloak was.

Walking outside, I noticed that Ellia was already sitting on a bench near the ring, looking like she had just arrived. She had a slight red tint to her cheeks, with her spectacles resting in her hand as she cleaned them with a piece of her long dress. Her gauntlets from this morning were fully discarded, the miraculous piece of technology they were.

I'm not even gonna try to understand them...I'll leave that all to Connor.

Speaking of my brother, Connor currently rested with one of his knees up sitting beneath the two, even though there were a wide variety of seats still available to him. He looked like he had just sat down, although based on the mud layering the knees of his pants he had been outside for a while.

The ground is so dusty...so I guess he just wandered off somewhere.

Avelina and Katrina chatted against the same box they rested against this morning, acting as if they had been here the whole day.

That girl named Mara was nowhere to be seen.

"Avelina!" I yelled out, causing her to sigh and slowly crane her head over to me, "I'm ready for our fight!" Avelina shut her amber eyes as she cracked her neck, standing up from the wall as she removed the large silver spear from her back.

"If you want to be thrashed that bad kid, don't be surprised when I deliver."

"Avelina..." Katrina cautioned, leading to a groan from the purple-haired woman.

"Fine," Avelina conceded as she lowered her spear only marginally, "I won't hurt you *too* badly. Just enough to both satisfy me and get a proper reading from Katrina." Both of us walked simultaneously to the center of the field, feeling the eyes of the others all drawn upon us.

"Remember, this duel is expressly for the assessment of Jack's skills and talents as a fighter," Katrina reminded both of us, "And that goes for both of you. Try not to make this day any more strenuous for Serena than it already has been." Avelina gave a nod as she drew the shaft of the spear behind her back, leaving the top quarter of the weapon exposed in her right hand. In the corner of my eye, Connor gave me a simple thumbs up, albeit with his usual complacent face while currently listening to something Serena was whispering to him.

"As you wish, Ms. Ward." Without any form of warning, Avelina gunned at me full speed, the spear still resting behind her back. I had enough time to draw my massive broadsword to block a strike from the shaft of her weapon, dust flying up past my legs as the strike reverberated around me. The silver dug into my blade, with a flurry of sparks sprinkling off as my sword ground across the metal surface.

When my sword slid from the shaft, the both of us swung at each other with the blunt end of our weapons, the hilt of my sword rebounding from the spear's shaft. From the recoil, I swung down with all my might, instead connecting with dirt as I yelped in surprise. In my peripherals, I barely managed to see a smirking Avelina lunging from my side, twirling her weapon with glee.

Striking me across the face with the hilt, I spontaneously released my sword without thinking, stumbling backwards as I grasped my now cut open face.

Crap!

Seeing the shine of the metal in the afternoon sun, I dodged to the right and caught the spear hand within my grasp, yanking as hard as I could as the back end of the tip dug into my clothes and the top portion of my skin. I could faintly hear someone on the benches cringe through their teeth.

After a brief struggle, and a rather mean look from Avelina, I managed to tear the silver spear from her grasp with one final, determined tug. As soon as I triumphantly had a grip onto the weapon, Avelina kicked the weapon out of my hands and up into the air, reaching up and preparing for it to sail into her awaiting grasp once again.

Instinctively I tackled her to the ground, feeling the air leave her lungs as the faint sound of the spear clattering against the ground resonated in the open area. Her back cracked against the hard dirt, sliding for a couple feet and protecting me from the brunt force of the tackle.

A gloved fist crunched against my face as we finally came to a stop, launching me off of Avelina from the pain. As my vision cleared back up again, an immense pain rocketed into my stomach, followed swiftly by a smooth strike to my jaw.

Throwing up my guard, my vision returned to me as two more strikes railed into my arms, making me wince from the dulled pain. Without glancing behind my arms I swung a frantic right hook, somehow connecting with Avelina's side. She grunted in pain, finally stumbling into my frame of vision.

Her purple hair splayed over her eyes, I lunged forward and cracked an elbow across her jaw, hoping the blow would be enough to knock her unconscious, or at the very least send her back to the ground where I could better maneuver.

The sharp elbow crashed into her, her jaw shifting slightly at the strike.

Yes! Right in the face!

Her neck reeling back from the force, Avelina's head snapped back suddenly, her orange eyes filled with nothing but irritation and burning rage as I recoiled back, feeling rightfully intimidated.

"How the heck are you even still standing?" Wiping the blood from her nose, Avelina rushed over to me in my shock, crouching down and drilling her right fist up into my stomach as she flashed a defiant grin up at me. I almost puked from the ferocity of the blow, feeling a billow of spit spray from my mouth.

"You think an attack like that will be enough to finish me? Keep dreaming kid." Avelina snapped, before whipping around and throwing another punch into my collarbone. The bone wobbled as I recoiled, but thankfully it didn't crack as I stumbled back, coughing from the amount of air being forced out my lungs by her strikes.

The dusty air irritated my already devastated lungs as the sun had begun to set, making my breath momentarily visible as I lay hacking up whatever oxygen was left in my system.

Despite the rampant fatigue coursing through my body like a foul disease, I sprung forward at my opponent, watching as she raised her arms in anticipation of the blow coming for her face.

It was a feint, used as a distraction to draw her attention away from what I was really throwing.

My knee came up sharply, digging into her stomach and eliciting a gasp as visible air and a minor amount of blood spilled out, staggering her back from the sudden blow to the stomach. Without letting up, I charged forward and slammed into her with my shoulder, knocking her back. She drew herself forward as she let out a snarl, my momentum carrying me forward as she drew her fist back.

"That's enough!" Katrina called out through the sounds of fighting, our fists both still reared back as we prepared to strike each other in one last ditch attempt for victory. I shined a grin toward Avelina as we both instead carried on, my intention clear to her as she too refused to stop, a smirk growing on her face.

This fight isn't over until I say it is!

As each of us sprung forward in our final attempt to win this battle, a yellow blur flashed in the corner of my eye, although I paid it no mind as all of my thoughts were focused on bringing my fist directly into Avelina's face. Her goal seemed the same as my own; her speed never faltering as we both came within a few feet of one another. I threw my fist forward, my grin becoming almost painful as I sensed my triumph was growing near.

Then, I felt someone grab onto my wrist.

My momentum continuing to pull me forward, my eyes widened as I turned towards the one responsible for the sudden shift of my strike.

It was Katrina. The yellow streak I had seen was her jacket fluttering to the ground as she appeared before us, grasping onto the arms of both myself and Avelina. For a moment, we both remained stunned; her eyes staring like purple daggers into us as she diverted the course of our fists away from their targets. Just as each of our fists passed by each other's faces, she instantly released both of us from her now crossed hands and slammed them both into our faces, halting our advance as she uncrossed her arms.

I yelled out in pain as I was swept off my feet from the force of the blow, landing flat on my back as I heard Avelina stumble, but not quite fall from the same intense pain. I propped myself up as I gripped my injured face, knowing my nose was bleeding but luckily not broken. I glanced up at my opponent, who was currently wiping off her nose as she stared between me and our golden-haired commander.

"I said that's enough," Katrina scolded, "Should've listened the first time. Both of you sit down and have Serena deal with you. I've clearly seen enough to gauge your prowess, Jack." Easing myself up with a pained groan, I sighed in relief as someone helped to hoist me up. Shifting my glance to the side, I let out a relieved chuckle as my own brother helped me to my feet, patting me on the back in a way that appeared sincere. I couldn't help but laugh further at the gesture, realizing that beneath Connor's cool expression, this was his way of making fun of me for getting decked in the face at the very end.

With shuffling footsteps coming my way, I took a moment to glance at the purple haired demon in all her frazzled glory, who at the moment was murmuring a swift apology to Katrina.

Her purple hair was covered in sweat and matted with various knots, with tangles poking throughout as she panted, eventually collapsing to her knees. I kicked the lance over to her, watching as it slid across the dirt mounds and kicked up geysers of dust. I took a step forward with a vague stumble, trying to ignore the bruising pain that tore throughout my face and chest.

If I wasn't putting effort into it, I would be doubled over right then. She peered up at me as I heard Serena swiftly approaching.

"If Katrina hadn't stopped us, I would've beaten you down easily." Avelina let out a light chuckle as she extended a hand up to me. I took it gladly as I helped her up to her feet, seeing her wobble slightly.

"Your overconfidence avails you nothing," Avelina laughed to herself, stepping in front of me to get to Serena, "I've been fighting for years before you. If Katrina asked for it, I would've beaten that sly cockiness right out of you." She gripped her face as she flashed a slight smirk, extending a hand out to me. I took it with a grin as I removed my hand from my tender chest, knowing it was a sign she wanted to fight in a more genuine manner sometime soon.

"All three of you have what it takes." I wearily turned to the side at the blonde woman's sudden declaration, garnering the attention of everyone present. She paid it no mind as she stared first at my brother, then to myself.

"Even though I wish that girl was here, I can say wholeheartedly that all three of you have the skill to be a part of us, so well done. Each of you showcased your ability, and your personalities through these matches. Do whatever you want for the rest of the day, rookies." With that final word, Serena rushed away with a dramatic wave as she finished healing the two of us. She was followed soon by the other three, with Avelina slugging me a bit too hard in the shoulder and Connor giving a tight-lipped smile and a thumbs up as he too left the dusty field.

Rolling my now sore shoulder, I turned to walk away before I felt someone grab onto said shoulder. Turning slowly, I stared into the indigo eyes of my new commander as she showcased a soft smile that juxtaposed the stern expression she held moments ago.

"If Connor was the one to gain your mother's insight, I can see now that you absolutely gained her impulsiveness." I let out a soft laugh as she made this comment, rubbing the back of my head as Katrina dusted off the jacket which had fallen into the dirt below when she halted our match.

"Dad always was the more level-headed one of the two. I remember one time when we were younger, mom chased down a thief over an entire town after she saw him steal a single loaf of bread from a street vendor. It took dad almost an hour to show her that the man was just a beggar trying not to starve." Katrina couldn't help but let out a snort at the final line, hiding it behind her hand as she chuckled softly.

"Your mother for sure had a bit of a...hot-headed streak, so that sounds just like her," she said with a reminiscent smile, "Always thought with her heart despite how sharp she was. Promise me that you won't be as reckless as she was, cause I'm not sure if I can handle that."

"Well...I'd rather not make that type of agreement with you, because I don't want you to be disappointed when I break it." She patted me on the shoulder as another soft chuckle came to her lips, staring at me with the same motherly warmth that was absent when she ended the duel earlier.

She's a kind woman, but damn did that second of rage almost scare me out of my skin.

"I shouldn't have expected anything different from Liza's firstborn," she chastised as she began walking away, adjusting her somewhat clean jacket onto her shoulders, "Both of you are excellent fits for the Sentinels. You both have raised my expectations because of how much you remind of her, so don't let me down alright?" I gave a joking salute as she turned her back to me, scooting away as I was left alone in the dusty circle, staring forward at the new base strewn in front of me; one that I now can call home.

17

Connor: Paranoia

I stood in front of the ornate door beside the entrance to Katrina's office, similar in design to it but I knew something else lurked within. My clothes flowed upon me in a smooth and comforting way, being washed alongside me earlier this morning. Rising early, I crept out to the river and washed myself off as swiftly as I could to prevent prying eyes. Feeling my skin without a disgusting layer of dust and grime upon it was almost euphoric, as everything from the past few days washed away.

I held a balled up, clean fist to the aged wooden surface, not sure if I should knock or if I should just let myself in.

I don't know why I was so indecisive. It's not as if the door was foreboding or ominous in any way.

Choosing the latter option, I grasped onto the ornate handle and pulled open the door, hearing its hinges creak painfully as it opened. I stepped hesitantly inside, hearing the hinges squeak again as it shut behind me. Upon glancing around the room, I stared slack jawed at what I was surrounded by.

Encasing me on all sides was a mountain range of books and novels; a flowing valley of literature that I could find myself trapped in for several lifetimes if I could.

I audibly whistled as I took a loud step into the chamber, with each minute sound I made absorbing into the many pages as they echoed off the walls.

The walls themselves were the same color as the rest of the building; a dark oak that made this place appear almost like a simple log cabin in the woods. The vibrancy of the room came from the many books, ranging throughout the color spectrum and giving life to what would normally be an incredibly mundane space.

The ceiling also cut incredibly low to ten feet above my head, which combined with the maze-like structure of the shelves created a room that was incredibly cramped to venture through.

"There have to be at least a hundred shelves completely stocked with books here." I mumbled to myself, the musty smell lingering in my senses as I took another apprehensive step, the tranquility of the large library almost unnerving me.

Running my hands down the surprisingly crisp spines, I passed by two fully stocked shelves as I rounded the corner.

There were more books in those two rows than I've ever read in my entire life.

Finally coming into a clearing of some kind, I noticed a wooden table with two chairs surrounding it, with nothing but a candle resting on top. Aside from this small area, the rest of the space was filled with the same bookshelves, looking like they would burst if any more books were added.

This library feels so...dead. My guess is no one really peruses these aisles based on how dusty this whole space is.

But why? It's such an extensive pool of knowledge to just leave alone.

My curiosity overwhelming me, I grasped onto one of the books beside me, examining its little red cover. Golden words adorned the front, almost as if they were stitched in meticulously with real golden string.

Inside the Mind of Cecilia Boldeveur by Judy W. Well, I was apparently drawn to this book so I may as well take it.

I placed the ancient book on the table nearby, seeing a cloud of dust puff out as it collided with the wooden surface. I traced my finger across its cover as I stepped away, my pointer finger now stained.

This book probably hasn't been taken out since it was initially placed here.

Granted, there are enough novels and tomes lurking within this place to distract someone for their entire life.

Glancing around the expansive web of books, I decided to walk into one of the many rows, knowing it didn't at all matter which one I selected.

I wonder if anything about these pendants exists in this library.

Taking a step into the row, I almost tripped over the crouched over woman who was sitting down in the aisle, intently invested in a little brown book she was reading. Her black hair was tied up into a ponytail; her eyes hidden behind fogged up spectacles that were clearly tracing across every word.

Ellia Rede...

Surprisingly, she didn't even notice my presence, nor did she notice me jumping back upon almost falling over her. Her body didn't even flinch.

Stepping away from her, I stared at her momentarily, adding to the overwhelming silence of the room. Raising my fist to my mouth, I discreetly coughed aloud in a last-ditch attempt to get her attention.

"Ah!" The spectacled woman yelped, slamming the brown book shut as she sprung up from the ground. Her spectacles fell off one of her ears, hanging on by a thread as her brain took a moment to recognize me. I took the liberty of speaking the first words.

"You're the woman from the photographs," I mumbled to myself as I extended a hand, "Apologies for disturbing you, but we never formally met when you were in Katrina's office or during the duels. I'm Connor." Shakily, she stretched out a hand as a light blush came over her cheeks.

"E-Ellia, but you probably already knew that," she stuttered out, pulling away from the confident warrior I saw fight Mara yesterday and back to the nervous woman I first met, "Sorry for the yelling. I d-don't normally expect anyone else to be in here is a-all." I gave her a light chuckle and a shrug as I glanced around at the walls of books surrounding us, entrapping us in a corridor of knowledge.

"That has perplexed me since I've entered here. Who in their right mind would pass up all of this knowledge?"

"S-Speaking of which," she mumbled out, "Would you be able to get the book up there? I'm a tad too short to reach it." Glancing to where she was gesturing towards, I shifted in that direction to spy a blue book, nestled between two brown tomes. I stepped in front of her as she backpedaled away with a blush, almost hugging the walls each shelf created.

"So, what is your position here?" I questioned to pass the time, reaching for the blue book she was pointing to, grasping hold of it eventually, "Judging by the photo on Katrina's desk you three must reasonably close." As I handed her the book she was reaching for earlier, she gave me a quizzical look as I examined the title.

A Venture between Two Worlds...doesn't sound like a traditional novel.

"Pho...Photographs?" Ellia curiously stated as she wrapped her fingers around the leather hinge, raising her eyebrows as her mind came to a realization. I gave her a puzzled look as she chuckled behind her hand.

"Oh, you mean the pictures on Ms. Ward's desk! That trinket used to create those was quite fascinating, but Ms. Ward is the only one who's used it very much." I took a step towards her.

"You're...unfamiliar with cameras?" I found this incredibly odd. I thought back to the house we lived in by the cliffs, filled with vast collections of pictures that my mother had taken of us with the camera she always kept around.

She was always fond of capturing candid shots of all of us, especially of our father.

The machine, and its various products were all swallowed up by the unforgiving flames.

"Of course," Ellia said as if it was obvious, "I'm not an expert on Bellhollow technology like Ms. Ward is. Never really researched the topic since Ms. Ward already knows so much." I gave another strange expression as she gave me a blank expression.

All of this seems so obvious to her...

"What are you talking about?" I questioned with some level of annoyance, "My mother owned one of those trinkets herself. She took so many pictures with that." Ellia gave a light shrug as she examined the book she desired laid in front of her.

"I don't know what to tell you Connor," Ellia murmured, "That um...camera device is a piece of advanced Bellhollow tech. Ms. Ward managed to snatch one from her time there, but..." I took another step towards her as she stared back, her brow furrowing in a confused manner as she looked up at me.

"What do you mean by Bellhollow technology?" I asked in as calm of a tone as I could muster, "I was under the impression that our technology was far superior to theirs." Ellia shook her head as she cracked open the book in her hands.

"Not true believe it or not," Ellia nonchalantly stated, "The rest of the public is unaware of it due to their secluded nature, but from our readings it appears Bellhollow outclasses us in regards to their technology. This is just one of the many things we've managed to smuggle out." Shrugging her shoulders, she leaned herself against the bookshelf behind her and slid down against it, sitting down on the wooden floor.

"By the way, since you asked previously, I serve as the head of research here. I know everything there is to know about our entire continent whenever it is required. I've...known Katrina for a longtime, so she trusts me with this." Glancing down at her book, she looked up and blushed as I continued to stand there silently.

"You seem rather close to her." I plainly commented, noticing her blush grow sharper. Her glasses fogged up slightly as her entire face lit up a distinct red.

"Um...y-yeah I guess...I guess you could s-say that," she stuttered out, "I mean...I trust her a lot I suppose and I w-would hope she feels the same about me." I smiled as she rambled on like this for several seconds, floundering and blushing harder with every new word she added. Eventually, it became too much for her as she collapsed back down, burying her tomato face back into the book she held.

"Anyways...c-could...could you leave me alone for a moment Connor? I'm not used to any c-company while I'm reading." I gave her a silent, somewhat awkward nod as I stepped away from her, snatching up a random book to make the air feel less still. I glanced at the title as I stepped out of the alleyway of books, leaving the spectacled girl to her own devices.

The White-Haired People by William J. Walker...if I had to assume, it's a book on the Zevron.

The white book looked incredibly pristine, almost as if no one had chosen to read it, yet ensured no dust or cobwebs formed upon its surface.

Clearly, I am fairly...uneducated about the rest of this continent. I suppose that's what I get for living in seclusion for so long. I may as well research more on the Zevron if I already need to cast aside my misconceptions about Bellhollow as well.

"Quite surprising to see you here." Spinning on my heel to face the sudden male voice, I turned to see the dark cloaked man leaning against the wooden chair, his blue eyes glued to the worn brown tome in his gloved left hand. He shut the ancient book as he placed it on the table, planting it right beside the book I had grabbed earlier.

"Henry," I replied as I set the white book down alongside the others, "Based on Ellia's reactions to my presence, I didn't expect anyone else to be here either."

I didn't even hear the door open for him to come in. Was he here this whole time and I just didn't notice?

"Neither did I." he retorted, uncrossing his arms. Sitting down on the opposite side of the table, Henry put his hands together as he stared up at me. I could hear the material of those gloves rub together as they collided.

"Although, I can't say I'm surprised you're in here. Of the three of you to come here, I knew there was some form of scholar lurking within that head of yours the moment I first met you specifically." Waving his hand forward, the hidden man motioned towards the chair on my right. I slowly pulled the chair back and sat down, staring into his regal eyes that bored directly into my skull.

I feel as if those eyes are glaring directly into my subconscious.

Tapping the middle of the table, I watched in confused curiosity as the center of the wooden table lifted up slightly. The square block of wood lifted itself away from the rest of its foundation as cogs screeched beneath it, filling the silence of the massive room with slow, mechanical clicks and shifts.

The square block split in two, with both equal ends lifting into the air and folding out as a smaller wooden block extended out from the center. Coming to a rest in a slightly elevated position, I glanced over at the gridlock pattern that spread across this wooden board, creating an eight-by-eight grid of different colored, yet equally sized

213

boxes.

A chess board.

"A gift from when I was younger," Henry monotonously interjected as he reached underneath the table, grasping onto a carrier of pieces I had failed to notice, "While far cruder than something Bellhollow could produce, it serves its purpose as a bastion of entertainment. Do you play?" I brought a confused hand to my chin as Henry wordlessly organized the pieces on each side. The pieces were carved out of wood, perfectly resembling each of the figures in an almost meticulous manner. My pieces were of a lighter shade, clearly carved out of some form of pine while his were far darker in their complexion, most likely made up of maple or mahogany.

Probably mahogany. Far cleaner and nicer for consistent use.

"I used to," I eventually divulged, "It's been a while since I've genuinely partaken in such an activity." Henry let out a single suppressed chuckle behind his left hand as he set down the last piece, placing his folded hands directly in front of him.

"That's perfect. No one else in this place has even touched a chess board, let alone sat down long enough to comprehend its rules. So, why don't we play a game?" Without a word, I grabbed onto the rightmost knight piece as I always have, feeling the grooves of its snout and ears as I placed it up and to the left.

He's speaking more than he did previously. Either he's incredibly standoffish to strangers, or he wants something from me...

"Diving headfirst into it I see," Henry acknowledged as he moved the pawn directly in front of the queen forward two spaces, "You think you have me figured out?" I remained silent as I positioned the pawn in front of the king one space forward, watching as he moved another pawn two spaces in front of his bishop. I took the other knight piece and placed it up and to the right, watching as he immediately placed one of his bishops two spaces in front of my first knight.

"If I were a Bellhollow soldier," Henry interpolated abruptly as I slid the bottom left rook to the right one space, "And I had just massacred several men and women I had encountered in order to steal riches and other goods from them, do I deserve death like my victims?" He moved his first pawn forward as I let out a sigh.

"No one deserves to die Henry," I countered as I eliminated his first pawn, sliding mine up and to the left as I took the first mahogany piece, "We're all people, but while killing is unsavory I would take his life if I ever encountered him to prevent the snuffing out of other lives." Henry gave a faint snicker as he moved the queen diagonally two spaces to my left.

"At least you're honest. But, what if I was doing this to provide for my starving family? Say times have been difficult in Bellhollow, and the only way I found I could ensure the health of my family was stealing and murder." I gave an audible sound of realization as I moved my rightmost bishop one space diagonally left. Hiding his features behind his mask, his icy eyes betrayed him as he realized I was not falling into any of his deliberate pitfalls and ploys.

"Evil is evil Henry. Whatever motivations you once had were thrown away the moment you resorted to murder to further your goals." Henry gave a dead laugh as I could see his mask curl up slightly, revealing that he hid a bemused smirk underneath. He moved his knight directly beside the queen, lurking behind a pawn that acted as bait.

His whole game appears to be baiting and luring away my smaller pieces.

"You're wise enough to not lie directly to my face. I'm not surprised though; it is a very human response. Most people like yourself would arrest or kill the man for his crimes, no matter the intentions; unable to control the runaway emotion festering in their heads." I castled my king behind the rook after he spoke, watching as he sent the other knight two spaces in front of his rook.

"What is your game in all this?" I questioned the darkened form sitting in front of me, sliding the pawn in front of the queen forward one space, "You want something from me, so you might as well just say it." His royal blue eyes narrowed as he slid the left most rook right beside his king.

"As perceptive as I expected, impressive," Henry remarked as I crossed my arms over my chest, refusing to play until he explained, "You're right. I did not challenge myself for a simple battle of wits." His cerulean eyes hardened as he glared into my hazel ones, threatening to burn through me with his gaze.

Every bit of joy and playful banter that existed previously just vanished.

"Why are you really here?" He questioned as I relented and slid the pawn on the far left two spaces up, my arm stiffening as I pulled it back.

"Same reason everyone is here," I simply stated as he pushed the pawn in the top left corner forward two spaces, "I didn't have a purpose before I discovered what you all were fighting back, something that could threaten so many lives. So, I choose to fight alongside you. You fight against this world's inner depravity, so it made sense."

"Don't give me that stereotypical rubbish," he maintained with venomous passive aggression, his words seeping into the quiet writings of the books around us, "Everyone has a purpose, and yet yours defies all reasoning." He moved the rightmost rook three spaces in front of my king.

"Are you accusing me of being a liar?" I questioned as I took another pawn, watching as he scurried his queen back and away diagonally one space, "If so, then you should know I saw evil plaguing that village: plain and simple. I was separated from Jack, and Mara discussed with me how you folks, the Sentinels, served a more refined purpose. As

I stated previously, I had nothing coming here, so you all gave me something to fight for."

"And I never doubted that was the truth," Henry cut in as I slid the furthest right pawn up one space, "What I am accusing you of is hiding an ulterior desire beneath that veil of truth." I remained silent as the blue-eyed shadow pushed the pawn directly in front of the mahogany king forward two spaces. I took out one of his knights with that right most pawn, watching as his bishop retreated one space.

"Katrina constantly tells me my paranoia is unjustified, but what would you do in my position Connor? Someone none of us have ever met appears at the doorstep of our base one day, claiming he wishes to join us because he has no purpose. A man who exists without a purpose is a dead man."

"Then why only question me?" I demanded as another pawn moved forward two spaces, oblivious of the arguments their creators were engaged in, "My brother and Mara are both in the same situation as I am. They both have nothing like I do."

"Don't be ridiculous," Henry spat as he edged the rightmost pawn two spaces up, "You're either too oblivious to notice something so obvious, or you yourself are purposely ignoring the truth of the matter." I moved the queen diagonally up and to the left one space, watching as he planted his queen one space right. I glared at him as I waited for him to finish his thought.

"Your brother has a purpose. He was undeniably connected to the people who died in that village. Although on the surface you two hold similar ambitions, his determination to be a part of us is fueled by watching so many people he cared about get cut down. Mara… I'm not absolutely certain what her story is, however I feel an odd amount of dedication within her. I will attempt to question her soon. So much harder to track down than you are." I nudged another pawn

217

forward as his last knight retreated away from the battlefield. The pawn in front of my king scuttled up one space as his bishop moved up to protect their king.

"The others saw an aspect of you they immediately trusted; something that constitutes someone worthy of being a part of us even though you've only been here for days," Henry rambled on as my left most knight moved forward, "So tell me, Connor Illium, why are you really here? Is your purpose for being here perhaps…different than we were led to believe?" He moved the rook one space to the left of his king, strangely not castling when he could have done so.

He couldn't possibly know every minute thought running through my brain. How could he possibly think I'm here for nefarious purposes?

Unless he speaks about tracking down the knight and mom, in which case how would he even know that?

He wouldn't, unless he spoke to Jack or Katrina that is.

That is entirely possible you idiot!

What's the matter? There's no shame in telling him what I also hope to accomplish by coming here.

But you don't truly know how the others would react to such a revelation from an almost stranger...

"I fight with you because you represent hope and change in this world, something everyone can appreciate even if they're unaware of who you even are. I desired to assist you because you were all I had, and as such I wished to contribute as much as I could to you in the hopes that tragedies like Eincrest, or what happened to my family, will never be repeated."

A stillness came over the air as the two of us stared at each other, his mannequin-like features glaring into mine. I could tell his eyes widened when I mentioned my family, a factor I mentioned to show him that I truly meant every word.

"Um…is something the matter?" the quiet voice of Ellia muttered beside us, causing both of our bright eyes to direct towards her, "Because i-if so I can take my le-"

"Nothing seriously important Ms. Rede. In fact, I was just about to depart," Henry relented as he stood up from the chair, its legs creaking as he stood and slid the dust from his gloved palms, "Apologies for disturbing you, Connor Illium." Without another word he walked around the table and began marching towards the doorway, his black cloak trailing behind him. I faced the incomplete chessboard as the door behind me creaked as it slid open.

Glancing at the board as Ellia scurried away back to her corner of this library, I noticed that the board had changed slightly as Henry passed me by.

The king...my king.

The brightly colored piece lay defeated on its side, the wooden ornament on the tip facing me as I became aware it was the only other piece knocked over.

Its pawns and other pieces surrounded their fallen leader, crying out as they realized that despite attaining no casualties in this battle, they had most certainly lost the war.

18

Jack and Connor: A New Calling

"**D**o you have any idea what Katrina could be summoning us for?" I asked, "I had a pleasant nap going there before someone violently punched my door." Serena shrugged nonchalantly, while Henry gave a grunt in response. His heavy footsteps almost startled me with every movement he made, although the loud thudding of Serena's boots within this space wasn't helping much either.

"I really wish I knew, but I honestly have no idea," she replied, "It's gotta be vital though to have us summoned in such a formal manner." Reaching the wooden gateway between us and her, she quickly flung open the large door of Katrina's office. I let out a surprised whistle at the mounds of paperwork that littered the wooden desk, ones which towered over us like deities.

Surprising that the desk has remained sturdy this whole time.

Glancing at Katrina, it looked like the blond woman hadn't slept at all last night. Dark bags lurked underneath her reddened purple eyes, and her blond hair was a matted mess of curls and wires. She was hastily scribbling on a piece of paper, the handwriting almost entirely illegible to me.

Obviously hearing us come in, her eyes darted between us and the paper as her frantic scribbling came to an end.

"You three," she blurted out, "Get in here, and close the door while you're there." Henry slowly shut the door behind us as we cautiously stepped closer, the only sounds being the heaviness of our trio of boots and the frantic writings of her quill.

She hastily threw that last paper off the table, my eyes drifting to the large pile surrounding her desk littered with discarded paperwork. Serena and Henry both exchanged glances, with the former appearing incredibly concerned.

Avelina rested on a wall nearby said desk, casually reading a book while taking fleeting glances at her leader. Her spear was attached to her back, freshly cleaned after our scuffle yesterday. Her outfit also had the addition of a black jacket to accompany her attire.

"Katrina," Henry declared apprehensively, "Was there...something you needed?" Katrina jerkily averted her attention away from us, glancing down at the paperwork wall slowly building around her.

This woman is...alright something's definitely wrong.

"I've been gathering...reports," she muttered while running a hand through her matted hair, "A supposed sighting of Zain, this time in a village maybe an hour away. It's unconfirmed...but it's reported that he went in alone, and reduced the town to a similar state as Eincrest was." I could feel the air in the room grow tense at her final declaration, my skin growing cold as the words hit me. Avelina's eyes narrowed at the discussion of Eincrest, taking a renewed interest in whatever book she was reading.

I involuntarily balled my fists together as I was reminded of what Zain did to Eincrest; of the men, the women, the *children* that were killed during that attack.

What if we had arrived sooner?

I shook the all too familiar thought out of my head, focusing again

221

on Katrina's words.

We did what we could, and that's all that matters.

"As you are all aware, this mysterious man first cropped up in violent capacity recently in that tiny village of Eincrest, where the two brothers and Ms. Rockwell encountered him and his forces. He also managed to pick a fight with the other three who left a while ago, although the Byron heir was the only one largely injured. Our spy couldn't get close to that village early on without potential harm coming to her as well, but he has apparently not scurried his way back to Bellhollow yet. It's possible that's where he will be heading now." I sighed aloud and gritted my teeth as I heard Serena grip onto her shirt, her hands shaking as her knees shivered along with them. Katrina took a long gulp from her drink on the table, setting it down with a slam that may have cracked the wooden desk she sat in.

"The reason I've called you three here is because we've been too careless in casting aside his threat for too long," she explained, "I have not informed the large wing of the military about this on purpose, as who knows what they would do. I've instead solely informed the Heartwood Senate. The government in Heartwood wishes for us to show zero tolerance for any terrible acts such as these, and the military cannot get its hands dirty without breaking out in full on war. Only members of the Senate know what is going on as far as I know." I pondered her words for a moment, before posing a simple statement.

"Ma'am with all due respect he's invading our territory," I pointed out, "He is literally a single man against an entire country, so if the military sent a squad out to eliminate him it wouldn't be cause for any war, as he's clearly a terrorist attacking on his volition. Besides, if the man is traveling alone then he can't grovel behind minions to throw up as shields."

"It's...not that simple," Katrina countered, "The government within

Bellhollow can be rather…volatile, as can our own. Both sides have been itching to prove their might to each other, despite the protests of the blue bloods in power now."

"Yeah, like they know what it's like to actually fight." Avelina flashed me an irate expression as I instinctively faltered under her gaze. I murmured a swift but biting apology.

"Why us?" I asked again, "I mean Connor was there as well when we faced Zain, so he knows fairly well what he can do." She took another gulp from her drink, gasping for air dramatically afterwards.

"I need a small group to lead," Avelina cut in, shutting her book and tucking it into a pocket within her jacket, "I have two people who work incredibly well together, with one of them being a gifted healer. Finally, I required one person who actually fought against him and survived." Avelina glued her eyes onto me, testing me to see if I would ask anything else.

"And besides," Katrina interjected, causing Avelina and I to face her direction, "I need both Connor and Mara for something major as well. I trust the four of you to track Zain down, but whatever happens do not engage. He is too dangerous to be faced with just you four. He'll kill all of you, and I don't know about you but I have quite the aversion to dying." Her indigo eyes, tinted red from strain or lack of sleep, glared into us as she waited for any objections or further questions. With none, she shut her eyes for a moment as she continued.

"Meet up with our spy near that village and send them back when you determine Zain's location. We'll send reinforcements as quickly as possible to capture him." She took one final gulp of her drink, staring into it with surprise upon noticing it was empty.

She growled angrily a slew of curses to herself before chucking the empty mug at a wall, shattering it into many pieces.

It was then when I noticed Ellia in the corner of the room near the bookshelf, who made a slight gasp from the sound of the exploding cup. She rushed forward and cleaned up the shards of porcelain, hastily depositing them into a nearby canister for trash.

She was already back in that specific corner nearby Avelina in an instant, staring worryingly at Katrina while daintily picking back up the book she dropped when she was startled, adjusting her spectacles as she did so.

Katrina held onto her forehead as she let out a raspy sigh, sweat running down her clearly tired face as she grabbed another piece of paper and began filling it out.

"All this stress and I still have to fill out all of this stupid paperwork," she murmured to herself, trying and failing to keep that comment to herself, "Dismissed, and please bring Connor and Mara here when you can." As we turned to hastily exit away from our clearly irritated commander, I noticed Ellia step forward, halting Avelina in her tracks as the rest of us continued forward.

"Be safe out there, Avelina." Ellia began, before shifting her eyes over to our departing forms, "A-And keep those three out of trouble as well!"

"Ah don't worry Ellia it'll be alright," Avelina reassured, pulling the book she was reading out of her jacket pocket, "I'll have the book I borrowed from you to keep me company while I'm gone. Now you focus on making sure Katrina doesn't throw all of those papers into a fire when none of us are looking." Ellia gave a big smile and laugh as Avelina patted her on the shoulder, hurrying to follow behind us she put the book back away in her jacket. Ellia returned to her position beside Katrina, who looked as if she was five seconds away from pulling all her hair out.

"Ms. Ward, you really need to take a break. I'm…a tad worried about you is all." Those were the last words I heard spoken from the room before the door shut, sealing in the exhausted blonde commander. I paused for a few seconds, ensuring we couldn't be heard through the door.

"What's got her all riled up?" I finally asked Avelina after taking a few steps away. She let out an exasperated sigh at the question, rubbing her temples.

"She's always been like this I'm afraid, or at least she has for as long as I've known her," she lamented to herself, "She's got a lot of responsibility on her shoulders to protect those people in time, too much responsibility in my opinion. The stress gets to her, and before she even realizes it, she's stayed up all through the night slaving away at her duties." The soft giggle of Serena to my right ended her speech, much to my surprise.

"That, and she despises all that stupid paperwork. And she hates it even more when she pumps herself full of coffee like she always does to power through those nights." I looked at her quizzically, thinking of the drink she kept reaching for throughout the briefing.

"She drinks a large amount of coffee whenever she's stressed," Avelina clarified as she walked beside us, "It's almost like an addiction, thinking it'll help her focus. It does a little...but she gets a tad irritating to be around."

"And she gives none of it to us? Not a good quality for a leader if you ask me." I joked, hoping to alleviate the mood. Serena giggled loudly at my proclamation, and I could see Henry's mask twist up slightly, his version of a smile I suppose. Avelina remained silent, although the quiet smirk she gave showed she was amused.

During this, I accidentally bumped into someone, not noticing them because of my conversation with the three others around. We both promptly fell to the floor, with a large stack of books and parchments flying up into the air as well. They fell all around us as I looked up, hearing the person groan in annoyance at their work fluttering around them.

"Darn it! Ah sorry about that. I just couldn't see anything ahead of me with all these books in my arms." A familiar voice sighed. I noticed the black hair covering his eyes, a fact which I frequently pointed out covered the brilliance that twinkled and shined within his shimmering eyes.

I smirked to myself, as I had just run into the exact person I was looking for.

"Hey Connor," I proclaimed as vibrantly as I could, "What are you doing storming through the hallways with that massive stack of books? I thought I told you to focus on socializing so you don't end up as some awkward, pale gremlin who stays hidden in his room." He rubbed the back of his head as he lightly smiled, one of the only traits he inherited from our father.

"Well…this place has quite an expansive library. Someone has to make use of it besides Ellia. She said it was okay to take them out of the library, so I took as many as I could." I laughed to myself on the floor as I helped my brother up from the ground.

Of course my brother managed to find a library here.

"Uh could you help me pick them up?" He asked. I nodded silently as I bent over to collect the fallen books, with the three others eventually joining along to help. A somewhat awkward silence filled the air as the sound of papers sliding and covers slamming resounded in the hallway.

Henry eventually broke the silence, picking up a large book off the ground.

"*The White-Haired People* by William J. Walker. This is a book about Pyrnesse and the Zevron." I glanced over at Connor.

Why would he be researching about the Zevron?

I knew one of his theories was that the knight who…killed our parents may have been a Zevron, but I still didn't understand the obsession he put behind this new race specifically.

Then again…it may tie back to that pendant.

Mom's pendant.

I saw that wind that Connor made during his skirmish with Katrina, whipping in and around his arm like a tornado. It was impressive, and I've never seen him use something like it.

It seemed that Connor discovered he was different, and learned how to use his gift through that pendant.

I even tried to build energy within the palm of my hand, seeing if I could do it like Connor could. Alas, to my dismay I could not.

I just ended up giving myself a light headache from the mental strain.

"I'd like to know more about them and understand them is all. I didn't study much about the other nations when we were little, so I thought it was time to learn" Henry paused for a moment, then ended up just nodding. I decided to examine a book's title myself.

"*Inside the Mind of Cecilia Boldeveur* by Judy W. Who is she?" Connor stopped smiling for a moment, shutting his eyes.

"It's an old war tale," Connor explained, "Tells the story of one battalion of an army attempting to seal away a god, but from the perspective of their tactician Cecilia. The story is…somewhat cliche in my opinion, but the tactics presented by Cecilia are incredibly fascinating. Her tactics appear to always be three steps ahead of the enemy at all times."

I laughed suddenly, startling my brother, "So she was just like you Connor?"

He shrugged, "I suppose."

We were interrupted by Serena's soft giggles, causing us to both turn and look at her quizzically.

"Not all of these are riveting tales like that," she sharply laughed as she held up a small blue book.

"*The Zevron and The Mage* by M. U. This is a famous romance novel," she teased, "I never took you for a lover of romantics Connor." Connor flushed a deep red as he snatched the book from Serena's hands. Not that it took much effort anyway, as she was laughing too hard to even notice.

Serena had fallen on the ground clutching her stomach, laughing harder than I've ever seen her laugh.

"You should've seen the look on your face!" she yelled out between laughs and gasps. Connor stacked his books finally and looked away, his face still flushed. Avelina gave a resigned grin, while Serena was down for the count and Henry remained as unreadable as ever. When the silence returned, I recalled why I was going to find my brother in the first place.

"Connor, Katrina asked that we fetch both you and Mara for something in her office. She mentioned it after giving us our mission ten minutes ago." Connor cocked his head quizzically.

"A mission?" he asked, "You four are going on a mission?"

Ah crap.

Avelina beat me to it before I could say anything else.

"It's a mission to track down Zain before he gets too far. She wanted a small group, so she asked the four of us." Avelina trailed off as she began walking away, with the other two following closely behind without another word. I could tell that his mood immediately soured at the revelation: his smile dropping as he glanced away from the four of us.

"I'll be in her office immediately with Mara," he said with his hair covering his eyes. Usually when I needed to know what Connor was thinking, I just needed to look into his eyes. To me, he always held a readable expression; a twinkling brilliance hidden beneath his bright eyes. The cogs in his brain never stopped turning.

But right now, I couldn't tell what he was thinking. His eyes seemed dull and glassy, an emptiness lurking inside that chilled me where I stood.

He better not go back to how he was before. I thought so much progress was made and yet.

"Be safe out there you four. And make sure you track down that pompous fool before he puts anyone else at risk." He flashed us all a hollow smile, before turning towards his room, leaving me alone in the barren hallway as Connor put all of his attention into balancing all the books in his arms.

Let's hope he doesn't do anything irrational.

I chuckled in defeat at that thought, plugging my pockets with my hands.

Of course he will. He is my brother after all.

I sighed as my brother continued down towards his room, walking opposite to me as I noticed his fingers begin to twitch, before turning away from him down the path the other three had already begun treading down.

* * *

Slamming the many books onto the desk nearby, my arms continued to shake profusely as my fingers gripped the leather coverings.

Easy Connor, you need to calm yourself down.

Calm down? Why on earth were we not sent on the mission that Katrina knew was salient to us?

Perhaps they required a small team? After all, they are attempting to track him down as swiftly as possible.

I fought him! Jack and I probably are the most knowledgeable ones here on how he engages in combat, so we would be an invaluable asset to this team. And...she knew above all else that I believed Zain could lead me in the right direction towards mom.

In a way it makes sense. After all, we are rookies to this group and need to participate more if we are to be trusted.

"Then why send Jack?" I yelled to myself, feeling as if the walls themselves were retreating from me, "It isn't fair! I'm equally as capable so why was I left out of the mix?" I sidestepped as the wooden chair beside me tipped over, the furniture clattering to the ground.

"Is it because I didn't beat her in our duel? Did she think I needed longer before I was ready for something real? Something that might actually lead me to what I've been searching for this whole time!" I was knocked out of the argument with myself due to the sound of two knocks to my left, softly pattering against the door beside me in a firm tone. I readjusted my shirt as I took a deep breath in, savoring the smell of aged wood as my heartbeat began to steady. Hoping nothing looked out of the ordinary, I stepped over and opened the door.

Standing in front of the door with her gloved right fist still raised was Mara, her green eyes staring directly forward in an almost unfocused manner. Her eyes refocused once she realized the door she was next to was suddenly wide open, and she took a half-step back in surprise.

"Oh, hello Connor," Mara said with a slight tint to her cheeks, noticing that she was glancing into my room behind me. Following her eyes, I saw she was staring down at the chair laying slain on the ground, along with a couple books I didn't realize I had thrown haphazardly off the table.

"Are you busy?" I shook my head firmly as I grabbed onto a black cloak Serena had been kind enough to give me earlier, replacing the one I lost in the fight in Eincrest. I threw it over my shoulders as I stepped through the doorway, relishing its warm embrace as I heard the door click shut behind me.

"Just reorganizing my room a little," I replied steadily, "Are you here to retrieve me for Katrina?" Mara gave a quiet nod at my question, already stepping away from me in the direction of the leader's lair.

Still as quiet as always it seems, despite being here as long as me.

But...at the same time she feels more comfortable in my presence. I don't know what it is...but her general vibe is...different to me. Perhaps our meeting in the forest helped her feel more open.

Coming to a swift pause in front of Katrina's door, Mara stood incredibly still with her back turned to me. Whirling around in an instant, I was blinded by a tornado of brunette hair momentarily as something latched onto my right wrist. I instinctively tried to wrench my hand away as my vision became clearer, noting that Mara had grabbed onto my wrist and was inspecting the top of my hand.

This scene looks familiar...

She threw the hand to the side as I gripped my wrist, watching as a puff of air exited her mouth as she groaned in dejection.

"You don't have it..." I sighed at the all too familiar verbiage as I placed my hands on my hips, pushing the soft cloak aside.

"This conversation seems all too familiar to me," I asserted with a huff, while still maintaining a tranquil visage, "Why are all of you coming up to me inspecting my hand like it's some ancient tome?" Brushing her gloved hands together, the woman crossed her arms as she stood in front of the office doors, staring away from me.

"The brand of the eagle," Mara finally announced, "Engraved in purple upon the skin of the right hand, soaring high into the distant sky. Supposedly the eagle flies off in search of prey, although others claim the bird is a protector of some sort instead." I narrowed my eyes in confusion at her vague explanation.

"The brand of a Zevron?" I questioned Mara, "Well, as you can see by my lack of blue eyes and white hair, I'm visibly not a member of that hidden race. Besides, a member of them hasn't been seen outside of Pyrnesse in generations."

I knew about the white hair and blue eyes from my mother, but thank that book for telling me about that brand. Helps find any Zevron who could be masking their appearance.

Tightening the folding of her arms, the woman silently turned on her heel away from me, grabbing onto the handle and twisting it with a screech before I could interrupt her.

Why would she ask me that? Is she joking?

I don't think she's capable of joking...or even lying for that matter.

In that case, then why on earth would she ask me that? Doesn't she have a pair of eyes that can undeniably see I don't look like a Zevron?

Henry asked me too, but at least Mara was courteous enough to slightly explain herself.

Unless she and Henry grew the personality to be in on the same joke.

Letting out a sigh, I rubbed the space between my eyes as I felt my brain fold in confusion. Shoving my hands in my pants pockets in resignation, I followed along behind Mara with my eyes pointed towards the ground, hearing the door click shut behind me.

Glimpsing up and out of my thoughts, I whistled to myself as I stared at the wall of paperwork that surrounded us on all sides, threatening to collapse and drown me in their treacherous depths.

The first figure I noticed was Katrina's assistant Ellia, who sat passed out in the corner of the room beside the emptied bookcase, existing outside of that library or her room for one of the first times. Her spectacles lay beside her, lying upside down on the ground slightly out of reach. In her sleeping lap rested various papers and parchments that were splayed out with neat writing, albeit for the last line where she clearly trailed off the paper as sleep overcame her. Her snores were soft and quiet, as a tired yet anxious smile crept onto her sleeping lips.

At the center table sat the blond-haired woman, who was at the moment frantically scurrying her words on a final line of a paper on her desk, the writing making even less sense than they already did.

At the final swipe of the black ink, the white feather found itself back into its well with a flourish. Her indigo eyes immediately shot back to us, a sense of calm filling her eyes that juxtaposed mine.

"Ah good you two made it," Katrina muttered as we both stepped forward, "Arrived right as I finished all this blasted paperwork those military men make me do. Sometimes I wonder if they're just handing me their own reports or applications to do for them. Now I can get a moment's rest before they pile more of this crap onto me in the coming days." Sticking her hands together as her elbows thumped against the wooden table, her worn down eyes reverted to us. Mara was standing slightly in front of me with her hands behind her back, while my own continued to rest contently within my pockets.

"As you two are new, and you two will be undergoing a mission without any senior members of the group...it would be best if I informed you of the system we have around here." Setting aside the papers so she could better rest her arms upon her desk, she stared at the two of us as I kept everything I wished to scream at her bottled up.

Let her explain, then I can calmly illustrate my gripes with this entire situation.

"Every month or so, I am given a set of missions from the higher ups in the military which matches our mantra, for which they desire me to pass this down to every Sentinel in this base. Oftentimes, it's miscellaneous complaints and tasks brought up at council meetings or directly to those in power, and some of them make their way to us. We simply proclaim we are emissaries of the military, or that we just so happened to arrive in town at the time of their problem. Either way, they always manage to believe it." Sinking back into her mighty chair, Katrina moved her hair aside as she stared at the two of us, pausing briefly with the expectancy of some form of question.

The two of us just remained silent, most likely for vastly different reasons.

"Anyways, as will become commonplace for you all as you spend more time here, I have granted you your first mission as swiftly as possible to ensure you attain a better sense of how we run things. Most missions will be smaller, such as clearing out a group of bandits plaguing a town or undercutting a corrupt mayor...or any other boring crap that the military spills on us despite being completely separate from their control." Her eyes had narrowed slightly as she spoke, her lips tightening as her nose curled up in disgust.

She seems to hold a large deal of spite for her higher-ups.

Curious...

Katrina let out a deep sigh as she pursed her hands together, shutting her eyes softly as she finished her mini rant.

"Forgive me for my outburst, I'm just a bit tired is all. Anyways, I have a task for you two." Both of us instinctively stepped forward, edging slightly closer to the overwhelming papers and desk.

"Eincrest," Katrina explained with conviction itching from her voice, "The village was utterly destroyed as you well know Connor, leaving nothing behind for Avelina, Henry, and Serena to find after recovering Jack. Even so, human beings have the distinct quality of surviving such drastic changes to their lives. Go there and find as many people as you can; injured or uninjured. We'll deal with housing and transportation once we have a better sense of the remaining numbers. That is the mission I give to you. It shouldn't take too long, so I thought it would be a pleasant rookie mission."

I stepped slightly in front of the brunette right beside me, steadying myself for the words I was going to proclaim.

"Katrina Ward," I began, watching as her eyebrow ticked up in curiosity, "While I understand that this mission is a necessity, I believe that engaging within-"

"No. Absolutely not." Immediately cut off, my mouth sat agape for a brief second as I stood in stunned silence, perplexed at her sudden interjection as she stared at me with the same sullied expression.

"I beg your pardon?"

"I absolutely forbid you from tagging along on the surveillance mission I sent the other four on earlier. I'm assuming that's what you meant to tell me, no?" My fists clenched together as I glanced down at the floor with a scoff, realizing I had just proved her point in silence.

"You and Mara are rookies Connor, newcomers to this group. I will not send you on such an imperative and potentially dangerous mission with no prior experience on the matter."

She has the nerve to spit out that lie to me...

"Then why would you send Jack along with them on such a paramount mission?" I countered quietly as I could fill my inner anger bubbling uncontrollably to the surface, "My brother is a newcomer just like the rest of us. So why is he allowed to partake in such a vital mission while we are not?"

"I needed to send someone who had already faced him previously, and could help guide the group in the unlikely scenario that things turn dicey."

"You know what I meant Katrina," I growled out, "I told you my theory over Zain and his pendant a while ago, so this would've been my chance to prove it. We both have faced him and seen what we could do, so you could've enlisted the help of both of us so that we can finally attain that lead we need, and kill him for what he's done!" A long silence filled the air as I realized that I had raised my voice exponentially, uncharacteristically shouting within the confined space. I swear even Mara took a single step back.

You damn fool. How hard is it to keep all those emotions in check?

Katrina's expression never differed as she stared into me, letting out a sigh as she shut her eyes and rubbed her forehead.

"...Henry came to me hours ago, and suggested that I only select Jack for such a mission if it ever were to arise." The silence perforated the air, weighing incredibly on me as I felt the weight of her words crushing me down into the hardwood floors of her office.

"I...I beg your pardon?"

"Henry has always been the most paranoid of us all, and while I believe he often focuses on that mindset too much, it's that mentality that makes him such a strong advisor to me." Staring into me with her piercing indigo eyes, the motherly softness that once lurked beneath had almost flickered away, replaced with another parental emotion: disappointment.

"While I don't share his sentiments about you, Henry distrusts you to a certain degree, believing you haven't proven yourself yet as a likely ally. Even if I desired to send you off with them, I will not willingly send two people together on a mission who do not fully trust each other. The mission could be screwed up in a deadly way."

"But what if I-" She held up her right hand to pause my argumentation, cutting me off mid-sentence as she lowered the hand back onto her desk.

"You're a good fit for this group Connor, but perhaps to a certain extent I agree with Henry on this. I see intense resentment and an unhealthy obsession growing deeply inside you. It's understandable why you hold so much raw emotion in your heart, but it's blinding you even now. This is a mission simply to observe first, then strike, and I worry that you'll blindly charge at him instead. That type of emotion is not boiling over within your brother, so that was another reason I selected him over you. Leave the butcher of Eincrest to them." I could feel the knuckles of my fingers turning white from how consistently I squeezed my fist tightly together, glancing to the floor to hide my fiery expression.

"That is all I have for you so please...do this mission as I have told

236

you so. If they find and require reinforcements to eliminate him by the time you are back, I will send you on that force to take him down. Don't put your own life at risk for no reason. As you said, your mother isn't likely to lie down and die. You'll have similar opportunities for information in the future, and you may even receive the same type of briefing if I were to send you on the secondary force." With that final note, she picked up a small brown book from her desk and began writing within it, plucking the quill from its ink well.

"Dismissed...and you may leave the base as soon as possible."

"But I-"

"Dismissed!" With that final note, I let out a resolute sigh and turned completely around, walking towards the door with my hands back in my pockets. I could hear the light, purposeful steps of Mara's boots right behind me.

You blew it, you could have convinced her if you didn't lash out like that.

Unlikely...she had her mind set already before I even entered the room.

Perhaps that is correct. I have to keep a level head about this.

Perform the mission. Find as many people as I can.

Bring them right back, so they can be safe and so I can prove myself to Katrina...and Henry.

"You really want to kill him, don't you?" I cracked my head to the left in surprise as I heard Mara echo these words, speaking for the first time since before we entered the office.

If I didn't know any better, she sounds almost conversational...

I let out a deep sigh as I pushed open the main exit of the base, making sure that I didn't bump into the nearby chair as I did so. From the looks of it, neither of us required anything from our rooms as we left, with myself ensuring that my dirk lay dormant within its sheath just in case it was necessary.

I held the door open for the green-eyed brunette before answering, slamming it shut behind her.

"I'd be a liar if I said I didn't," I confessed as I began to walk in the direction of where Katrina said Eincrest was relative to here, knowing it would probably be a couple hours of mindless walking. I glanced up at the sky, noting that the sun hadn't even come to rest directly overhead.

At least the morning is still young...and the air is reasonably chill.

"I watched that man butcher so many for a pendant like this," I recounted as I pulled the accessory out of my own shirt as a demonstration, "Items like this hold so much power and yet, how much power would it need to possess to convince a man to commit such atrocities?"

Instead of answering me, her eyes became transfixed with the green jewelry I gripped by its band, her eyes of the same shade scanning over every detail.

"So that explains it," Mara muttered to herself as we resumed walking, her head turning back to the path ahead, "You use something that doesn't require Zevron blood to activate. It all makes sense now." I gave her a questioning stare as our feet crunched into the gluey mud beneath us, threatening to swallow our boots into its repulsive depths.

"You assumed I was a Zevron because I could perform this...magic?" I asked, to which she replied with a stern nod, "I thought that fact would be obvious. I don't possess any of the distinct characteristics those people carry with them." Mara shook her head softly as she ran a gloved hand through her brunette hair.

"Not if you're half," Mara elucidated in a matter-of-fact tone, "For the rare people who are half-human half-Zevron, they often lack the hair and eye color of their magical guardian." Pausing for a moment, I noticed that her eyes seemed to trace throughout the nature around us, scanning through the ranges of green that surrounded us on all sides.

This staring is different from her usual glancing around, the type she's still implementing periodically to scan the road ahead.

No...it's almost like she's staring in...admiration...

I smiled internally to myself as I realized where her eyes were wandering.

Towards the same green seas that have so mesmerized her.

"Those who are half possess the brand of a purple eagle on their right hand," Mara continued as she raised her own gloved hand as a demonstration, pointing to the very center of the back of her hand, "No matter who you are, if there is any amount of Zevron blood within you, then that crest will appear there without fail." Lowering her hand, Mara readjusted the glove to ensure it remained steady on her hand as it fell to her side. She turned her head back to the foliage around her, her blank eyes twinkling with the same warmth she directed towards the verdant surroundings.

"These half-bloods can perform magic like the Zevron, although often it will be far weaker than full-bloods. That pendant is a tool that allows humans to perform certain magic like the Zevron do, however the power will be far weaker and more limited if you don't possess any Zevron blood. I do not believe the full power of those pendants can be utilized by humans, forcing humans to either have limited power through a pendant or lack it entirely."

"Then what about Serena?" I interjected as her words sunk in, "She possesses the ability to heal most wounds and yet I've never seen a crest on her hand."

"That...is a factor I've been trying to figure out myself," Mara admitted as her eyes constantly switched between scanning ahead and watching nature bloom, "She is in no way a Zevron who could be hiding using magic, as she requires an extraordinary deal of energy to even heal a broken bone or a substantial gash. True Zevron do not possess that handicap." I nodded my head along as I waited for her to continue speaking, before shortly realizing that this conversation was over.

And she doesn't seem to be one who enjoys small talk.

I placed the pendant back around my neck as we continued to walk, pondering the new information Mara had just blessed me with.

All Zevron possess a crest, whether they are full-blood or not. And they can all perform magic.

All the others must assume that I can do that...wind punch or whatever it was because I have their blood. But no...

This pendant does it all I suppose...thank you mom.

Is it possible that mother or father could've been a Zevron in hiding using magic?

But why would she hide who she was even from us?

Better question, why would any Zevron hide who they were from us?

As soon as the thought entered my mind, I let out a cynical chuckle to myself, suppressing it so Mara wouldn't hear it and have questions.

Of course, because of the way our ignorant species would react to another race with powers beyond our comprehension.

The ugliness power like that brings out in people unnerves us all I suppose. Perhaps everyone in Aelton just assumes Zevron are all just like Zain: power hungry killers.

I sent myself into deep thought as we continued our path towards Eincrest, as the two of us went off on our first mission, utterly silent.

19

Jack: The Hopeless Search

"We should be almost to the village he supposedly appeared in. Keep your guard up. We have no idea what the state of this place will be." I strode as quickly as I could alongside Avelina with a huff, hearing the individual steps of Serena and Henry behind me, our steps sounding heavy after a full day of traveling. Although all of us appeared to be glancing around the area vigilantly, Avelina appeared to be doing the opposite. Instead, her eyes were glued to the book she was still reading in the office.

"You don't seem to be paying much attention," I commented with slight irritation, growing tired from the constant walking, "All you seem to be focused on is…" I bent over dramatically as I stared at the book title, with Avelina never breaking her stride as she continued to read aimlessly.

"*The Dragon Slayer* or whatever." Avelina let out a single dry laugh as Serena and Henry trailed close behind, with the tangerine haired girl listening intently with the same cheeky smile.

"I'm paying enough attention, plus I have you three to also keep watch," Avelina said as she gestured to us with her off hand, "Ellia recommended this to me a day or so ago, but I just haven't had the time to read it until now. She picked out something that's almost perfect for me, although that makes sense considering how long I've been friends with that woman. I'd recommend it to you, but I think it's above your reading level." Saying the last part with the same stone-cold expression with the right amount of snark, Serena giggled behind us as Henry kept his eyes trained on our surroundings.

"Never really been a reader myself so that doesn't count," I shrugged as I gestured to the sword on my back, "Fighting's all that I really care about, so unless you have a picture book on swordplay I'm probably going to be lost." Avelina let out a single snort at my words, our boots kicking up dust with every step.

"Jack is that all you think about?"

"Eh, probably. A little unfair considering at the moment I just wanna fight you again so I can finish beating you." Avelina finally shut the book as a smirk came to her face, shutting her eyes as she shook her head and tucked it back into her jacket.

"Does it hurt sometimes Jack?" I cocked an eyebrow at her words, unsure as to what she meant.

"Does what hurt?"

"Does it hurt to be this dense?" The true meaning of her insult finally dawned on me, I feigned a dramatically offended expression as I lightly pushed her, trading the first few insults that could come to my mind.

Avelina fired a few more back at me, both of us attempting to keep a stern expression as our inner snark rose to center stage.

However, we were horribly failing. Every insult that flew out of our mouths was accompanied by a toothy grin, until eventually the both of us couldn't stop ourselves from laughing at the ridiculous level of the barbs that were shot out of our mouths.

Avelina wiped a tear from her eye as she shook her head, shining a bright smile towards me.

"You really are a handful kid," Avelina exclaimed with a laugh, "What am I gonna do with you?"

"You're the one who picked me for this mission, so now you're stuck with the consequences of your choices."

"Suppose so."

"So um," I heard Serena mutter slightly, tilting my attention towards her, "I don't want to interrupt this...tender moment, but we appear to be here and uh...something tells there was a discrepancy in the report we were given earlier." Coming to an immediate stop as Avelina and I both turned, our expressions hardened and simultaneously glanced over to see what Serena was talking about. My eyes widened as I stared upon the village.

Zain was supposed to be here...but this place...

I heard Avelina gasp as I scanned the immediate area up and down, my mouth widening as I stared upon the overhanging sign, telling me this town was known as Stagmire.

It's perfectly fine...as far as I could tell it hasn't even been touched by any form of violence.

A man who resembled a merchant based on his attire rode by on a large brown horse, giving us a smile and wave as he trotted by. The four of us continued to just gawk at the town that appeared to still be incredibly crowded, our expressions stunned.

"I...I don't understand," Avelina eventually babbled, "Were the reports wrong somehow? Did we...did we somehow end up at the wrong place?" As soon as the words exited her mouth, our current commander violently shook her head as she began taking steps towards Stagmire's gates, her spear clattering against the plate on her shoulder.

"Never mind that. We still need to explore this area to ensure that the report really was faulty. Hopefully, what we see right now is accurate, and we were luckily spared from a repeat of Eincrest."

Henry immediately hurried behind her, with Serena and I doing the same.

The streets were insanely packed with people, laughing and talking as if they had just gotten out of work or school.

"None of them seem perturbed in anyway," I commented as we moved through the bustling crowds, "How could anyone be dumb enough to not realize this place is perfectly fine?" Avelina's brow furrowed as she further examined the crowd, finding nothing except the smiling faces of men and women who knew nothing besides the life they currently lived. They didn't even notice the four of us were staring at them in such a way. Snapping her head back up towards the many buildings, Avelina turned completely around and stared at the three of us.

"Henry; you and I will try to meet with the politicians or military if there are any in the area, and we'll march straight to the town hall if we have to in order to get some answers. The military insignia will make them listen." Raising two fingers up, she pointed at the two of us, then pivoted her fingers towards the surrounding crowd.

"You two. Mingle with this crowd a little bit to find some answers. You two are the most sociable of the four of us, so try and gather as much information as you can about Zain, or if our spy is still in this area. Don't ask too many questions though; we don't need the locals confused, or worse in hysterics if they find out our reasoning." Without another word, the two of them made their way through the shifting crowds, making a beeline for the building at the far end of the road.

I felt a small force slug me in the arm in a non-threatening way as Serena smiled up at me.

"Welp, I suppose they're just gonna leave us on that note. So like them to be all moody and serious," Serena remarked as she raised her fist in the air, "Let's track him down Jack!" A couple people looked our way due to Serena's impassioned outburst, although it didn't appear Serena noticed at all, maintaining her same proud stance.

With an excited whoop and another bright smile, Serena led the way through the crowd, randomly grabbing onto people strolling by and asking them if they've seen the robed scoundrel we were looking for.

"Hiya mister! I'm looking for someone with long purple robes, pretty noticeable. Have you seen him?" "Can't say I have ma'am, I apologize."

"Miss, did you happen to see a man in purple clothes walk by here? Has a stupid pendant hanging from his neck if you need anything else to go off of." "No s-sorry kid, I can't be of any help."

"Mister I'm looking for some purple robed guy have you-" "Look little girl can't you see I'm busy with something? Run along now." Serena's eye visibly ticked at being referred to as a small child, looking like she was five seconds away from kicking his kneecaps in. I grabbed her by the shoulder and dragged her away before she could do anything.

"As much as I would like it, we can't beat up every person we come across for answers," I jokingly scolded, causing her anger to turn into slight pouting, "Forget it. Did you find out anything, because currently these people don't seem to be very cooperative?" Serena shook her head as she stared off into the distance, flashing that same resentful expression to the same well-dressed man who skulked by.

"Not a thing. There has to be someone in this town who knows where Zain is."

"Unless he was never here to begin with." Serena's brow furrowed slightly, while still maintaining that genuine smile.

"Someone hired by Ms. Rockwell would never be careless enough to not realize that," Serena defended in an uncharacteristically serious tone, before reverting to her usual smile, "If we can't find out if

Zain was here, we can sure find out where this spy is—so come on!"
Without another word, Serena sprinted off into the crowd of people
with the same boundless enthusiasm. I let out a groan as I followed
swiftly behind her, my legs sore from all our previous walking.

How does this girl have so much energy within her?

Following swiftly behind her in this massive crowd, Serena occasionally would ask random people the same question repeatedly,
receiving the same indifferent result each time as she rushed by. I
could tell Serena was slowly getting more and more agitated the more
the same result was given, her smile fading.

A sudden feeling gripped my psyche as we made our way through
the bustling group of people—a feeling that shouldn't be foreign
within such a large crowd, and yet goosebumps still traced their way
across my skin as my paranoia grew.

Someone's watching me.

I whipped my head around the entire crowd, my dirty brown hair
fluttering in my face as I scanned all around me to find the source of
this sudden surge of paranoia.

And there it was.

A brown hood ducked into the crowd around us, an appearance
that wouldn't be out of the ordinary in such a massive group of people.
However, it was clear they had swiftly looked away when my gaze
locked onto theirs. I tapped Serena on the shoulder.

"Serena, I don't know if I'm going crazy or something, but I feel
like we're being followed somehow."

"Fantastic, I thought I was the only one," she whispered to me as
we continued walking, albeit at a slightly quicker pace than before,
"Let's try and move deeper into this crowd to see if we can shake 'em."
Rushing forward at a slightly faster pace, I tugged the new brown
coat that I had been given recently close to my face, hoping to be less
suspicious despite the crowd.

The coat is okay, but it doesn't have the same charm my old one had.
I'm gonna have to slug Zain a couple times for ruining that coat.

I felt like whoever was watching us was still maintaining their gaze upon us, despite how deep we had entrenched ourselves in the crowd's depths. I maintained a sprint as I glanced back to see if I could spy the stranger that I had noticed earlier.

The crowd was thinning, and yet I couldn't find the figure anywhere.

Coming into a clearing, the two of us continued to walk as I glanced over my shoulder another time, watching as the crowd faded behind us. Turning back, I noticed that we had run into a random stretch of road where only a couple people currently perused. A couple vendors littered the streets, with other sporadic people brought from the stalls. Other than that, it was almost completely empty.

"Alright...alright Serena I think we lost whoever it was. Now let's uh...let's just keep looking to see if anyone has seen that Bellhollow bastard skulking around recently."

"You're not going to find him here anymore." Serena and I both recoiled from the hollow female voice that echoed behind us, staring wide-eyed at the woman who announced such a claim.

Or at least I think they're a woman based on their voice. It's a tad hard to tell with the porcelain mask she was wearing.

The woman was standing with her arms crossed behind us, her brown cloak flowing past her and into the dusty ground. Her long black sleeve tunic had several red lines streaking across it, extending down to her wrists where a pair of black gloves currently lurked. She stepped up to us as her knee-high armored boots crunched against the ground, keeping her bracer covered arms crossed. The hood clung tightly to her head but didn't hook onto her mask the same way Henry's did.

"If you wish to find him, looking around here won't help you at all."

"Oh yeah?" I questioned as I took a proud step towards her, watching as she remained stationary, "And how do we know that you aren't protecting his sorry ass from getting kicked back to the despicable pit he crawled out of?" As she glared into us with her chocolate brown eyes, I further examined the unique porcelain mask that currently adorned her face.

The mask had a white base, which allowed me to know it was made of some form of porcelain. However, whoever made this mask made no attempt to shape it into anything that resembled a human. There were no indents; no spaces that resembled a nose or a mouth.

There were just two eye holes, from which her bright brown eyes glared through.

Slashing diagonally across the mask was a long orange and red streak, one which contrasted the white surface it lurked on.

Her demeanor felt incredibly familiar, although I felt like I was supposed to be more unnerved than I actually was.

"Because she works for me, Jack." I darted my eyes over to the familiar voice of Avelina, who was currently walking up to us with a smile, noting that Henry wasn't present at the moment. Avelina waltzed up to us as she placed her bent elbow on the woman's shoulder, causing her to let out a restrained grunt.

"Serena and Jack, allow me to introduce you to the one and only spy of the Sentinels. Or as I like to call her...my younger sister." My own eyes widening at the revelation, Serena's grey eyes also lit up with glee as she stared at the masked woman, letting out a little squeal as she put her fists together.

"I didn't know you had a sister Ms. Rockwell!" Serena gushed, "That's so cool!" Avelina let out a light-hearted chuckle as she patted her sister on the shoulder.

"For ease you all can refer to her as Fox, as it's pertinent to keep her identity concealed even from you. She's the only spy in this country that works solely for me and not the military, and along with being my family I trust her with my entire life." As her lenient expression fell back into a stoic one, her younger sister took a confident step towards us.

Her demeanor feels so similar to Avelina's, and yet something is so much more...standoffish about it.

"He was here at one point," she stated in a light, albeit cold voice, "When I sent the report it was in anticipation over what he was planning to do, but he never did. He didn't do a single violent thing while he was here, but I hoped to eliminate him by surprise while he was alone. However, Avelina advised against it before I ever set off." Her sister let out a sigh as she shook her head, as if the two of them have had this same conversation several times before.

"I advised against it because we're in the middle of a village, and a reasonably crowded one at that. If you even made one misstep, Zain could have unleashed mayhem upon this town. Luckily, he doesn't appear to have done anything to this town, despite what your report said." Shaking her head, Avelina began walking towards the direction she came from, with Fox swiftly following behind.

"Henry and I may have found ourselves a substantial lead. I was hoping that all of us could investigate it, especially now that you found my sister." Following closely behind the two sisters, I leaned over to Serena as we exited the clearing we had just entered, receiving a few strange looks from the crowd who were now thinning behind us.

"I thought I could only deal with one, now there are two of them." Serena let out a giggle as the two in front of us rounded the corner into an alleyway, allowing us to follow swiftly behind.

"I can't believe I've never met Ms. Rockwell's sister until right now," Serena commented as we stepped into this random alleyway, "I've known her for years now, so it's weird I'm only meeting Fox now."

249

As soon as the words left her mouth, the healer let out a shrill gasp as she stared into the alleyway. As I took steps into the same place, I immediately saw why.

A man much older than us was in this alleyway with Henry. Judging by the wrinkles and balding grey hair he was in his fifties or his sixties. His attire made him appear to be a member of the upper class, based on the expensive looking black suit he wore with white frills and lining that were all clearly fit for a younger man.

The most obvious thing that I could see was that this man was currently being gripped by the collar by our blue-eyed compatriot; pinned against the wall as his feet didn't even touch the ground beneath him. His suit jacket was unbuttoned, revealing the wrinkled white collared shirt beneath. A platinum pocket watch was hanging from the shirt, clearing dislodged and steadily swinging in the chill air around us.

"Henry!" Serena shrieked, "What on earth are you doing?" Henry extended his left hand out at her interjection, silencing her before she could say anything else. Surprisingly, Henry was still able to hold the politician up with one hand, his slit-eyed gaze never deviating away from the man.

"He's the lead that we need Serena, don't worry," Avelina explained, "We caught this weasel skulking out of the council hall as soon as we mentioned that Bellhollow fool. So, I was simply wondering if our friend here could explain himself…" The old man grunted to himself as he attempted to escape from Henry's grasp, squirming around fruitlessly as a pair of fiery blue eyes glared him down.

"You defiant military dogs! I'll have you court-martialed and thrown in prison for this…" The gloved fist let go of the politician as he crumpled to the ground, clutching at his chest as he stared on in wide-eyed terror.

I took a step towards the interrogator, but Avelina extended a hand out in front of me to stop my march.

"Let him handle this."

"He's an old man Avelina," I insisted as I tried to push past, "We can't just beat up somebody to get information out of them."

"Henry isn't going to hurt him Jack. Just scare him a little bit to properly interrogate him. It's what he's best at." A scoff to my side halted my forward march, drawing the attention of all three of us as Fox glared forward with crossed arms.

"He won't get anywhere through such methods," Fox growled out as she pushed past Avelina's arms, "Scum like him don't give anything up unless they are genuinely threatened, something that…child can't possibly do. I'll take it from here." Hearing Avelina yell out in protest next to me, Fox pushed Henry to the side and off the man far harder than necessary. He glanced up in shock as he cracked against a wall, his eyes widening from the sudden collision. Fox now was the one who stood over the downed man, her porcelain visage glaring into the quivering politician.

"Get up," she deadpanned as she reeled back and kicked the politician in the stomach, eliciting a sharp grunt from the man, "You sold your own village out, didn't you? What deal did you make?" Receiving no immediate answer, Fox pulled her leg back and slammed it square into one of his knees. Although obviously not broken, the man wailed out in pain at the sudden strike, gripping at his leg as I cringed at the attack. I attempted to sprint past Avelina's arms again, but they remained firmly planted.

I glanced over at the sister of the current interrogator, fire brewing in my eyes as I heard several more devastating blows connect with the politician, along with his yells of pain.

"I can't stop her once she does this," Avelina lamented, looking genuinely defeated as her hollow eyes turned back to me, "Just…just let her go through the motions and hopefully she won't do anything drastic." The man now lay crumpled against the ground, hacking up blood as the brooding figure of Fox stood above him. Clouds above had begun gathering near the sun, blocking out the precious light as the alley grew far darker.

"I'll ask again. What did you discuss with the man known as Zain?" Mustering the strength to sputter out a combination of spit and blood, the man attempted to pull himself up as his now dirtied clothes clung to his sweaty skin.

"I-I don't know what you…you're referring to you…you swine…"

"Don't lie to me," Fox snapped as she picked the man up by the collar again, "I saw you speaking to that purple robed insurgent. Speaking in secret; making some sort of deal before Zain disappeared in the shadow of darkness. So talk, or this alleyway could be the last thing you'll ever see." Rushing past Avelina before she could react, Serena sprinted under her arm and past Henry, who was still crouched down from the hard push. She came right up to Fox and latched onto her wrist, which was currently pulled back to deliver another powerful punch. Ducking past Avelina as well, I came to rest beside Henry, looking back to see that Avelina was attempting to look away from the entire scene.

"Just stop it!" Serena rasped, "This way of dealing with people is absolutely wrong, no matter what he knows about Zain. So just let him go!" Both stood in silence momentarily as her plea rang out like a whisper in the alley—grey eyes hardening and glaring into the same piercing slits that hid behind the mask. Her fist was still drawn back for a powerful blow, held firmly in place by the hands of the peppy young healer.

"She's right Fox," I interjected as I reached a hand down to Henry, who gladly accepted it with a groan as I pulled him up, "I may know nothing about you, but I can't watch in good conscience as you beat the crap out of the defenseless old man. It makes my stomach turn just to even listen to. Besides...the man can't talk if you're just gonna beat him to death before he tells us anything." Staring at the two of us in general silence, the spy seemed to be weighing her options as Serena continued to glare into her, refusing to release her even for a moment. Avelina still hadn't said anything, her mind clearly elsewhere as her sister unleashed her assault upon the politician.

Finally, she released the politician from her grasp, letting out a single scoff as Avelina breathed a sigh of relief.

The old man crashed to the floor with another grunt of pain, as Serena was already upon him with her hands glowing the same green hue. Fox let out an annoyed sigh as she stepped away, walking towards the opposite side of the alleyway to apparently keep watch that way.

"Thank the Goddess for that girl and her blasted heart." Avelina sighed as she stood beside me, her shoulder slumping back down as the tenseness of her body washed away.

Serena removed her hand from the man's knee last as the light fully faded away, flashing a light smile as she brushed her clean orange hair out of her face.

"Thank you...young lady..." As soon as the healing process ended, his old features evolved into a downward facing snarl as he smacked Serena across the jaw. Dazed, our healer fell to the side as he rose to his feet, bolting in the opposite direction of the alleyway.

As I took a single step forward to chase after him, Henry held out a hand to stop my movement. Turning my head to him in angered confusion, a loud thump met my ears and emanated throughout the stone hallway.

Whipping my head around, the old politician was now lying on the ground in a crumpled heap, gripping his leg as it appeared he only made it a couple steps before collapsing. In a flash Henry stood directly over him, his back to Fox as his eyes glared into the deceitful man.

Serena slowly propped herself up from the ground as she panted, still gripping her face with her right hand as her left sat limp at her side. Her tangerine hair falling slightly over her eyes, the woman stared up and glared at the fallen man in a manner I never thought was possible from her.

"I can't believe you right now," she breathed out, almost giggling as an unnerving smile came to her face, "I healed your wounds; stopped your attacker from bombarding you with vicious blows to get answers in a more diplomatic way. And what did you decide to do? You struck the very woman who was trying to help you." I instinctively took a step back at the very sound of her distinctive snarling tone, completely throwing me off as she sounded like a totally different person. Gone was the bubbly healer I had grown accustomed to upon joining this group.

Now in her place stood an incredibly upset one.

One factor I noticed right away was the pink hue that surrounded Serena's hands rather than the traditional green aura, fading almost as quickly as I saw it. She brushed her hair back with her hands as she stepped towards the snake lying helpless on the ground.

"So, in the very moment you ran from me," she continued as she walked over to the groaning politician with the same giggly smile, coming to a stop directly opposite of the equally as pissed off Henry, "I did a little trick and reversed my healing powers on your leg. I even managed to inflame your muscles so badly that you won't be able to stand comfortably on that leg for a while." Standing over him now, Henry rolled over the now quivering man with his foot. His visage held nothing but horror as he stared at the two Sentinels.

"Serena can be a lot...scarier than I thought she would be." I mumbled to Avelina, who let out a snort at my remark.

"Serena is a sweet girl at heart, but all of her other emotions are just as strong as her radiance whenever they arise." As the politician attempted to crawl away, Henry planted his foot on the man's hand, letting out a crunch that elicited a whimper from the old man.

"Someone...someone will hear us...and t-they'll utterly shut your petty coup down!"

"Oh this isn't a coup mister," Serena mockingly whispered as she crouched down next to the man's face, "This was a test, and it appears you have dramatically failed to pass. When I first gained these powers, I promised a long time ago to never use these hands to kill, but I never said anything against bringing harm upon someone, especially someone as callous as you are." Gripping him by whatever hair was left, Henry lifted him up slightly as Serena glared into him with narrowed eyes.

"Now I find it quite rude that you so quickly hit a girl mister politician," she taunted in a gleeful tone as the two of them both cracked their knuckles, "Wouldn't you agree Henry?" Henry gave a silent nod as he drew his leg up, preparing to stomp down.

"Okay! Okay I give I give! Just don't hurt me anymore..." Mumbling the words out, the politician held his hands out as Henry lowered his leg, seeing as a cloud of dust manifested around where his boot stamped down.

I marched over to the prone man, standing directly over him as I crossed my arms together.

"Alright you old pig," I began as I glared down at him, "Start talking."

He paused momentarily as he stared in terror at the area around him. Glancing to both exits to the alleyway, he was greeted by the two sisters who were standing in front of each entrance—ensuring there would be no prying eyes to interrupt. He let out a sigh at this realization, knowing all of his options were now exhausted.

"I...I encountered the man you speak of just before I entered the town hall two days ago," he started as he remained quivering on the ground, "He wore those long purple robes and amber pendant like you described earlier." Henry stared down at the mumbling man; his blue eyes glaring through the holes of his mask and making him look even more terrifying.

"When you met him....what was it you two did?"

"...he promised me that he would alleviate the drought and food problems that have been facing Stagmire for some time now." The air itself stood still as we all stared in disbelief at the fallen politician, not believing what seemed like such an obvious lie.

Waltzing up to the man I grabbed him by the hem of his shirt, pulling him up slightly so that we ended up face-to-face.

"You're lying," I asserted as I bore into him, "Zain torched Eincrest to the ground and led a massacre of its people. Why on earth would someone as deplorable as him do something like that? What did he ask for in return?" I roughly released the man from my grasp, grabbing at my wrist as he fell back to the ground.

"I am not a liar," he replied with renewed confidence, "We've had a water shortage problem for months now. The rivers were blocked by debris none of us could move, and as such our crops were losing a substantial amount of water. He promised me he'd find a way to alleviate all of our problems. I thought he was crazy first of all, since not even our entire council could change such a thing."

"He wouldn't do something like this for free though," Avelina cut in as she remained on the opposite side of the alley, "Did he actually do this, and if so, what did he ask for in return?" The old man paused as he turned to himself in thought, before his eyes gazed back at us.

"He did. I don't know how he did it but the river came rushing forward without fail, and still is doing so today. In return, he asked simply for the quickest route to get to Bellhollow, although why anyone would attempt to enter such a barbaric land is beyond me." I could hear Avelina let out a small scoff as I turned away from him.

"He can't be serious," I insisted, "Zain would never do something so humane, even if it was for something like that." Instead of answering my declaration, Avelina turned towards the direction her sister was currently standing.

"Does this information match yours Fox?" The masked woman gave a simple nod to the question.

"Almost exactly. Zain left in the southeast direction about a day ago. He stayed in this village for two days, not even bothering to hide his presence." Avelina gave a light sigh as she shook her head, rubbing her forehead in deep thought.

"Doesn't make sense," she mumbled to herself, before staring back at the three of us, "Well then, if we manage to set off right now, we can make it decently far before sundown. Let's move out." With that note, Serena and Henry both gave a silent nod as they followed Fox out of the alleyway in the direction that the old man pointed us to. Serena gave a small wave and smile to the man as they left. I followed closely behind, with Avelina coming from the rear.

"Oh and sir?" The politician tensed up as he was called, before he cautiously turned around and stared at our commander.

"Don't tell anyone this encounter occurred. Having to cover something up myself is so bothersome." The politician nodded frantically as he laid there on the stone floor, still attempting to move as his leg remained immobile.

As Henry, Fox and Serena all began marching ahead, I felt an arm grasp onto my own, halting me in my stride. Turning around, I realized it was the hand of Avelina, who I gave a quick smile as I prepared to ask what she needed.

That grin quickly disappeared as I gazed upon her; her hand visibly shaking as some form of emotion attempted to stay bottled up inside her.

"I'll...tell this to Serena at some point on the journey, but I'm sorry you had to see what Fox did. She is my sister after all, and I had hoped for a better first impression." Preparing a snarky reply to her comment due to the previous situation, I halted my initial thought as I gazed upon Avelina's face. It almost appeared completely empty; devoid of emotion as she appeared genuinely ashamed of the actions her sister had just taken. She couldn't meet my gaze, with her eyes instead staying glued to the floor.

Just like Connor...

"It's alright Avelina," I assured, mincing my words, "It's nothing I haven't seen already, although perhaps you should be telling her this so she doesn't do something stupid like that again." I almost instinctively covered my mouth as she cringed at my statement, the weight of my words coming to me.

Idiot! You were supposed to censor your words, not supercharge them.

"No, you're right," Avelina mumbled, rubbing her arm as the forms of the other three appeared to halt in their march, "I...never mind. Let's just...go on our way." Not letting me respond, the woman released me from her grip as she began walking away, already pulling out the book as if pretending nothing had happened.

Letting out a sigh, I walked away in the direction that Fox said Zain began down maybe a day earlier, my mind still grappling with the revelation that came from that slimeball of a politician.

The revelation of someone like Zain benefiting the lives of people, rather than annihilating them where they stood.

20

A Momentary Respite

The rising sun blazed over the heads of Captain Anderson and his large group of companions, barely shining through the dense tree line and further covered by clouds as they crept through the almost marshy terrain. Even though it was the afternoon, this combination made the area the soldiers were in appear almost as if it was dusk. No one ever visited this section of their land, even if it was for hunting trips or simple family gatherings. No matter how much the people of Stagmire disliked it, somehow an outsider in the form of Captain Anderson hated it the most. Every step of his was filled with purpose and increasing anger, hating the denseness of the tree line and how the moisture in the air clung to his skin like clothing. Sweat was pouring down his bald head, sticking into his blonde mustache as he groaned in annoyance.

"Stay vigilant my soldiers!" he growled out in the proud baritone voice he was famous for, "Our mission is to end this man before he becomes a significant danger, so watch every direction for someone matching his description." He glanced over his shoulder, scanning over the combination of rookies and veterans that made up his current crew.

About forty counting him.

Captain Anderson grumbled to himself, wondering how he managed to be in charge of the expedition to kill the man called Zain. Or the Butcher of Eincrest as the Senate so lovingly called him.

Word traveled fast to the capital, and within a day of the event the entire political section of Heartwood knew of the transgression.

The Senate had narrowly passed a measure to simply survey Zain's actions before executing him with a larger squad. They sent a group from the Sentinels to do the job.

The captain laughed to himself pessimistically at the thought of that underground hodgepodge, startling an especially squeamish rookie who was gripping his spear as if his life depended on it.

"The Sentinels," he mumbled to himself quietly, "Those dogs up in the Senate highchairs have too much faith in a band of spies. Luckily, the Chancellor knows we're the ones who can get things done." Every higher up in the military who was aware of them greatly despised the Sentinels as an organization, despising how much they often defied military orders and dared to consider themselves reasonably independent from military control. The old and honor bound Anderson could not help but loathe them.

And that is where his squad came in. The Chancellor himself called upon the aged captain to kill this menace before he could go any further, almost laughing at the idea of simply observing before taking him out. Both thought that the Sentinels were not worthy of being their own separate organization and were not well-equipped enough for such a task, and their agreement led to the secret transaction and the likewise deployment for what essentially amounted to extermination.

Although, the captain would never express these opinions out in public as openly. The very thought of that blond haired devil sent terrified quivers up the spines of even the most experienced of military commanders, present company included. Even though most soldiers knew Captain Anderson may carry with him an intimidating presence, everyone was aware that it paled in comparison to the aura of authority the elusive Katrina Ward carried with her, despite how rarely she appeared in the public eye nowadays.

As thoughts like these filtered through his wrinkled mind, the familiar sound of metal piercing through the air met Anderson's ear as his soldiers froze in place, clearly raising their weapons at something—their armor quivering on their bodies even as they stood like frozen statues. The mighty captain glanced over in indignation...

Several feet in front of him sat a man fitting the exact description Anderson was briefed on: a man garbed in purple with a pendant colored an amber hue bouncing against his chest. Frozen in his almost lackadaisical stride, the man known as Zain could only look on as Captain Anderson took but a second to process the situation, before drawing his mighty blade. His cool auburn eyes glared into green slits that hid within the confines of his hood, motioning for his underlings to surround the still frozen Zain. Many of them formed a large circle around him without much fuss, leaving only the most experienced few standing beside the captain. To Anderson's dismay and Zain's surprise, the sound of armor plating rattling against skin was audible as many soldiers couldn't help but shake in the presence of a man they knew nothing about. All they could go off of was the vile presence he carried.

"Heartwood soldiers," Zain realized in a gravely tone which shook even the most experienced of soldiers, freezing their blood as he glared them down. Some of the rookies almost dropped their weapons through involuntary quivering at just the voice of the man they were sent to hunt down. The captain remained vigilant, drawing his sword as his teeth ground painfully together, almost generating sparks as he glared down at the Butcher of Eincrest.

"By executive order from the Chancellor of Solaton, we have been commanded to bring you down with whatever force necessary! Try not to make this difficult for us; my squad and I have you utterly outnumbered." Instead of shrinking back or faltering as the grizzled captain had expected, the robed man from Bellhollow let out a dramatic sigh, almost as if this ambush were a burden rather than a problem. His shoulders slunk back down as he decided to stand normally, no longer feeling a need to stand utterly still.

"Oh I'm well aware how far you outnumber me, but sadly none of you could possibly be aware of just how much of a distance in skill level there is between you and I." He flicked a knife up and out of the sheath on his leg, causing a couple soldiers to flinch. Others chose the former half of the fight or flight reflex, taking another nervous step forward.

"If any of you wishes to see another day as a mindless soldier, walk away now," Zain growled out as he repositioned the blade within his hand, "If you do not actively attempt to stop me, I will not go out of my way to end your life." Even though the shaking never subsided or even lessened in any way, no soldier took a single step away from formation even at the sight of such a threat. Captain Anderson for once felt a glimmer of pride within him, knowing even as cowardly and fresh as these men were, they still respected the orders of their superiors. Zain let out a weary sigh, annoyed.

"Why do I even bother?" he grumbled to himself as the soldiers nervously took another step forward, "You all blindly follow the word of your Chancellor as if it were your own religion, not even bothering to think for yourselves. It may not be as troublesome of a situation as it is back home, but that doesn't matter. It's people like you and them that have made this world such a worthless place." Unbeknownst to the crowd, Zain's grip on his dagger involuntarily tightened at the mention of the home he so despised.

"No matter. I can at least know that I tried to show you a shred of mercy, one that you don't even deserve." He growled as the captain gripped the hilt of the sword, preparing to swing down at a speed he knew would cleave right through the man. If his strike didn't accomplish this task, his men could do the job just as well.

"Now die!" There were forty soldiers that came from Heartwood and now surrounded the Butcher of Eincrest, many of which had spent a multitude of years training for moments like these.

No matter what they did, no training could prepare them for this.

None of them could have realized this would be where they would take their last breaths.

In a flurry of purple and silver, the men closest to Zain all collapsed to the ground in an instant, slashes dug into the gaps in their armor. Captain Anderson had already begun swinging down with a loud yell, hitting nothing but the dirt below as his target had already lunged away. As he stood up in his stance again, Captain Anderson was met with a sight he couldn't believe.

In that instantaneous moment, half of his men were already slain, lying on the ground as their blood coagulated together. He spotted the man responsible, watching as he nimbly dodged out of the way of a spear strike from one of the rookies. The glow of his amber pendant was evident in their forested surroundings, beaming proudly as the man called upon its mighty gift.

Another soldier ran up behind him with a spear, hoping to skewer him in place while his opponent was distracted. Instead, Zain dodged yet again while mumbling indiscernible words to himself, the poor soldier unable to stop as he ran through his comrade with the spear. He didn't even have time to process what happened before a dagger strike tore into his back, ending him.

Enraged, the captain of all these corpses pushed forward and swung again, watching with growing anger as his strike slashed across the surface of a tree instead. Leaves alive and dead fell above him as he whipped around again, noting only five soldiers were left standing of his group of forty.

Intelligently, all five of them nervously gathered in a formation of some sort, all lunging forward at once as the captain did the same, pinning the man in all directions as they hoped to make this mission finally mean something.

In the shadow of the tree line, what almost every soldier including the captain failed to notice was the large sheath of knives and daggers that was wrapped around Zain's arm and leg, making up more blades than any of the soldiers could count. Anderson at once noticed his arsenal as he charged, and something within him stirred. A survival instinct that had kept him alive for so long made his body jump away without thinking. Unfortunately, his men lacked the same honed impulse.

A gleam of silver met his eyes, as Zain threw both of his hands up as various throwing knives littered his worn hands. He leapt up and back as his final defiant opponents charged on, leaving their captain to watch in horror as the blades left the madman's hands, and with a marksman's ability found their way into his soldier's throats. They all instantly fell dead, with Zain still staring down without appearing to even break a sweat.

Where once stood forty, now only stood one.

Without youthful hesitation the captain charged, almost gleeful to see the man didn't dodge this time.

With unparalleled strength, Zain threw a dagger behind him and blocked the downward strike of the blade without even turning, surprising the captain but not utterly shaking him. He dug his sword further down into him, hoping to push him down enough to make his arm falter in its defense. He could see a crooked sneer beneath the veil of the cloak as Zain craned his head back, a grin which even in his years of experience chilled every ounce of blood in his body.

"Your blade will slip and dig into the earth below." As if by magic, Anderson's sword slipped off the dagger with a resounding screech and dug into the earth below, pinning him in place. Anderson pulled at his favorite blade for one fateful second before forgetting about it and turning to face Zain, one second which was long enough for his appreciative opponent.

Three knives dug into Anderson's right arm as he threw up his guard just in time, cringing in pain as he already felt the blood begin to seep down. As he lowered his arms to continue to fight and pull the blades out, his opponent was gone. Instead, a sharp pain erupted in the small of his back as he stumbled forward, realizing two knives had been dug into it. In the corner of his eye, he spotted a purple blur before another few dug into his left shoulder, narrowly missing his neck. Irritation grew as Anderson could hear the man mumbling to himself, words which he realized too late were locations on his body.

"Find a home in the tendons in his knees!" Almost immediately the captain felt two sharp pains dig into the back of his leg, sending him involuntarily to the ground in a cry of pain as he attempted to push himself up. After a similar sentiment, a knife dug into his right elbow, sending him back to the ground. At this point, it finally dawned on the injured captain the power this man held and why it was so easy for him to ransack a whole village, but by then it was too late. Over a dozen knives stuck out of the experienced captain, leaving him brutalized on the ground as everything about the situation hit him at once. Unbeknownst to Anderson, Zain's stomach dropped as these knives dug into the man, knowing full well that the targets for every knife were completely different. The power defied his will, and he didn't understand why.

However, he didn't linger on this thought for long, as his single opponent was still crumpled to the ground.

"No it can't...how can one man hold this much power?" Anderson bellowed to himself in a fearful tone which he didn't think he could muster, attempting to crawl away as the blood pooled around him, "I can't...I won't let this be my end!" Anderson felt the familiar tearing of cool steel enter through his chest, piercing completely through and digging into the ground underneath him. He sputtered out blood as the figure clearly let go of the dagger, leaving him as a living pincushion dying on the ground. Zain dusted off his robe, relieved he had somehow managed to avoid garnering any crimson stain on its surface. He didn't bring any spare clothes along with him, so avoiding anything to make it any dirtier was optimal.

"Strange...three of those were supposed to dig into your head," the hooded figure snarled as the grizzled captain began to choke on his own blood, not caring about why his intentions deviated despite his uncertainty, "Every one of you was so persistent to blindly march to your demise, stupidly clinging to your devotion to that mindless fool in your capital. You don't stand any form of chance against the might of this pendant. Even if my purpose is for something else back home, testing out how truly powerful it is surely doesn't hurt. I apologize for all of this, but it was all of you who chose to walk the shadowy path towards your own demise." The dying captain could do nothing as the Butcher of Eincrest walked away down a path only the man from Bellhollow knew, leaving another mountain of corpses in his bloody wake.

21

Connor: Sole Survivor

"Your mother was taken, correct?" I escaped my mental world momentarily as I processed Mara's blunt question, realizing we stood at the fallen gates of what used to be Eincrest. The charred sign rested below where it once hung, a skeleton of its former self.

I glanced up at the sky.

A little past noon, and one full day of endless walking.

"Yeah, she was," I replied with a depressed sigh, "Taken by some blasted knight that struck down my father. I...I know she's alive somewhere, I just need to find out how to reach her." Mara stepped underneath the entrance way as she walked into the small town, forming footsteps in the combination of ash and dust that littered the ground.

"Hope is a precious thing to have, especially when it concerns someone as treasured as parents," she lamented to herself without even bothering to disguise her verbiage, "Hold on to that ideal Connor, because some people will hope every day for someone they love to return, only to be met with the cruel silence the world provides instead." I was somewhat taken aback by her declaration, likely prompted by the amount of death surrounding us.

Is she...talking about herself?

Gazing at her, something new twinkled within her eyes that was slowly bubbling to the surface. Her eyes were narrowed and withdrawn, and while she attempted to maintain that same blank expression around me, I noticed how small her pupils were becoming as she truly traced around the area.

It's almost like it's...some form of fear, or perhaps regret.

I swiftly followed behind her as our boots crunched beneath the ground, sounding as if we were marching across a macabre beach.

"D-do you...do you think that we'll find anyone alive?" Mara atypically stuttered out, her eyes scanning over the carnage I witnessed unfold days ago.

"I...I don't know," I answered honestly, "When...Jack and I came here, this whole place was already burning down. We didn't find anyone alive except a girl named Catherine, and then Avelina. But...I honestly have no idea if she survived afterwards." Mara nodded as we walked through the blackened wood, occasionally stepping over charred bodies that littered the streets.

The other bodies must have become trapped under rubble.

"I...don't like being in this place," Mara murmured as we continued to walk, "I know that should be ordinary considering the state of this village but...everything about this place makes me uncomfortable." As I moved forward to respond, a cold shiver washed over my entire body, sending harsh chills up and down my spine as I froze in my tracks, my heartbeat accelerating. Mara clearly felt the same, with her emerald eyes scanning over the surrounding village as goosebumps formed across her skin. The two of us both instinctively gripped onto the hilts of our weapons.

"Someone else is here Mara. I can't tell if they're a survivor...or something else." Skulking several steps forward, our boots crunched against the ground beneath us as the faint scent of burnt wood continued to invade my nostrils.

A faint tapping noise came emanating somewhere around us, sounding like it came from all directions as we both attempted to pinpoint the source of the repeating sound.

Someone barefoot by the lightness of the boards creaking, but other than that it's hard to tell.

It sounded almost like someone trying to sneak around on creaking wooden floorboards, trying not to be spotted but not being overly cautious.

They're watching their footing for nails or sharpened pieces of wood, walking carefully but not like someone attempting to stay hidden.

As we both pinpointed the sound's location, a loud thud shook through the semi-destroyed house beside us, startling the two of us as we fully drew both of our weapons.

Creeping up to the destroyed house to our right, Mara grasped the burnt, corroded handle, and nodded to me as the metal creaked with the slightest of movements. She turned the knob slowly with a rusty screech, before ramming her shoulder into the wooden door, almost breaking it down by forcing it open.

The wooden room we had burst into was blackened completely, making it obvious the flames had easily forced their way inside days before. Chairs had caved completely in, and those that hadn't were clearly knocked over as their occupants attempted to flee as fast as they could. Part of the roof had also collapsed, with the foundations of the ceiling resting where the beds were. The combination of wood and stone rested where it appears children would sleep, which luckily were empty at the time.

Although, they most likely didn't make it far.

At the center of the room face down on the charred floors rested a young girl, who appeared to be passed out based on her ragged breathing and the way she was resting currently.

Her black hair cascaded over and on top of her like an explosion, allowing me to notice that every strand appeared to be laced with some form of dirt, ash, or both.

She wore a blue shirt that had a single tear at the bottom, along with various stains from dirt and mud that caked the sides. A single blackened streak bore across the middle of the back, looking as if fire had crawled across her like an animal.

Wait a second...

Glancing at her once again, my eyes widened as I recognized the long white skirt that flowed down to her feet, covered in similar abrasions and stains as her upper garments.

I sprinted over to the prone girl and slid down beside her, sheathing my dirk as my pants collected soot and splinters. I could hear Mara take a single step forward, clearly confused at my reaction but hopefully understanding. Her sword remained hesitantly drawn.

I crouched down beside the young girl and turned her over, noting that her breathing had remained steady. Her sunburnt cheeks were completely covered by soot, and portions of her face were littered with specks of dirt.

She's still alive, but incredibly malnourished. Most likely hasn't eaten much since the village burned down and she just collapsed.

"Catherine..." I breathed out as I stared at how gaunt she had become.

At least she took my advice and hid. Who knows what would've happened otherwise.

What if we came to this village just a day later? Would she still be here?

I picked her up and pulled her close to my body, feeling her quiet heartbeat that luckily still hammered defiantly on. Her body was unhealthily light to carry, almost as if she were a living skeleton.

I'm so sorry for not arriving sooner...I was so distracted. I should have been here earlier.

I turned towards Mara, watching as she herself finally sheathed her regal blade.

"This is...the girl I mentioned meeting that day," I declared as I stared at her, "Although death didn't steal her away that fateful day, she's lost everything, all because of one man I couldn't stop in time." I extended the unconscious Catherine out to Mara. She stared at me in the same blank way; her eyes shifting between my gaze and the girl in my arms.

Hesitantly, she took the young girl into her grasp and hoisted her up, pressing her against her shoulder as she held the young girl close.

"If you can, find a river and clean her up as well as you can," I maintained as my brain snapped into action, "After that find her a new set of clothes anywhere in this village if there is any. If there's nothing, try to clean off her clothes as well." Mara seemed incredibly conflicted and hesitant, staring down with softer eyes at Catherine. Her breathing had slowed down and steadied slightly, as if she found instinctual comfort in Mara's arms.

"Hey...you are the only other girl here," I explained as well as I could, "So in other words, I am not comfortable with being in charge of that particular task." A tint of pink went over Mara's cheeks, looking incredibly foreign as her expression remained the same. Giving a faint nod, she ensured that Catherine remained secure in her arms, before walking right back out of the building.

I sat down cross-legged in the center of the house, contemplating what to do moving forward as I waited for their return.

Is it possible there could be more people alive in this village?

"No," I pessimistically announced to myself, "If anyone else was here, they either found a way out somehow or perished already. Otherwise, there would be at least someone watching that young girl." Sighing to myself I stood up to try and make use of my time instead of doing nothing.

Let's hope it's the former...and that I wasn't any later than I already am.

"You were right...Katrina," I begrudgingly whispered to myself as I paced around, "I shouldn't have doubted you. If you had allowed me to be selfish then, this girl might have fallen like the rest. I'll thank you for your level-headed judgement when I bring her back."

Pushing aside an abundance of rubble, I dragged out the three beds from underneath where they were crunched and hauled them near the center of the house.

Two of them were clearly for children based on the size, both having the same turquoise sheets tainted by the rubble they lurked underneath.

The other was a queen-sized bed, one which looked like it once held the two leaders of this family before they fled during the attack. A nightstand nearby was unusable, having been crushed by the roof itself.

Modest living. These people most likely weren't wealthy merchants or penny-pinchers based on this house.

Finally setting both of them down, I laid back on the family sized bed as the quaking of my knees ceased. My legs were on fire from a day of endless walking, and finally being able to sit down let out an involuntary sigh of relief.

With nothing else to do, I groaned as I knew I was being left alone for a while with the thoughts inside my own head. Sadly, I left any books on the right side of my desk in my room, so reading was out of the question.

Thinking to myself, I pulled the green pendant out from the confines of my shirt, staring into its emerald pools. Looking at it now, I could almost see faint energy crackling within the misty green pendant, like a thunderous storm was swirling throughout its depths. The item which may have many more equally different copies around the world. Their distinct nature and their connection to both mom and Zain may be the tool I need to press on.

I'm still incredibly unsure on how this pendant works...could it grant me the ability to bend the air around me to my will?

No. The attack doesn't seem to be ranged in any way. It balls around my hand no matter what I try.

Perhaps it's a way to strengthen my attacks? Drawing the air around my fist in a way that could make it similar to gauntlets?

It's possible, however if this is the case then I lack the power to properly control it. Dammit.

Staring into the swirling pendant I had carried with me through this entire journey, I attempted to steady my thoughts back to the one man the other group was desperately searching for.

The only rules I can gather is it requires incredible willpower to conduct, but that each of these pendants have a unique set of gifts. It's possible there are more considering that Zain had one.

His abilities can't constitute mind reading or any proper form of fate manipulation, as he would've ended my brother and I easily if he could.

I still don't know what he can do...Damn it all!

Shaking my head as I attempted to solidify the increasingly conflicted thoughts flowing through my head, I snatched a small stone from the ground. Weighing it slightly in my hand, I hurled it at the corner of the wall directly opposite of me, hoping to bounce it back to me to pass the time.

Instead of this, the rock collided with the corner and ricocheted off it at a slightly lower angle than anticipated, causing it to fall almost directly below where it initially hit. I let out a defeated sigh at having lost my one tool of entertainment, feeling too lethargic at the moment to get up and grab it just to potentially lose it again.

Should have known better...the way those two walls connect would've made it impossible for it to exactly bounce back to me-

My eyes widened suddenly as a single thought panged through my head, jolting me to my feet as my single act of boredom created the connection I so desperately needed.

That...that's it! That's the key!

That makes the most probable sense. All other options are ruled out... that must be the secret to Zain's power.

I pumped my fist in a way reminiscent of my brother, a foreign sense of triumph washing over me.

I'll relay this back to Katrina once we get back...this could change everything.

Placing the pendant back under my shirt with a renewed feeling of success, I instead directed my eyes towards the other object of my interest.

The stolen dirk.

Its blackened teeth grinned at me as I stared at it down, curious as to why I hadn't replaced it with something else, instead of carrying around the weapon of a deceased enemy.

I feel...drawn to it somehow. I don't understand it myself, but for some reason I wish to hold onto it.

It's just a simple dirk. I can let go of it at any moment.

For whatever reason I remained transfixed by the slashes of black and silver that tore throughout the blade, giving it an almost rusted visage. And yet for whatever reason, it looked almost elegant.

Requiem...

I jerked back as a name shot into my brain as I stared at the piece of metalwork in front of me, startling me for a moment as the thought rang louder than all the others. It pierced through the crowded network of interwoven thoughts and screamed out that single name.

"Requiem." I murmured as I continued to stare at its edges, "Since I appear to have such an affection for you, I suppose that is what I will call you. Requiem..." I sheathed the dirk again, the one I now had a proper name for.

I was stirred from my thoughts when Mara suddenly came back in through the door, cradling a still unconscious Catherine in her arms.

The dirt and grime that initially caked to her face was almost completely gone, and her arms and legs were no longer coated by the same lingering dust.

By the look of things, it didn't appear that Mara found any other clothes for Catherine to wear. However, her slightly damp blue tunic and white skirt were much cleaner than they were previously, which aside from the holes made them look relatively well.

"She needs food," I stated obviously, "Put her on one of the beds I pulled out and try to look for any proper tinder and wood we can use to light a fire. I'll do my best to look for something reasonably edible." She nodded silently as she slowly deposited her onto one of the children's beds, her gaze lingering on the child in a way that resembled compassion. Catherine's chest heaved in and out; a complacent look still present on her face. I sighed as I glanced away from her, with Mara already vanishing yet again.

I took one moment to place Catherine further under the covers, ensuring that she was at least comfortable in her long slumber.

* * *

I raised my hands above the fire that Mara had created about five minutes earlier, taking comfort in the warmth I felt beneath the cool night sky.

On a spike above the fire was whatever remained of a small wild boar I found about five minutes away from the village. He was incredibly difficult to catch, but the animal was enough food for the three of us once Catherine awoke.

I let Mara be the one to cook it, as knowing me the beast would simply catch fire at me even touching it.

Speaking of her, she had also chosen to only eat a small amount of food in front of her, leaving the rest for me and the unconscious girl.

That's the first time I've actually seen her eat, even if it was only a little.

I had consumed my fill briefly before leaving the rest of the roasting pig, noting that we had eaten about half of the animal all-together.

We both sat in relative silence, preferring not to speak until Catherine had stirred from her slumber. Or at least, that was my reason for it.

A vague, indiscernible murmur met my ears as I heard the rustling of sheets behind me. Glancing over, the young girl had finally sat up in bed with a fatigued slouch, rubbing her eyes free from the land of dreams she was just entrenched in.

Turning to the left, her eyes immediately widened and fully awakened as they glanced upon us. A hand drifted to her mouth as she stared at us, slack jawed.

"Hey Catherine," I announced nonchalantly in an attempt to break the silence, "Um...Long time no see?" A single tear rolled down her face as she sprung out of the children's bed; the dust that once caked it flying into the air along with the discarded sheets.

I was promptly tackled by the almost emaciated girl, who had finally let the tears run down her face as she slammed into me. I steadied my body to prevent it from falling over as I instinctively wrapped her in my arms as she did the same, burying her face in my dark cloak.

"Easy there," I consoled, patting the back of her head, "It's alright Catherine. I told you I'd come back." She let out a soft sniffle as she released me from her grip. She stared up at me with tear-soaked amber eyes, gripping my cloak with her tiny hands.

"I...I was so sure you left me alone," she sobbed as she lowered her head, allowing for her black hair to cascade over her face, "Thinking I'd be stuck here to d-die." Another sob involuntarily choked out of her throat as she finally released me, looking up with reddened eyes.

"You'll be fine Catherine, don't worry. I do have a couple questions I need you to answer for me, but for now they can wait. I know a lot has happened in the past couple days, but I need to know everything at some point. For now, you need to eat something before you starve to death." She let out a gasp at my statement, a faint sniffle echoing from her nostrils. I almost kicked myself again at my wording.

I'm getting better, but I need to figure this out before I scar some kid for life.

"We left quite a bit for you," Mara commented, staring down at the fire as she poked it with a large stick, "Have as much as you'd like Catherine." Catherine didn't say anything, glancing at the two of us with minor concern. I tore off a large chunk from the boar and placed it on a pointed stick, handing it to the young girl.

"This is Mara by the way, and she's a companion of mine," I clarified, reading her confused expression, "We purposely left much of it for you, although I do appreciate your concern for us." Seemingly alleviating any apprehension that she had, she ferociously snatched the stick from my hand and began tearing into the roasted boar. I smiled at how viciously she consumed it.

Before I could even blink, the piece was completely devoured. Mara moved to place another piece onto the stick, which was also soon gone.

The process repeated until the boar was nothing but a coalition of roasting bones, with the sounds of tearing and chewing of meat being the only one in the area.

The three of us sat in relative silence for a short while afterward, enjoying the comfort of the crackling fire, until Catherine's soft voice eventually echoed throughout the world again.

"Why did he have to come here?" she whispered, "My mom... my dad...my best friends. He...he took them all." She hugged her knees close to herself. Her amber eyes were glazed over and faraway, refusing to focus on anything as her entire world became blurred.

Mara scooted closer to her, allowing Catherine to lean against her if need be. It was a rare moment of affection I didn't expect from her, and while she did look somewhat uncomfortable, she still sat beside her as the pillar of support she needed right now.

"I know this is difficult for you...Catherine," I announced in a way that echoed the first moment I met her, slowing down the way I spoke so I didn't say something else stupid, "But before we can take you back...I need to know everything that happened. The man who came here that day is called Zain, and he's a very bad man. So, we have a couple friends tracking him down. If you tell us what happened, we may be able to take him down for good." Letting out a soft sniffle, Catherine pressed herself further into Mara as her face scrunched up, attempting to recollect.

"My full name is Catherine Belladonis. My f-friends called me Cat for short. I'm....I was the only child to the mayor of this town, Joseph Belladonis." My eyes perked up at the mention of her lineage. My mind shook as I recalled the large town hall, the only location that was spared from the terrifying flames.

We fought him there...he got the pendant there.

"Zain took an amulet of some kind when he went into the town hall," I explained, "Cat...did your family possess it before his arrival?" Seeing her eyes gain some of its life back at the sound of her nickname, her eyes continued to gaze down at the floor as she strove through all of her memories she had obviously lived through many times already.

"My father...gave it to me," she explained, prompting the wheels in my head to turn even faster, "For a year I...I think. He told me that it was something strong he wanted to keep out of the wrong people's hands. That our family has had it for generations." Her hand fell limply back down to the ground, crunching into the dirt below.

Her fingers were already beginning to collect dust.

"When...when that man came, my father hid with me to try and keep safe until he went away. He burst through the door and hurt my mother before he g-grabbed me and tore the pendant from my neck. Before he could k-kill me, my father tackled him out of the way. He told me he l-loved me, and threw me out of a nearby window. When I turned around and ran, I saw him get...g-get..." Another sniffle, as I saw her mind shutting down as the memory of it all became too excruciating.

"He...he took everything," she continued, staring off into space, "I could've been taken too. Why...why why?" She promptly crashed into Mara's side, causing the brunette to run her hand through the child's hair softly, no longer uncomfortable with her presence.

She's a sole survivor. Everything she has is gone.

We have to take her back immediately. Who knows how much more damage being out here will do...we have to-

"We'll get him," Mara blurted out suddenly, causing Catherine to perk up in her grasp, "We'll make sure he pays for what he's done. We work for a sizable military organization, so we were tracking him down in fact, right after we searched through here."

What the...?

Motioning to interrupt, Catherine glanced up at Mara and spoke up wide-eyed before I could say anything.

"Really?" she radiated with renewed enthusiasm.

"We'll make sure to track him down little one. I promise."

"Thank you," she breathed out, "Thank you so much..."

"You're welcome...Catherine," Mara replied in a way that actually resembled compassion, "Now go get some rest. You'll need it if you are to come with us." She smiled for the first time lightly and nodded, scurrying back inside the house and shutting the rickety door. Its hinges almost popped off as it slammed shut, the damaged wood bending.

As soon as she left, I glared forward at Mara, my eyes narrowed into slits.

"You lied to her," I accused plainly, "Our mission is to bring any survivors, a la Catherine, back to the Sentinels' base. You aren't serious are you?" Mara firmly nodded a single time as she poked again at the fire, the once roaring flames dying down as the evening stars became clearer.

"We have the ability to provide her with enough food and water as we go, given that she is the only one. They should find Zain soon, and the notion that he won't notice someone spying on him was ill-advised from the start. We need to be there as soon as they find him to provide the proper backup at that moment." I contemplated her words, the fire reflecting off our eyes as I sat in deep thought.

You really want to kill him, don't you?

Everything became clear as her words rang within my head, my mouth bending into a frown.

She planned this from the start, and thought that I would willingly follow along with her plan because of my disdain for the madman.

Does she not care for the life of that girl? We'd be putting her in substantial danger by taking her.

Not only that, but Katrina would notice quickly we didn't arrive at our expected time.

While she has a point about reinforcements, bringing Catherine is idiotic. She's a child, and her life cannot be put into jeopardy.

All this lying, all this deception from this one woman.

"We would be stopped from leaving right away if we attempted to bring Catherine back, and sending us off as reinforcements would be too late of an effort," Mara commented as she stared into the flames, the fire illuminating her furrowed brow and contemplative expression, "This is our only chance, and we both have the ability to protect her from anything."

"Please...take me with you..." I stared back up suddenly at the semi-collapsed doorway, seeing Catherine leaning against the wooden frame. Her hair was flowing directly over her face, disguising all of her features except her eyes, which looked at us with subdued concern and longing.

"You should be resting Catherine," Mara chastised sternly. Catherine looked down at the splintered floorboards and clutched the door frame. The wooden surface shifted and bent momentarily in her grasp.

"I will, don't worry," she mumbled softly, "But...I want to come with you. Please...I don't want to be alone here, and I can handle myself." She looked down again, tears welling up in her eyes.

"Don't worry Catherine, we'll be bringing you along with us. I'm sure Connor and I will be able to protect you." Mara glanced over at me. I froze, before my body decided to nod in response, unsure of what else to say.

What else am I supposed to do if the girl is looking right at me?

"Now get to sleep," Mara instructed from afar, "We need to have enough energy to move swiftly in the morning." Giving a nod, Catherine rushed away and shut the door behind her.

"I'll take watch duty first," I proclaimed to the brunette who had just put me in a difficult position, "You go get some sleep too." Giving a slow nod, Mara kicked some loose dirt over the already dying fire, killing the last of its smoldering embers.

As I heard the door shut several seconds later, I stared into the abyss of the night sky, watching as stars twinkled and glimmered in the sky above.

I sighed as I sat next to the smoking pieces of wood, now blackened like the rest of the village around us.

A village that now only had one true occupant from it left.

Their future...spared from the jaws of death.

I could only save that one girl to prolong their future, and yet here I am, willingly letting their future march right back into that despicable maw...

22

Jack: Discovery

"He was here," Avelina announced to us all as we stumbled upon a broken-down campsite, complete with a half set up tent and an already deceased fire pit. We had been marching for the rest of the day since receiving that tip from the politician, and now the sky was turning dark as the sun began to set.

"What gives you such an impression?" Henry questioned, "In theory, it could simply be any random person camping out in the woods for a weekend." Fox turned her head at these words, her eyes beneath the mask shrinking as she glared at Henry.

"Don't question her," she growled, "My sister is far more perceptive than you could ever be."

Her attitude had been bugging me ever since we left the village, but every jab she made in Henry's direction pushed my buttons even more. Her rampant jump to extreme violence earlier today was anger inducing, but this downright pissed me off.

Could she be just super defensive of her sister?

Said sibling sighed to herself as she crouched down next to an extinguished campfire, examining the charred wood and ash still littering the pit.

"Lose the attitude sis. Henry's just being his usual skeptical self is all." Fox's eyes widened underneath her mask as she gave her sister an incredulous look, crossing her arms in a huff.

"Avelina...don't you realize that he's..."

"I said drop it!" Avelina snapped in a tone that suggested consequences if the topic was to be brought up again. Fox muttered to herself and stepped away, averting her attention to another place in the campsite.

Avelina continued to stare into the dead campfire, riffling her hand through the layers of chipped apart wood and ash.

"To answer your question Henry, I know because of this." Pulling her hand out of the depths, Avelina revealed a semi-charred and blackened book that had been buried within ashen remains of the campfire. She blew the grime off the cover, revealing an almost illegible title, and a golden metal piece. The piece itself read *Property of The Stagmire Library*.

"I actually checked this book out while we were stationed here by Katrina a long time ago," she remarked, "It's title is relatively nonexistent, but I do recall it was some story about the war so long ago. Zain must have nonchalantly checked this out while perusing the town, but disposed of it once he finished it." Serena excitedly pumped her arms multiple times as her ever present smile beamed in the light.

"That means we're close," Serena cheered, "We'll track this guy down if it's the last thing we do!" Avelina smiled tiredly at our medic and stood up, brushing off the dirt that had coalesced on her knees.

"I've missed your attitude so much on my travels across this country Serena," she said as she motioned for us to glance over near her, "He stamped through the bushes here, so it's obvious he's keeping a steady pace towards Bellhollow. However, night is rapidly approaching. For now, we should set up camp here, and pick up the trail in the morning at breakneck speed. If he does the same, then we should be able to triangulate his location by tomorrow." Motioning to Fox, the woman removed a large pack from beneath her cloak that I hadn't noticed when we were walking, probably because of how far in front of us she was when we walked.

Setting the massive bag down, Fox began pulling out several clothes and sheets, clearly there to be used as camping equipment to sleep with while we went along.

Looks like enough for all of us to have our own small, individual sleeping arrangements.

Despite Henry being directly next to her, Fox went to the trouble of walking all the way over to Serena to hand her a cloth for her tent, before deciding to set up her own nearby. Serena gave a smile at receiving the gift, but looked fairly uncomfortable at being picked first. Avelina sighed, handing Henry and I one as she rubbed her temples in annoyance.

After several minutes, the five of us had set up our own tents with thicker tarps underneath them. Although there were no blankets of any kind, it wasn't particularly cool out tonight due to the changing seasons, and the enclosed nature of the tent left us relatively protected from the harrowing wind.

Avelina's tent sat at the end of the row we had established, whilst her sister sat on the direct opposite end. On Avelina's right was Henry's own tent, followed by Serena's in the middle and my own to the left of Fox, who had already fully set her tent up before I had even started.

After the tents were initially set up Avelina came forward in front of all our blue tents with her arms crossed, staring down at us as she brushed the dust off the metal piece on her shoulder.

"I'll scout ahead momentarily to see how much ground we'll have to cover tomorrow if we wish to reach Zain soon. In the meantime, Fox I want you and Jack to be on watch duty for now until I return.

Serena and Henry, you two can get some well-deserved rest." Serena let out a whoop and a cheer at Avelina's declaration, immediately turning back to her tent and closing it. Henry said nothing, instead silently returning to his arrangements.

Avelina gave a smiling salute before walking in the other direction, tracing through the trampled bushes in search of the direction Zain went despite the overwhelming darkness that was soon to come.

Her sister and I both sat nearby several trees, bridging the edge of the camp from where Avelina departed and facing the row of tents. I chuckled to myself as I already could hear Serena snoring loudly, already sound asleep.

I wonder if Henry sleeps with his mask on?

The hilarious thought of Henry shot my gaze towards the other masked member of our group. Fox at the moment was still staring down the path that Avelina had just gone through, with her cloak disguising the rest of her outfit. I tugged the edges of my coat closer to my face, staring at the standoffish woman.

"What is your problem with Henry?" My effort to break the silence ruptured through the air as her gaze shot to mine, stiffening at my sudden proclamation. Her eyes shifted underneath the porcelain mask, narrowing as she crossed her arms and propped herself against the tree beside mine.

"I do not have any sort of gripe with that man." I snorted to myself as I leaned against my own tree, pushing my arms behind my head to better leverage my sword in a more comfortable position.

"Right...and I'm secretly Solaton's military commander." Her eyes narrowed to slits as she bowed her head down slightly, hiding even the mask beneath that blasted black hood. Instead of letting her reply, I decided it would be best if I spoke up again as my tone turned aggressive.

"Perhaps a better question would be what is your problem in

general? You for some reason think that openly insulting someone's character would go unnoticed by the others, although I'm fairly certain they all in some way recognized the absolute amount of disrespect you have given Henry. They're all ignoring it I'm sure just like Avelina ignored your actions in Stagmire, but you're not so lucky when it comes to me. I may not know Henry well, but that gives you no right to belittle him the way you have. So why don't you knock it off before you get on my nerves any more than you already have." A dead silence perforated the air around us as the words sunk into Fox's psyche, hopefully digging into where it hurts the most.

Raising her head up to the moonlit sky, her eyes were still narrowed to slits, barely even shining the brown light through the mask.

"Would you care to repeat your petty sentiment?"

"Depends, would it hurt you more than the first time I said it?" The masked woman flashed her gaze over to me, glaring into my soul with those bronze eyes that were somehow filled with far more malice and ego than the eyes of Avelina's ever had, even when she was upset with me.

"Watch your tongue boy," she hissed through the echo chamber her mask created, "That man, Henry, is far different than he appears. He's right to be paranoid of all of us, as I feel that same paranoia when I'm even near that boy."

"Perhaps that paranoia is actually some form of delusions you're facing. Because if so then you may as well just leave now." The two of us glared at each other with shrunken eyes soaked in the moonlight. Brown eyes bared down on one another as our clashing insults finally subsided, but probably not for long.

Before another venomous word could be spat out by one of us, the bushes rustled beside us as a layer of purple hair appeared from the rough.

With a tired expression present on her face, Avelina stepped out from behind the layer of bushes, brushing off the leaves that had lodged themselves on the edges of her clothes. Pushing aside the stray hairs that hung directly over her eyes, Avelina noticed where we were currently standing and stepped towards us. She gave a toothless smile as she stepped forward.

"Continues the same path forward as we expected," Avelina confirmed, "However the path ahead feels recently torn through, so I think I'd rather take one of you with me. Don't want to get taken out by surprise."

Cracking her knuckles and adjusting her wrinkled green shirt, Avelina leaned against the perpendicular side of the tree Fox was already leaning against.

"If either of you wants to turn in early, be my guest. I only need one of you to watch my back, and then we can take over the watch once we finish."

"Jack can go with you." Fox's declaration clearly surprised her sister, as Avelina stared at her with a wide-eyed expression.

"You...sure sis? You usually prefer tasks like these."

"I'm fine," she replied in a deadpanned tone that reminded me of that girl Mara, "Just...feel a little tired today is all." Without any confirmation from Avelina, Fox already began walking towards her own tent without another word.

Her sister let out a sigh as she motioned for me to follow, shining her metal plate for a second to pass time—breezing over the indent she clearly gained from Eincrest. We pushed past the layer of bushes to go through where we believed Zain entered, noticing the path continued for several feet into darkness.

Walking for several silent seconds, Avelina let out a sigh as she turned to face me, not halting her stride.

"What did you do to make her angry Jack? It must've been atrocious to make her up and go to bed like that." I involuntarily sighed as I thought back to the insults traded previously, where all of our malice bubbled viciously to the surface.

"I called her out for being a jackass. Plain and simple." Her complacent face immediately shifted as her left eye ticked in anger, glaring back at me with slits.

"Jack…"

"I mean it Avelina," I insisted as I noticed a bent branch nearby, hanging loosely over the path of footprints, "Your sister was being nothing but an absolute jerk towards Henry, through and through. That in combination with what happened in Stagmire has driven me to a breaking point. You saw it; we all saw it Avelina. In fact, I'd like to have a word on how blatantly you all ignored what she was saying. Serena I get, but you have no excuse." Avelina, in a similar manner to her sister just five minutes ago, raised her eyes to the moonlit sky. The light cast down from the moon illuminated her eyes, accenting the copper tones rather than the yellowish orange.

"She can be a bit…much around Henry," Avelina relented as her sighs made the air around her mouth visible, "While this is the first time she's met Serena and you, she's encountered Henry momentarily before. She harbors some form of unnatural dislike for the boy, no matter how hard I try to knock it out of that stubborn head of hers." With another sigh she examined the steel spear she hadn't yet put on her back, studying the slightly rusted tip as she flipped it around in her hands.

"To answer your other gripe, I know I should've done more in the village. Like I said, she's an incredibly stubborn woman. I love her, but she often takes things to an…extreme degree. I…I've tried to get her to stop…but there's only so much I can do with someone who's had this mindset for their whole life." Even though I wasn't an expert like Connor is, I could immediately tell this discussion about her sister was dampening her mood. Her expression fell as she continued talking, looking like she did at the village.

Looking away, I chose to keep my eyes peeled on the road ahead, trying to tell how recent any of this was despite not being as knowledgeable as someone like Connor.

Aside from the occasional branch that had been knocked to the ground, the only sign someone had taken this path was the pair of shallow footprints indented into the still wet ground.

Maybe somewhat recent...can't tell how recent though like Connor could.

"I find it all quite annoying considering she won't shut up about it," I continued the previous conversation probably far more than I should, "I mean, if you really dislike the guy at least keep it to yourself." Seeing her eye twitch again in her distinct sigh of annoyance, I let out a nervous chuckle as I rubbed the building sweat off of my forehead.

Although, I felt a sense of relief that she did get ticked off actually. Being annoyed is much better than being depressed about something.

"Sorry, you know how I am with these types of things. Why don't we change the subject?" Avelina gave a quiet nod as I glanced behind me, still faintly hearing the booming snores Serena gave from the tent, even though we were traveling far deeper than Avelina probably went.

I stared back at the woman who had watched over me every time I entered Eincrest, even if she didn't want to admit it. She always made sure Connor and I were sustaining ourselves well enough in our secluded little home; always made sure I didn't get jumped as soon as I walked through those gates.

She fought like her life depended on it in Eincrest, which to be fair it did.

And yet, she could still do all that and manage to secretly be a member of the military, serving as some sort of spymaster to this entire regiment.

"Tell me, do you have any aspirations in your life besides serving

Katrina?" Avelina seemed taken aback by my sudden question, averting her eyes away from her twirling spear which was illuminated by the moonlight poking through the dense tree line. Surprisingly, she chuckled plainly to herself as she shook her head.

"You act as if I'm some mindless drone of the army, serving my queen without question or second thoughts…"

"I don't, which is why I asked you that question." She paused again at my words, brushing off the metal plate again as she finally hooked the spear back onto her back, never breaking her stride.

"Maybe you can be as perceptive as your brother," she said as her amber eyes stared back at me, "Tell me, Jack: What do you think I seek to gain from all of this? Of being a part of the Sentinels I mean."

"I could come up with a lot of things, most of which I'm sure you wouldn't like." I snickered to myself as she let out a huff, her eye ticking for the third time today.

"Seriously though, I find it difficult to think of any other reason besides your devotion to Katrina. It's almost creepy how much you follow what she says." She sighed to herself in deep annoyance, a factor which had become commonplace the further we traveled. She rubbed her eyelids, blinking several times as she obviously struggled to keep awake, refusing to avert her eyes from the continuous roughed up path ahead.

"Have you ever pondered on the leadership of this country?" Unprepared for such a question, I instinctively shrugged my shoulders. I felt my sword grate against a tree I breezed by, cringing at the obvious clang and hearing bark slide down to the dirt below.

"Besides the fact that every politician is either old, corrupt, or out-of-touch with the rest of us, I don't have much of a clue." Surprisingly, the purple-haired demon of a commander let out a suppressed snicker, before cracking up into a long chorus of chuckles and chortles. Echoing out in the quiet landscape of towering trees and shrubbery, her head was raised to the sky and her eyes were completely shut, lost in her own world of laughter.

Finally settling down, Avelina wiped a final tear from her eye as a final chuckle choked its way out, finally reverting her gaze back to me.

"Jack for the first time in your life you've managed to say something profound," Avelina teased with a smile, "I'm proud of you, really." My eyes involuntarily rolled as she let out a single hearty laugh, amused. Almost instantly, her smile became rueful as her eyes reverted to the illuminated sky.

"Your sentiment isn't that far from the truth believe it or not," Avelina lamented, "The dogs in charge of us, of this entire state are nothing but lazy old fools who sit in their highchairs all day, scooping up wealth while the rest of us scrounge on our own." Scoffing to herself, I could sense the older woman's discouragement over the matter through her tone, one which was far more cynical than anything else I've heard from her.

"At least we agree on something," I joked with a slight laugh echoing in my voice, "But what does being self-aware have to do with any of this?" Avelina for once actually didn't react physically or audibly to my declaration, instead opting to stare down at the path ahead.

"I hope that…one day I can move up the ranks of this…putrid establishment. Countless corrupt bargains and shady backstabbing goes on up there that the public is none the wiser about. Maybe in a year's time once we catch Zain, I can rise to a more senior position in the military. Then I can finally clean up that den of thieves in Heartwood." I grinned to myself as I repositioned my sword so it didn't crash into anything else, preventing any more damage to the path.

"That's quite the noble goal Avelina. Wouldn't expect something like that from you," I teased, "I'm guessing our great leader fits somewhere into that mix."

"Another magnificent guess, Jack good job! Keep this up and maybe you'll actually activate some brain cells." I let out an annoyed yawn as my eyelids fluttered, making me want to pass out on the dirt below. I frantically rubbed my eyes to ward it away, all the while hearing Avelina chuckling quietly to herself at my side as our boots marched almost in rhythm.

"I...I was in a stronger position in the military at one point," Avelina reminisced with a light smile, "I was poised to be one of the youngest people ever to become some form of commander within the military. Then one day, I met a rookie commander named Katrina Ward with a new idea, and then everything changed." She let out a sigh as she hugged her shoulders, obviously thinking back to that moment with a twinge of nostalgia.

"Katrina is the most genuine person I have ever met in the entire military, and I dropped everything to follow her. I don't regret that moment at all, because to be honest I think I have done more good here than I ever did back in Heartwood. While we're only considered a simple covert operations group by the military, I'll help Katrina to change that. I hope that one day our group will number in the thousands, with the people looking up to us with the knowledge that the higher ups truly care about their well-being. To put it bluntly, the military would rather keep things the way they already are. Why else do you think Nathaniel is the one funding this entire organization?"

"I'm sure the people appreciate an alleviation from more taxes," I snickered quietly to myself, "Although I wouldn't know. Part of the reason I think dad moved out into that magnificent land of nothing was to dodge getting taxed." Avelina let out a faint chuckle as I heard a bird chirp softly in the distance, followed by three more as the group darted through the tree line. I glanced up as I saw a fifth larger bird following up behind them, trailing at a much slower pace behind the others as if it was injured.

"Your parents must have been wonderful people," Avelina lamented as she stared forward at me, "I do hope you manage to find your mother, but I'm sure you'll find a way. After all, they did manage to raise two able and kind-hearted children." My eyes widened as my head shot over to Avelina, genuinely surprised and a tad bit touched at her declaration. My cheeks briefly burned red as she leaned her head back with another laugh.

"Don't get too big of a head over that kid," Avelina said while attempting to suppress another laugh, "That's the one and only compliment I'm ever going to give you. Cherish it cause you're never going to hear another one come out of my mouth." Feeling quite awkward, I released an embarrassed smile as I rubbed the back of my head. A single laugh escaped the two of us, looking like two friends having a refreshing chat rather than two people supposed to be looking out for the enemy. I tried to not think about any of it, just relishing this moment of calm I had missed so much.

A long silence followed as the laughter soon died down, filling the air with nothing but the sounds of squirrels leaping through the trees and soft winds rustling leaves. I turned towards Avelina, who looked like she had finally managed to beat back the drowsiness and sadness that was threatening to overcome her. I knew in about an hour my eyes would grow heavy, and I would pass out maybe minutes later. I wanted to say something to fill the silence, but I couldn't conjure up anything to say.

Avelina's bright orange eyes widened as she suddenly gasped, lunging forward past my vision. Swiftly turning to see what caused such a reaction, I stared forward in silent shock as Avelina came to a stop within a small clearing. She shakily glanced around at what we saw.

More bodies than I bothered to count were lying face down in the mossy dirt; a dried red wave coalescing around their contorted forms. It was obvious they were each only pierced once, but based on each attack they were done by swift slashes and pierces. A group of five each had a knife protruding out of their necks, each slain in an instant.

At the center sat a larger man Avelina was now crouched beside, one who was absolutely littered with knives protruding out of his body. Only the one sticking through his chest appeared to be fatal, although I'm sure with how many there were he would've been dead anyway. Avelina turned the body over as a widened look of recognition dawned over her face.

"Captain Anderson," Avelina whispered as she stared at the fallen man, "You proud old fool. What the heck were you doing all the way out here?" I stepped forward into the clearing myself, unable to comprehend the multitude of bodies littering the area.

"It...it could just be a random patrol." I attempted to rationalize, although Avelina immediately shook her head at my statement.

"It could've," Avelina relented as she neared a tree, "But, what're the chances some random attacker would have this lying around?" Raising up the head of a spear that was through the body of a sickeningly younger looking soldier, Avelina snatched something from the tip and waved it in the moonlight, walking back from where we came as she showcased it.

A single strip of purple cloth.

He...this was him again...that elusive bastard.

My body tensed up in anger as she ran her hand across the ground where the red had coalesced. She paused for a moment, before sighing to herself as she pulled it back up.

"The blood isn't wet, but it hasn't dried well enough to fade away into the dirt. They must've been attacked earlier today, but the Captain must've sputtered on a little bit longer." I still couldn't believe what I was seeing, staring down at a man who resembled a bloody mess rather than a man. The symbol that emblazoned his armor rang familiar to me: the same image of a wolf growling into the sky. I glanced up toward Avelina, her hand gripped over the metal plate that guarded what I knew was an identical symbol.

"Why would soldiers from the capital be all the way out here? Or even have the chance of encountering Zain?"

"Someone over there clearly didn't trust us," Avelina growled out as she stood up, her fists balled, "Some officials clearly didn't think we could pull this off and sent this team to their deaths behind our backs. Now I know for certain that our idea of this being a reconnaissance mission was sound." She sighed as she took a final glance at the fallen, before turning around and walking back down the path.

"We've seen enough to know he's near, but remember to relay this to Katrina when we get back. For now, let's make sure camp is still standing." I hesitated only for a moment, my eyes pivoted between the purple haired woman and the soldiers.

In the end I walked after her, refusing to linger.

So many people dead from this one man...how many more will fall if we don't find him soon?

We just have to find him. Only then will this blasted mess end.

The walk back was as silent as I expected, with Avelina clearly lost in thought as her brain attempted to figure out Zain's location relative to us. If we were lucky, we'd be close enough to prevent an event like this from happening again.

Hating the way this blasted silence perforated the air, I turned to the older woman as I recalled our conversation moments prior to our morbid discovery.

"Do you really think you can accomplish a dream as monumental as yours Avelina?" Avelina glanced over at me with mild surprise on her face as if it were an afterthought, before reverting her attention back in front of her and the events the path initially led to. I could almost see her own determination and ambition burning within those bright eyes.

"Without a single doubt in my mind Jack," she hollowly chuckled to herself, staring forward down the path where the others slept, unaware.

"Without a single doubt."

23

Jack: Training, More or Less

For the first time in my long existence, I missed that wretched darkness that used to cling to me with my every movement I made. The darkness that swarmed throughout me, embracing me in its cold, lifeless arms. With every step, I felt as if I had taken none at all as the background shifted and swayed in the same manner it did every day. By all accounts, back then I was a prisoner.

And yet, my imprisoned past felt freer than I do at this moment.

"**Damn you...damn you all**," I murmured to myself as I lay crouched on the ground, clutching at the hairs that stuck out of my splitting skull, "**I'll kill you...I swear you will suffer the most prolonged and painful death I have ever wrought upon another being. You should f-feel honored.**" I felt a laugh tickle the back of my throat involuntarily, my eyes widening as I further gripped the sides of my skull.

"**I'm losing my mind in here...somebody.**" Finally gathering the strength to stand, I brushed off the same blackened clothes I carried with me since The Abyss, keeping it in as pristine of a condition as I could maintain.

A cool wind strangely rushed over the air, making me stare towards the door that taunted my every move. It stared down at me with the faint glimmering light behind the door, all the while mocking me with my own visage.

A sudden blow struck me in my shins, startling me as I was propelled forward in the small space. I let out a loud embarrassing yelp as I struck the bars full on, my body launching off of it as currents ran up and down my body. Skidding across the ground like a stone in a pond, I slammed into the back wall with a loud groan.

Lying flat as I attempted to regain my composure, I planted my palms on the ground as I attempted to push myself up. My right arm faltered as pain shot through both of them, sending me back down on my face.

"**What...what the...**" Propping myself up, I glanced down at my pained arms, only to notice that my knuckles had become bruised in some way.

"**How the...I don't understand...**" Another blow, this time to the ribs, followed swiftly by a devastating strike to the stomach. I crumpled over at the attacks, frantically glancing around as I attempted to discover the source of this misery. As my right hand contacted the ground as I fell, it immediately recoiled as if they were filled with the same power as the bars. I paused to ensure no more of this barrage continued, eventually jumping to my feet.

"**Show yourself!**" I bellowed, the room shaking as my threats echoed out. I panted in a way where pain shot through with every breath. The attack had finally died down, but the pain still lingered. Pain unlike anytime I had hit the wall or even touched those damn bars.

Pain...only a human could know...

* * *

"Correct me if I'm wrong, but Zain doesn't appear to be moving at as fast of a pace as us, correct?" Avelina glanced back at me as we were running through the forest in almost complete darkness, her eyes lighting up the shadows and her own silhouette.

Two hours earlier, and several hours after my shift at watch duty was replaced by Henry, Avelina awoke the three of us with a start. I remember groaning out some harsh expletives, before Avelina dragged me by the leg and threw me out of the tent. We got ourselves ready and left within five minutes.

We avoided the path which ran along the bodies of the soldiers. There was no need to tell them. We would bring it up to Katrina privately to gripe against those that willingly sent those people to their demise.

I rubbed the small of my back as we continued along, still in pain from colliding with the hard soil earlier.

Serena was rubbing her eyes dramatically to try and stay alert, her orange hair frayed as she kept decent pace with us. Fox and Avelina led the pack, with Serena and I trailing behind. Henry was guarding the back, his eyes staring throughout the darkness. Thankfully, a glint of sunlight began creeping out just beyond the tree line, meaning I'd actually be able to see something besides the two sister's silhouettes soon.

"That should be correct," Avelina acknowledged, skidding to stop in her tracks, with Fox doing the same. Since awakening a little before I did, she hadn't said a single word to anyone but her sister.

Although, I think I actually prefer it this way.

"Awesome," I grinned as I turned around and stopped, watching as Serena and Henry did the same, "It'll only take a couple minutes, but I'm itching for a little sparring against both of you." Serena looked startled by my exclamation, while Henry probably lifted an eyebrow as he crossed his arms.

300

"Really?" Serena asked, "Right now? Um…Are you sure?"

"Definitely," I continued as I cracked my knuckles with a grin, "We have the time and this mission doesn't involve fighting, so even if it was, we'll be rested enough to be at our full potential when we find him."

"And besides," I rambled on as I pulled my fist up confidently, "Avelina wants to save our fight for later, but I'm going a little crazy from all this endless walking and I'm dying for any kind of fighting. So let's do this, as long as that's alright with you Avelina." Instead of audibly answering my question Avelina gave a simple shrug, leaning against a tree nearby. She pulled the same book out of her jacket yet again, mumbling to herself something about me and my denseness or some other insult directed at my intelligence as she began to read, the minor amount of sunlight being enough to see. Fox scoffed to herself in annoyance, before turning around to apparently keep some form of lookout.

"If it's a fight you desire then so be it," Henry plainly announced in his usual monotone voice, "Come on Serena. Let's try and make this quick." Serena pouted as she followed behind, crossing her arms as she dragged her feet along the dusty ground.

"But I'm so tired!" I chuckled as I walked into a small clearing across from Henry and Serena.

Henry brought his gloved fists up, taking a standard fist-fighting stance I had seen my dad utilize countless times. His left hand was held high to block his face, while the other was just a tad lower. Serena half-heartedly did a stance of her own, although I wasn't sure what the technique behind it was.

Bringing up my own fists, I was surprised to see Henry motioning past my present hands with a simple turn of the head.

"Use your sword." I heard Henry say it bluntly. I hesitated momentarily, knowing I had used my sword previously when fighting

Avelina earlier, but I still wasn't sure if I should.

"Don't worry," Henry explained, reading my thoughts, "You won't land a scratch on either of us." I smirked at his apparent cockiness, pulling my beautiful blade off of my back with the same flourish I had done countless times.

The metal gleamed in the slight sunlight, the fireball beginning to rise from beyond the tree line. I pulled the sword back and over my right shoulder in my traditional stance, pointing the tip of the blade directly at Henry's mask. Standing ten feet away from each other, I could feel four pairs of eyes staring into me as I repositioned my stance. I made sure my own remained locked on Henry's as I did so.

Henry rocketed towards me immediately, his fist already pulled back behind him as a geyser of dust shot into the air. Instead of ducking as he most likely anticipated, I drew the sword's hilt down by the left side of my hip and flipped the blade, letting Henry's fist collide with the flare side of my guard. I stepped back once from the force, before swinging the already vertical blade across. Henry simply stepped out of the way with an agility that rivaled Avelina's, and maybe even Katrina's.

This is gonna be a challenge...sweet!

Spinning around, I sprung forward with a high kick to his jaw, connecting with his sudden shielding arms instead. I instantly pulled that leg back and jabbed at him again, swinging at him with my offhand in a somewhat clunky manner. He caught it with ease, gripping my knuckles tightly within his gloved grasp.

Growling slightly, I launched an elbow down at his wrist, forcing him to let go of my hand as he yelled out in pain. Jumping away, I sprung forward and dragged the broadsword across the ground with one arm and swung it across his chest. He leapt back in surprise, although the blade managed to barely scrape across his leather armor as dust littered the air around us.

In a flash Serena was in Henry's place, launching through the cloud of dirt, landing in a dramatic fashion in a way that almost resembled a pose. What soon became obvious was the faint translucent pink glow overwhelming her hands like some sort of glove, shining in a similar way to when she healed others. Even after seeing it before, the pink glow somehow seemed more...menacing.

"I'm not really sure what that glowing around your hands is," I proclaimed with a grin, "But something tells me I'd rather not have them hit me." She giggled to herself as she gazed over at her partner, with the both of them not saying anything.

Henry nodded towards Serena, who in an instant glanced back and rushed forward. Although she wasn't as fast as Henry was, it was clear I had to pay proper attention.

I swung my broadsword sideways towards Serena, who managed to slide underneath the swing while keeping her forward momentum. Trapping my right leg between both of hers, I was swiftly swept off my feet, colliding with the ground as my eyes now stared up at the sky.

Dammit! How'd she do that so fast?

Popping up off the ground, Serena went for a hard jab to the face while I was still collapsed on the ground. I lazily rolled sideways and sprung myself up, minus my sword.

Taking a fist fighting stance I glanced to the side, just to see Henry just standing there, watching with his icy eyes.

"You better pay attention Jack." I panicked while frantically glancing back just in time to duck past one of her pink jabs, fighting far faster without my sword.

Leaning back, I struck her once in the nose, causing her to step back with a stumble as she groaned in pain and annoyance. I rushed forward without letting up, wrapping my arms around her waist in a fierce tackle before slamming her back down to earth. Serena gasped out in pain as her arms flew outwards, the pink light dulling and eventually fading from around her hands.

With her normal hand, she cracked me in the jaw with a surprising amount of power, propelling me off of her with a yell of pain. She rolled backwards and stood up to her feet, blood steadily dripping down and out of her left nostril. She held up a now green hand to her nose, causing the blood to slow down to a trickle. I held my jaw in frustration, annoyed I couldn't do the same trick.

She's small, but she hits like a damn horse!

Instead of facing me one-on-one like before, the two of them rushed me at the same time, with Serena's hands lighting up with that same pink glow yet again. I raised my fists to my face as I prepared to defend against them, staring almost longingly at the discarded blade.

"Alright then you two…come at me!"

Henry was far faster than Serena was, ending up directly in front of me first with a drawn back fist.

Raising an arm to block the first devastating swing, I almost gasped in surprise at how unresponsive the appendage was as I attempted to defend myself. I could barely get it up in time to block the strike, cringing in pain as the block wasn't timed well enough.

"What the…?" I wondered aloud in confusion, pushing Henry away from where I blocked. The edges of Henry's mask curled up as he dusted off his arms, stretching them out as I shook my right arm. The arm was incredibly stiff, almost as if I had gone through hours of training without breaks, maybe even with rocks strapped to it as well. Gritting my teeth together, I attempted to lunge forward at Henry with my offhand, my stupid right arm weighing down my approach.

"Do you forget so easily what she did only a day ago?" he taunted while he vaulted backwards, easily dodging my slow strike, "Those palms are gifted at the art of healing, but at the flick of wrist she can take that all away. Should've watched what she was doing when you tackled her!" I growled as a reinvigorated Serena charged at me again with those pink palms, with Henry not too far away. I pulled my stiff right arm back, pulling my left arm up.

As Serena went for another overhand strike with her right hand, I ducked past and snaked my arm up and around, passing her magic. I caught onto her wrist as she yelped in surprise, the pink energy flickering on her hand as her fingers twitched.

Desperately trying to wrench herself free, she jabbed at my face with a normal strike with her left arm, which I narrowly dodged with a swift turn of my neck.

In the corner of my eye, I noticed Henry fast approaching from behind Serena, a factor she foresaw as well.

I swung my knee up as hard as I could, sharply striking her in the stomach. As she exhaled in pain and surprise, I pulled my head back and headbutted her perfectly, rewarding me with dull pain afterwards instead of a sharper one. As she began to sprawl backwards, I lunged forward and struck her in the jaw with my offhand, finishing the fight.

However, before she fully collapsed, she suddenly flicked her left hand down as a dim smile came to her face. I could only watch in horror as a pink coated hand brushed against my other arm, unable to dodge right away. The light flickered out completely as she fell to the ground barely conscious, my eyes widening as the muscles in my other arm contracted and stiffened painfully.

Crap crap crap...

With my other arm now lying stiff at my side, Henry charged right in front of me preparing to strike, knowing full well that defending myself was out of the question. In a panic, I attempted to dodge out of the way of the devastating blow, only to have Henry strike me full on in the chest. Pain enveloped and spread throughout my rib cage as I involuntarily coughed, stumbling backwards before another strike bombarded me. I felt my back crash into a sturdy tree, its branches quivering and shaking as the masked man approached.

Henry charged forward at me, knowing full well that one final strike would be enough to end this little sparring match. What the man didn't know was that although the aching remained pervasive with my left arm, it had already begun to die down in my right. So, even though it wasn't perfectly back to normal, I could still swing it at almost the same speed. I sat there with my arms down, waiting as he came scarily close.

As he lurked within ten feet of me, I shot my head up as I raised my right arm, pulling it back and swinging at the right time when I knew he would be in striking range. I could see his blue eyes widen in surprise beneath his mask, clearly not anticipating the move. I almost grinned at my triumph.

But something inside me flickered, causing me to hesitate before fully committing to the attack. It was almost like...that innate feeling you get when something goes wrong. That sinking in the pit of your stomach as dread overcomes you; the fight or flight instinct kicking in before the unease even enters your thoughts.

I chose flight midway through my strike, jumping to the right as swiftly as I could manage in my position. Weighed down by the heaviness of my left arm and my position of already swinging at him, my arm was nicked slightly as I sprung out of the way. Even from the minor attack, pain shot through my entire arm as the material of the sleeve tore at the point of attack.

I landed face down in the dirt a foot or two away; my face crunching against the ground as my left arm became pinned under my body. I let out a pained groan, one which became easily overshadowed by a sudden crash, followed by wood splintering and cracking as if they were rotten. Another crash swiftly followed, as a gasp rang out behind me. I built up the strength to prop myself up with my right arm, glancing over my shoulder.

The limber tree I had been leaning against previously was now lying on the ground, its branches crunching into the dirt as already dead leaves splattered across the ground. Vaguely connected by a few splinters and loose bark, the trunk sat out in the air as wooden spikes formed from where the rest of the tree broke off.

Henry stood there with his fist still extended, his eyes wide as he shakily uncurled his gloved fingers. His blue eyes frantically stared between the splintered trunk and his open palm, shaking in utter disbelief and shock.

"I...I didn't mean to..." he stammered in a voice that wasn't its usual monotone, almost condescending tone. It was the voice of someone who felt genuinely afraid of something. The closest thing it resembled was the tone I took whenever my brother and I did any play fighting as kids. I would always hit Connor way too hard, and end up frantically trying to console him before dad came through the door and brought his wrath down upon me.

"That's enough!" I heard a female voice yell out from behind. I turned on the ground to see Fox standing afar, her bright brown eyes furrowed. At that moment I noticed the multitude of daggers and knives hidden underneath her cloak and attached to her leg. She was currently gripping onto one of them still within its sheath, although for how long it would stay there I wasn't sure.

Avelina was farther away, as she was still near the tree she was leaning against. She appeared perplexed, but at the same time there wasn't an ounce of worry similar to what her sister carried. In fact, the book remained open in her hand, showing that she was nearing completion.

Serena had gotten back up after resting on the ground in pain, the green light fading from her injuries as she gasped at the scene in front of her.

"Everything…is alright Fox," I breathed out as I unsuccessfully attempted to ease myself up without my arms, only to crash back down to the ground, "Something tells me…we're done now." Fox's expression soured even more based on the way her eyes narrowed more than I thought possible.

"He could've killed you!" she yelled out in anger, "You're lucky you only have a couple scrapes on you from this match. That…that bastard could've caved your skull in if he really wanted, and you're sitting here acting like it was no big deal." She stood there with her hand on her weapon still as Serena applied the healing aura to my arms, flashing me a nervous smile as I finally was able to push myself up comfortably. She also applied her hands to the small cut that Henry had managed to dig into my arm, although I had just barely first noticed it before Serena made it fade away. The blood had already stained that sleeve and my skin.

Fox refused to move, keeping her hand on one of her daggers as she stared down at the still immobile man. His arm slowly began to lower, but his eyes remained wide. The masked woman took a single step forward.

"Hey you!" Fox yelled out towards the still immobile Henry, "Yeah I'm talking to you monster boy. I'm five seconds away from doing something drastic, so you'd better give me a solid argument for why I shouldn't. Can you even hear me you stupid beast, or are you that flustered about this?" My jaw tightened as her words flew into the clearly dazed man, ready to spring up and knock her ass out for daring to say such a thing to him. However, someone else was much closer to the same solution.

Serena…

For a brief second, the green around Serena's hands flickered to pink as she stopped her healing, her palms crunching to fists as her grey eyes hardened into an emotion I didn't think was possible from her.

Pure, unbridled hatred.

"How dare you…" Serena whispered at a volume only I could hear, taking a step forward.

I sprung up immediately, putting a firm hand on her shoulder. Her eyes softened as I shook my head, although the angered glare never truly left as I stepped in front of her.

"It was an accident," I insisted, trying to diminish the hostility as I stretched my arms out, "I really don't understand what happened but all I know is I didn't get hurt, so your words are moot. So why don't you chill out on the threats and back off before one of us does something…drastic."

"Jack's right sis," Avelina exclaimed in just as affirmative of a tone, "Henry didn't hurt anyone, so go ahead and stand down Fox." The masked woman stood motionless at the sound of her code name, before finally shutting her brown eyes and moving her hand away from the dagger with a scoff. Moving the cloak back around her, Fox turned back around and walked back toward her sister and the lookout area.

With the moment of tension somewhat gone, I shook my arms in glee as I was finally able to move them without too much trouble. Serena laughed to herself as she walked to her masked companion, giving a sideways glance Fox's way. However, the refined anger was suddenly gone, her bubbly joy returning.

Henry still stood in front of the tree silently, however he now turned in Serena's direction as she bounded over. His eyes squinted back to normal as the fear dissipated.

"Well," I announced through the pervasive silence, "I guess our break is over. If we would've kept going, I would've found a way to win by the way." Henry gave me an eye smile as he shut his blue eyes, rolling his shoulders back and forth as Serena finally finished her healing procedures on everyone.

"The fact you could barely move once we finished tells me otherwise," he called back in the same deadpan tone as I walked towards a sighing Avelina, "But if you wish to test that, I'd be thrilled to go again." I heard Serena let out a groan of annoyance as I flashed Henry a swift thumbs up, confirming my interest to fight again later.

"All that healing and fighting tired me out even more," she whined to herself as I could almost audibly hear her cross her arms in a pouting manner, "Now you'll have to carry me the rest of the way Henry." I heard the masked man sigh as Avelina had already started walking ahead, waiting for the rest of us to catch up before we resumed our sprint from earlier. If my read on the fight was accurate, then we probably sparred for ten minutes at most.

"I'm well aware that you can still walk on your own Serena."

"Well did you ever consider I don't feel like walking, Henry?" she pouted, "So you'd better prepare yourself, because I'm jumping on your back whether you like it or not!" I chuckled, relieved that the jovial energy had returned after being sidelined by that single moment of tension.

But as I walked, I thought back to the fight we had just endured, one that had begun as a simple sparring match. Thinking about how the tree had almost come down on top of me once it had collapsed.

How Henry was the one who caused it.

24

Connor: Split Perspectives

"I'm taking her back Mara." Those were the last words I'm sure she expected to hear from my mouth, as her once blank expression swiftly shifted from nothing, to surprise, until finally settling on some form of anger.

The sleeping Catherine was currently resting on my back as we walked, as I knew she might not have the energy to properly walk any long distances. She barely weighed anything, so I didn't care much. Her soft snores echoed into my back, her patterned breaths already sounding better than they did yesterday.

I hope she's feeling better. Once I get you back everything will be okay.

We had only just left, dusting dirt over the fire one final time to ensure no prying eyes would trace our steps. By my estimation it was around six, maybe seven o'clock in the morning. The sun had barely started poking up from beyond the tree line, providing enough light to follow the trail despite being heavily shielded by clouds.

We left probably fifteen minutes ago. Judging by these steps it's been about an hour or less. They were walking based on the stride distance of the people.

It could easily be another group of four...or perhaps five people.

Correct, but considering the timing, the creation of a new path, and counting on the inclusion of a spy to go along with them, this must be them.

That...and one of these footsteps has the occasional dragging of something behind them. Someone I know happens to always get aggravated when that happens to him.

Fantastic. Now all we need to do is move backwards from these steps and we'll make it back to the Sentinels' base by the end of the afternoon.

Mara turned to me clearly shocked, glaring at me with a betrayed glint in her emerald eyes.

"What do you mean you're taking her back? I thought you agreed with me earlier?" I attempted to maintain my stoic expression as we both halted our stride.

"I...thought about your original idea all night Mara," I explained as I reaffirmed Catherine's position on my back, "And to bring her along on this excursion is simply inhumane. If we run into Zain, we would be putting her life into serious jeopardy." She stared at me in shock as I turned over to stare at the still sleeping child.

Even in just one night of proper rest and food, she's already looking so much better than she did when we found her. I don't want to think about what would have happened if we hadn't arrived when we did.

"We need to bring her with us Connor," Mara replied in a rising voice, "As I stated Katrina will stop us if we attempt to sneak away after returning her. We're close enough as reinforcements to not take too long if Zain is far from the base." Mara crossed her arms at me after her exclamation, taking her eyes off me with a light scoff.

"We can go back, and then Katrina might send us as reinforcements later," I growled out as I became increasingly frustrated, "Even if we are decently far out, we can still assist if we hurry and bring Catherine back." I now stood face-to-face with the woman who I had been traveling with for almost a day. By my counts she was only an inch shorter than I was, but that didn't really matter.

312

The amount of anger brewing in her narrowed expression gave her the intimidation she needed.

"She needs this Connor," Mara snapped in an almost pleading tone, "She *needs* to come with us." I stepped closer, noticing that both of our voices were continuing to rise.

"But why!" I uncharacteristically yelled in her face, feeling myself losing control of all these bottled-up sentiments and emotions, "She is a child! She just lost everything and could have easily died herself, and you wish to willingly throw her life back into a stream of danger. And for what? Necessity?"

"I'm trying to take her pain away Connor!" she screamed out in a way radically different from her usual voice, startling me with the sudden juxtaposition.

"Even if she isn't able to fight, seeing the one who caused her so much torment beaten into the ground can make some of that pain disappear. She may never have an opportunity like this, and we have to take it. For her sake." Mara looked down at the ground as she said this, her auburn hair covering the determination that was absolutely brewing in her green pools.

How...How could she say something like that? I get the reasoning behind it all, but why would she even consider putting her life in jeopardy? She escaped death once. I don't know if she can do it again.

"Is...is that all you care about?" I rasped out, my voice quivering as I spoke, "Does her well-being mean nothing to you Mara?" She looked back up at me with burning indignation present in her eyes. I backed up as I set Catherine down on a tree nearby. She let out a light groan, but other than that remained fast asleep.

"Of course I care about that," she replied, anger reverberating through her calm and level voice, "I've seen that look before Connor, and I never wish to see it ever again. It's the look of someone who has nothing left in their life but vengeance and hatred, and this is her only chance to return back to a normal existence before it swallows her whole." Mara was looking back down, her entire body shaking in a way that defied the calmness her tone had become. I wasn't listening to any of it.

I'm not going to allow this girl to die. I couldn't stop her village's destruction, but I can do this.

I won't fail her again.

"I don't care what your reasoning may be Mara because whatever it is I know I'm going to disagree with it. So therefore, I will be taking her back whether you-"

My entire vision shook as a gloved fist connected with my chin, slamming into me as I recoiled in surprise. Dazed, I grasped onto my jaw as I attempted to recollect my thoughts, only to have another swift strike rock my vision yet again. I fell to the ground, clutching my pained face as I groaned. I looked up at Mara standing above me, her teeth grinding together and her squinted mossy eyes containing nothing but anger and hatred.

I sprung backwards in the opposite direction, watching as her fist dug into the ground where I once was. A geyser of dirt and grass flew up into the sky as her hand burrowed into the earth.

"You're willing to attack me just to bring her into unnecessary danger? Just like that?" She charged at me and went for another strike, only for me to catch it with relative ease. I twisted her wrist back, causing her to yelp out in pain.

"You would never understand!" she yelled as I rammed into her stomach, causing her to double over in pain. My leg swiftly cracked against her side, knocking her back down. While she was still on the ground, I sprinted forward for another kick, hoping to end this swiftly.

She was baiting me in, and I should have seen it. Spinning on the ground, her two legs wrapped around my front leg and tripped me, sending me through the air. With the momentum of her spin she sprung to her feet, slamming a foot into my stomach as soon as I connected with the ground.

The wind knocked out of me, I could barely react before Mara had her hands wrapped around my collar. With a sound that almost resembled a snarl, she drilled her fist into my stomach as she held me with a single hand. Her arm almost looked like a blur from the speed of the strike, but it didn't take away how strong of a punch it was, almost making me puke from the pain.

Pulling me closer, she reeled back and smashed her skull against mine.

I yelled out in pain as a cut tore across my forehead, scrambling wildly and managing to connect a kick to her stomach to stumble away.

"You think you're the only one who's seen pain like that before?" I pleaded as I recoiled several steps back and pressed a hand to my forehead, the red already beginning to rush down my fingers, "This isn't the way to do this. I've seen trauma like hers, and I won't let you ruin whatever chance of recovery we have by dragging her off to die." She panted to herself as she ran back at me, somehow unfazed by the headbutt she had delivered only seconds earlier.

I can't think...that hit from her gave me a monster headache.

I need to incapacitate her somehow, before she does the same to me and drags us into the maw of death!

"You'll never get why I'm doing this Connor!" she screamed out in a tone that ran shivers up my spine, "I've seen more than you'll ever see in your entire life!" Waiting for her to be right on top of me, I narrowly dodged out of the way and kneed her in the stomach full force. She gasped for air as I threw another punch. It was clunky due to the previous knee and was easily latched onto by both of her hands. Rolling down the length of my arm, she kept one hand on my arm as she latched onto my face with the other, slamming me to the ground below. Before I could even attempt to stand, she had her arms wrapped around my wrist, locking me in an arm bar as her legs kept my right arm trapped. I tried to wriggle free, but her grip only tightened as her boot heels pressed down on my chest.

"Submit," she plainly demanded, "We're taking Catherine with us. I'd rather not be forced to break your arm since you need that to fight, but you're making this difficult."

Seeing an opening, I struck the interior of her calf twice, hearing her growl as the pain shot through her. While it wasn't enough to free me, her grip instinctively loosened as the pain reverberated.

Giving my arm enough space to shake loose just barely, I had enough space to swing up and drive my trapped elbow into her chest. She gasped out for air as she finally released me, but not before I slammed the back part of my fist into her face with the space I had. While not particularly hard, the strike to the nose was enough to crack her back down to the dirt below.

I frantically scrambled away as Mara stood prone in the same spot, easing herself up as she spit a coagulation of her own blood out. Through the brown hair that splayed over her face, she stared back at me with those malice filled eyes.

She's far faster than me, and judging by the tenacity by which she fights she's trained longer than I have.

She's also a sufficient grappler and has enough power to bring me down with a couple strikes. I don't have the advantage of distance either.

I truly am on my back foot with this.

I just need to incapacitate her at any opportunity I see, whatever it takes. If I drag this out any longer, her superior skill will be the end of me.

Springing from the spot with a renewed determination, Mara was already in front of me with her enraged visage, sending me reeling back with a heel kick to the jaw. As soon as I looked up she was already upon me again, her right fist at the ready. Rolling out of the way, the fist found a home in the base of a tree instead of my face. Tearing a hole straight through the base of the relatively thin tree, the swordswoman took a second or two to pull it out as I tried to steady my breathing.

How could she possibly possess that much strength behind her strikes?

Charging in front of me with an incredible dash of speed, I barely had enough time to block against the flurry of kicks and punches that soon came my way. My arms had become dulled to the pain, which combined with the adrenaline made me more capable of withstanding strike after strike.

She's far faster than I am, and her strength could rival mine blow for blow.

I can't keep this up, and I won't use the amulet on her for this. I promised to only use it if my life was truly threatened.

Smacking one strike to the side, I lunged forward at her face to try and end this here and now, only to have the fist caught with a quick flourish from Mara. Seeing her lean her head back to go for another headbutt, I used my placement in front of her to knee her twice in the stomach. She released me from her grasp as she gasped for air, unprepared for her attack to be anticipated. Stepping back, I knew I only had a couple seconds before she went after me again.

"Listen to my reasoning Mara! You're going to get that girl killed if we go there!" With another burst of speed, she was already right in front of me with her fists raised again.

This time I was ready for the bombardment to come. I rolled out of the way of her fist, sliding along the length of her arm. Grasping her right arm, I spun my body around and slammed her back down to earth. She choked on her own breath from the devastating impact, gasping for air as dust billowed up in its place.

She stared up at me as she attempted to wrench herself free, the hatred vaguely disappearing from her eyes as she poured all of her energy into escaping from my grasp.

"She needs to go," she whispered out in a raspy tone as she continued to struggle on the ground, "I won't...I can't let her be consumed by all of her suffering." Just as I thought Mara was going to continue fighting, I stared down at her, seeing into her eyes a glimmer I never thought would be possible coming from her at this moment.

Compassion swirling within the pools of rage...

At first confusion reigned supreme in my mind, not fully recognizing that the emotion was truly there and present.

Is she...actually doing all this for Catherine? She couldn't be...

Those had to be lies...justifications she created for her own motives... right?

I glanced back at the young girl Catherine, the only one who survived the tumultuous attack we failed to stop.

I couldn't quite tell what emotions she felt, but...I knew they had to be violent and ever present. Feelings of sadness sure, but I know there has to be some form of anger brewing inside that young mind of hers.

And what should I do Jack? Stand on the sidelines like you do while our mom is still out there? While that demon is still out there?

I glanced down at the woman in my grasp.

You...you know what it feels like.

"You see yourself in her too...don't you?" Her eyes lit up in surprise as I released her from my grasp, lowering my fist back down to my side as the black hair covered my eyes. Immediately jumping up with her fists up, I raised an open-palmed hand to halt her advance.

"You're doing all of this for her," I realized as her green eyes widened at my proclamation, "You see yourself in her, just like I have. The difference comes about through our own philosophy." Lowering her fists, her gaze came to rest upon the ground by us, staring at small tufts of grass that had poked their way through the abrasive soil.

Trauma. I hadn't seen it before but now I just couldn't ignore it.

That blankness in her stare; that cynical gaze she brought upon all things as if they weren't even worth a second fleeting glance.

Something from her past had dug its way into her being, locking her ideals into a single mindset. And whatever it is, it's making her believe this is the preeminent course of action. Every lie she has ever told; the deception she put behind every sentence in a conscious effort to not reveal too much information.

"Just what on earth have you gone through Mara?" She remained wordless at my questioning, rubbing her cheek at the spot I struck her. I let out a sigh as I shook my head, placing my hands in my pockets.

Something about you makes us so similar Mara, and yet at the same time so different. I feel almost...sympathy for you, and I'm not sure why.

"I will bring her to this fight," I begrudgingly relented as I walked over to the still sleeping girl, raising my hand as I did so, "But first, I have two terms I wish for you to agree on before we set out." Craning my head back as I kept my arm raised, Mara gave a hesitant nod as she kept her eyes on the distant tree line.

Thankful she was listening this time instead of lashing out, I raised my index finger as I turned my head back.

"Under no circumstances will Catherine face any combat or even be on the same battlefield as said combat. She may watch from the sidelines, but she must stay with one of us at all times instead of approaching." Without waiting for any form of affirmation, I raised the second finger, hoping she was listening closely.

"My second condition is just as simple: When the time comes where we will be reprimanded for this action, you will be the one to explain why we directly defied orders." Hearing her stance shift slightly, I knew that she must have glanced up in surprise at my proclamation.

"What? You thought Katrina would just be alright with this little excursion?" I rhetorically asked, "When we chose to join the Sentinels, we chose to exist under a distinct section of rules set by them. While I believe we have every right to disobey orders if we feel it's the right thing to do, someone's still going to have to explain why we directly defied the orders of our superior. Understand?" Turning back around to see how she would react, Mara hastily nodded her head to my two conditions.

"Then alright. We'd better get going if we desire to make it on time to be reinforcements." Hoisting the girl back onto my back, I could hear Catherine faintly grumbling to herself as she finally awoke.

"Con...Connor," she sleepily mumbled.

"Easy Cat," I consoled as I turned my head to the girl on my back, "We just took a small break is all, and I had to pick you back up to get going again. Now get some more rest." Almost effortlessly agreeing with me, Catherine set her head back down and within five seconds was snoring peacefully again.

Following closely behind me, Mara finally passed me and walked up ahead, following the trail of the others and keeping a sharp lookout as I had the girl on my back.

We're going to get that man, and I'm going to find the lead I've been searching for, but I'll make sure that you remain safe while we do.

"I promise you." I thought aloud in a soft whisper, the young girl shifting again from my proclamation. Thankfully, she didn't stir from her slumber in the slightest.

I promise...

25

Jack: Fundamentally Flawed Plan

The effects of this endless walking were beginning to drive me insane.

We had been walking for five straight hours now I think, seven if you count the two hours of running scattered between the walking. Needless to say, I was about ready to pass out with each resounding step.

The afternoon sun was currently beating all of us down, threatening to scorch us in its deadly light as the thin tree line offered minimal protection. We all attempted not to show it, with Henry and Fox remaining silent whilst Avelina and I attempted to maintain the banter. Well…all of us except Serena, who was currently complaining about whatever she could while still resting on Henry's back. Clearly despite how loud she snored last night, she did not have a pleasant night's rest.

"Hey you two." I asked as we kept walking, hoping to make the air less awkward.

"What do you two think of my brother?" I questioned both of them to pass the time. Serena gave a tired smile as she nestled into Henry slightly, her eyes lowering to half-lids.

"What's there to think?" she lazily proclaimed, "You, your brother and that Mara are some of the most incredible people we've met in a long time. You even managed to stand up against the three greatest fighters we have with us. Hen Hen and I couldn't even do that the first time around." Henry glanced up at the healer on his back, watching as she giggled softly at his somewhat puzzled gaze.

"Hen...Hen?" Henry questioned in a way that sounded both annoyed and slightly amused. Serena just giggled even more.

"I think it is rather fitting for someone with as gloomy of a personality as yours." I could tell he gave a smile underneath the mask as he reaffirmed her position on his back, along with probably weighing whether to just drop the girl on the ground.

"As you were saying, Jack," Henry continued, "He's a capable man, and while he certainly didn't beat Katrina in their fight, that's a match almost no one has ever won. While I...do not believe he is the most accomplished of this group, he may grow into something far superior if he can prove his worth to us." Serena's expression turned from tired to miffed at his words, striking the masked man on top of his head. To his credit, the man didn't react at all to the blow.

"He's proven himself enough Henry," Serena hissed, her tone losing its usual giggly nature, "Stop being so paranoid, it wouldn't bother me usually but you caught me when I'm sleepy." Henry shook his head, although I swear beneath his mask he released a small grin.

"You always get like this when you're tired. Sometimes I wonder if you are even fit for trips like these."

"I need a lot of rest to function Hen Hen," Serena replied as she nestled back into her spot, "As soon as we get back I'll get all nice and cozy and sleep until next year." Henry let out a single, muted laugh as he repositioned her on his back, letting out a deep sigh as he did so.

"What do you think of your brother then Jack?" Henry asked calmly as he looked back at the girl on his back, "You've known him for all of his life, so obviously you should know him best." I pondered to myself momentarily, thinking back to the brother I hoped to protect, and yet oftentimes I found myself looking up to him instead.

"My brother..." I wondered aloud, "To say we weren't as close back before is an understatement. He'd stay in his room most of the day, while I spent most of my time training or just hiking around our new place." I glanced down at the ground, noticing in my peripheral vision that Avelina was staring back at me.

"But then, dad was killed, and mom was...whisked away somewhere. We had nothing else but each other, and while he still stayed in his room, I feel closer than I ever have to him. Sometimes, I kinda wish he would branch out a little, because just having me as a support system isn't that great for either of us." I could hear Avelina snort in front of us as she turned her head back, glancing to the path ahead.

"In many regards, he has far more potential than I do," I continued as I noticed Avelina nod to my statement, to which I raised my eyebrows towards her in feigned betrayal, "His perception by itself is incredible, which can be shown in him latching onto certain traits like eye color when first meeting people. He notices the technique you use to fight and exploits it, or sees the way you speak and can pick apart everything about your family history somehow. While I have him soundly beat in the technique category, Connor has always been far more quick-witted than I was. If given enough time to prepare, he'd knock anyone down as if they were nothing." I let out a chuckle at my final statement, drawing a somewhat confused stare from Henry as I pointed my thumb to myself.

"Of course, no amount of preparation time he's ever put down has ever beaten me in a fight. Not once in his sixteen years of life has he ever bested his older brother." I could hear Serena snicker at my statement, glancing up from his back as she gave a tired smirk.

"If he fights anything like you Jack," she joked, "We'd knock him flat on his butt quicker than we will when we fight you again." I huffed loudly at her jab, while Serena laughed even harder to herself, sounding far more awake but still incredibly sleepy.

As Serena began her laugh, Avelina's eyes widened in front of us, crouching down to the ground as Fox did the same. She frantically turned back to us, her skin a sickening pale.

"*Be quiet you three,*" Avelina rasped out in a panicked tone, one which was almost inaudible, "*We have a situation to deal with.*" I immediately halted the thought I was about to yell out as I crouched down, hearing a low grunt as Henry dropped Serena onto the ground. Serena quietly murmured to herself about the pain in her legs and how tired she was as Henry held a gloved hand to her mouth, an action done to Serena's obvious irritation.

Waddling over as stealthily as I could to the nearby bushes where Avelina and Fox currently sat, I gazed over their shoulders to see what was causing all the ruckus. My heartbeat began to pick up immediately as my eyes locked onto their object of despair.

That...that bastard...

Zain...

He was still wearing that long purple robe he wore back in Eincrest, along with the same minute tears we managed to put into him there. His hood was currently down, exposing the bald head of a man who looked older than Avelina and Katrina, but not by much. He didn't have any traditional weapon at his side, as instead it appeared he had picked up a multitude of knives he had attached to his right arm and leg. At the moment he was poking a campfire with a long stick he grasped in his hand. He huffed to himself at the dying flame, unable to make it grow any larger.

"Never been good at this sort of thing," he murmured to himself, freezing all of us in place with his gravelly voice, "Hopefully I'll be back to them and home cooked meals soon."

Across his neck, beaming proudly, was the same amber pendant he snatched from Eincrest. The one that almost made him appear to control fate itself, ruling over it through his words alone.

The one he willingly sacrificed so many lives for...

"What do we do?" Serena asked as quietly as she could, shock evident in her features.

At least she seems to have shaken off how tired she was...

Avelina frowned sharply as she stared at the robed man, clearly questioning within her head what would be the correct course of action. Turning back to us, she placed a hand by her mouth to muffle her voice. We leaned in closer to make sure we didn't have to hear her commands twice.

"Fox and I will head back to the Sentinels' base since we are the quickest and least winded of us five," Avelina finally whispered, "We'll get some adequate reinforcements as quickly as possible. Just keep track of him until we get back, and don't get too close. We're almost squarely in the middle of this country, so leave a suitable trail we can follow since he won't get far." I nodded at Avelina as I motioned for Serena and Henry to get closer, making sure they could see through the bushes as well as I could.

"No way we're letting the bastard get away now," I rasped out, "Be quick about this, otherwise we could be in some serious trouble we can't wade our way out of." Avelina gave a nod of approval before standing up with Fox, making sure the bushes concealed herself adequately enough.

Turning to go back to our surveillance, a darkened form of something darted through the brush, whizzing by my face at speeds I almost didn't recognize. Maybe if we paid more attention, we could have seen Zain murmuring to himself. Or when he put down the stick, and picked up something else.

"...the blade I hold will fly through the air and connect with one of those lurking in the bushes."

It was a steel short-sword that flew perfectly through the brush, tearing a hole through the interwoven patches of green and brown in front of us. I almost felt the terrifying force behind the throw. In that split second of time, Avelina's eyes shot open in shock, springing forward and leaping in front of her sister. Extending her arms with all her force, the woman I had known for months shoved her shocked sister forward with enough strength to knock her completely down.

The distinct sound of hardened metal piercing through human tissue rang through the air as Fox collapsed to the ground with a surprised grunt.

Shock was evident in her eyes as the shadow of her sister beamed over her. She was frozen in place, her body shivering as the rest of us finally began to process what just shot through the silence. Serena's face grew incredibly pale as a hand flew to her mouth, Henry's cool eyes widening in horror.

Through Avelina's chest stuck the shimmering steel short-sword, the blade just barely poking out through her body in a sparkling glimmer of silver and red.

She stared at it for a moment, her hands clutching at the weapon through her as she wordlessly gasped to herself. She shakily stared downwards towards her sister, flashing a faint, pained smile, before her body collapsed to the dirt below.

"Avelina!" Fox shrieked, springing up and drawing one of her knives at a speed I couldn't even register. She tore through the brush and bolted towards Zain, tears already welling around the porcelain eye holes of her mask.

"You bastard!" she screamed out through choking sobs, "I'll…I'll kill you!"

Jumping into the air, she slashed down onto Zain, only to be swiftly dodged as he whispered again to himself.

"You all are nothing but fools. Did you really think I didn't know someone was following me?" Serena was already at Avelina's side, staring at the foot-long sword pierced through her chest.

"Oh my god oh my god," Serena gasped to herself as she activated her healing palms, the comforting green enveloping her hands, "H-Hold on Ms. R-Rockwell I got you." I almost yelled out as Serena wrenched the sword free of her, causing Avelina to yelp out in pain. However, the instant it was removed Serena had placed her hands upon her and began attempting to seal it.

Already Henry was rushing past me with his gloved hands extended, pushing aside the green to assist the crazed Fox.

I squatted down near Avelina, my eyes welling up in tears as I placed a hand on hers. My teeth involuntarily ground together painfully as I stared down at her, shaking and choking back a sob. Her jacket was torn through its center, blood soaking into her clothes as well as the ground below. Poking through her jacket was a page of the book she was so insistent on reading during this whole trip, the paper already turning a crimson red.

Avelina...

The woman who I considered like an older sister since that day.

Who guaranteed our well-being even if she chose not to show it.

Who held dreams and aspirations to mold this world into something better than it is...

Now lay dying at my feet, another person who suffers just beyond my reach.

She limply squeezed my hand back, letting tears fall as her hand was already beginning to grow colder by the second. Her skin was already looking sickly and pale.

"Don't you dare die on me Avelina, we still have our r-rematch later remember?" The woman somehow managed a smile as the green light swarmed over her stiff body, hopefully giving her some form of comfort from the pain.

"...don't...don't worry k-kid I won't..."

"This pendant..." I could hear Zain rant behind me, "It's remarkable! I can't believe that village wouldn't use something so valuable." I scrambled away from Avelina and Serena with a loud bellow, drawing my sword as I rushed forward. I ran next to Henry and Fox, the latter of which was still continuously swinging one of her daggers at the man. Each swipe was followed by a yell of formless anger and agony, blindly swinging at the man without any form of technique or rhythm.

Not that it mattered to her. All she cared about was digging one of those daggers into wherever it hurt Zain the most.

Pushing her away with a tremendous amount of force, the masked woman slid back beside the two of us, dragging the dirt across the ground with her feet. Her dagger was raised to the side above her head, with her masked face directed towards the ground. She was obviously still crying; her arms shaking momentarily. Henry approached her from the side.

"Fox," Henry began in a commanding tone, "You need to get out of here and retrieve reinforcements as quickly as possible. We can hold him off for some time, but after that I can't guarantee either of us will survive." Fox gritted her teeth and tightened her grip on her knife.

"I don't...take orders from you..."

"Well you'd better start," I commanded with a hiss, watching Zain intently with my sword drawn, "With Avelina out of commission at the moment I know you're the fastest one here, and Henry should know that too. You need to go and get help or we'll all die here for nothing." Her masked visage paced between her sister and Zain, who strangely was simply staring at us rather than implementing any form of attack plan.

"I...I can't just leave...she did that so I could live and f-fight him."

"She...she did that so you could survive past today," I cut in, "Would you rather that you still end up dying along with us and Zain keeps running around? Don't squander the chance your sister gave you, or our lives for that matter." Fox stared forward, choking back tears as Zain just stood there, watching us with his robed arms crossed—the amber pendant continuing to taunt us. She closed her eyes, her teeth audibly grinding against each other.

"Don't you dare let...let that monster get away," she demanded as she turned around, beginning to run as fast as she could down the path we originally came down. Zain obviously noticed this and sighed to himself, pulling one of the many throwing knives out its sheath.

"Where do you think you're going child?" he taunted as he steadied the point towards Fox. Right before he hurled it, Henry was already there and attempted to strike him across the jaw.

While Zain managed to dodge out of the way of the attack with ease, the act of doing so caused the weapon to veer slightly off course from the stumbling throw, grazing Fox across her shoulder instead of somewhere much worse.

She stumbled slightly but continued to run, taking off faster than ever and disappearing into the deep foliage.

Leaving us with Zain, I turned towards my only fighting companion during this stand, knowing that his strength rivaling mine helped immensely in this moment. Avelina being taken out so swiftly was immensely bad.

"You know this is basically suicide right?" I rhetorically asked Henry with a broken smile, to which I received no reply.

Zain...first you take the lives of everyone in that village and those soldiers, and now you have the audacity to try and kill Avelina right in front of me. You have no idea the world of hurt I'm about to put you through.

"Alright you snake," I proclaimed as I gripped my sword with two hands in front of me, hoping to stall for time without having to engage in as much combat, "While your very presence is driving me to a breaking point, there's been something that's been bugging me for some time." Henry took the hint and stepped back beside me, raising his gloved hands in a defensive manner.

If I can stall with words for long enough, then we may be able to last far longer than we would otherwise. Maybe Avelina will be back up by then.

"You know unless you have some voodoo magic powers or something, I'd really appreciate it if you had something like a weapon or literally anything besides your fists." Henry snarled at my whispered sarcasm and kept his attention on Zain, who was continuing to curiously stare in our direction. His green eyes lit up, somehow looking less frightening now that they weren't concealed by a bulky hood.

"Ah, I remember you. Jack, wasn't it?" Zain finally announced in that gravelly voice, "One of the two boys in that village who tried to stop me from taking this." He motioned to said pendant as he recalled the story, grinning slightly as it glimmered in the afternoon light.

"Did the other one run off with his tail tucked between his legs?"

"Afraid his presence would hasten your demise?" I taunted in as threatening of a tone as I could manage, "Now as I was saying I have something I've been meaning to ask you." He let out a single harsh laugh to himself, hiding the cackle behind his left hand.

"I may as well indulge in your curiosity. I won't die here, so very well...what is it that plagues your mind about me?" I glanced back behind me at Avelina, ensuring that Serena was maintaining her healing stream on the woman. Much to my relief she was, but... Serena's panicked expression never wavered.

Is something wrong? Please tell me I'm simply misjudging the situation.

"Why did you help the people of Stagmire?" His green eyes looked at me with ample confusion, although the amusement didn't fade entirely.

"What on earth do you mean?"

"You burned the entirety of Eincrest to the ground with your no-brained goons," I continued, hoping to prolong the conversation for as long as I could, "And yet when coming upon another village you actually alleviated some of their troubles. Why would someone as rotten as you do something like that?" Zain scoffed at my accusation, looking the most irritated that I've ever seen him.

"You think I'm some oaf from Bellhollow, running around destroying everything I see in my enemy country?"

"I do actually. Which is why such a personable action partaken by you in Stagmire rubs me the wrong way. I wanna know what you did to them, Zain." A long, pained silence followed as the two pairs of eyes glared into the sharp green ones. Part of me hoped the silence of it all would last just a tad longer.

If I can't buy enough time for Fox to get back, I need to at least distract him until Avelina's recovered a little.

"They required assistance," he calmly replied as he shut his eyes, "Nothing more. One of their main council members was kind enough to provide me with the fastest route back home, and in return I used this pendant to unblock the river a little faster. He chose not to deceive me, so I paid him in kind." He motioned to the pendant as he did so, allowing me to watch as that damned controller of fate swayed in the breeze.

"You lie!" I yelled out, "You had to have done something else. Did you promise to assassinate a rival candidate for his spot or something?"

"As much as I love to hear the sound of your yelling," Henry interrupted sarcastically, "It doesn't appear he's lying in any way. The politician gave us a motive, and the village from the council members right down to the poorest of peasants remained the same." I scoffed to the side in annoyance as my hair whipped around my face.

"Then why did you kill all those people in Eincrest?" I demanded with a growl emanating from my throat, "It's like two different people made both decisions, and all I've got for reasoning is that you're a sadistic asshole."

"Those people in Eincrest were fools," he grumbled as if it were fact, "I tried to reason with them, but they just wouldn't listen. They were resting on a powerful tool they could use for so much good, and yet they decided to keep it locked away in their town hall instead. They stood in my way, so I was left with no other choice but to annihilate them." I felt my grip on the sword tighten as I stared him down, my own knuckles turning white.

"If your information on me was accurate, then you should know I'm an...estranged Bellhollow resident. You all should know how dirty and corrupt that nation of thieves is. I killed all those people yes, but I did it to take this from them and ensure it fell into better hands. With this, I can do far more good than anything those fools in that village, or even this entire country could do."

"You...you moron," I growled out as I pointed the tip of the sword at his throat, even though he stood a mere ten feet away, "What good could be possibly worth all of that suffering?" Zain let out a sigh at my words, as if he were a parent whose child didn't understand their in-depth lesson.

"You wouldn't know," Zain murmured, although he appeared to be staring towards a still defensive Henry, "After all, your entire country doesn't see us as worth a damn do they?" Seeing the light flickering off something metallic, I instinctively sprinted over to Henry's direction right beside me. In a flash his left arm reached over to his right and onto one of the sheaths holding the knives, one of which he flung in Henry's direction.

Without even thinking I tackled the masked man, hearing us both grunt at the sudden force. As we fell, a foreign object dug forcefully into my right shoulder, sending pain shooting down the entirety of that arm as the knife pierced through it.

"You're all diseased," Zain muttered, his tone taking a more unhinged sound, "You all watch on as our nation falls to ruin, with the gap between people like me and those in power rapidly expanding, ripping us away from our homes. And even when our suffering first began, you all sat there on high thrones and watched as we died in dirt caked droves. I will not allow it anymore, for with this pendant I can lead my people against those who wish to drain us of our livelihoods and completely remake this continent in a more fitting image! I wished to show mercy to you all, but it's clear you idiots don't deserve it. Before I save them, I'll destroy every one of you for your sins!" Hoisting me up with a groan, Henry glanced down at me and the knife sticking through my shoulder, glistening as the afternoon light shot down at us. I cringed as I stood, the jagged weapon jostling around painfully as I moved.

"Can you still fight?" he asked apprehensively, still glaring at Zain's still form. Taking only a moment, I tore the knife out of my shoulder with a pained yell and hurled it to the floor, panting as I gripped my bleeding shoulder. It clattered against the ground right beside my sword, which was currently resting with its blade touching the dirt in my offhand.

"Of course I can," I glowered as I took my now red hand off my shoulder, "I think I've had it…with talking." I picked up my sword shakily and jammed it directly in front of me with the point directed up in a traditional defensive stance, knowing full well my right arm couldn't handle my ordinary stance.

Is…is he right? I've heard Bellhollow was a wreck but…could there really be people fighting to change what we've been ignoring?

I shook my head as I stared Zain down, my own stance shifting as I prepared to lunge forward.

Doesn't matter right now. All that matters is making sure our asses stay alive for as long as we can. He's still a murderer who has a habit of being quite insane, and we have to make sure his path ends here.

Zain gave a crooked sneer at our approach, laughing to himself as our talking finally ceased.

"To fulfill that ambition you must die here," Zain proclaimed with his right hand near his face, revealing two knives lurking within, "If your people cannot save us with power right beneath their noses, then I must take matters into my own hands no matter how bloody the affairs become." I maintained my grip on my sword as Henry charged forward, somehow managing to duck past both the blades. They clattered and skidded against the dirt as Henry came in close.

This absolutely could be the place of our deaths, but I can't think about that right now.

I know what you stand for can be just, but from my angle you've taken things too far. People like you can't be allowed to stick around.

I'll protect the world by ridding you of it, Zain.

With that final thought I charged forward to clash against the purple mage alongside Henry, letting out a final yell as I leaped forward into the awaiting arms of death.

26

Connor: Shifting Existence

Walking in utter silence for hours now, the only comfort I could find in the situation was the occasional mumbling of the girl still resting on my back. I chuckled to myself due to her sleeping remarks, ones which came out as full-on sentences instead of jumbled up gibberish.

While I found myself comforted by the charming nothingness silence brings, Mara's utter avoidance of me in both voice and action was beginning to unnerve me.

Her silence when we first met and even now I could write off as some unique character trait of hers, but the closing off of character made me feel shunned.

I finally agreed with her after all this time. Was she that hurt by my initial rejection of her plan?

Walking always just slightly ahead of me, I sighed to myself as she wouldn't even look at me with her gaze.

Strange to find company in a sleeping child rather than my current partner on this mission.

I thought she had moved past the no talking phase, but this is somehow even worse.

I sighed bleakly to myself, hoping that we would encounter the others sometime soon.

And hopefully not get reprimanded by Avelina or someone else like Henry for disobeying orders.

"Help!" A voice rang out to my left, instantly causing me to spring forward and draw Requiem from its sheath. Mara had somehow managed to do the same with her sword. Catherine, somewhat startled by the jump awoke suddenly, letting go of my neck and landing on her feet on the ground. She rubbed her eyes as she gazed at me, perplexed due to the sudden interruption.

"Wha-"

"Stay behind me Cat," I commanded, "Not sure what it is but keep close just in case it's a bandit of some kind." Almost immediately answering my question, a darkened silhouette darted through the tree line nearby, skidding to a stop along the path we assumed was made by Jack and his company.

Instead of some form of bandit or even a random citizen, it appeared to be a younger woman in an all-darkened attire.

Wearing a long-sleeved black shirt with red lines streaking across it, mixing together with blood that appeared to be pouring out of a slash wound on her shoulder. She gripped onto that wound with a pair of black gloves, most likely staining the material with the still leaking crimson. Her knee-high armored boots dragged across the dirt as she limped into our view, panting to herself as if she had sprinted full speed even with her injury. A brown cloak surrounded her entire body, with the hood somehow still drawn over her head.

The most distinguishing feature of hers that I noticed was the porcelain mask that donned her face, which combined with the hood shielded her entire head from prying eyes. The flattened white disguise only contained two eye holes, from which a pair of bright brown eyes shined through. Streaking across the mask's white surface was an orange and red slash, adding much needed color to the mannequin-like design.

Still makes her stand out extremely...

I steadily lowered Requiem and placed it back in its sheath, however Mara kept her sword's point trained directly on her. Catherine was just staring at her intently, now fully awake. This mysterious woman held up her gloved hand as a sign of peace, leaving the other one to cover the wound on her shoulder.

"I need...I need help in any way possible. I don't care who you are, I just need help." My eyes widened as I stared at her, noticing that she didn't tear through any new path to arrive where we now stand. She traced down the path we were following, meaning she had either just come from there or knew the path herself.

Furthermore, the hood covering her head was pushed back slightly, and while it still covered her entire head it exposed something that piqued my interest.

A single hair peaked through the veil of her disguise, and while normally that wouldn't matter, the recognizable color was drawing my attention.

The woman's hair was a distinct purple shade.

This woman has purple hair...although I would more likely call it indigo based on its lighter shade.

Bright brown eyes with a hint of orange-gold in them, almost a complete inversion of someone else I know.

Similar build to her as well, but slightly smaller in stature, probably a sibling based on vocal inflections and depth.

Attire fit for a military spy, fitting under the bill that Avelina is currently the head of that field. And considering the mission they went on, it makes sense the only spy Katrina would trust would be the sibling of one her closest friends.

"You must be Avelina's sister. I'd like to ask what you're doing out here?" Her bronzed eyes lit up underneath the milky mask, showcasing her surprise along with her confusion.

"My name is Connor, this little girl beside me is Catherine and the woman pointing the sword at you is Mara. Besides the girl, we're all members of the Sentinels, and I'm going to assume you are as well." She looked at me with the same surprise after my swift rundown, but a sense of relief overcame the confusion seeping through her eyes, her stance slouching.

"Thank the Goddess," she panted, "You…may call me Fox. I don't know who you are but we need help. I'm not sure if anyone else was briefed on this mission, but we are currently engaged in a fight against an incredibly violent man. Jack and Henry have been holding them off all this time while I gathered some form of reinforcements, but we can only do so much." I paused at her words, taking in all of this new information.

They found him, but they're fighting him now?

They must've been ambushed or somehow attacked by surprise. Unless one of them disobeyed orders they wouldn't engage.

"Take us to my brother Fox," I exclaimed as I drew the black dirk back out of its sheath, "We'll offer as much support as we possibly can." Her eyes widening again, she turned herself around and faced the direction she came from again.

"So you're the one the others were talking so fiercely about," she realized as she nodded her head, "No time for any more formalities. Follow me before anything else goes…goes wrong."

She sprinted off towards the direction she was running from previously, with all three of us attempting to chase after her at a similar speed. I hoisted Catherine up onto my back and immediately ran after. It was a little difficult, but due to her weight and the dread beginning to fill my system I pushed forward, ignoring the pain in my legs.

Mara's blank expression fell away completely as we ran, replaced by a powerful look of resolve. Her sword was drawn at her side, staring dead ahead with a furrowed brow as we sprinted through the tree line.

Coming upon the battle after fifteen agonizingly long minutes, a gasp escaped my throat as the full scope of the affair came into view.

Avelina lay still on the ground, a red hole torn through the center of her chest. The blood continued to leak out of her body, staining the once green grass below a violent crimson and tainting her green and black clothes. A blood-soaked book poked through the veil of her stained jacket, cleaved through on the side closest to the hole. A discarded sword sat in the grass, guiltily showcasing its vermilion aura.

She appears to be alive for now, but based on the wound's placement clean through her body some vital organ has to have ruptured in some way.

Serena was on her knees right beside her, mumbling to herself as the green light flashed from her hands, attempting to pump more life into Avelina's rigid body. Cuts that resembled those caused by paper were slicing across the skin of her hands, continuously opening the more the magic pumped. She was already beginning to sweat, her limbs shaking.

She's already losing energy. Those scrapes must be forming through the overuse of her magic, and if she continues who knows what will happen.

Let's hope that magic of hers can seal that soon...

I skidded to a stop right beside the two women as Fox continued to run, bolting in a direction I wasn't paying attention to at the moment. I felt myself experiencing tunnel vision as I stared deeply at the other two, crouching down as Serena gasped in realization.

"Connor!" she yelped out, refusing to remove her bloody hands from Avelina's body, "O-One of you made it!" I gave her a soft smile as I set Catherine down, turning to her before I did anything else.

"Stay with Mara, do you understand?" She showcased a shy nod at my words, sprinting over and latching onto said woman right beside me. She didn't react to the force, instead choosing to stare directly at Serena's work. I glanced back at Avelina.

Every breath sounded as if she was fighting the toughest opponent there ever was, and failing at it. Every single time a gasp of air came out, a soft cough sputtered out of her throat, the frailness of her pale body becoming apparent to her. Her amber eyes glanced over, now tinged with pain and even fear.

"Con...Connor?" she rasped out, barely managing to say my name "...I thought you two were still at home...home base."

"Well, it's a good thing I'm not right?" I replied as I stood back up, turning my attention elsewhere, "Don't give up hope yet Avelina. You've got the finest medic in the world watching over you." Serena actually let out a single giggle at my words, probably the first in a while considering the tears and a sniffle she had to choke through in order to do so.

"I-I know Connor," Avelina replied solemnly, "I...wouldn't p-put my trust in anyone else..." Staring back at the battlefield, my eyes latched onto the most obvious figure at the center of this clearing.

Zain...

That man was currently being forced on the defensive, opting to dodge out of the way of attacks by his three opponents.

Fox, Henry, and Jack.

They were all stumbling around Zain, attempting to get some sort of attack through his evasions. Jack and Henry looked far more tired than Fox did, with both having distinct scrapes across their clothing. Specifically, I noticed the red puncture wound on Jack's shoulder that almost mirrored Fox's, although it didn't appear to be only one he carried on his marred body.

Zain had a few scrapes as well, although the most notable feature of his attire was the ever-present amber pendant that swung in a taunting manner along his neckline.

Not even processing another thought, I flipped Requiem around in my hand and sprinted towards the battling three, making sure that Zain didn't notice my approach and that Mara was staying with Catherine.

Henry noticed my attack first, jumping out the way as he was in the direct line of fire. Noticing me at the last second, Zain threw up his arms as I kicked into his awaiting guard, watching as he stumbled from the attack. I went for another as his guard was down, colliding with his chest as he further backpedaled away from me.

"You three!" I yelled out as I shakily steadied myself, motioning for them to all fall back. With all of them instantaneously registering my words, all three of them retreated slowly towards the others, refusing to turn their backs to the enemy. Sliding to a stop, I flipped around with Requiem ready, gathering us all up in one spot to better anticipate a full-scale barrage from the madman. Instead, he simply sighed to himself and sat down in the dirt.

"I have the ability to end you all," he remarked, "It doesn't matter when, I'll eventually be rid of you lot and finally go back home to make things right." He closed his eyes and crossed his arms, thinking to himself as he left himself wide open in a moment of pure egoism. At least, that's what he was attempting to put up as a convincing facade.

It's a trap, we can't just rush him head on without a plan...

Jack and Henry made it to me beside Avelina and the others, where Serena was still pumping all of her energy into her with the same lack of results. Avelina was still alive at least, smiling up at her sister who had crouched down beside her. Mara was standing deathly still, staring towards Zain with the hair covering her eyes. Catherine clutched at Mara's shirt, hiding behind the statue-like woman and directing her golden eyes towards Zain's direction.

I doubt he would even remember her face...

"I'm not...even gonna ask why you're here Connor," Jack panted with a slight smirk, the sword appearing to be incredibly heavy in his quaking grasp, "But...I'm sure glad that you are." He pressed down on the shoulder that was currently red from blood, holding it there for a moment before releasing. Staring at his hand afterwards, he let out a sigh of relief as the blood had largely stopped flowing and dried.

Besides Avelina, he looks the worst out of everyone here.

"Well...since you're already here, could you help provide some sort of plan to help us along besides swinging my sword at his face?" I nodded seriously despite his apparent taunting, standing towards the edge of our group while keeping a sharp eye on Zain for any sort of movement.

He hasn't moved in the slightest...he genuinely believes he can survive without being truly on the offensive.

"Alright...give me a second..." Henry and Jack nodded at my statement, switching their gaze between Avelina and Zain.

Henry's not questioning me...perhaps he's giving me a chance to make this all right.

"He's an insurgent or something within Bellhollow." My gaze shot away from Zain as Jack's proclamation shook me from my train of thought. I stared at him with surprise, noticing the way he stared solemnly at the dirt below.

"Come again?"

"I guess he took that pendant to fight for his people there. I don't know what kind of person he was before all of this, but right now he's a fanatic. He believes all this murder is a justified action if he believes it'll lead to some good. I just wanted to bring everyone on the same page just in case it helps your planning to take this madman down." I stood there stunned at his sudden proclamation, before turning back to my own thoughts.

Could he have...good intentions? No, even if he did his methods are not those of someone who still holds those intentions. He has gone completely mad. I need to focus on how to beat him as quickly as possible, and I can focus on that and how he can connect back to mom afterwards.

His knives seem more dangerous at longer ranges, but up close he's still a threat. Henry and Jack could probably handle that job to keep him at bay.

The issue of the pendant: Something's wrong with it and I can't quite figure it out.

Whatever the case, I don't desire to be caught off guard, so I'll treat the jewelry as if it were at its full potential.

If I have two people wearing him down progressively, sending more people slowly at a time would not only surprise him but overwhelm him. We can't all fight at once or otherwise he'd take advantage of the fact we can't all fight in such close quarters.

Standing fully up, I shrugged my shoulders back as the plan finally came into focus within my head.

"Before I begin," I calmly announced to the crowd that I had managed to gain the full attention of, "I believe that a certain piece of information is imperative if any of us are to continue." I paused to make sure everyone paid attention, before continuing.

"I believe that I now truly understand how Zain's pendant functions." The eyes of those watching me widened at my sudden proclamation, even Henry's. In fact, the blue-eyed man appeared to be the most stunned of the audience, shown very clearly by his slumped over posture and the movement of his mask, showing he went slack jawed.

"You do?" Jack asked incredulously as I nodded, causing him to shake his head, "Of course you do. Well in that case, spill it already."

"Yes Connor," Henry interjected, catching me off guard, "Please continue."

"While many of us have theorized that the pendant could read our minds, or perhaps even mold the strings of fate itself, this couldn't be farther from the truth." Making sure all their eyes were on me, I explained further.

"The pendant can change the probability of an action occurring." Their shock somehow grew at my proclamation, watching as they each prepared to shout something back. Jack probably already had fifteen things to say to me, whilst both Henry and Fox leaned forward to ask questions most likely. Serena listened but at the same time remained focused on her task, although her eyebrows did rise from my comment.

Mara remained unnervingly still, clearly registering what I said, and yet she kept her gaze solely on the man we had been sent to find.

I raised an open palm to pause them, wanting to continue before anything else could be presented.

"Everything that he has done so far was within the realm of possibility, from the dodging of slashes to the crashing of rocks upon my brother. My guess is that the pendant itself allows Zain to see all possibilities of the actions playing out in front of him, and through his voice he can draw forth whichever one is most likely. That's why he doesn't just say we die on the spot, considering the probability of that random occurrence isn't quantifiable." Before I could continue, a strange single sound came to my ears, confusing me for a moment before its slow, purposeful continuation allowed me to realize what it was.

Clapping, all coming from the man sitting on the ground, a small sneer present on his features.

"Well done well done," the fanatic commended as his clapping ceased, "I must admit that is quite impressive, I have to commend you. While it won't help you any, I can still praise anyone who could make

344

such a connection from nothing." I balled my fists up as I turned away from him, proud that I was right but focused on dedicating all of my efforts towards not rushing him right there.

"Anyways," I said in a slightly lower tone, making sure that he couldn't eavesdrop on us, "I believe if my plan goes right, we could overload that pendant and present too many variables for him to keep track of. With enough variables in place, multiple actions will have equal probability and make understanding any of them unfeasible, or perhaps prevent any choices from properly standing out. This is a live or die situation, so I need everyone to pay close attention. Any questions?" Hearing nothing from those around me, I shifted my gaze towards the two men who would be leading the charge.

"Henry and Jack, I need you two to charge at him as you have previously before. Be fast and avoid getting injured, but also be as distracting as possible. Do just enough to keep him on his toes and go for a killing blow if you can. However, don't take unnecessary risks. I need you two to be what he's focusing on at all times." They both nodded to me as they readied themselves for another wave of attacks, with Jack flashing a weary smile that screamed his usual defiance.

I glanced over at the masked woman, who was still clutching the arm of her sister on the ground. Her purple hair was beginning to gather red stains, and her eyes were losing their usual brightness.

"Fox," I called out, causing her to look up at me with water at the tinges of her eyes, "Are you still capable of fighting?" She wiped the tears from her eyes, standing with a renewed strength as she twirled one of her knives, drawing it by her face.

"Of course, sir," she confirmed firmly. I was taken aback slightly, not used to being referred to by such formalities, "What is it you need of me?"

"How unnoticeable can you be?" I quickly asked, knowing what the answer would already probably be.

"I'm trained as a spy for a reason." I smirked, thankful for this stroke of luck.

"Alright then Fox. I need you to sneak to a spot Zain cannot spot you from, and if not, act as if you won't be engaging in the fight. When his attention is completely on the other two, do whatever you can to bring him down. Hurl knives. Run up behind for a quick slash. Do whatever you can, but only do it when you know for sure that he is occupied." She nodded as well, taking hold of one of her knives. Jack glanced over at me with his usual smile.

"Look at that, my usually stoic brother just smirked. Oh now I know we're about to kick that magician's ass." I snorted to myself as I glanced over at the young girl who had now found herself next to me, staring up at me brightly. I smiled at her.

"So you all know this girl's name is Catherine, and we found her in Eincrest during our mission. Catherine, you'd better stay beside Serena. Don't leave her side, no matter what happens." Catherine swiftly nodded as she bolted towards where Serena was sitting. I balanced Requiem in my hands, methodically ensuring once again that it fit to my liking.

Still does...the universe didn't swap it out to screw with me or anything.

"Now, if Fox doesn't land the killing strike on him, Mara you and I wi..." I looked up to speak with her directly, but she wasn't standing where she was only a moment ago. The others clearly noticed my surprise, only to also notice that the silent woman I was about to address had suddenly vanished. I frantically spun around searching for where she was, hoping she didn't just run away or something.

And then, I saw her.

Oh god...

Sword already drawn and at the ready.

Charging full speed at Zain's sitting form...

"Mara no!" I yelled as I sprinted right after her, trying to stop her from bolting straight towards her demise.

"Connor what're you doing?" Jack yelled directly afterwards. I knew in that moment that they all thought I was being idiotic for chasing after her.

I kept on running, my lungs aching and legs burning as I ran at speeds I didn't know I could reach.

I wasn't going to let Mara die so carelessly, even if she was the one who was putting her life in jeopardy.

Zain had opened his eyes already, staring at Mara with a dejected grin ever present on his aged face.

"Ah charging towards your death without a care in the world?" he rhetorically chuckled, "Unexpected, but I'll gladly take it."

She wasn't even close enough to land a single swing. She had to know that by now, and yet she kept sprinting towards him with a repressed snarl.

Pushing forward with all of my energy stored in my body, the burning sensation in my lungs grew ever more painful as I continued to rush towards the running form of this woman.

No one is dying while I'm here!

I was right there when she began to swing down at his crouching form, only for him to jump back and raise his right hand, revealing three knives facing the glistening sky.

"These will be the source of your pitiful demise!"

I tackled Mara from the side as the words left his mouth, sending her elegant sword flying into the air and launching us both to the ground.

I let out a sigh of relief as we were about to collide into the earth below, thankful for my good fortune but ready to spring back up and fight.

Until I felt something tear through the side of my neck, splattering red across the ground as my vision instantly became spotty and dark…

* * *

I breathed a deep sigh through my lungs, contempt that I could use them but displeased with the amount of effort I had to put into utilizing them. I hated every moment of this.

Feeling like this…

Feeling like a human.

Hurting like a human.

It was an extreme level of putrid that even made my skin crawl.

I've had to heal a multitude of wounds I've received over time, most of them relatively minor considering. But the fact that anyone had the audacity to lay a finger on me at all was far worse.

I growled to myself in exasperation, pacing around in the confined enclosure, trying to determine the source of my confinement, and my suffering.

Could there be anybody here with me?

Doubtful. There isn't anywhere for them to go, much less to torture me from.

Some form of advanced magic perhaps?

It would be possible, but no. Magic of this scale would need to be done in person, and far closer in range.

You could set timed magic traps, but they would have to have a specific trigger and time, both of which were clearly shown not to matter. Each time the pain arose, it felt more like someone was beating me up rather than inflicting magical damage upon me.

I growled at the painful bars in front of me. I felt like a caged animal, trapped, and never allowed to leave without some pitiful human's allowance.

"Treat me like an animal and be prepared to be murdered by

one."

What was strange about this confinement was that I felt feelings other than pain…occasionally anyway.

Visions of unknown people flashed occasionally in my vision. People of unknown ages and origin came before me, but most common was this brown-haired girl with green eyes that stared deeply into my soul.

I saw these visions of some distant world, but I knew for whatever reason whoever was watching these visions were not from my own eyes. This became obvious from seeing the figure's reflection, viewing events from the hazel eyes of a black-haired boy. I could never hear dialogue, which made seeing these visions all the stranger.

I then felt it once again.

The pain flowing back into my senses. I was about to groan and prepare my energy to nullify it when I instantly doubled over in pain and grasped onto my pulsating neck. Blood coursed through my hand, staining my skin with its ooze. When I glanced down, I chuckled to myself in a deadpan manner.

An incision was torn straight across where the jugular would normally run along the neck of a human. I tried to apply some of my energy to the slashing wound, but whatever it was I couldn't. The incision while not necessarily deep was deadly, and the blood continued pouring out despite my attempts. It was slowing down the bleeding somewhat, but my energy couldn't seal it no matter how hard I tried. It was as if my power was suppressed in some way. All I could do was pump more blood into my system to keep me alive. I sneered again as I stood up shakily.

"So you have decided to cut the torture short you sadist?" I continued to try and try to close the dramatic wound, with nothing productive happening that curbed the pain or the bleeding. I held my head with one of my bloody hands as a wave of nausea began overwhelming me, collapsing me to my knees.

"**It's about time you did it.**" I laughed, still trying to pump more energy into my neck, refusing to die within the confines of such a dark and disgusting room.

Not until the one who did this suffers for what they've done to me...

I survived eternal damnation within the Abyss; I can survive this disgusting torture...

27

Connor: Hidden Within Us

"Oh my god C-Connor! No...god no please...d-don't die because of this..." My vision remained blurry as I heard this scream unfamiliar to her own voice tear through the silence, the ground beneath me already growing wet from the dark red.

It's so hard to think...my head feels like someone's slamming into it with a club...

Tearing a piece of my own cloak off, Mara desperately pressed it to my neck as tightly as she could, gasping as the red already began to taint the gloves she wore. In a matter of seconds her gloves and the cloth were stained an eerie murky red. I dizzily chuckled, seeing spots begin to form in my vision as the sun beamed on overhead.

Or I'm already getting woozy from the blood loss...any deeper of a cut and I would be dead in seconds...

"...That...That was quite the kill sprint you went for Mara. I knew you wanted to kill him...but you somehow wanted it more than I do..." I murmured softly. Mara shook me frantically, noticing the blood continuing to cascade out despite the amount of pressure she was exerting to keep me alive.

"You didn't have to save me you idiot!" she screamed, "I disobeyed you…you s-shouldn't have paid the repercussions for it."

"If I knew that getting injured like this was the fast…fastest way to bring out your emotions, I-I would have d-done it a while ago." Mara's palms began to quiver as her hands continued to apply pressure, despite the cloth becoming nothing but a container for my own blood.

"D-Dammit Connor," she mumbled, lowering her head as her eyes glazed over slightly, "I-I d-didn't…please n-not again…" Barely hearing a dry scoff, I tilted my head on the ground as slowly as I could without hurting myself more. Mara craned her head over her shoulder, glaring at the robed man with a fiery gaze that contained nothing but hatred in her eyes.

"I apologize that it had to come to this kid, but I can't let you dogs stand in my way. I will not allow any of you to impede on what I have already accomplished, no matter how determined you are to stop it." Zain said this all as he raised another knife to his side, watching as the amber pendant bounced against his chest. Running at us with a yell, he charged at us with the full intention of driving through Mara with the weapon. I tried to move anything to fight back, but even trying to flex a finger sent sparks of pain shooting through me.

Mara shot forward, dragging me to the side by my shoulders as the knife dug into the ground where we once stood. Just the act of dragging me a few feet caused pain to tear through me, forcing a pained yell to expel out of my throat, along with a sputter of the same putrid, darkened blood.

In the corner of my eye, I could see Henry charging at Zain full speed with Jack by his side, managing to strike him in the jaw while he was distracted by us. Jack followed up with another overhead swing in the hopes of ending him, but I knew it wouldn't connect as soon as Zain began mumbling to himself.

Attempting to focus on the scene any further proved futile, as my vision blurred from the lack of blood and my body convulsed as Mara hastily dragged me across the forest grounds, not caring how she did it as long as it was quick.

I don't...I don't know how I haven't passed out yet...I feel like I'm going to vomit...

"S-Serena!" I heard Mara scream in a volume and panic I never could have imagined her speaking, let alone screaming in, "Serena!"

I heard Serena let out a sharp gasp behind me. Mara proceeded to drop me on the ground in front of her, ripping off another piece of my cloak and pressing that against my neck. In a second, I was suddenly glancing up at a pair of frantic grey eyes, ones that were attempting to focus on both of the injured laid out in front of her.

"The knife heading for me went straight across his neck! P-Please Serena..." Mara gasped out, as Serena examined me in a panic while still applying her magic to Avelina. Craning my neck to the left as slowly as I possibly could, I could see the hole that tore through the woman's torso still refused to close despite Serena's attempts. The muscles and tissue continuously attempted to fuse together, but always ended up falling limp within the confines of her body. My eyes widened in realization.

She's handicapped in her abilities by not being a Zevron...her magic can't seal a wound with that much internal and external damage...

Serena was beginning to not look as good either, as cuts appeared to be growing at a faster rate. The skin on the tips of her fingers had begun to peel as more slices formed across her arms, mixing the blood of the doctor and her patient as she fought to keep her alive.

"Dammit! His jugular has been severely damaged," Serena exclaimed as she stared at me, never moving her hands from Avelina's still body, "I...I don't have a clue as to how you're still conscious, let alone how you haven't b-bled to death yet Connor. The amount of blood you're l-losing should've already k-killed you." Still focused on the woman lying beside her, Serena turned to Mara in a panic as a layer of sweat began coalescing on her forehead. Just as the thought came a slice dug across the surface of her forehead, and while it was relatively shallow it began to bleed as much as most head wounds do.

"Mara, I need you to try and maintain pressure with whatever cloth you can find," she ordered as clinically as she could muster, refusing to wipe the blood that was beginning to fall across her face like a curtain, "Don't completely cut off blood flow but try and calm the stream. I have some towels in my pocket you can try and use."

"I tried to...Serena," Mara replied, "He just keeps bleeding; I can't get it to stop!"

"Well I'm working on Avelina right now!" she yelled out, the stress oozing from her words, "I've got nothing but that so please just do what I say!" I heard the pattering of feet rush up to me as I shot my eyes to the left, careful not to turn my neck too fast.

Standing over me was the young girl Catherine, who was currently doing the exact opposite of what I told her to do and was now at the center of the battle, standing over me with a wide-eyed expression.

"Mi...Mister Connor?" Her expression turned sour as her eyes grew watery. I flashed her a faint smile that sent pain throughout my entire body as I maintained it.

"H-Hey Cat..." I murmured as I heard Mara gasp, not realizing the young child was currently standing beside me, "I...I thought I told you to stay put until we had this handled."

"What...what happened?" Mara's grasp around me tensed as her head remained lowered; her brunette locks tickling my face as the young girl collapsed to her knees.

If I could reach out to comfort her I would...

"Just a little banged up at the moment Catherine but don't w-worry. I'll be back up in no t-time." Catherine looked away from me as she buried her face in her hands, refusing to glance upon the entire scene as the two women attempted to heal their fallen patients.

I took another glance forward at the battle that was still ongoing, feeling incredibly lightheaded as the blood rushed out of my body.

Jack lurched forward with his massive blade, panting harshly as he dragged it sluggishly behind him. Ducking underneath a slung dagger, Jack charged forward and swept the blade horizontally across aiming directly for Zain's exposed neck. Sometime when I was glancing away, Zain had lost the specific knife he had carried with him in his hand, causing him to be completely open to Jack's attacks.

Another mumble and Zain had dodged out of the way like always. However, despite everything his robe was still nicked by the towering blade, creating a hole in the garment as Zain's eyes widened in surprise.

He must have said he would completely dodge the attack, so how on earth did he still get struck if that is what he saw as true?

Could his effect on probability be weakening overall? Could he be-

My thoughts were cut off by the sudden pain that racked through my body, causing me to spasm as Mara attempted to steady me on the ground. No matter how much pressure she applied, the bleeding wouldn't stop, a factor which all of us had to know considering the nature of the damage.

Veins are much easier to heal than other wounds like arterial injury, but with this amount of damage and no proper medical attention...not so much.

Crouching underneath another side sweeping strike, Zain came up with a powerful strike with the hand that gripped the hilt of the knife. The fist collided with Jack's jaw before he could react, rocketing him back as he slammed into the ground nearby, dropping his sword with a loud clatter.

As a set of bandages began to wrap around my neck and instantly grow wet, I noticed Fox approach swiftly behind the distracted Zain, who was currently walking over to Jack to kick him while he was down. The spy had a dagger drawn above her head, as her eyes spewed nothing but hatred towards the Bellhollow insurgent.

Without even turning around, Zain drew one of his knives up to parry the strike, causing her weapon to cascade through the air before it was flung back down into the earth.

Turning around, Zain railed a dazed Fox in the stomach with his knee, knocking the wind out of her as her eyes widened in surprise, nearly bugging out of the porcelain mask that somehow stayed attached to her face. A wisp of indigo hair remained motionless in the air as time appeared to stop, with Fox caught by the brutal strike.

As quickly as the air around us came to a halt, Zain swiftly dropped his knee and grabbed Fox by the throat, slamming her into the ground. Her eyes rolled back into her head as she was knocked out cold, the porcelain mask becoming stained with the dirt and mud.

Pulling her own knife from the dirt, Zain raised the blade over Fox, preparing to end her life almost immediately. Tackled backwards, Zain glanced down to see the blackened silhouette of Henry rampaging into him full force. The knife hurtled through the air as it escaped the robed figure's grasp, trying to elbow Henry in the face mid-flight.

Hearing a sputtering cough beside me, I painfully craned my neck to my left to see the injured Avelina, slowly clawing at the healer's arm as the hand remained firm on her chest.

"...S-Serena..."

"Save your energy Miss Rockwell," Serena replied hastily, her skin further peeling back from her fingers as her hands became engulfed in red, "I'm trying to keep you alive here."

"...cut off your healing on me..." Serena and I both popped our heads up at her statement, with my action of surprise causing pain to shoot through my neck and skull. Mara remained utterly still, applying as much pressure as she could to prolong my life for as long as she could.

"I...I don't think I heard you correctly Miss Rockwell?" Serena nervously laughed, "Because I'm pretty sure I heard you tell me to stop doing what's currently keeping you alive?" Avelina gave her a grim smile at her words, causing the nervous smile that Serena held to vanish.

"You heard correctly S-Serena," she croaked, "You k-know that your healing is the only thing keeping me alive. Connor...Connor's going to bleed out soon if you don't start applying your power to him. If you k-keep this up on me, we'll both die at this rate." Serena shook her head, her tangerine hair whipping violently around as she pressed her hands harder onto her chest. Another slice dug into her cheek, one which she barely noticed as the sputtering magic continued to tear apart her flickering hands.

"No! I-I can save both of y-you! I'll s-seal this w-wound of yours and then fix Connor while Mara's keeping him s-steady." Serena replied frantically, "Mara! I need you to t-try and cut off as much bleeding from his neck without killing him!" Her voice lost the clinical nature she was attempting to maintain, her tone becoming wild and more frantic with every word spoken. Mara just stayed utterly still while holding the garment at my neck silently, knowing full well that Avelina's words rang true.

"Even if you managed to heal Connor, the sword definitely pierced a portion of my heart or one of my l-lungs," she rasped calmly, "I'm d-dead the second your healing stops." Serena lowered her head, her eyes beginning to water as her blood and tears dropped onto the dying woman.

"No, I...I can save b-both of you," Serena repeated through sobs, "N-No...no one's dying while I'm h-here." The woman chuckled sadly to herself, staring up at the clouds above that littered the afternoon sky.

"Serena..." she whispered, "You're a medic. You should know... when someone is b-beyond saving." She glanced up at the sky as I heard Jack grunt in pain, his body slamming into a tree as I heard the air leave his lungs, almost certainly knocking him unconscious. Henry remained as the last man standing, raising his fists as he silently charged at the magician's red and purple form.

"And besides...you shouldn't waste your energy on me when you have someone else you a-absolutely can save. Your b-body is breaking down just trying to keep me f-functioning, and there's no use in all t-three of us dying." Serena began to sob more to herself, staring down at the woman who she knew for much of her life. Even now, the green light shined brighter than ever as she pumped everything she had into the woman, willing to sacrifice herself in one final push to keep her alive for even a second more. The slices had already begun digging up her arms, luckily missing prominent veins and arteries, but creating a patchwork of bloody skin and muscle on both of her arms.

And her hands...despite the green glow they were still giving off, the crimson that overwhelmed it was almost just as prominent. If I didn't know any better, then I'd say both of her hands were utterly covered in deep cuts and bruises. Even with the threat of her own death, she persisted.

"You...you idiot," she cried, "Katrina still needs you Avelina! Your sister still needs you!"

"And Connor has a whole life ahead of him," she countered, "It's not fair to l-let him bleed out when I don't even have a chance in the first place." Serena sat there, sobbing to herself as she refused to remove her bloodied hands from Avelina's torso. The blood around me began seeping into my hair and shirt as it continued to pour out like a macabre fountain.

"Just…Just tell Katrina that…to be her confidant…and her friend have been the greatest years of my l-life," she lamented with a withering smile, "…I did my best, and I wouldn't trade this life that I lived for anything." Serena didn't move a muscle, refusing to halt her power as her green tinted palms quivered in place.

"I won't…I c-can't." Avelina faintly raised her right hand up and gripped onto Serena's sliced up and bruised wrist, causing the healer to tense up in her grasp from pain and surprise.

"It's okay Serena, you did all that you could…" With hesitation, and tears flowing like rivers from her eyes, Serena steadily and shakily removed her injured hands from Avelina's bloodied torso. With a final and content smile directed towards the shimmering afternoon sky, Avelina's head fell back as a visible tuft of air left her mouth—her eyes turning glassy, and empty.

The pale hand clutching Serena fell at her side, now cold and lifeless.
No…

Instantly, a cool feeling washed throughout my neck as Serena laid her bloodied hands on it, the wound beginning to seal itself up slowly. The process took a minute or two before the pain began to subside slightly.

The blood slowly fell to a trickle as the wound began to close fully, as Serena was already running on fumes regarding her own power. The blood itself was already realigning back to my head, no longer spilling out as it once did.

I took another fleeting glance at the woman who Jack knew so well. The woman who fought so hard in Eincrest and dedicated her life to the Sentinels.

The woman I wish I knew better.
It shouldn't have been you. I…I'm sorry.

Mara sat next to Serena as she sobbed, eventually collapsing into

Mara's shoulder as the cries of agony overtook her and the green light faded from her quivering hands. Mara for some reason didn't look uncomfortable with Serena's contact, even willing to place an arm around her and pull her closer into her warm embrace, her sobs cracking louder than the battle around us. Serena gripped Mara's shirt as she visibly shook, further covering Mara with blood that continued to seep out of the still open wounds.

Her hands and arms are completely wrecked...she's lucky she has the ability to heal herself as well. One more minute of that constant stream, and Serena might've actually done far more permanent damage to herself.

The fact she was willing to give up her own life to save Avelina...

Serena...there's no one else in this entire continent more deserving of the title of medic than you are.

Catherine had finally glanced up for a moment and stared up at me, her mouth agape as the blood no longer poured out as it once did.

"Why do you all have to be such troublesome rats?" I craned my head back to the battle sorely, noting that the pain was still there even though the bleeding had mostly subsided.

Fox was lying face first on the ground, unmoving from where she was struck down before. Jack was slumped against the same tree that he collided with previously, remaining in the position he was in before just like Fox.

The last of us still standing was Henry, killing intent burning in his azure eyes as he launched himself at Zain. Henry flew at the purple robed man with a flurry of rapid kicks and punches, only to have the man parry every one of his devastating blows.

There were large tears in each of their outfits, with Zain's robes bearing several noticeable holes. Henry had tears and slices forced into it, his clothes looking incredibly tattered.

Zain has to be slowing down. That strike by Jack wasn't a fluke; it was a sign that something was wrong.

He appears incredibly capable even without it though...

Zain charged first this time, swinging his right fist forward towards Henry's chest. Henry deflected his punch with the back of his hand, hammering his skull with a strong headbutt. The crack that emanated through the air sent chills up my spine as their skulls collided.

Falling back, Henry struck Zain in the stomach with his fist before elbowing his jaw, ending with him whirling around and kicking Zain in the side of the knee. As Zain fell onto one leg, Henry pulled his own back, swinging his leg forward with all of his force. Zain had managed to jump out of the way of the devastating strike, drawing two daggers in his left hand. Henry stared him down a solid ten feet away, glaring at him with his fists raised.

"For all the people you've killed I'm ending you where you stand extremist, here and now!" Zain let out a grin as his eyes shifted away, averting his gaze to something else.

"Not everyone can defend themselves like you can!" At the same time Henry and I both shot to where his crazed green eyes were staring towards, a look of relief and glee present on his expression.

Fox, still unconscious on the ground and completely helpless to what Zain was attempting to do.

Without even taking time to process the change, Henry rushed towards the unconscious spy, lunging forward as fast as he could while almost forgetting about the pendant user behind him. Zain twirled the knives once, before throwing them both at the helpless girl.

Henry was too far to move Fox out of the way of the attack, he and I both knew that. If he attempted to take the hit himself, he would be taking one of the few capable fighters we have out of commission. His options were few, and yet he still charged directly in the path between Fox and the knives.

My mouth widened as he did something I didn't expect: he pulled his right fist back and struck the daggers midair in the split second he had. A mighty wind shook the battleground around us, making dust fly into my eyes as Zain stumbled back, almost falling to the ground below. A small pillar of dust exploded up around him, which combined with the wind in my eyes made him difficult to see.

As my vision cleared, my jaw dropped as I noticed where the two knives were now.

They were completely shattered, lying on the ground in defeated heaps of scrap metal.

Zain grinned as he reaffirmed his stance, with Henry still standing with his fist drawn.

"Well," Zain laughed, "I wasn't expecting someone like you to be in this merry band." Henry's blue eyes bore into Zain's as he clenched his raised fist in anger.

His hand...

Whatever force was behind that blow had enough power to annihilate the glove that resided on the hand he punched with, exposing the pale skin beneath. That...and another prominent feature.

The brand of a purple eagle.

Its wings were spread wide, and its mighty maw was gazing towards the sky. One bright visible eye was on the side of its head. Its talons looked like they were clutching onto something, but that something couldn't be seen.

His hood was cast down from the power of the strike, the hooks attached to his mask digging into nearby trees and the ground. His cloth mask lay discarded, looking almost lonely on the dirt below.

The skin on his face was pale and sickly, looking like it hadn't seen the sun in several years. Henry clawed at his face as he realized what just happened as his lowered hood swayed in the breeze, shock evident on his features as he ran a terrified hand through his snow-white hair.

28

Connor: Henry

I froze momentarily, the shock probably evident in my wide-eyed features.

I should have seen it sooner. His eyes, his reserved attitudes, his attire for crying out loud.

It was so obvious...I'm such a fool for not figuring it out myself.

Both Serena and Mara didn't look surprised in the slightest as they still held each other tightly, with Serena's being the only one shifting to something that resembled sadness.

They seem inseparable, so it would make sense that she would have known a long time ago.

Mara must've somehow figured it out before I could, as perceptive and paranoid as she is.

Zain sneered again as Henry grasped at his face, his pants turning into loud, terrified gasps as they both glared at each other.

"A Zevron in disguise amongst humans," Zain snickered as he repositioned the blade in his hand, "Afraid of revealing yourself to those closest to you? Although, considering the ignorance of people I don't blame you." Henry didn't respond to his insinuation, still holding onto his revealed face. His entire body shook as his features shifted in a way that a mask could never represent, standing in his defensive stance in front of the still prone woman.

"Although if that is the case, why did you only use your power as a last effort to defend that woman rather than during our fight?" Zain taunted, "Are you incapable of using your power Zevron?" Henry just stood there, his shaking becoming stronger.

"Or...are you afraid?" Zain continued, causing all of Henry's shaking to cease. He stiffened like a board as Zain smiled with a predatory grin, "Ah that's it. You're afraid of this immense power, and based on how strong that strike was you lack the ability to control it. Even what you wear shows how afraid you are of your true self. I thought Zevrons were supposed to suppress all emotions inside of them, including fear." I heard Serena grit her teeth, thrashing in Mara's arm, who had gripped hard onto Serena to keep her from moving.

"Shut up!" Serena yelled, "You don't know anything!" Zain glanced at Serena with disdain, flicking a dagger he had at his waist at the two. Mara was already up on her feet, deflecting the dagger with her own swing of the blade.

"Medics are some of the only individuals I respect in this country, so I have been leaving you alone. I could change that instantly." After he turned back to Henry, I planted my palms onto the ground as I pushed up with every bit of strength I had in me.

Come on Connor get up! Your wounds are healed so stand up and fight!

My arm gave out underneath me for a moment; my face collapsing back into the dirt as I gasped for breath, the coarse dust entering my lungs like a disease.

Come on...Come on!

Another motion. I pushed myself up with all the strength I could muster as my arms straightened, pushing all the way up into a sitting position. I panted as I repositioned my legs, standing one leg up, then another.

Two feet on the ground.

You have the ability to fight for what you believe in, so stand up and prove you have the strength to do it!

"This is new to me," Zain began as my body rocked back and forth, slightly uncomfortable with standing, "A Zevron who fears their own abilities. Why be afraid of this power? It's a gift that could be used for so many purposes." I noticed during my crawl that a tear actually fell down Henry's pale face, splattering against the dirt floor below.

Serena was the first one to notice that I had fully stood up from the ground, letting out a whimpered gasp as she saw me.

"C-Connor...what do you think you're..."

"I respect your race of people, but all of you cowards who leave your own country are weak-willed," Zain taunted, "You can't handle your own gifts or the minute taunts of the ignorant masses, so you hide behind masks and other people. By shirking your own abilities, you forgo training that could be used to hone your abilities and turn you into something. And yet you choose to be nothing but dirt, and you will always be a coward for it." Henry had stopped his shaking, as his hands lay dormant at his sides. I took a single step forward as I raised my head up, my entire body swaying at the slightest of movements.

The pain is there, but it's dull enough where I can push through it.

"Henry you dense idiot!" I yelled as I grasped onto my neck with my offhand, "Are you actually listening to him?" Zain cocked his head to the left examining me. His green slits looked incredibly curious, tinted with a feral deadliness. I glanced back behind me to see the two women still beside each other, with Mara's gaze meeting my own.

"Keep these two safe, Mara."

"Hmm...I thought I brought you down with a single strike? No matter…" He flicked his wrist again, flinging one of his many daggers at my face.

I lurched to the side as quickly as I could, narrowly avoiding the dagger that flew by me and dug itself into a tree nearby. I took another determined step as I drew Requiem from its sheath, shakily drawing the black dirk in front of me.

I have to do some damage here and now, no matter what it is.

"This man will say anything to break your spirit Henry…Don't let him get inside your head! Your powers are your own to control, as is who you are! Not one of us will judge who you are, because you'd be using that gift you were born with for good." With a loud and pronounced yell that hid the stiffness my body was currently experiencing, my feet dug into the earth below me as I sprung from the spot I was on. Charging as fast as I could muster at the robed man, his eyes grew wide as I swiftly came within striking distance of Zain.

"Your strike will utterly miss!" His words falling completely on deaf ears as the strike dug into his shoulder, sending him staggering back as that portion of his robe turned red.

"You're right…" I remarked as I dug the blade deeper into his body, causing him to yell in agony, "I utterly missed going for your wretched heart…your power seems to be weakening Zain." Letting out a snarl, the robed man smacked me across the jaw with the back of his hand, launching me to the side as Requiem remained embedded within his shoulder.

Pulling the jagged dirk rigidly out of his body, Zain hurled it to the side as the revealed Zevron still stood motionless, the hair covering his eyes as he stared at the ground.

Standing back up slowly I shined a satisfied smile as I glared towards the man who was currently rushing towards me.

I knew that something was different about this…

Before he could reach me, a brown and red form flew past me and crashed into the charging form of Zain, the man barely able to bring up a dagger to defend himself. Mara's tear-stained eyes glared into him as metal slid across metal, slicing through the air itself as she unleashed a flurry of sword slashes upon the backstepping Zain.

Wanting to offer proper backup, I rushed forward with my fists drawn as a cocky smirk spread across my face, Zain's pendant lurking in my head.

"From what I can see Zain there's a crack running along the middle of that amber pendant. My theory is that these gems aren't meant for humans, potentially being given to half-Zevron members who couldn't do magic as strong as theirs. You tried to break past that limitation and over-exerted its power, making you use its maximum power consistently. You don't possess the willpower or the bloodline to control that power!" I ran up to the battle just as Mara was battered to the side, stumbling as the tip of her sword clinked across the ground. With Zain facing me faster than expected, I raised my fists up as he struck me in the side of my stomach. I tasted iron as I staggered to the left, lifting my fists again fast enough to block another fierce strike.

Rearing back, I rocked him in the jaw with a powerful strike, revealing the bald green-eyed man that lurked within. The expression he held contained absolute terror.

Another strike aimed for his face, albeit this one was blocked by his own crossed arms. As he staggered backward, gripping his chest, my mind flashed to my final resort; one tool that could potentially end this battle. Mara rushed at him full-speed before he could get his bearings, giving me the time I needed.

Attempting to do it as fast as possible, I gripped at the pendant resting against my chest with my left hand and put my entire will into harnessing that energy again.

I need you...I need your power to protect them!

I refuse to let anyone else die while I am here...no matter what it takes I'm going to keep you all safe!

Immediately, the jewel began to grow hot against my chest, right as Zain knocked Mara away with a powerful strike to the chest. Almost grinning, I lowered my right hand to my side as I felt the now familiar hurricane like winds coalescing within my grasp and whipping around my entire hand in the same glove-like formation. Continuing to let it build up, I rushed forward at Zain, who had just recently removed his hands from his bleeding face. His eyes widened as he saw my approach, although they never gazed upon my right hand.

"How in the world are you even still standing? You should be dead!"

"I told you exactly what I was going to do back in Eincrest, " I yelled as I was almost upon him, "I won't let you hurt these people anymore, even if it's for your twisted ambition! No matter what you throw my way I'll always stand against people like you even if every bone in my body is shattered and every drop of my blood has spilled!" Finally registering my approach, he whispered to himself and instinctively threw his hands up to block.

I dug my fist as hard as I could into his guard, his eyes widening as the wind enhanced blow slammed into him. A grunt exploded out of him as my fist connected, before a brilliant green light met my eyes as the power exploded out.

The winds propelled him backwards at incredible speeds, somehow managing to keep his feet on the ground as the force of the blow utterly decimated him. Dirt and rocks kicked up around us as the wind exploded out. However, I soon realized why the power behind the strike was not as substantial as it was before.

I had rushed the process too quickly, and suffered the painful repercussions.

Instead of dedicating the hurricane's full power towards Zain, the rest of the force rebounded and dug into me, sending me away as well as the sharpened winds cut across the surface of my skin. They tore across my clothes and arms, acting like miniature daggers slicing across my skin.

My vision went spotty as one stray torrent of wind slashed across my neck, reopening the previous cut just barely. I collapsed to a single knee as a wave of nausea overwhelmed me, the wetness flowing down my neck again.

As my brain attempted to formulate a backup plan to this scenario, I heard heavy footsteps pattering against the ground, causing me to look up.

With a new hole blown through the surface of his purple robe exposing the black tunic underneath the garment, a surprised looking Zain marched toward me with renewed vengeance. He clutched at his chest with every heaving step, most likely having been severely bruised by the strike.

"So, you yourself have a pendant…incredible. That's how you knew about mine in Eincrest. Perhaps I'll take yours off of you once I'm done with this. You won't mind, will you?" My vision further blurred as his palm slammed into my face, making me collide with the dirt below as pain shot through my body like bolts of lightning. The red splattered against the ground along with me, my body shivering.

"Go…go on and die you sick bastard," I growled out as my body refused to stand, "I'd give my life for all these people if it meant one of them put an end to your measly life." Zain snarled to himself as he grasped me by the throat, bloodying his hand and lifting me up with the same strength as he did back at Eincrest. He swiftly threw me aside, my body crashing to the ground as I groaned in pain.

"I've had enough of this and your insistence on dying," Zain growled, "I think it's time I ended you and take the power you can't use properly." Zain turned to himself, picking up a discarded knife off the ground. He turned it over in his hands, gripping it by the tip of the blade as he prepared to hurl it at me. Everyone else was too far away or lying unconscious in the dirt, with even Mara still coughing on the ground as she desperately attempted to stand. I tried crawling away so I could stand up, but the familiar pain shot through me again at the worst possible moment.

Dammit...not now!

As he prepared to hurl the blade, my mind clung desperately to the memories before all this chaos.

The memories of times where my younger self didn't have a care in the world besides his books.

Or the tactics taught by his mother...

Mom...I wish I could read one more chapter of your book with you...I wish I could be there to save you from that monster.

I chuckled to myself, noting the gleeful times where my mind wasn't aware of that knight, or what he would do to our family...

You're really screwed up in the head aren't you Connor?

Just as I closed my eyes to accept my blasted fate, I heard the faint sound of metal clashing against something else. Wind rushed by my face as I gradually opened my eyes, almost recoiling. The knife Zain was going to throw now was buried in the dirt by my face, clearly missing its target.

But...But how? There's absolutely no way he could've missed from that distance.

A darkened shadow soon washed over my prone form. I glanced over my shoulder, my hazel eyes widening as an uncommon gleeful grin came over my face.

Standing above me with his fist still raised was Henry, his white locks almost floating up in the sky as his blue eyes stared directly at the purple man. His blackened cloak swayed in the breeze as his right fist lay extended, glowing a bright blue similar to how Serena's hands became.

"Connor, you damn fool," he mumbled, sounding far clearer now that the mask was no longer hooked onto his face, "How could you protect someone who's doing nothing to help the fight?" He drew his fists back into his traditional stance, albeit with the blue glow ever present on his hands. Zain recoiled back as fast as he could, unnerved by this sudden development.

"I shouldn't be afraid of something I know I can hone and train," he said proudly, glancing back at me, "I won't be afraid, just as you weren't." With renewed strength, Henry charged down at the man who had taken so much from all of us.

I felt someone grab onto my legs as Henry rushed forward towards Zain, his hands glowing as Zain drew several more knives.

"That…may be…one of the dumbest things I have ever seen a person do in my lifetime," Serena huffed, "Dragging yourself over there injured like that." Serena sighed as she dragged me closer to where we were initially, applying her power to my neck once again. Her hands up to her elbows were completely covered by a white gauze, whilst the small cuts on her face had stopped bleeding. The green glow shined through despite it.

The trickle of blood died down once again, although the closing of the wound was incredibly sluggish at the moment.

Serena's running out energy. She's pushing herself to do all this.

"Although, I have to admit your stupidity did something incredible," she acquiesced in awe, "I've…never seen him use his powers before like this, even when I first met him. Now that he has, I know without a doubt Zain is completely screwed." I glanced over my shoulder as I lay on my back on the ground, making sure Catherine was staying with Serena. She was, with her back facing the battle and probably not even noticing I was back. Mara stood there staring at Zain as she finally stood, her mouth agape at the sudden change. I glanced back at the battle myself.

Zain frantically showcased four knives in his hand, desperately hurling all of them at Henry's charging form. Almost with a refined flourish, Henry deflected two to the ground with his blue-coated hands and sidestepped the others, acting like it was simply child's play for him. Zain gasped in surprise, reaching towards his many sheaths only to find them ironically empty.

"No!" he yelled out, directing his green eyes back towards Henry, "Stay away from me!" Clearly not heeding his warning, Henry charged forward with his fist drawn back, preparing for a strike directly aimed at his face.

"Your strike will easily be blocked by my guard!" Raising both of his arms in an X-position, Zain sneered as he knew that because of the pendant's power, he could block any attack as if it were nothing.

Or at least…that's what he assumed. After all, as far as I knew he had only tried dodging with the pendant's power and as I pointed out he had weakened it through overuse.

Connecting with Zain's waiting arms, I heard a sickening snap echo throughout the clearing as Zain screamed in agony. Mara involuntarily cringed at the aftermath.

Zain fell to his knees as he stared at his two arms, now both obviously broken in some way by the force of Henry's blow, much to my disgust and his misery. He stared at his two broken limbs in shock, panicking to himself but not able to properly release any words to show it. Henry stood silently over him, his hands still glowing blue as Zain cowered beneath him.

"No…I won't die to you gutter rats! I will fulfill my ambition!"

"You've dishonored the idea of your ambition the second you used it as an excuse for murder. Even more so, you did it with a form of focused Zevron magic, which I find quite disgusting. I believe that those who you've massacred deserve retribution." Drawing his fist, I saw a faint glimmer in Henry's eyes as his hands glowed even brighter than they had before. Zain closed his eyes, knowing not even the power of the pendant could save him now as Henry reeled his fist back.

"Forgive me...Holly..."

Striking him across the jaw with full force, I heard another sickening twist and snap as Zain was catapulted through the air with enough force to snap the chain that held the pendant around his neck. As the gem flew, his body crashed into a thick oak tree headfirst, eliciting another faint snap. His body fell back down to earth, collapsing to the ground below as his green eyes grew dim.

Falling limp, and dead.

Henry stared down at what he had done, looking down at the hands that somehow held enough power to snap human bones and launch people into the air with a single strike.

It's...remarkable how much power he holds...

Much to my surprise, he smiled.

Not a fake or forced smile that never quite reaches the eyes, but a true, full smile as the blue light faded from his palms. He stared up at the afternoon sky, the sun's warming rays hitting his face for what was probably the first time in forever.

He soon collapsed face first into the dirt, the dust billowing up as every combatant now lay in the dirt below, with most unable to take in the fact that the mission was somehow a success...

29

Connor: Aftermath

Propping myself against the tree as the dust settled, Serena ran in the opposite direction towards Henry. She turned him over on the ground, revealing that Henry was actually wide awake, simply staring forward now towards the sky. Serena breathed a sigh of relief, seeing he wasn't unconscious.

"Oh thank the Goddess," she murmured to herself, "You didn't have to exert yourself that much just now you know. Now, just sit still for a second so I can keep you from keeling over on the walk back." Henry grunted as he lowered his head back down to the earth, staring into the sky that almost matched his eyes.

"...thank you, Serena." Serena's eyes lit up in surprise at his words as she swayed her green hands across Henry's bruised body. She lowered her head as the tangerine hair fell over her face.

"Don't g-get all sentimental on me just because you almost died," Serena replied, flustering between words, "I'm just gonna believe you're going crazy from the magic or the blood rushing to your head or something." Henry let out a snicker as the dust began to congregate in his normally clean milky hair, the dirt making clear blotches on his pale skin. He shut his eyes as he expressed another smile that we would not have ever seen him flash without that darned mask.

"Whatever you say…Serena."

Jack awoke slowly as well, rubbing the back of his neck as the aftermath came into view for him. He bolted up with widened eyes as he scanned around him expecting a raging battle, eventually laying his eyes on Zain's limp body. I eased myself up, able to somehow stand and shuffle towards Jack's direction. I gripped the many spots where I knew bruises had obviously formed, but I tried to make them less obvious.

Serena needs to save her energy for those more gravely wounded.

Jack grinned solemnly at me as I gave him a weary smile back.

"Is that…Henry?" He expressed suddenly, his eyes locking onto his prone form. I gave him a swift nod.

"Indeed…it appears he's been a Zevron this whole time." Jack's eyes widened in tired surprise, letting out a chuckle as he did so.

"Ah," he relented, "Surprised you didn't even know. Gotta pay more attention brother of mine." I shrugged my shoulders as he laughed, examining Henry as Serena continued to heal him.

I really do…

"While that absolutely went against any sort of plan," he continued, "We somehow got him." I rubbed the back of my head as Fox began to stir.

"We did, Jack," I simply declared, "We did…" Jack grinned again, staring into the sky. The sun had already begun its descent down, meaning it was around five, maybe six. His grin vanished as his eyes glazed over, lost in thought.

"It makes me wonder; do you think he meant to do this?" Jack mumbled as he peered into the sunset, "He believed that his country fell to ruin and became a corrupt power because of us; because of our inaction and how we didn't offer any form of assistance." I shook my head as I walked to the slouching corpse, my hands in my pockets as

I peered at the battered body of Bellhollow's insurgent.

"He had good intentions at one point, Jack, but those ideals appear to have been lost to time. From what I could gather he still held the idea that what he was doing would protect his people, and who knows. Maybe the justice and morality that lurked within him that became twisted and malformed still held true, but the madness he portrayed showed otherwise."

"Do you think…we just doomed any form of rebellion, or that we crushed any form of hope and optimism he could have generated?" I didn't respond, knowing his words most likely rang true.

"Answer me Connor!" I swiveled my head around rigidly to my brother, seeing him shaking as he glared down.

"Was what we just did right?" he spat with venom oozing from his words, "I know we had to do it Connor, and I'm somewhat glad that we killed him over everything he's done. But at the same time, did we just doom so many others to damnation in Bellhollow because of this? Did we…just prove him right?"

"Do you see any other path we could've taken?" I responded honestly, "I don't honestly know what will happen in Bellhollow, but what I do know is that Zain was a fanatic; a man who needed to be cast aside before he caused anymore death. Another disenfranchised soul will pick up his torch; we are a stubborn species after all. His ideals were corrupted, so maybe another will come with a fresh sense of justice, and morality." Jack breathed through his teeth as he glanced away.

He's right, and you know it. He may not realize the true implications to that doubt...

This man was a killer, no matter what he stood for he sullied it all with the path he tore through this nation.

But could we have doomed them; cursed them to rot in that eternal pit of solitude that Bellhollow is?

Maybe...perhaps that is true.

Every action has consequences; the same could've been said if we just left him to his own devices.

If he never told us anything, we probably wouldn't have even considered any reverberations in Bellhollow from his death.

Turning back, I noticed in the corner of my eye a familiar amber hue that shined through the dust and tufts of grass that poked through the earth's surface.

Glancing around, I bent over and grabbed onto the exact item I was looking for.

The amber pendant...

Zain's pendant...no

Eincrest's pendant...Catherine's pendant.

It didn't seem to glow or shine as brightly as it had before, however there was still a faint glimmer within it that gleamed beneath the surface, even with the surface level crack across the center.

You put everything on the line for this, no matter how twisted your dream became. I may as well make sure it doesn't fall into any more morally corrupt hands.

This is the next piece of the puzzle...A firm step towards finding my mother even without more knowledge on Zain.

I shoved it into my right pocket, snatching Requiem off the ground before turning back and limping towards where everyone was gathering.

I need to study this gem further and find a connection to help me track her down, and then I'll give it back to its former owner.

You're the key I've been looking for all this time...with you I'll fulfill my own dream.

Catherine was the first to notice my presence and immediately rushed towards me, wrapping me in a tight hug as I was planted against a tree. I smiled as I rubbed her dark hair in a calming manner, hiding my cringe as her hug pressed against the bruises in my stomach.

"D-Don't…don't do that again C-Connor." She muttered out.

"I won't Cat, don't you worry about it." I felt a sob tear through her body as her face dug into my shirt, the dirty clothing growing damp from tears this time.

Mara sat with her arms crossed, her clothes covered in thick blood stains and dirt. She stared towards the center of the circle, panting heavily as her eyes traced me over with the same reserved stare.

As for Fox…

She was now fully conscious and her face was down, buried into the still smiling corpse of Avelina. Sobs were raking her whole body, causing her to visibly shake as she clutched onto the dead woman.

Her sister…

God…

"No…" I heard Jack gasp, with the sound of metal clattering to the ground as Jack sprinted to the body.

Jack ran up to Fox and rested a shaking hand on her vibrating shoulder. Jack, my brother who had known the woman longer than I ever had, collapsed to the ground as well, unable to quell the emotions stirring within him.

"Dammit Avelina…why'd it have to be you?" he muttered to himself, as I heard the shrill, unfamiliar sound of a sob rake through him. Fox grabbed onto Jack's arm instinctively as she cried, leading to Jack embracing the sister of the woman he had known for so long.

The two held each other as the rest of us lay tired and yet restless; two souls who had lost such an indispensable piece of their lives.

I laid my head down as well, the wind brushing by us as I grasped onto the young girl who sat defeated in my arms.

We beat him. We really did it.

I stared out at the group of men and women who lay injured or broken in some way in this clearing.

The Sentinels…people who protected Solaton without anyone even knowing.

Many of them now sat in deep thought within a distant clearing, sobbing the only sound that pierced through the silence even though the mission had been completed.

None of that mattered…did it?

None of that mattered…

* * *

It…It stopped.

At first, the bleeding began to trickle out slower, flowing much slower than the river it once was. Then suddenly, it stopped completely.

I was startled as I turned back to my neck, widening my eyes to see a green aura surrounding it in the corner of my vision, until it was completely sealed after a couple minutes.

Sealing in a way completely antithetical to the way I enacted.

My teeth gritted together with a shrieking grind, as I bolted up from where I had collapsed in the first writhing pain I had ever experienced throughout my long life.

"**Anula!**" I yelled, "**You devious witch of a woman! How dare you even think of touching me with your vile power!**" As I yelled, a sharp pain shot through my skull that felt as if a knife drove through. I groaned loudly in irritation as I banged my head against one of the black stone walls, taking solace in the fact that the pain rang far duller than that of the pain that cracked through my skull.

That damned black-haired boy again…and I knew it was him because of the black tufts in my peripheral vision.

He was lying on the floor, with that same human girl beside him.

The usual complacent face I had come to know looked deathly afraid. She raised a hand…a hand coated in red.

A new face appeared: an orange haired girl with grey eyes. She was staring down at him with that same mix of human fear and compassion.

Her hands were surrounded by Anula's vile aura.

But…

The boy had a blow through his neck, one that was bleeding strongly as a vein was clearly split in some way. The girl applied her healing through tears, placing her glowing green hands onto the neck of the black-haired boy.

I rubbed my neck as I stared down, my similar black hair covering my eyes, but I could still see it.

I could still see the wound, the very wound that somehow acted the same as mine.

The wound on the neck of Rennak the fallen god, my neck, my body.

Lingered mockingly in the exact same spot as the human boy in my visions.

No…

No no no…

"No!"

* * *

Henry eased himself up as Serena turned to the others, ensuring their wounds were healed and that those who were knocked unconscious wouldn't suffer any permanent head injuries. There were tears in her eyes, but she remained focused on the task of healing everyone's injuries. Henry stretched his arms out as he stood, making his way over to us.

381

"Fox..." Fox just sobbed in response as Henry proclaimed her moniker, her face still burrowed into Avelina's blood-stained shirt.

"We have to leave at once," Henry continued, "But, you can find a suitable burial site for her. We'll meet up with you later down the road." Henry turned around to face Serena as Fox stood firm, shaking her head.

"No..." she rasped out, causing Henry to pause, "I...I'll be a little ahead of you, and bury my sister at home base. It's...It's what she would've wanted." Henry, now standing with his back to Fox and Avelina's corpse, nodded and continued on his way, with Serena swiftly following behind. The tangerine haired woman took two steps forward as the green light faded away, before the lights upstairs completely vanished as she suddenly fell unconscious.

As her eyes rolled up into her head, the next involuntary step she took twisted suddenly, causing her to slip forward as she had already passed out before she hit the ground.

Henry was already upon her, catching her in his right arm before any part of her touched the ground. Without a word, he threw the collapsed form of Serena haphazardly onto his back.

"Her body had already over-exerted herself, and her mind is now just realizing it," Henry rhetorically explained as he continued to walk, now with the Sentinels' healer in tow, "Didn't have to heal every sore portion of my body Serena, especially with your hands still bandaged up."

Jack followed closely, rolling his muscles in his right arm as he walked.

I took a careful step forward, gripping at my side as pain shot through it. I glanced down in dismay as my hand grew slightly wet, just now remembering my entire body was still littered in bruises and scrapes I didn't have Serena heal.

She barely had enough energy to heal the others...I wasn't as important.

As I attempted to move with the group, the edges of my vision went black as I collapsed to one knee, my entire body spasming in pain.

Jack, hearing my exclamation of pain turned around and stepped towards me, already crouching down to lift me up. He suddenly stopped, a smile curling onto his lips. He gave a salute to someone behind me before turning back around.

Almost like a sign of...gratitude?

Just as I thought this, something warm brushed beside me as something came under my left shoulder. I turned to see a familiar brunette girl next to me, pulling my arm slowly over her shoulders.

Mara...

Hoisting me up slightly, she placed her right arm underneath my left as my left leg propped up slightly. Acting as my crutch, I was able to steadily walk without as much pain as we both took gradual steps towards the others, attempting to find a speed to walk that would suit both of us.

I ignored the dissipating pain with each step and craned my neck back, watching as Fox carefully threw Avelina's body over her shoulder. Her eyes still carried tears as she still mourned the loss of the one we were unable to save.

30

Connor: Promises and Penance

The ceremony was rather short.

As soon as we had arrived, Katrina was already standing in the doorway waiting for Mara and me to return, most likely to give us a tongue thrashing. Her entire body froze as her eyes shot to the body of her friend, her face turning a ghostly white. She just stood there...frozen in time as our battered forms and her friend came into view.

Without another word, she led us to a small clearing nearby the base as she was briefed on what happened, water coalescing on the edges of her eyes. Her and Henry went back into the base in search of something to fashion a headstone out of afterwards, along with informing Ellia of what had happened. They came out with a linen sheet to wrap her body in preparation for burial.

Now, all of us stood around the single grave that now rested in that clearing, every member present paying respects to the woman who had somehow affected everyone's life.

I don't remember any of the words; it was hard to pay attention without zoning out into depressed thoughts.

I disliked ceremonies like this, and I knew the words were always the same: valiant stories of friendship and hardship, and how different the world will be now that they're gone. All meaningless words to the dead that should've been told while they still drew breath.

We didn't have a priest or a holy figure of any kind, so we did the next best thing and had Serena preside over the ceremony. She knew Avelina for a long time, and her art as a healer and her dedication against killing people made her the holiest person here.

Katrina delivered the eulogy, clearly staying as stoic as she could to maintain her face as a leader.

But, I'm sure everyone knew better. Beneath every word came the choking back of tears as she lamented the loss of a true friend.

Henry had put his hood back over his face before we even arrived to avoid prying eyes just in case the others were here as well. After all, this ceremony was for Avelina.

Ellia and Serena were both crying the entire time, even with the medic presiding over the ceremony.

Gripped tightly within the spectacled woman's arms was the battered and bloody book I had seen in Avelina's jacket when I first arrived. The pages were crinkled due to the dried blood, and the cause of her murder created a hole that tore straight through the book, making the words indecipherable.

Ellia clung to it like a keepsake, tears flowing as she could barely glance upon the body, her hands quivering as she hugged the book close.

Maybe it was lent to her or something by Ellia...I'll never know.

Jack remained close by the grave, occasionally running his hand over the gravestone as he too choked back several tears.

Mara and Fox both stood at a distance, watching but not getting too close. While Mara seemed like she was handling it fine, Fox was far different. An occasional tear would flow down her neck.

The young Catherine stood nearby. I gave minor introductions to

Katrina before all this, giving a genuine smile to the young girl.

She sat confused during the ceremony, but clearly understood the gravity of it all.

I stood right beside my brother, placing my hand on his shoulder to ensure he was alright. Even though I was devastated by Avelina's loss, I knew Jack was hurting more, and I had to be the brother he desperately needed right now.

The ceremony ended just as quickly as it began, and most swiftly vanished from the clearing back to the base upon the burial done by Henry and Fox. Katrina stared forward at me with a blank expression, one I was unable to read at the current moment.

"You and Mara, in my office," she deadpanned as she already began walking away, "I'll give you time to recollect your thoughts, but I expect you both to be there before nightfall." Her body swayed as she exited, her yellow jacket clinging loosely to her shoulders as she took one final glance at Avelina's final resting place. Her eyes held a flicker of regret and heartbreak as she shuffled away.

Jack and I remained the only ones present, the breeze causing both of our clothes to sway in the wind. My clothes remained as torn and bloody as they were previously, whilst Jack had swapped his out for a similar pair Ellia provided upon our arrival. He stared at the grave, his eyes glazed over as he was lost in thought.

"I always thought she was too stubborn to die," he finally lamented as a single tear fell down, plopping into the fresh dirt below, "That she would personally beat death away before he could ever snatch her up." He raised his fist up into the air, grinding his teeth together as he threw it down with a pained scoff.

"Why do good people die Connor?" I was taken aback by the question, unprepared for such a thought-provoking inquiry from my normally jovial brother.

"Why does anyone die Jack?" I replied back, "Why do children die before they experience their full lives? Why do parents die before truly teaching their children? Why do good leaders die so quickly, whilst the corrupt stay alive for much longer? We will never know the answer to that question, and to dwell on it is a useless endeavor." Jack sneered to himself, letting out a sigh as his hands fell into his coat pockets.

"She had dreams Connor! Dreams of molding this continent into something better through the military. You know this whole system is corrupt, and she hoped to fix it all herself."

"Everyone has dreams like that Jack, and inadvertently those dreams happen to die with the person." I knew I was being harsh in this debate, but my brother needed to hear all of this. My brother said nothing to my remark, instead opting to scratch the spot on his back where his sword would normally rest.

"I'm gonna do it," he finally announced, squeezing his fists shut, "I'm going to do what Avelina wanted to become. I'm going to rise through the military ranks, and I'm going to fix everything broken about it. I'll finish what she started." I glanced over at my brother in surprise, although I made it clear admiration shined through that initial surprise.

"Do you really think you can do that Jack?" I genuinely asked without any form of malice or taunting, "Everything is swamped and broken in every system. To undertake an endeavor like that would be suicide. Perhaps it would be easier to remake the system from the ground up."

"I don't care," he murmured, speaking in a way that was completely separated from the jovial prankster I knew Jack was, "Her dream is now mine, and I'll do it for her. I hope you'll be there along every step of the way Connor, because I'll need your guidance if I want this to be done." Without any forethought I gave him a swift nod, flashing him a quiet smile as he ran his hand along the tombstone one last time.

"You promised me a while ago that you'd always stick by my side through whatever turmoil we faced; it would be selfish of me to say otherwise." Jack let out a hearty laugh as his hand ended its journey on the stone, falling limp to his side as he began to walk away. He tugged his brown coat close as he stepped along the path, careful to tread where everyone else had to ensure he didn't disturb any wildlife.

"I'd expect nothing less of you Connor," he chuckled out as he continued to walk, "I'd expect nothing less..."

Hearing his footsteps begin to fade away, I rested my hand on the loose dirt as I crouched down next to another tombstone.

"Did you see us Avelina, wherever you are? We did it, we stopped him." I chuckled to myself after those words, realizing what I was doing.

Maybe I am crazy; this is the second tombstone I've talked to in recent days.

I stood up from the ground, dusting off my torn pant legs as I began to walk down the same path he went down only a minute ago.

"Thank you Avelina Rockwell, for being the support that Jack needed that I never had through all this turmoil. May your soul drift on to whatever place allows you to continue guiding him." Without another word I strolled away from the lot we now built for graves, the sun hitting my back as I escaped the tree line. Back to the home base...

Away from all this death...

* * *

Arriving within my room just after the ceremony, I briefly noticed that my wardrobe door was slightly ajar, the door creaking as it hung on its side. Easing it open, I was amazed to find stacks upon stacks of clothes strewn throughout the small appliance, almost to the point of spilling out.

Ellia or Serena must have snuck in when I wasn't looking.

Examining my own clothes, the wear and tear of trekking and engaging in fights left them rather tattered, something Jack and Serena had commented on before Avelina's funeral in their own way. Even the blue shirt Mara gifted to me was also torn, with miscellaneous holes and tears stretching throughout my back and sleeves. Taking it off, I cringed slightly at the bruise that remained on my stomach where Zain had struck me.

Hurling the ruined tunic onto the ground, I took a glance into the mirror at my beaten and battered form. Bruises and scrapes littered my body, but many had already begun the process of fading. I raised a hesitant hand towards my neck, tenderly touching the newly formed skin which had molded itself into a discolored scar on the side of my neck. I could almost see the point where the veins were severed and were eventually healed by Serena.

Strange. The lesion appears to be far lighter than it was before.

I don't get it...it's been less than a day and my wound should still be incredibly dark and blotchy, and yet it's already scarred over and lightened.

Staring closely at it, I wouldn't describe the blemish as ugly or disfiguring in any way. If you weren't paying attention, you probably wouldn't even notice it was there. It looked like someone traced a jagged and sloppy line across my neck lightly with some form of ink, one that made it almost invisible in the right light.

Shifting my gaze back into the cramped space, I rustled through the overabundance of options that littered the floor and walls of this cabinet.

I might as well change into something nicer before I receive my lecture.

"Who even owns this many shirts?" I mumbled to myself in slight annoyance at having to dig through many.

I'll give most of these to Jack, or maybe even Nathaniel if they are to his accented taste.

I settled on a shortened cloak that hung against the right side of the cabinet, one that I soon realized was double sided. The outside of the cloak was a vibrant, forest green, a shade or two darker than Mara's eyes. The inside was an inky black void that existed within the interior of this cloak. A bronze clasp adorned the center of it with the letter "S" emblazoned on the front, proudly showing off the several scuff marks on its once immaculate surface.

Speaking of Mara, she took off somewhere as soon as the funeral was completed.

"I hope she's at least conversing with someone instead of going off on her own...especially right now."

Randomly digging through the piles and piles of clothes, I threw on a brown tunic and a pair of black pants I found lying within this mess. Changing my lower clothes, I made sure the amber pendant was transferred to my new clothes as I did so. I snatched up a pair of brown boots and gloves off the floor, securing them properly as I examined the cabinet one final time. I left the leather plating inside the cabinet, preferring to be comfortable over anything else.

Clasping the cloak around my neck and lowering the green hood over my head, I glanced over myself repeatedly within the slightly dirty mirror.

From an opponent's perspective, I looked like any ordinary person, willfully fighting for one's cause without standing out in any way.

This looks good.

Satisfied with the new outfit I had established for myself, I stepped towards the door as I glanced at myself one final time.

Don't know if this is what people would think of when they think of a dog in the military, but that's alright. After all, my point isn't to stand out.

I reverted my gaze back to the exit of my room, placing my hand on the slightly creaky handle.

It's what they will have to get used to now.

Swinging the door wide open, I gasped in surprise as I saw Mara standing right in front of the freshly opened door only a couple inches away from my face, her own gazing at the floor. Her clothes were still the same from our conflict with Zain, an obvious factor when seeing the bloody handprints which remained from Serena's embrace. My own blood was mixed in the dirt and grime as well.

"Oh you surprised me Mara," I exclaimed in a somewhat deadpan manner, which I attempted to infuse with brightness halfway through, "It's good to see you walking around a little." She didn't respond to my exclamation, continuing to stare towards the ground.

"Well...I suppose we shouldn't keep our leader waiting. Would you care to walk with me?" Standing in silence, she stiffly nodded her head once as if it took all of her energy to do that single action. I sighed to myself as I closed the door and began to walk past her, hearing Mara's feet drag as she shuffled slowly behind me.

Glancing back at the recreational hub connected to the entrance before I made my walk over, I smiled as I noticed Catherine frantically chatting with Ellia about something I couldn't decipher due to the speed. I could tell the introverted assistant was trying to get to Katrina's office for some form of task, but was currently being held up by the chatty child's talking. She smiled nervously at Mara and I as she tried to escape from the conversation, but I knew the smile was plastered on for one particular reason.

Grasped within her right hand still was the book Avelina once had, with Ellia's thumb poked between several pages showcasing that she was indeed trying to read through it.

Henry and Serena were both nowhere to be seen, and as far as I know Jack made his way to the training grounds almost immediately.

The other three still appear to be on their mission as well.

I smirked for a moment as I kept walking, once again rubbing the faint scar on my neck as I walked down the claustrophobic hallway of doors. For many more awkward seconds, Mara and I walked side by side just barely as we passed door after door, dreading the final moments before we came upon the large one at the end.

At least this silence doesn't feel as malicious...almost feels like the first time we met.

"...I'm sorry." I jolted up at her sudden interjection as we finally arrived in front of the ornate doorway, the dragging of her feet becoming more accented due to the enclosed environment. I turned to her as I lowered my hand away from the handle I was about to twist, letting it fall to my side.

"Excuse me?" I asked eventually, not sure if I heard her correctly. She stiffened momentarily as her gaze remained fixated with the ground, her fists curled up slightly at her sides as her eyes continued their staring contest with the wood below.

"I'm sorry...for almost killing you," Mara whispered, "Serena and some of the others kept calling you reckless for charging at Z-Zain like you did, when I was the one who got you in t-that situation by charging in. None of the blame rested on m-me. I j-just..." She paused to recollect herself as she stared away from me, refusing to meet my eyes as she attempted to compose her breathing and tone.

"You were right," she admitted, "I let my emotions cloud my judgement the whole way through. No plan. No prior thought. I just wanted to see him die." She rubbed her arm somberly as we stood motionless, her eyes hidden by the shadows of the light peeking through the small windows cast.

Her now hazy emerald eyes were red and vaguely puffy, with a single tear rolling down her face as many more threatened to rain down upon the aged wood below.

"I've...I have made it my mission to eliminate people like h-him," she choked out, "I told myself that I would hold that mission above everything else. I told...I told myself that it even stood above other p-people, and I would do whatever it takes to ensure I completed it. But..." She raked out a quick sob, which she concealed quickly with a swift movement of her hand.

"But when you see someone d-dying, and you know it's all your fault..." she let out another pained sob as her palms violently shook at her sides, threatening to vibrate into the walls at the speeds they were moving. She wasn't even attempting to conceal the motion.

"You must hate me," Mara mumbled, averting her eyes once, "You could've died, and I would carry with me for the rest of my life the fact that your blood would forever linger on my hands. It would be normal for someone to hate the one who k-kills them." I turned to fully face her as we stood in front of the office door, trying to stare into the swirling green pools of emotion.

This is the exact opposite of how she was when we first met, and yet she is just as hard to read.

"I don't hate you Mara," I replied simply, "Confused and a little hurt? Maybe, but that is given. However, hate is a strong word that should only be used for the vilest of people, so therefore there isn't a fiber in my body that hates you for what you did back there." She glanced away from me with a flinch, clearly surprised by my interjection.

"W-Why?" she shakily breathed out, "I jeopardized everything we were working towards. I put everyone's l-lives in danger because I couldn't keep my emotions properly in check. You should've just let me run towards Zain and pay for my f-foolishness." I violently shook my head, softly glaring at her with conviction burning in my hazel eyes.

"It's because of why you did it Mara," I professed, "I may know absolutely nothing about you, but I do know that you're a good person.

A rotten person who I would direct my hatred towards wouldn't have saved me back in Eincrest, nor would they have told me about this group I could be a part of to further everything I stand for. And because I know that, I am aware of how valuable protecting those who have been beaten and broken down is to you. Even though we differed in action, I saw that compassion you directed towards Catherine. It's instinct for you…and even though it directly defied what I proposed as a safer option, I can still understand why you did it." She stared at the ground as she took in all of this information, giving an incredulous laugh as she shook her head.

"I don't understand you at all, Connor," she admitted, "A normal person would hate me for what I've done, so why don't you?"

"I could never hate anyone who truly means good with their heart and actions," I replied, "You charged at him because you perceived him as a present danger and a threat to everyone. You ran at him to protect our safety, and as such in those moments you weren't being selfish. If I died right there, I would at least know you'd still be there to fight against Zain and protect people like Catherine who need it most." I extended my gloved right hand towards her, one which she hesitantly took.

"Perhaps…we should start over," I suggested as I released her hand and gripped my fist in front of me, "You already know me as Connor Illium but, if I am to work with you, you have to learn more. My goal in life is to track down and save my mother, who as far as I know was taken by an unknown man who I…intend to find. I stand with this group because I know they'll change this country in a brilliant way if we work with it, but more than that I know that they have the resources and pathways to lead me in the direction of my mom. I didn't tell the full picture to anyone else, but I now share much of it with you, as a sign of complete faith in who you are." Mara stepped back as she stared at me, taking in everything I had to say before placing her own gloved hand on her chest.

"My name…is Mara, and my goal is and always will be to defend this continent with everything I have," she stated, "While I shared this with you, I didn't think you'd be one to understand my reasoning behind this, along with bearing this burden all by myself." Her gaze diverged from me again, a look of shame dawning over her features.

"I've…I've lied a lot while here in order to stay on the right path, and I know for a fact I will attempt to lie again. I don't like doing it and I'm rather lousy at it, but I find it necessary if I am to ensure the protection of everyone." I smiled at her as I gripped onto the doorknob again, preparing to turn the ornate piece of metal.

For once, she smiled back at me.

It was an awkward grin she showcased to me, as she was obviously not used to smiling the way she did just now. But I had to admit, there was a purity to her expression that made me wish to see it again and again.

"Now…let's hope Katrina doesn't get too upset with us."

31

Connor: A Bittersweet Achievement

"I honestly don't know what to do with you two right now. Either congratulate you on your success, or remove you from this base immediately for disobeying direct orders from a superior."

Mara and I stood alone in Katrina's office, standing utterly surrounded by the judgmental gazes of the papers and the seething woman sitting in front of us, her eyes burning with disappointment and a strong, vindictive anger. I rubbed the neck wound again instinctively, across the tender skin that I still couldn't believe healed. The sun was just beginning to settle back down through a window nearby.

"First, you directly disobeyed my orders by not immediately returning from your search for survivors, not only with you two but with a child whose life was absolutely threatened by your little escapade. You then did not return for several days, edging towards the one location that I forbade even a glance at with any form of ambition."

I stepped forward instinctively, passing the brunette who glanced up in surprise at my sudden steps forward. I placed my hands behind my back.

"I take full responsibility for the actions that occurred these past few days," I interrupted with as much conviction as I could muster, "And, while I will take any punishment from you, I must say that I believe that the mission would not have been as successful without Mara and I's assistance." Mara looked incredibly shocked by my proclamation, considering the promise she made earlier to explain this entire scenario when it came. Katrina extended an incredulous finger in my direction.

"That scar on your neck tells me otherwise," she contradicted, "While I am incredibly elated that Zain was defeated, you two could have needlessly died because of your insistence on defiance. Someone did die because of Zain. That could've been you two!"

She slumped back into her chair as I flinched at the reference to Avelina. She picked up the picture that sat on her desk when I first came in that day, the one with her posing beside Avelina and Ellia. I could see a faint tear coagulating in the corner of her right eye.

"Avelina…" she whispered to herself, her eyes glazing over as she set down the old photograph, "I still recall the day we first met… thank you for believing in my future, my friend."

These people are so tight knit, I'm so sorry…

We explained as much as we could from our perspective of how the events transpired earlier, aside from Henry's Zevron blood. Ellia was still absent from the room, probably still held up by the noble girl's antics.

I had no idea how she would react to it.

"You took the exact risk I specifically instructed you not to take Connor!" she yelled, startling me as she refused to let that single tear fall, "Don't you see? The mere idea risked the lives of not only you, but Mara and that girl too." She held her forehead, pushing the blonde hair out of her face.

She was making every point that I made towards Mara when she first decided to defy orders, but that didn't matter.

I'll cover for her as much as I can...I don't why but I felt the need to do so despite what I stood by previously.

You and your blasted heart Connor...

"I lost not only a good troop today, but I also lost one of my closest friends." She stared at Mara, who was staring at the floor silent. She would cringe at every reprimand delivered in my direction, stiffening as Katrina's gaze fell upon her. Instead of a brief glance, Katrina continued to stare down at the increasingly small looking woman, her eyes narrowing as Mara quivered under her gaze.

If I didn't know any better, she may already know the truth of it all even with my cover story.

"If...I may interject..." Katrina jerked away from her staring contest with Mara, startled at the voice she heard. Mara for her part let out a sigh of relief, thankful to not be stared at as deeply.

"Henry," she breathed out, "You're...you're not wearing..." I turned around myself, noticing that he stood in the doorway behind me.

His outfit was nowhere near the blackened outfit he wore when I first met him. His cloak was the same icy blue as his eyes with his hood currently being worn down, revealing his Zevron white hair and eyes. He only wore a glove on his left hand, revealing the eagle on the back of his right, and black boots. His long-sleeved tunic was a faded grey, with black leather armor on top of it, and black pants with black leather knee pads. He leaned against the door frame, his blue cloak flowing past his knees.

Serena stood behind him, her mouth curled into a distinct smile as her clothes were freshly cleaned. It was also blatantly apparent to me that she was the one who picked out Henry's clothes.

The distinct white bandages still lurked across both of her arms, concealing the grievous wounds she cast upon herself in a last-ditch attempt to save Avelina's life.

She's still fairly worn out and depleted from the battle, as she would've already healed those wounds if she could. Some of them will probably scar at this point.

"Not wearing that mask?" Henry replied coolly as he stared at me, "It's alright, I don't need it anymore." Katrina looked startled as she stared between Henry and I, looking at me in a quizzical way.

"I lost it during the fight," Henry explained, "And…I suppose it would be better if I went on without it." Katrina folded her arms as she leaned back, flicking her hand to bring them inside. They stepped slightly in front of Mara, who stared at the two incoming people and took several steps away to give herself room.

"I assume you didn't come here just to showcase a change in attire?" Katrina questioned as Henry and Serena fully entered the room, taking a sip from her drink. I could smell the distinct scent of coffee, noting that the caffeine within must be incredibly strong.

"No actually," Serena cut in, "We…may have a tiny proposition for you." Katrina raised an eyebrow as her indigo eyes stared into them.

"A proposition?"

"A position here for Connor," Henry deadpanned, "A position as the Sentinels' primary tactician." She spit up her drink as she sat straight up, staring at the other two incredulously.

"What?"

"You and I have both seen what he can do firsthand," Henry commented, "As much as I'd hate to admit it, I've seen how well he can think on his feet. He had concocted a decent plan for us to face Zain, which would've worked if not for some…issues." I saw him visibly hesitate at that final word as Mara and I stiffened. I explained the story at first, so I left out the part where Mara charged at Zain and blatantly ignored the plan.

I just stated that I was caught by surprise by one of his attacks.

"He notices things that none of us would and can come up with strategies on the fly. He's a good candidate, although even if you listen to our advice, I'm still keeping my eye on him." I somehow rolled my eyes through the somewhat flattery, sensing his paranoia seeping through the minor amount of praise.

Still doesn't seem to be a fan of mine, but at least he's warming up to me.

"And besides!" Serena cut in, catching Henry by surprise as she nudged past him, "I can already tell he's well-liked by everyone here! He's witnessed us in combat and already knows how we all fight. He's a super genius Katrina!" Now I know my cheeks were completely red as I was hammered by so many compliments, making me almost shrink in my chair. Katrina leaned back into her own chair as she bored her eyes into mine. Mara continued to stare at me, a look of complacence present on her features as the words continued.

"That specific position has always been left empty..." she trailed off to herself, glancing back at Henry, "What dissipated all that paranoia you had towards him Henry? It's unlike you."

"Of course I'm still paranoid about him Katrina, but there's something about him I just can't ignore. Even when his life was threatened, he put everything on the line to ensure the rest of us could survive, a good fit for someone in a leadership role."

"I absolutely support this as well!" Mara blurted out to us all, before the volume of her proclamation dawned on her as she crumpled down yet again, "I believe that he would be a good fit...that is all." I couldn't help but smile at her sudden burst of nervous support, showcasing a woman who I hoped was the real Mara.

A woman I hope to learn more about.

Serena gave another smile as she stared towards Mara's direction, pumping her arms with a laugh.

"Thank you for the support, but don't sell yourself short," Serena beamed, "You're so amazing too! That fight wouldn't have ended as well without your help!" Mara paused momentarily at her yells, her mouth slightly agape as she absorbed it all. I smile slightly at her surprise.

Katrina said nothing to all of this, thinking everything through as the cup went to her mouth once again. Setting it down, her eyes stared back at me with renewed determination.

"Hmm...perhaps you are correct in all those regards," she finally relented, "And although Connor you did disobey direct orders from me, you all still managed to kill Zain, along with the monumental task of not only gaining Henry's trust, but also making him more trusting in general." She stood up from her chair and crossed her arms, towering over my sitting form.

"Your punishment for disobeying orders will still stand. For the next three months, you will be going on no missions whatsoever, and afterwards for another three months the missions will all be minor. At the end of every week and after this three-month handicap, you will be tasked with cleaning and organizing the entire library until it looks pristine. This stands for you as well Mara, so don't think either of you will be punished disproportionately more than the other." Finishing this all in almost one breath, she let out a deep sigh as I logged all of this information, making sure I wouldn't forget it somehow. Mara nodded along with a lowered expression, looking deflated.

Don't be too hard on yourself Mara.

"Stand Connor Illium." she announced. I immediately stood up and brushed myself off, unsure of what was going on, "If we're going to do this, we appear to have sufficient witnesses, and I have the power of authority here so may as well do it now."

"Are you willing to serve the Sentinels to the best of your abilities? Through times of peace and of war?" Realizing what the process truly was, I stood proudly as I stared back.

"I am willing."

"Do you promise to fight whatever enemies are against us, even willing to kill them where they stand?"

"I promise."

"Will you treat every person within this group as an equal?" I gave Henry a smile before I responded, watching as Serena giggled behind bandaged hands.

"I will."

"And will you follow my command, even through the greatest of conflicts and troubles?"

"I will do what is right, commander." I maintained with a slight curl to my lips. Katrina sighed and shook her head, faintly smiling to herself.

"You sound just like your mother," Katrina sighed, "Funny, she was the one who filled this position back in the academy, and the one I hoped to fill this role once I created the Sentinels." She extended a hand towards me, which I gladly accepted. Turning back, Serena was flashing me her usual smile with a bandaged thumbs up, with Henry giving a solemn nod.

Mara stared at me momentarily with her usual blank expression, before a look of realization dawned upon her as her mouth curved up into that same awkward smile she showed before we entered. Serena seemed taken aback by her show of affection, one which I couldn't help but smile quietly at as I turned back to Katrina.

I appreciate her at least trying to not stay hidden behind that mask of emotionlessness she used to hide who she was. Maybe during our time together without missions, I can get to know who she really is beneath that facade.

"I now dub you the tactician of the Sentinels," Katrina announced as she released my hand, "Congratulations Connor. I'll explain all of your duties once the six months of no major missions ends. In the meantime, wear the title you now carry with pride, Connor Illium."

Epilogue

As the last of the flames within the village of Eincrest flickered out, and as two distinct brothers sat crumpled miles apart, a figure sat miles away, softly humming an unknown tune. He balanced a small, blackened dirk within his ragged hands, grinning as the teeth of the jagged blade glistened in the sun. He smiled as he sheathed the weapon, knowing full well whose hands he would hope the magnificent blade would fall into.

A blade that would serve as the perfect channel between humanity and its creators. He faintly chuckled at the idea, giving the jagged teeth of Requiem one final look before he finalized the sheath's position.

The man readjusted the frills of his black suit jacket as he stood up, clasping the golden buttons as he straightened the cuffs of his white dress shirt. He knew he was overdressed for both the weather and his surroundings, but he didn't care even slightly. It was his pristine outfit of choice, and he would be damned if he allowed anything to change it.

Confirming twice that his suit was meticulously clean and smooth, the man of shadows turned to the silent figure who stood in front of him. Years ago, the man would be unnerved by the chilling silence men like him would provide when joining his fold. Now, he found a sense of pride in it, knowing full well their silence meant progress.

"Are you ready for this mission of ours?" he asked the cloaked figure as he wrapped the sheath around his waist in his smooth, almost whimsical voice, "Make it realistic, but I'm counting on you to lose this so try not to kill him alright? Oh, and make sure you keep Requiem with you at all times. If you die with it, it is all but guaranteed he'll take it with him with my influence involved."

He chuckled to himself callously, knowing full well the husk in front of him wouldn't reply.

"I hope my little ploy works; otherwise Rennak is going to be incredibly confused and incredibly pissed off." Affirming that Requiem remained in the sheath of his thrall, the man's unnatural bright purple eyes twinkled as he became lost in the machinations of his own mind.

"Fusing you to a human could be the key to securing my desires, or I'll have to do this the hard way again. That damn girl, making this entire situation so troublesome." The man of shadow slapped the drone who possessed Requiem on the back, eliciting a fatigued groan as he wordlessly marched forward. His thralls followed swiftly behind, marching forward with an alternative goal in mind.

Kill the girl, whatever the cost.

The man knew his scheming was flawed, knowing full well his two mindless soldiers weren't going to be enough to take down the girl. She was too capable to die from that, but the man had some extra troops and was feeling especially petty today.

He needed to bide his time, build up strength in this land until his power could return to its former glory.

"Maybe I'll pay Rennak a visit soon after this is all done. After that, I can formulate a strategy of some kind in Bellhollow." He grumbled to himself as he turned around, briskly walking down the opposite path of his still marching soldiers. He clung a worn grey cloak tightly over himself, hoping to shoo away prying eyes who might take special interest in the noble attire he refused to shed.

The sharp point of a blade suddenly met the back of the man, halting